Cthulhu Lies Dreaming

Twenty-three Tales
of the Weird and Cosmic

GHOSTWOODS

THIS IS A GHOSTWOODS BOOK

2 3 4 5 6 7 8 9 10 11 12 1

This volume copyright ©2016 Ghostwoods Books.
"The Red Brick Building" copyright ©2015 Mike Davis. Originally published in *NecronomiCon Providence 2015 Souvenir Book*. Reprinted by permission of the author and Lovecraft Arts & Sciences Council editors.
"Babatunde" copyright ©2014 A. Leeman Kessler. Originally published in *Arkham Horror Book Club Anthology Volume 1: Shadows of the Past* edited by Frederic Norton.
All other stories copyright ©2016 their respective authors.
All stories, artworks, fonts, and textures appear under license.

Executive Editor: Salomé Jones
Cover Design: Gábor Csigás
Cover Sculpture: *Key of Cthulhu* by Lee Joyner
Copy Editor: Tim Dedopulos
Image Credits: Cover image "Key of Cthulhu" by Lee Joyner (joynerstudio.com). Cover textures by Mercurycode (www.facebook.com/mercurycode) and Siriuz-sdz (sirius-sdz. deviantart.com). Fonts "Selfish" by Eduardo Recife, "Baron Neue" by Frank Hemmekam, "Metalista" by Tomáš Brousil, "Duerers Minuskeln" by Manfred Klein, "Courier New" by Howard "Bud" Kettler via IBM and Monotype, and especially "Garamond" by Claude Garamond via Christophe Plantin and Adobe. All artworks, fonts, and textures appear under license. No part or whole of this book may be reproduced without express permission, except for quotation and citation purposes.

Gábor Csigás can be found at gaborcsigas.daportfolio.com

ISBN: 978-0-957627-17-8

This edition published February 2016 by:
Ghostwoods Books
London
United Kingdom
http://www.gwdbooks.com

Cthulhu Lies Dreaming

Twenty-three Tales of the Weird and Cosmic

Edited by

Salomé Jones

For Tim.
He's a deep one.

Table of Contents

Foreword:
Cthulhu, Lies, Dreaming
by Kenneth Hite

Ph'nglui mglw'nafh Cthulhu R'lyeh wgah'nagl fhtagn.

As H.P. Lovecraft tells us in his epochal short story "The Call of Cthulhu," that inhuman, primordial text – the liturgical chant of the worshippers of great Cthulhu – means something like this: 'In his house at R'lyeh dead Cthulhu lies dreaming.'

Cthulhu, the titanic alien priest-king trapped below the surface of the Pacific when the stars changed and his ancient city of R'lyeh sunk, can never die. His ultraterrestrial matter and incomprehensible life-force rest in a kind of interphase, a quantum indeterminacy beneath the unified field, or perhaps a lemma in the great un-life equation in which he is the key variable. Until the stars come right again and Cthulhu solves or re-solves himself, humanity may scrabble and squabble on the surface of the planet.

And at night, under the not-quite-right stars, humanity dreams. As Lovecraft quotes the Cthulhu cult leader "Old Castro" saying:

> *Even now They talked in Their tombs. When, after infinities of chaos, the first men came, the Great Old Ones spoke to the sensitive among them by moulding their dreams; for only thus could Their language reach the fleshly minds of mammals.*

Cthulhu and the Great Old Ones dream, and we dream in response. The dreams of Cthulhu thus filter out into our fleshly minds. Dream molds dream, and from those dreams comes waking knowledge, spoken by shamans and written down in that hellish book, the Necronomicon. Cthulhu dreams, and his initiates dream, and we read the result; beats in a sequence, perhaps even an inevitable, inescapable fugue composed by the Great Old Ones and played out in religion, and warfare, and madness, and art.

Art such as ... "The Call of Cthulhu." You see, H.P. Lovecraft experienced two of the crucial motifs for that story in his dreams: the risen Pacific island covered in noxious weed and slime, and the young artist who creates a bas-relief based on an image from his dreams. Yes, that means Lovecraft dreamed about having dreamed about an enigmatic image "older than brooding Tyre, or the contemplative Sphinx, or garden-girdled Babylon." And then he wrote it down for his followers to transform into ritual.

His followers, such as the authors of the stories you are about to read. Did these stories likewise come from dreams? And if so, from Whose? Remember that we remember barely any of our dreams: out of an average of 5 (or as many as 10) dreams in a night, how many do you recall when waking? How many just remain hidden in your hindbrain, molding your fleshly mind? How would you know? How can you know?

Even if you remember the dream, and write it down – or guard against it and never tell a soul – do you remember it truly? And even if you remember it truly, was it a dream of truth? Dreams, Homer reminds us, come through two gates: the true gates of horn, and the deceiving gates of ivory. Dreams can be lies, and those who tell them can be liars – or be driven to lie by their dreams. Old Castro was insane, after all, and speaking under interrogation. So it's probably nothing.

That's probably the best, the safest thing to believe. That all these fictions, all these lies, all these uncorrelated contents come from nowhere but the authors' imaginations. They certainly don't come from a mountain-sized unearthly insanity, slumbering beneath the global unconscious masked and symbolized by the

Pacific Ocean. They didn't appear in the authors' dreams, not night after night, digging away insensible and invisible until they emerged onto the page or the screen. They did not will themselves into existence, nor did some monstrous alien will transmit them through fleshly minds and into yours.

There is no Cthulhu. These are all lies. Pleasant dreaming.

Nikukinchaku
by Matthew J. Hockey

In thirty two years working at St. Andrew's Community Primary school, this was Margaret's first time there after dark. It had been built of black stone, in an era when every building looked like a church. It had a steepled roof, high arched windows, even a belfry. It didn't creak as it cooled at night, but moaned, deep in the foundations. She hoped McEnroe would arrive soon. It was starting to get to her.

She waited on one of the half-size plastic cafeteria chairs. The room felt somehow sad and lonely without the children in it making a mess. The pale yellow of the energy-saving light bulb played across the student self-portraits lining the walls. During the day, their misaligned eyes and radar-dish ears seemed cute and charming. Now they gave her the creeps. Flared nostrils, blood sausage lips, sharp teeth, livid pink skin and egg-yellow hair.

The wooden floor was plastered with laminated food-chain displays done by the after-school clubs. When she'd been at school, a food chain had meant grass to herbivore to apex predator. Now there was a big drive to teach kids just where their food came from – field to collection to storage to wholesale to distribution to supermarket to plate.

The kids were taught about food groups and recycling and sustainable farming and fair trade, and the importance of nutrition and a balanced diet. The hope was that they'd go home and pester their parents into cutting down on salt and sugar. All the while, they reduced her budget – fifty pence per student per day, thirty pence per student, twenty, fifteen, ten pence per student per day.

The parents paid for the lunches, and the government paid for those who couldn't afford it, but she never saw a penny of it. The money disappeared into the school's black hole, and the head didn't like her asking questions. So she didn't.

A week ago, Mr. Propp, the headmaster, had broken the silence. He called her into his office, and said she needed to give him a list of names. "Three names from the dinner staff, and the reasons they're going to be sacked without pension or redundancy. Pilfering supplies maybe."

"I can't do that," she said. "There's only five of us."

"Then I'll make it easier for you. Give me the name of the person you want to keep. It's either that, or you bring it down to eight pence a child a day. Or you hope sixty of them suddenly decide they'd prefer mum's sandwiches."

She hadn't written that list yet. If this meeting went to plan, she wouldn't have to.

The car was so quiet she wouldn't have known it was there, except for the headlights on the wall and the crunch of tyres over the gravel. She peeked out through the curtains. Her blocky Fiat looked frumpy and ridiculous beside the freshly waxed silver Mercedes estate.

The driver got out, took a cold-box from the boot, and slung a holdall over his shoulder. He was every bit as highly polished as his car. His paper-white hair was pulled back into a tight bun, he had frameless oblong glasses perched on his broad nose, a black-on-black tartan suit, and a club tie that hung right down to his belt. He looked up and down the length of the school, as if he knew he was being watched.

"Mister McEnroe?" Margaret opened the door to greet him.

"Sandy. Please, just Sandy." He stepped inside and walked around the hall as if he had been there a hundred times. He set the box and his papers on the foldout table she'd prepared. "Just a tête-à-tête, is it?"

"I'm sorry, the head couldn't make it. He had commitments."

"Why talk to the horse when you can talk to the jockey, am I right?"

"Excuse me?"

"Let me put it this way." He popped the tabs on the cold-box and steam poured out of the crack. "From the first time you called me, I knew the way it was. It's the headmaster's school, but it's your kitchen. You're the captain of this particular ship. What you say goes, am I right?"

"Well, I suppose you could put it that way. Yes."

"Then it's you I need to impress." He took a toaster oven from his holdall and hunted around for a place to plug it in.

"I really appreciate you coming out like this. It must seem a little strange."

"Margaret. Can I call you Margaret? Well, Margaret, I've been pitching for sixteen years and this..." He gestured around the darkened cafeteria. "This doesn't even come close to my top ten of weird venues. Just last week I did a tour of drilling platforms in the North Sea. Earlier this year, I went out to a pitch at a Buddhist temple in far, far, far, *far* Northern China."

"Wow. I didn't think you'd be so... so..." She physically groped for the word.

"Global?"

Margaret nodded.

"People, wherever they are, they have to eat. I've got clients all over – Argentina, Bosnia-Herzegovina, California. Three research bases out in Antarctica. Hell, the Royal Navy have got it on their Tridents. They're out there somewhere eating Epikurea products as we speak. I'm sorry..." He took his buzzing phone out of his pocket, checked the name and then dumped the call.

She drummed her fingers on the fold-out table while she waited. It sounded so much like somebody stepping into the room behind them that she had to stop. "I've read your prospectus. I've got to say the testimonials are very impressive, but..."

"But you've got one question, am I right?" He took a covered metal platter from the cool box and put it into the tiny oven. He cranked a dial and it ticked.

"Yes, it's just..."

"Hold that thought." He tore a swatch of paper from his pocketbook and uncapped his Montblanc pen. "I bet I can guess what your question is."

He wrote something down and then twirled her hand for her to go ahead.

"What exactly is it?" she asked.

He smiled and turned the paper to show her. *What is it exactly?* was written on it. "Damn, one word out, but still pretty good, am I right? Honestly though, I could do this talk ten times a day for a year, and that trick would work every time. But, to answer your question, in Japan they call it Nikukinchaku. In South Korea, they call it Badagogi. Both countries claim to have discovered it, and neither wants to back down." He blew out a big puff of what-are-you-going-to-do air. "We go with the Japanese because it looks better on the marketing copy."

"But what actually *is* it?"

"Well..." He took his glasses off and chewed on the arm. She could see little grooves in the plastic where he'd done it before. The oven's bell shrilled. He took an insulated wool glove from his pack and laid the platter out on a rollout rubber mat in front of her. He took the lid off and used it to waft the steam towards her. "Smells good, doesn't it?"

"It does actually. It really does." She wasn't just saying it. It smelled as though it had been wok-fried, not pre-cooked and reheated in a glorified Fisher-Price oven. He handed her a knife and fork and she shied away from trying it.

"What's the matter?"

"Does it have a radiation certificate? What with Fukushima and everything."

"It's very refreshing to meet a customer as well-informed as yourself," he said, and she blushed. He took a sheaf of papers from a binder, one long index finger tap-tap-tapping at the gold seal. "Tuck in."

She speared the browned meat with the fork, and turned it around in the dish. There was no sauce, no heap of salt or spices like some of the more insalubrious outfits had used to hide the cardboard bland meats they'd tried to push on her. It was firm rather than spongy, white flesh with a brown sealed outer edge. It looked like a cross between chicken and steak.

She closed her eyes and bit into it.

"Oh my God." She grunted with animal pleasure, and then blushed even harder than before. "Sorry. It's just... wow. That is actually delicious."

"Good, right?"

She didn't answer, except to go back for a second mouthful. He watched with badly concealed delight. She ate as if he was going to take it away from her, and didn't speak again until she'd finished the whole bowl.

"You know my predicament," she said, once she was done. "It wasn't a clever ploy to bring your price down."

"Yes." His smile didn't move.

"I really meant it. This has to be the cheapest of the cheap, or I can't take it. This Nishi..."

"Nikukinchaku."

"This," She pointed her fork at the empty platter. "There's no way I can afford this on my budget."

"You can. Eight pence per child per day, just like we agreed on the phone." He handed her an invoice in a plastic wallet. Their fingers touched for a second and she pulled away, even wiped her hand on her skirt. He pretended not to notice.

"How?" she asked.

"I'll show you."

They went outside together.

She jigged from one foot to the other trying to look over his shoulder as he opened the car boot. She kept one eye on the gate to the schoolyard, and pressed the short blade of her car keys between her knuckles. He seemed nice enough, but her brain kept sending her images of him bundling her into the back of the car. Nobody would ever know. She'd kept everything about their meeting a secret.

She needn't have worried. There was no room for her in the car, even if he was a psychopath. The back seats were folded down into the floor compartments and a huge plastic tray took up the full space.

He took a penlight from his jacket, clipped a red gel to the end, and shone it inside. Margaret recoiled, almost stabbing herself in the stomach with her key.

There were six of them. Pale flesh-pink rugby balls, like pigskin conches with jagged vents and spines in ridges along the upper lip. Twists of gristle trailed out of livid pink cracks where they'd been wrenched out of the sea bed. Their surfaces rippled with clots of varicose veins that glowed faintly in the red torch beam.

"I thought you said..." She put her fingers to her mouth to stifle a retch. "You said you sold them to a Buddhist monastery."

"I did."

"Buddhists can't eat meat."

"They're not meat."

"Fish then."

"Not fish either. Nikukinchaku are officially neither meat not vegetable."

"What are they then?"

"Unclassifiable. They have the taste, texture and nutritional content of A-grade beef, yet they have the same general behaviour pattern as a plant. Except the sunlight. Sunlight's anathema, because of the depth they're found. They're happiest in a cold, dark place, in an inch of sandy soil. Treat them right and they grow quicker than green bamboo. Harvest them two, three times a week and you're golden. Once you've got over the initial outlay, they won't cost you a penny. They just keep right on growing."

"For how long?"

"Indefinitely. My very first customer, Little Acorns Elementary School in Great Oaks, California, they're still on their first batch after six years."

"I'm not sure."

"Look. Margaret. It's late. I've had a long drive. Are you interested or aren't you?" He took his glasses off and pressed his thumbs into his eyes.

"I'll take them."

"How many?"

"How many have you got?"

They talked through the details and arranged shipment.

"I'm in town for the week," Sandy said. "Chasing up a few more leads. I'm staying at the Seagull. Look me up if you need anything."

She waved him away, turned the lights off, and locked up behind her. She climbed into her car and sat there for a moment, motionless in the dark.

"Anything." She clucked her tongue off her bottom lip "Anything. *Any*thing. Any*thing*." She said it again and again, trying to catch his exact inflection, the subtle spin he'd put on the syllables. Had she imagined it?

She started the engine. Her mind flashed on the way his laugh lines crinkled when he chewed the arm of his glasses–

She shook her head and pulled out of the yard.

The Sean Connery eyebrow he'd cocked when he got the call–

She got out and padlocked the gate.

His strong hands opening the binder, the soft skin of his knuckles when they accidentally touched. Had he hesitated for just a second too long when they brushed together?

"Margaret, you mucky pup." She laughed, and drove home.

She ate a miniature single-serving green tea ice-cream and went to sleep in front of the shopping channel. That was her Friday night.

*

The next day, she walked hunched over across the fallen stones at the foot of the bluff, stopping here and there to scoop tide-bound fish out of the rock pools and carry them to the sea. Thick tendrils of predawn sea fog reached towards her across the salt-rotted groynes that protruded out into the waves. She was lit only by the intermittent beam of the automatic lighthouse as it swept the cove. There was no need for it these days. There hadn't been a boat launch from the harbour in four years.

Nobody in Mossport really knew for sure why the local fishing industry had collapsed. That didn't stop the town's UKIP delegate insisting it was Brussels bureaucrats in a conspiracy to stifle British spirit with draconian EU fishing policies, of course.

The town was still going through a painful transition period, changing from six hundred years of fishing tradition to gaudy plastic tourist town. Despite how much money the local government pumped into regeneration and marketing, it would always play second fiddle to Blackpool just to the south and Morecambe an hour north. The only tourists that ever usually came were down to the last day of their holiday and the last few coins in the kitty.

Businesses were dying on every street – no matter how brightly they painted the fisherman's cottages on the seafront, no matter how many times a day the restored Victorian tram ran. None of it brought the fishermen back. None of it brought the sights and smells of the barter on a fresh haul, the excited chatter and wheeling gulls of an especially large catch. The line of skiffs, tugs and trawlers dotting the horizon. None of it brought her Donald back. His boat was still at the bottom, right in the harbour mouth where it rolled. She and the other seven widows still had to fight the legal challenges, to stop it being moved so millionaires could get their yachts up to the wharf. They still had to beg the council for a memorial.

The sound of an outboard startled her out of her thoughts. It drifted towards her and then cut out again. The boat's prow sliced out of the mist. It was small and sharp, piloted by a young black man in golfing clothes worthy of a fancy-dress party.

"You Margaret?" He had a scouse accent. She nodded in reply, too cold to speak. "Margaret Handley?"

She nodded again, and he threw a coil of wet rope so she could pull the boat in.

"Where are they?" She caught the rope, but held it loose, ready to cast him back out if she needed to.

He kicked a pike hook up into the air and grabbed it, then swept it in a fan behind the boat. He pulled up a blue plastic barrel weighted down with ballast in netting.

"You brung something to stick 'em in, like?"

She pointed to the wheelbarrow on its side in the sand. He popped the barrel lid with a flat metal file and tipped them into the barrow on a wave of yellowed brine. Then he unfurled a Looney Tunes bedspread from by his feet, dipped it in the sea to soak it, and draped it over the fleshy pink shells. She threw him a foil wrap of crab sandwiches as agreed, and he tipped an imaginary hat.

"As you were." He pushed off back into the mist.

She waited until the sound of the engine had faded before taking the barrow back up the bluff to the school.

*

She closed herself in the walk-in fridge. She'd prepped it exactly the way the brochure said – removed everything but the shelves, swept and mopped, even got down on her hands and knees to pick stray fibres from the tile grouting. The light she'd replaced with a low-wattage red bulb. Once the floor was clean, she'd spread a mixture of sand and soil on the ground and mixed it with a rake.

Now that she had the things here, she took a sealed jar from her tote bag and opened it. The smell made her gag. It was a chunky red-black mulch of three-week-old fish and kelp she'd ground up in a blender. She tipped it on the sand and spread it as best she could.

She gulped in air, and drew back the bedspread. Ten of them, as agreed. She had to put rubber gloves on before she could bring herself to touch them.

They were heavier than she expected. About the same as a bag of sugar. A cold, gently pulsating bag of sugar. She set them on the sand and left.

The things started clicking to one another as soon as she closed the door.

*

Saint Andrew's five dinner ladies met first thing Monday morning in the 'the war room', their nickname for the storage shed that housed the school's splintery Victorian rowing boats. Margaret stood at the head of a loose semi-circle. Anina, her right-hand woman, stayed in place by her side.

"Is it true?" Bethany sounded as though she'd smoked herself hoarse waiting for news over the weekend.

"It is," Margaret said.

"Is what true?" Sally chewed on the split-ends of her unkempt hair, and fiddled with the ludicrous green stone earrings she wore.

"Could've bloody told us. I was expecting to come in to a P45 today." Bethany got up in Margaret's face. Her breath reeked of mints and nicotine.

"I just found out myself." Margaret backed up against the coal bunker. She had nowhere else to go.

"Is what true?" Sally asked.

Cath sighed. "Linda and Pam were let go."

"Who?" Sally sucked her hair so far back into her throat that she choked.

"The girls who watched the yard, you ignorant get," Bethany said.

"I only knew them as Mrs. Morton and Mrs. Barraclough." Sally pulled the wet string of hair out of her throat and inspected it.

"That means I need two of you to step up and take over yard duty. Bethany. Cath. I want you." Margaret pointed to both of them. "Sally, I want you to work front of house with Anina."

"Front of house! It's not a bloody restaurant," Sally said.

"Take some pride in what you do for a change." Anina poked a stubby finger into Sally's collarbone – not hard, but it didn't have to be. She was a big woman, an ex-Bavarian bierkeller maid who'd done twenty years lugging kegs on each arm with seven steins in each hand.

"That leaves me in the kitchen," Margaret said. "It'll be a stretch for one person, but if you all keep out of the road I can manage." They all talked at once, arguing with her. She cut them off with a waved hand. "I mean it. Kitchen is now out of bounds to everybody but me. It's their first day back after the holidays, so let's make it a good one. Chop chop."

*

The things had grown overnight. Three-foot clutches of pale fleshy fingers that lolled out of the vent in the front. Silvery veins and tubers had sprung out along their length, and sucked audibly at the red mulch underfoot.

Margaret breathed heavily as she drew the knife out of the block. She knelt down in the bloody soil, trying not to inhale through her nose. She gripped the nearest cluster of growths in one fist and pulled them taut, gritted her teeth, and sliced them away. The sound of escaping gas was so much like a scream she had to take a break in the main kitchen before she went back inside. Back to the cutting and the escaping gas screams. Back to the feeling of wet flesh sliding in the sand. Back to the sprays of black blood that gouted up the wall.

*

The kids loved it. Couldn't get enough. First time in years they'd come back for seconds. First time they'd eaten anything she'd made with smiles on their faces. Even the shy children were chatty in the queue. Anina gave her a wink and a thumbs up when she brought another stack of spotless plates to the serving hatch.

Bethany and Cath had no problems in the yard, none beyond the usual scraped knees, 'he hit me' and 'she pulled my hair' dramas. Even Sally pulled her weight, wiping tables, mopping spilled milk, and consoling a boy who had his food stolen by three of the older girls.

"We'll make sure you get an extra big helping tomorrow," she said, and little Bryon stopped crying. "That's right isn't it, Mrs. Hadley?"

"You can count on it," Margaret said.

Little Bryon left smiling.

Mister Senior, the PE teacher, caught up with Margaret as she was leaving for the afternoon. He was still in his shorts and a T-shirt, smelling pleasantly manly from a day spent playing football.

"Whatever you're doing, keep it coming," he said, with one hand on her open car door.

"Pardon?"

"Three One are usually a nightmare after lunch. Running around, screaming, spitting at each other. Today, good as gold. Good. As. Gold. Did everything I told them first time without me having to raise my voice. On a normal day that's amazing. On the first day back after a holiday? Unheard of."

"There's less additives in the new stuff."

"That'll be it. I always said these E-numbers are turning our kids into monsters." He bumped his fist off the car roof and she drove away.

*

The black water swallowed her. Bubbles ran up her nose. In her ears. In her eyes. In her throat. Couldn't see. Couldn't breathe. A light somewhere above her. Far away. She kicked out. Swam up. Had to be the surface. Had to be. Swam faster. Up and up and... her clutching fingers hit the silt. The bottom. Strands of kelp wrapped around her. Ankles. Wrists. Waist. Clouds of fish burst and reformed as she approached, crabs scurried away from her along the bottom, worms retreated into their burrows.

There was an abandoned shopping trolley half-submerged in the sand. 'Aldi' faded but still legible on the handle. She saw his boat. Her Donald's boat. On its roof. A pale silver light shone out of its depth. Her lungs strained, her shoulders bunched and burned. Black threads filled her eyes.

She dragged herself in through the broken bulkhead. There was Donald, draped at the control station, as he was. Young. Smiling. The current played through his hair, spreading it out as if he was lying on a pillow. His bloated abdomen glowed from inside. Silver white light. Black threads below his skin.

He saw her.

His eyes wide and dead, he saw her. He raised a hand to wave her away. To warn her. He held his head and screamed. No bubbles came out. His jaw snapped down.

White silver fingers of meat pushed out of his mouth so hard that his teeth smashed out of their sockets and floated around him, his tongue forced dumb against his lips. The fingers grew and grew. The reached for her.

They wrapped around her head. Her neck. Her chest. Her elbows. Her...

She woke up soaked with sweat. She lay still, looking at the ceiling, the lamp, Donald's roll top desk. Her stomach cramped and she ran to the bathroom, vomited clear salty puke into the bathtub.

She sat down with her back to the toilet and cried. She would have stayed there all day, except the alarm went off in the bedroom and the neighbour thumped against the wall.

*

A huge flock of birds flew overhead as she pulled into the schoolyard. They came wheeling and wailing away from the sea and further inland. Something had panicked them. They shed feathers and sprayed dung as they went.

She'd never seen so many different species of bird flying together like that – gulls, gannets, curlews, dunlins, and more. They squawked and shrieked, thrashed their wings and pecked at each other in a frenzy. Fighting one another to get away from the water.

A dead bird pranged off the children's slide. A second later an oystercatcher plummeted onto her bonnet, where it lay broke-necked and twitching.

Then they were gone. Away over the slanted roofs and dead chimneys.

She waited ten minutes to make sure nobody was watching. Then she collected the dead birds in a plastic Londis bag, and took them inside.

She plucked their feathers on the kitchen worktop, fed them into the blender and whipped them until the beaks clacked and clattered off the blades. She opened the fridge door and threw the paste onto the sand. They clicked even louder this time.

She drew the longest knife out of the block and waited, waited until she heard the growing meat scraping off the inside of the door.

*

Over a hundred students arrived for dinner in the seconds after the bell rang. They stretched out of the cafeteria and snaked three times around the narrow corridor.

"There's enough for everybody!" Anina yelled. The children ignored her, pushing and pulling each other. Squabbles broke out. Arguments. Fights. The school nurse had to get involved.

Eventually they fed them all, and retired to the war room, each with their own vice to keep them company. Caffeine. Cigarettes. Energy drinks. Margaret's was a bar of chocolate as big as her thigh.

"Lively today, weren't they?" she laughed.

"What do you mean?" Cath puffed out smoke and drew it back in through her nose.

"You didn't see? It was like world war three in there," Anina said.

"Bedlam," Bethany agreed.

"Not outside it wasn't. All quiet on the western front. No offence, Annie love."

Mr. Propp poked his head around the corner, whistling to let them know he was there. They all dropped their cigarettes, hid cans behind their backs, and shoved half-melted chocolates into their pockets.

"Margaret," Mr. Propp said. "A word."

She followed him into his office. It reeked of leather. None of the furniture was leather. He made sure the door was firmly closed, and handed her an envelope.

"What's this?" she asked.

"Open it."

"This is ridiculous. I did everything you asked," she said.

He sat on the edge of his desk and swung his short legs. "You're not being let go, Margaret. You're far too valuable." He broke the word down into its component syllables. *Val-you-ah-bul.* "It's a formal raise. A tidy bonus, too. I had to check your figures to make sure they were accurate but..."

"Thank you."

"You did it. I don't want to know how you did it."

"Well I—"

"I'm serious. I don't want to know. Enjoy the money, though. Buy yourself something nice. We both know you earned it. Don't tell the other girls though, eh?"

She hid the envelope in the same pocket as the chocolate and went back outside. When they asked what it was all about, she told them he'd got in her ear about the queue situation at lunch. Only Anina didn't believe her, and she kept it to herself.

*

Margaret decided to take Mr. Propp's advice. She stopped at Boots on the way home, bought herself some perfume from the locked cabinet by the counter, and a new lipstick. A bright red one.

"You're just going there to thank him." She touched her new haircut and watched it spring right back.

"You're just going there to say thank you." She kissed excess lipstick onto a tissue.

"You're just going to say thanks." She sprayed another dose of perfume onto her wrist and rubbed it on her collarbone.

She pulled her Fiat into car park of the Seagull, a white and black Edwardian mansion perched up on a cliff by the sea. Sandy's car wasn't there. She went in anyway, tottering on a pair of high-heels she'd never broken-in. She smoothed her houndstooth skirt, and clutched her purse to her side.

"Has Mr. McEnroe checked out already?" she asked the Polish girl on reception. The girl shook her head, didn't know. She asked Margaret if she'd like a drink. Margaret took a gin and tonic, and sat in the window.

The gin made her brave. The tonic made her red. She wouldn't just say thank you. She knew that now. She'd ask if he wanted a drink. Maybe go for a Chinese. She'd ask him if he'd seen the sunset from the bluff. She'd ask if he was staying for long. He'd say he was leaving tomorrow.

They'd...

The bell chimed over the door. Sandy walked in, coral-coloured polo and fresh sunburn, patches of wet sand on the knees of his chinos.

A woman walked in behind him. East-Asian. Skinny. Blue-black hair down to the middle of her back. Flowers on her skirt. A flower in her hair. They weren't laughing, but they had been. They threatened to burst into uncontrollable fits of giggling at any second.

Sandy tapped on the counter to get the receptionist's attention. The woman slipped her hand into his belt loop.

Margaret downed her drink, then dropped the magazines and walked out through the dining room onto the beer garden patio, and from there to her car.

Her phone rang halfway home.

"Please don't be him. Please don't be him. Please don't be him."

SANDY MOBILE.

She let it ring.

*

Another ringing phone woke her. She couldn't find it. They had to ring back, which was when she found it, in the bottom of the linen basket under the houndstooth skirt. "Hello."

"Sally's disappeared." It was Anina.

"What?"

"Her grandma called me, asked me had I heard from her. I told her I hardly know the girl. She thinks she's run off with an old boyfriend."

"What do you think?"

"I think she's slovenly, depressed maybe. Could have done herself a mischief."

"I think you're probably right."

*

The girls met in the war room.

"Cath, you come in, and cover for Sally until she turns up. I'll plate everything up an hour before lunch and leave it in the heaters, then I'll join you outside and watch the yard. Unless anybody has any better ideas."

Nobody had any better ideas.

*

The queue was just as long today, longer even. Nobody shoved, though. Nobody pushed. They'd had all their territorial disputes the day before, and now they got their trays and they waited. The silence was unnerving. Total silence and a tense atmosphere, as if every class had just been yelled at by their form teacher. They weren't sheepish, though. No bowed heads, no averted eyes. They stared straight ahead at the food.

Margaret kept serving until the first students made their way into the playground. Then she tapped out, checked the lock was secure on the fridge, and made her way outside.

It was eerie quiet. Children always made a lot of noise. The St. Andrew's kids were famous for it. Local curmudgeons had been submitting noise complaints for decades. The windows of the old folks' home were swaddled in soundproofing to drown it out.

Margaret joined Bethany at the top of the stairs down to the bottom playground. The lower playground was a sponge-coated pit for the reception, year one, and special needs students. It was full to the brim, but none of the students were playing. They just walked around in ones and twos, with toys strewn all around them, untouched. Even the push-along scooter, usually the trophy of any child strong enough to hold off the others, was leaning against the railing.

"Do you think that they heard about Sally going missing?" Margaret asked.

"Don't see how they could have done. Even if they did, it wouldn't have bothered them this much. Miserable cow never so much as smiled at them." Bethany broke off to wave at a tiny girl with bone-white pigtails. The girl waved back jerkily, once left, once right then her right hand fell back to her side.

The playground filled up around them. Hundreds of students poured out. It didn't get any louder. They muttered to themselves, the ones and twos and rare knots of three. They walked around and around in set patterns, almost like formations.

Margaret found Simon, a year four boy who loved sport. Today, like every other day, he was wearing a Blackpool football strip in place of his uniform. His mother had got special permission from the school – it was the only way they could get him to come. Margaret threw him a ball. He watched it all the way to him until it hit him in the face and he fell down. He didn't even put his hands up to block it.

Beth stifled a chuckle. "I won't tell anybody if you won't."

Margaret didn't laugh. She went over to pick Simon up and dust him off. He had flecks of gravel stuck to the snot on his lip. He didn't wipe it away.

There was a sound from the direction of the beach. She recognised it, and ran for the gate. She picked up Annabelle, a year three, and pulled her out of the way.

A horse leapt over the fence. Its eyes rolled and its tongue was clenched between bloody teeth. A lather of sweat ran from its flanks. Strings of shit hung from its tail. Its back legs clipped the fence post, and it went down heavily, slipping forward in a spray of gravel and blood.

Margaret yelled, but there was no need. Cath tackled the children in its way, picked them up and ran. The children didn't scream. The children didn't laugh. They made no attempt to chase the horse as it ran. They stood rooted to the spot, pivoting on their heels to watch it run out of the yard.

A van hit it as it got to the junction, and it rolled up onto the bonnet and shattered the window. The driver's head slammed forward onto the horn, and stayed there.

The horse whinnied and screamed for the whole time it took to get the children inside. They didn't cry, they didn't shout. They barely seemed to notice.

The horse kept trying to get up. Its back was broken, and it kept trying to drag itself away. It used every last moment of its life to get a few inches further from the beach. Away from the sea.

The vet put it down.

The children didn't cry. They didn't sob. They didn't even ask what had happened to it when Mr. Propp called a special assembly.

*

The black water again. In her nose again. In her eyes again. In her throat again. Choking. Burning bubbles in her bones. She pulled herself down towards the light. Wrapped her hands in the orange rusted bars of the Aldi shopping trolley. Along the bottom now, her fingers in the cracks, on the slime-covered rocks.

There were no fish, no crabs scurrying away, no worms to slide back into their holes. The sea had been scoured, picked clean. Everything living had fled.

She pulled herself through the ragged puncture in her husband's boat. He was still up against the command console. Rotted now. Withered. No light burning in his belly. His eyes gone. His nose gone. His hair snagged on the broken glass of the wheelhouse. His scalp pulled away to reveal the tarnished plate of his skull. The planes of his face eroded. His lower jaw hanging by a brown thread.

The water surged forward. Out to sea. It dragged her with it. Dragged her into Don's corpse. Then came another surge as though some immeasurable weight was stirring out in the deep water. The boat rocked under her feet, tremors and groans that worked up her spine and into her brain.

Something was coming. Something was headed for the coast. Headed for her. She felt it. Drawing closer and closer and ...

Don lunged at her, and shoved her away with his flesh-flaking hands. Frantic for her to leave. To get away. Even though his tongue was gone, she knew he was screaming.

Screaming and screaming and screaming and screaming and screaming for her to get away. To get away from the water.

*

She had been holding her breath in her sleep. She opened her mouth to drag in air, and instead puked off the side of the bed. Clear brine. Nothing but stomach acid. She hadn't eaten in days.

It was still dark. She pulled herself into the bathroom and climbed into the bath in her pyjamas.

It didn't lift, the nightmare surety that something was coming inland. A pressure behind her eyes like a skull full of dirty water.

She clicked on the radio, and turned on the shower with her feet. She didn't take off her pyjamas.

"... for four hours before reportedly turning the gun on herself. Once again, that is the story of an as-yet unidentified elementary school teacher in Great Oaks, California, who is alleged to have opened fire with an automatic weapon during an early morning student breakfast club ..."

Margaret let the warm water wash over her. Into her eyes. Into her ears. She opened her mouth and let it fill her up. A radio jingle played to dispel the bad vibe before the next news story.

"In local news now, a school of dolphins has swum up the Calbridge shipping channel after taking a wrong turning in Mossport harbour. Joint efforts by RSPCA and lifeguard officers to divert the animals back into open water have been unsuccessful... excuse me... unsuccessful after the dolphins apparently attacked them. Officials have urged members of the public to avoid the dolphins, which they describe as confused and frightened."

*

Margaret arrived at the school before dawn. She left her car in her spot by the gate, and walked down the shingle to the beach.

She wanted to go down and touch the water, maybe to roll up her trousers and paddle like she had when she was a girl. She hoped that would convince her she was just being silly, that it was just stress catching up with her. All the things she had to do, that she was still doing, the scrimping and the saving. The people that depended on her for their jobs, their livelihoods.

She dipped her hand in, and recoiled. She rubbed her fingers on her sleeve. The water was dirty. There was no other way she could explain it to herself. There was nothing in it, no rainbow of spilled petrol. It was corrupted somehow, and she needed it off her skin.

There was a splash to her right. A fish flopped on the sand, gasping and gaping. Its fins fanned madly. She picked it up and threw it back in the sea. It turned circles in the water and threw itself back at her feet.

"Stupid bloody sod," she laughed.

It flipped and sprayed her with droplets of the tainted water. She picked it up and threw it further out. It swam six feet up the beach and rolled out of the surf, exhausted now. It whipped its tail back and forth to propel itself up the beach away from the water.

She brushed the sand out of its gills and turned it around to look it in the eye.

"Listen to me. No matter how bad it gets, it's not worth it. Believe me." She threw it as far as she could.

There was a splash before it hit the water. And another. Two more fish had leapt up onto the sand. She tried to push them back in with her feet but they fought her, wriggled and jumped to get round her onto the beach. Another jumped out. Another. Then another three. Four. Five. Soon a wave of hundreds of fish jumped out and landed, choking in the burning air.

More and more and more, until they piled on top of each other, a writhing silver wall of tails and fins. Slapping and thudding against the ground, shedding scales and droplets of black blood.

Margaret ran. She ran until her heart hurt and her hips burned. Something was coming. Coming towards land. Coming towards her. From out there.

*

The children left their classrooms in silence. They got their trays in silence. The teachers hid in their rooms, and pretended not to notice. The students got their food in silence. They ate in silence. They ate the white meat in silence. The silver meat in silence. They came back for seconds in silence. Margaret fed them and then went outside to watch the yard. Monday through Friday.

*

She dreamed again over the weekend. Saturday and Sunday. She dreamed she dragged the horse into the fridge, twitching and rolling, its back broken. She dreamed she butchered it. She dreamed the white fingers grew over it and sucked it, with a sound like the last dregs through a straw. With a sound like water running down a drain. With a sound like waves beating at the shore.

*

It was in all the papers. A man had killed himself in the Seagull – drowned himself in the toilet bowl. A Mr. Sandy McEnroe. No word of his companion.

*

Monday morning came, and she drove herself to school. She kept her head down in the car park. She watched her feet as she went to the kitchen. She unlatched the padlock, and opened the door.

The fridge was a foot deep in black water. It came out in a wave, and soaked her up to the knee, rolling away along the sloped floor and out of the back door into the yard.

The Nikukinchaku sank back to the sand as the water dispersed, clicking and clacking. There was no leak. Nowhere the water could have come from.

She mopped and sopped and wrung out, and mopped some more. She got down on her hands and knees, and brushed the fibres from the grouting. She scrubbed caked blood with a wire brush. There, in the sand, in the centre of a nine point star etched into the tiles, was Sally's ludicrous green stone earring.

She took it and buried it in the bottom of the bin, piled rotten veg on top, and pretended she'd never seen it. She carried the bag down to the beach, and buried it in the sand.

The white fingers grew five feet by lunchtime. The most she'd seen. The dinner bell rang. She moved in with the knife. The fingers moved, and she bit her hand to keep from screaming. They slid away from her against the wall as if they were trying to get out. As if something was calling them.

She heard it too. A low, low moan in the centre of her skull. The fingers stroked and caressed the wall. They pinched and poked at the wall. They scratched the wall. The plaster cracked.

She walked out into the cafeteria. It was deserted. No queue. No children. No Anina. No teachers. The dinner bell rang and rang, and that same low groan tolled in her head.

Calling her.

She went out into the yard. No children. No Bethany. No Cath. No teachers. The moaning dragged her down to the beach. The groan rose into a pulsing scream that throbbed in her eyes.

The sea receded to the horizon, pulling back and back and back and back. A vast stinking brown-grey strip of land. The walls of the harbour were usually just tips breaking the surface, but now they towered thirty feet tall. Don's boat was smashed in the harbour mouth. Her stomach crunched down. The rupture was the same as in her dreams. The same popped bulkhead. The Aldi shopping trolley was submerged in the seabed beside her.

The sand underfoot was crisscrossed with footprints. Hundreds and thousands of footprints. Tiny footprints. She ran after them, yelling. Through the harbour and out onto the wide black fan where the river silt spilled into the sea.

She saw them, then. Every student from the school. They walked hand in hand, in silence, towards the roaring wall of water in the distance. Until they were just black dots.

The moaning turned to groaning turned to singing, and the wave broke.

Something was coming inland.

Something was coming for her.

She felt it.

Babatunde
by Ayobami Leeman Kessler

To my good friend Arthur,

God bless you, and may this letter find you well. I am in desperate need of feeling some connection with the civilized world and so with your permission, I would like to jot down some of my thoughts and experiences as they come to me on my journey home. It is so strange to use that word in reference not to London but to the place of my birth, which I thought I would never see again. I speak of a small town in the backwoods of Nigeria, near Ogbomoso. You will not have heard me speak of it and indeed, in my sudden departure, I failed entirely to mention it at all. I hope you'll forgive me.

It is foolish to think one can escape one's family. They hold a special power over your heart, and no reason can overcome it. When my mother died, I said to myself I had nothing keeping me there and left, thinking I would never return. But as I now see, that was hubris. God has ways of making fools of all our vain promises. Now I find myself, barely able to write for the way this auto is jostling and bouncing on this dirt road, on my way to pay respects to my late father.

I never said much about him for there was little to say. We did not get on, and now that he is dead, I will speak no ill of him. Let me just say that I was not saddened to be parted from him, and I think he likewise felt relieved of a burden when I left. With him passed, I am well and truly rid of this place, and once I have made my expected appearance and avoided the worst of my family, I will make my way back to London with all due speed.

I once heard a very inebriated magistrate's assistant joke that if an officer passes out drunk on duty somewhere in the British Empire, chances are he'll wake up in Nigeria for his troubles. I am inclined to believe him. There is nothing here but *wahala*, as we like to say. Big trouble. Ah well, this whole affair shouldn't take too long and when I am back, we can look over these lines and laugh down at the club.

*

Well, I have arrived. I am alarmed by the absolute lack of change around the old hill. Dirt roads, mud huts, and no sense of progress, no sense of these people making anything of themselves. It sickens me, but I should not be surprised. When I think of all that England has offered the world, all the opportunities it presents us, it fills me with pride to consider myself well and truly one of her own. These people, however, take no such advantage. They are happy to sit and let history move past them without even wanting to know what else there might be. I tried to ask my driver his thoughts on the Great War, and he shrugged as if he'd barely heard of it.

I consider myself very blessed to have found my way to London, Arthur. You were born there and so maybe you only see the traffic and the noise and the pollution, but believe me when I say it is a paradise compared to this squalid Hell to which I've returned.

My uncle Ayodele came out to meet me and show me to where I will be staying. I had hoped I would lodge with the missionaries, who have certainly made themselves as comfortable as they can, but no such luck. I am to stay in my father's house – as is my right, or some such. Uncle Ayo has been unpleasantly laconic but that's just as I remembered him from my youth. He is a dour, unfriendly man, absolutely redolent of the stoic close-mindedness I sought to escape.

It was rather shocking to hear my old name again though. You have known me as Robert these many years, but I was born Babatunde, a name given to children in honour of a deceased patriarch. It means "Father Has Come Back To Us", and I never cared much for it. The sailors I befriended on my escape shortened it to Bob during our long journey. By the time I made it to London,

I'd decided that Robert was a far more fitting name with which to introduce myself to better company, and so it stuck.

Here, however, I am once again little Babatunde, and I feel as if I am expected to run around barefoot in the dirt after the dogs. It is, to put it mildly, highly frustrating.

I tell you, Arthur, if there's one thing that is jarring my memory it is the smell of this place. Everywhere I turn, I come across a scent that sends me tumbling down a rabbit hole of past thoughts and experiences. I stepped in a rotten mango, and while scraping it from my shoe was transported back to countless childhood days. I was forever running around and slipping in the slimy things. They fall from the trees with great regularity in the season, and attract countless iridescent flies to their burst flesh. So odd to see how little things have changed here, whilst I am hardly recognizable.

The funeral is to be tomorrow, but Uncle Ayo keeps hinting at further duties. It's becoming something of a bore. Every time he says it, the other men and women simply nod their heads silently as if they know something I don't. When I say that my time is limited and I must return to London, someone invariably sucks their teeth disapprovingly and says, "Babatunde, why disrespect?" It is more than I can stand, but I just keep telling myself it won't be long.

My fear is that my suits will be ruined by dust and sweat.

*

I had a very odd dream just now which I feel the need to jot down, even though the images are already receding. There was a distinct, earthy smell that seemed familiar, although I am at pains to remember just how. I also recall smoke, although not a particularly acrid one. What I remember most of all however was hearing my own name being said again and again. "Babatunde. Babatunde." The whole business has put me off entirely, and I doubt I will find sleep again tonight. Forgive my prattling, my friend.

*

Today was actually rather pleasant, Arthur. There was such a festive mood in the air that one would hardly think a funeral were in the offing. I made my way to the fires where women in brightly-dyed cloths were cooking up mouth-watering delights. Fried *dodo* (which you might know as plantain), spicy *akara*, steaming *moinmoin* – oh, there are a few things I miss about my old country, I will admit. British fare is hearty and goes well with a good pint, but there is something about Yoruba cooking which calls to me from time to time.

I tried to linger by the women, with their pots and their mortars. They pounded yams with such ferocity that I was surprised none of them lost a hand! Too soon though, I was chased away and my uncle swooped upon me like a moribund bird of prey. He wanted to tell me of my role in the funeral, which to your mind would probably more closely resemble an odd festival. There is to be a panoply of music and food and colourful attire. No doubt it would look garish and outlandish to your cultured eyes, but these are my people's ways, and one must do as the Romans do. Damn, but I will be happy to be rid of these flies!

*

Arthur, I must jot this down while the outrage is still fresh in my mind and there is enough paraffin left to light this pitch-black hut. My uncle took me aside after dinner and showed me my duties for tomorrow. I am *most* put out. I assumed they would be limited to standing around and perhaps making a short speech in honour of the old man, but no! I am to don some ridiculous outfit and scamper about like a savage and, worst of all, I'm meant to impersonate some old, daft spirit. The whole thing is quite absurd, and I would laugh if it weren't such an imposition. I respect that there are traditions that must be upheld, but there are also limits past which a gentleman can only be pushed so far.

Slowly I feel my heart begin to calm. Writing to you is a true balm for my frayed nerves. Perhaps it's just the heat, or my constitution being somewhat unprepared for the richness of the food this evening. I shall try to sleep and hopefully by tomorrow, I will be in a better place to handle all this nonsense. Thank you, my friend. At least I'm not required to kill myself to be a horseman for my father in the hereafter. As a child I heard stories in that vein that haunted me most terribly! Always count your blessings!

*

Another of these blasted dreams. Very much the same as last night, only my burdened mind added the detail of the strange and unwieldy costume I am to be forced to wear as part of the funeral festivities. I could feel the very weight of it around me as I moved through the smoke and the dust, still smelling of old earth. Through it all, my name was repeated again and again. "Babatunde. Babatunde."

I am not a superstitious man, Arthur. I gave all that up after getting a proper education, and my introduction to the right sort of people helped ease me from my ignorant past. Still, I cannot shake the notion that this dream has some portentous design. Forgive the trembling of my hand, but I am very much still affected by this whole matter and the light grows dimmer with every scratch of my pen. I shall stop now and try to reclaim what rest I can.

*

Oh, Arthur, my good, good friend. You are long suffering, and if you are still reading this, you are a patient old fool. I am almost of a mind to tear these letters up and throw them on the fire for their rank silliness. I joke, of course. I must keep these as a reminder of how one can become so worked up over nothing!

Today was the funeral, and allow me to try to paint the scene. The missionaries asked one last time if my uncle was certain he did not want a proper burial for my father. Ayodele shook his head and said, "No, today is not for the hanged god. He has his days. This day is for us." The missionaries did not quite know how to take that, and I offered what apologetic glances I could, but I fear it was small comfort.

The promised festivities were just as I had imagined, bright and musical and full of wondrous foods whose smells and tastes still linger with me. Hopefully they will continue to do so as I begin my journey back to London tomorrow. At the established time, I was taken away and draped in my outlandish attire. I swear to you, although I expect you will find me half-mad, I rather got into the spirit of the whole thing!

I danced and I shouted as if I were indeed one of these old spirits walking the earth, praising this man for his good work or castigating that woman for letting her children run wild. As I moved through the village, others in similarly styled but wildly different outfits likewise danced about. The laughter and the excitement and the sense of truly being home again was remarkable, Arthur. There has been nothing like it in my experience.

By the end of it all, my father was laid to rest. I feel we were all of us made whole by the experience. All my fears and my worries were such silly things, born of old disagreements and time spent away. I certainly have no intention of remaining here and trading my good suit for a bright *agbada*. All in all though, I must admit that it has been a remarkable trip, well worth the distance.

I think I shall carry these letters with me and hand them to you upon my arrival. The look on your face as you read these brief words will well repay my pains over my undeserved fears.

Until we meet again, my dear friend.

*

The dream came again, only now I am unsure whether it is dream or if I am going mad. I woke to find scratches upon my feet and the smell of earth on my fingertips.

Dear Arthur, what is happening?

In my dream I was running, still encased in that leathery outfit, the sounds of clattering cowry shells echoing as I heard that terrible call again and again and again. "Babatunde," it beckoned.

At first I ran from it, trying desperately to shed the awkward attire, but my clumsy fingers could not find my way out of it, no matter how hard I tried, so I just kept on running. Eventually, with my legs on fire and my way lost, I turned and began to walk towards the sounds. Up and up the old hill I marched, my vision obscured by the mask on the costume.

As I felt my legs begin to buckle beneath me, I saw smoke, and soon came to a clearing on the crown of the hill. There had gathered all the other costumed figures from the funeral, and many more besides. They beckoned for me to join them in their chant. The drum, which I had mistaken for my own heartbeat, echoed to their solemn words. "Babatunde. Babatunde."

"Why do you call my name?" I asked, unsure even as I took my place among them. "What do you want from me?" My words had slipped back into Yoruba without my mind even noticing.

One of the masked figures turned towards me and answered, "We do not. We have never called you." At those words, I joined in their chanting, unsure what the figure meant, but knowing that it was my place to be here and to join with them.

"Babatunde!" I called out, the name – no longer my own – rushing past my lips on that windswept hill, swirling with the smoke and the drumbeat and all the fears of the long and terrible night. "Babatunde!" The word lost all meaning. Suddenly it was no longer name or honorific but promise, in that darkness. "Babatunde!" *Father has returned to us.* In that moment, I felt the hillside quake and eyes that were not eyes opened before me, and then there was nothing.

Arthur, this dream has me shaken beyond all comprehension. My muscles ache and my throat is raw. Tomorrow, before I leave, I will speak with my uncle about all this. I must know just what is happening and what it all means. Once I have such answers as he will give me – and I do not expect many – I will gather my things and take the first auto out of this place, never to return. Thank you for your friendship, Arthur. It means the world to me.

*

Dear Mr. Goodale,

You do not know me, but my name is John Copeland, and I am a Southern Baptist missionary working in Nigeria. About a year ago we found an old, moldy copy of *Paradise Lost* in one of the old residences here in Ogbomoso. We were going to burn it in the trash heap when my wife noticed that there were yellowed papers stuck inside. These turned out to be letters addressed to your father, and we've included them in this envelope. We didn't quite know what to make of them, but wanted to make sure they got to their intended recipient.

After many inquiries, we eventually discovered that your father had passed away not too long ago, but your name was given to us, as well as your address. I hope you will not find this too distressing, but we felt that these should go to you to do with as you wish.

We tried to find out what we could about the writer but no one knew anything about him, so we concluded that he must have passed away as well, if indeed this man existed at all. My wife is convinced that the letters are a work of fiction. The writer does seem to have had some familiarity with this area, although he appears to have mistaken a crater for a hill – unless the locals were experimenting with dynamite decades ago!

Either way, the letters truly are a remarkable example of the rich, imaginative lives these people lead here, and how connected they are with their innate spirituality. We honestly believe that the Nigerians are a blessed people, and we consider it an honor that the Lord sent us here to do his work.

God bless you and keep you well,

John Copeland

April 7th, 1975

The Myth of Proof
by Greg Stolze

The Georgetown lecture hall was surprisingly full. Joyce and Glory worried, briefly, that they wouldn't be able to find adjoining chairs, but there was a space, and they seated themselves.

"People do love their red-meat debates," Glory said.

Joyce tilted her head noncommittally. She was in her forties, and her expensively uninteresting work skirt and sensibly feminine heels suggested that if she wanted to be gorgeous, she would, but she had chosen collected and intelligent instead. She was slim, short, discretely made up. No reasonable observer would have been surprised to find a government ID in her Coach clutch. Any such observer who knew the INR's function within the State Department wouldn't have been surprised that she worked for that organization.

Glory was younger than her colleague, with shorter hair, looser clothes and the face of a Greek statue. She readily conceded that her statue was one of the less popular ones, representing martial valor or domestic responsibility. Most people assumed she was ugly, since it was easy to think her fat. She didn't mind. If those same viewers had seen an Olympic shot putter in baggy clothes, they'd think the same thing. But if you saw her move something, it was clear that she was unusually strong. Especially if that something was a high risk prisoner, hauled from transport to cell.

Up on the stage, an academic came out to stand between the podiums and introduce the evening's speakers. His clothes were as formal as Joyce's, but looked cheaper—which they almost certainly were.

"Ladies and gentlemen," he said. "Questions of faith and religion are central to the issue of man... Of humankind's place in the universe. Here to discuss the matter tonight are the Reverend Jill MacCray from right here at Georgetown..." He paused, as a number of students reflexively cheered, "... along with the bestselling author of *I, Antichrist*, and *Gene, Genus, Genius,* Dr. Ward Maddox!"

The cheers for the atheist had a raw edge to them.

"Did you read his Tweet about Palestine?" Glory asked.

"I read his book on biology," Joyce replied. "It was very well thought out."

"I can't say the same for his hundred forty characters on politics."

"Religion," said Dr. Ward Maddox, "is the engaged parking brake on social progress. Religious belief serves the same purpose for individual cognition. Instead of pursuing original ideas, the lazy mind clings to the orthodoxies of a book, one that was ancient to cultures which died from old age! Instead of basing social policy on the rational maximization of happiness, archaic principles forged by priest castes in order to control behavior and even emotion are cited as justification for the suppression of dissent, the creation..."

"He's a good speaker," Joyce whispered to Glory approvingly.

"Anything sounds smart with a British accent."

"Hmph. They like him in England, too."

"Has anyone gone broke telling the English they can kick Christianity to the curb?"

Joyce made a little *moue*, and they returned their attention to the podiums, where Reverend MacCray was having her first say.

"To judge religion by the criteria of science is as unfair as judging science by the criteria of religion. Faith is not meant to measure facts, and dismissing it as just 'a story told to explain the thunder' is far too easy. Today, we know what thunder is, we have physical explanations, but humanity's faith, and our love of God, is undiminished. Religion is a foundation for community, a primer on how to become our better selves..."

"I don't like her scarf," Joyce whispered. "It looks like a knockoff."

"Whatever," Glory replied, brow furrowing.

"This is what religion always does," Maddox said, surging up for his rebuttal. "It moves the goalposts. Consider the doomsday prophets who give a time and date for their lord's great day of wrath." He rolled his eyes, mouth drolly pursed. "They're barking mad, but they're at least coherent and consistent and honest! They give you a *testable hypothesis*. But when their predictions fail, as they inevitably do, as William Miller's did in 1844 and Harold Camping's did in 2011, they don't step back and reconsider, they *double down* on their delusions and recalculate a different date! Miller said, 'Oh, no, the world's going to end in 1845 instead,' while Camping changed the rules and claimed *Jesus* was running late. It's not only these loony end timers who do this, they're just the clumsiest and most obvious.

"Once faith can no longer claim the grandeur of thunder, it becomes all about morality and community. But I would assert that you can have plenty of community without needing to share an imaginary friend in the sky. Moreover, morality based on appeasing a god who might as well be the monster in the closet is terminally fragile. Once a believer has a 'moment of weakness' (which is what they call it when you're strong enough to ignore the Holy Writ) and does not get struck down and punished, the entire system of enforcement collapses beyond resuscitation. The only exceptions are those who internalize the culture of abuse so thoroughly that they punish themselves. In their meek abasement, they fail to realize that the only 'god' smiting them is their own entrenched neurosis!"

The atheists in the audience erupted in cheers. Joyce politely applauded. Glory just sat, expressionless, as Maddox recited a litany of religious war crimes and genocides. Some of his followers even booed when Reverend MacCray came back to speak again, while others shushed their rowdy fellows.

"If the function of religion has developed, is that in any way a bad thing? Certainly, by the standards you set for science, constant improvement is, um, desirable. No one needs to discover the electron again."

"Religion didn't do that the first time!" someone shouted.

The minister continued. "The conflict between faith and science is needless and artificial. One is a tool for dealing with what we don't know, and the other is for coping with what we can't know. I'll freely admit that churches have been... that horrible things have been done in the name of belief. But it's always the greatest goods that do the most damage when corrupted..."

"If god was real, and involved," Maddox interrupted, "religion would be incorruptible! Religion would be something you can test! But its myriad failures have..."

"Please, I was speaking," the reverend said.

Maddox bulled on ahead. "Science tests facts and reveals truth or falsehood! You give me a positive test for religion and I'll believe it! I'll have no choice, my scientific integrity would, would demand it! But I've issued this challenge time and time again, I'll pay a million dollars, one million US..."

"It's not about money!"

"Tell that to Jim Baker and Peter Popoff!" Dr. Maddox sneered. "The Bible, like the Koran and the Torah and the Bhagavad Gita, is a counterfactual narrative! Revering these idiotic books means embracing lies over truth!"

"The point of the Bible is not mere facts!"

"*Mere* facts? The truth is now a negligible concern to you? Mrs. MacCray, I've dealt with some frothing, simpleminded fundamentalists but at least they have the courage of their convictions! You don't even believe the Bible is *factual*?"

"Neither do you!"

"I'm not a Christian! What kind of Christian denies the, the Bible itself?"

"You seem intent on defining Christianity from the outside!" Reverend MacCray's face was flushed and she, like Maddox, was starting to shout. Unlike him, she was clearly unhappy and uncomfortable doing so. "You exclude anyone with any doubt, any nuance—the *vast majority* of Christians can't meet your standards..."

"Only because I demand consistency!"

The audience was starting to boo and catcall.

"I've had about enough of this," Glory said to Joyce. "You want to go get gelato?"

*

After his speech, Dr. Ward Maddox took off his shirt and undershirt, and toweled his armpits triumphantly. His chest was sunken and frail above the dome of a modest paunch, but he felt vigorous, young... Dominant. He'd go out after, with some fellows from biology, and charm some undergrads from the campus chapter of the CFI with well-tested *bon mots* they'd never heard. He might get drunk. He might get laid. But he was certain he'd get admired, and that put a smile on his face even as he wiped the doughy prominence where his solar plexus blended into belly.

He heard the door open behind him, and instinctively brayed, "Don't you know how to *knock* in this country?"

"My apologies." The voice was quiet, barely masculine, tinged with the ghost of an accent. "I shall try anew."

Maddox turned as the door closed, and was immediately knocked upon. He rolled his eyes. "James, is that you?" he said, voice loud and just starting to ramp up to its fullest sarcasm.

"No, my name is..."

"If you're not James, do be a dear and *piss right off*," he bellowed, applying underarm deodorant, and pulling on a clean polo shirt.

"I'm afraid I have a matter of some importance to discuss." The voice was barely audible through the door, but it had a serenely persistent tone.

"If it's a speaking matter, James sets the schedule, and for anything else my agent is Parveen Sasooli..."

"It's about the million dollars."

Maddox shut his mouth, and his shoulders dropped a little. "Oh for fuck's sake," he muttered, running his hands through his thinning hair. He didn't say it loud enough to get through the door.

"May I come in?"

There was only one way out of his dressing room, and the intruder was blocking it. Maddox turned the knob, pulled, and was immediately struck by the man's smell. The intruder was dressed neatly, but his coat had traces of dust on the shoulders—traces only. It must have sat in his closet, since the last funeral, Maddox guessed. He'd dusted it, probably gone over it with tape, but hadn't taken it to a proper dry cleaner. His tie was inoffensive, but showed fine lines of distortion across its midsection where the tiepin (a curious onyx affair with gold chasing) had snagged threads over and over and over again. The cuffs of his shirt were frayed. He presented a deeply-tanned hand to shake, its nails bitten and with tarry black matter under disgraceful cuticles. The knees of his pants were shiny, and his shoes were too old.

"My name is Mateus Quiroga," he said. "I have traveled a long time to see you." He had a neatly trimmed white beard and coarse white hair struggling out of a left-side part. His eyes were so dark they seemed to have no iris, just light-devouring pupils.

Quiroga held an old, distressed, leather bound book against his ribs. The hand clutching the book looked burned, or perhaps deformed. But it was the scent that curled Maddox's lip. Quiroga didn't stink of after-workout perspiration, but of old sweat gone stale and layered and ignored to ferment. It was the reek, not of someone who needed a shower, but of someone who'd needed one for a week.

Still, he shook the man's hand.

"Another million-dollar challenger, eh?" He shook his head. "Come in. I can't give you more than ten minutes. If you need to make a longer argument you must schedule it with James..."

"It shouldn't take too long," Quiroga replied. Perhaps it was his confidence, or the blackness of his eyes, or the inhuman brightness of his false teeth that pushed Maddox's heart, sped it up, made him sweat as if to catch up with the sheen on the man's face. "May I use this table?"

"Sure, but it's going to take more than a Bible verse to..."

"The *Bible*, pah!" Quiroga actually spat on the floor. He gave it more than a token drop too, taking his time to generate a noxious bolus of yellow phlegm. "The only belief more ignorant than your denial of the sublime is to put one's faith in 'Jesus, meek and mild.' What a narrow life of coddled safety one must live, to believe that a god is just, and loves you!"

"No argument here," Maddox said, glancing at the door. When he looked back, Quiroga had the book open to a diagram, drawn in a cramped and tiny hand. He started muttering.

"Look," Maddox said. "Maybe we can reschedule?"

"Giving in so easily?" Quiroga looked up, his expression contemptuous and sly. "It's simple to play at the superior intellect, when one is only in front of an audience of gullible god-lickers and smug agnostics with advanced degrees, scoffing to think that anything more powerful, important or real than themselves could bestride the earth!"

"Look, just calm down..."

"Don't tell me to calm down, you fatuous *tit*," Quiroga snarled. Despite his nerves, some part of Maddox noted the man's command of colloquial English. "The things you disbelieve, I *know*. Now, about the million dollars..."

"Yes?"

"I prove, to you, the existence of a incomprehensibly powerful inhuman entity, and I get the money? That's how it works?"

"Er, yes... I have to say, if you can *prove* god exists, why not form your own church?"

"Who says I haven't?"

"Well, it's just... I never heard of you. Sorry..."

"No need to apologize," Quiroga said, consulting a small pocket calendar and looking back at the chart in the ancient book.

"I'd just assume that a church which can prove that which other faiths merely assert would, ah, grow quite rapidly."

"Public relations," Quiroga said, "are a bitch."

"Ah."

"Besides, can you think of a better P.R. maneuver than converting you, the loudest and proudest scoffer in the intellectual arena?"

"Um..."

"Have a seat."

"I'd prefer to stand," Maddox said, glancing at the door again.

"We will not be disturbed," Quiroga said, with maddening certainty. "I must insist. *Sit*."

"Er..." He sat.

Frowning at his book, Quiroga uttered a series of syllables unlike any language Maddox had ever heard. They sounded more like a melding of birdsong with the deep croaking of camels.

...and then Dr. Maddox's excellent mind fell down.

His identity, the sensations from his eyes and ears and the nerves of his flesh, his memories and instincts and epistemological fundaments plunged downward into something below, like an unsuspected step into quicksand. He was not in his body, not in time, nor in place, nor even inhabiting the structure of thoughts and judgments that he had accrued throughout his life, surrounding his epicenter of ego like a snail's protective shell.

Quiroga spoke, and Dr. Maddox was subsumed.

*

The vastness of time engulfed a mind, and Maddox beheld it.

It was wordless, beyond the structures of verbal thought the way an eagle is beyond the need of a wheelchair. Past alive and dead, past self and other, past belief and doubt, past all order, this chaos of knowledge lurked. Its incalculable mass dwarfed Maddox's thoughts the way the sun might outshine a matchstick, but there was nothing bright to it. It was all glacial dark, it was that into which light fades, into which heat sinks in entropic surrender.

Pulled beneath the surface of this alien genius, this psychic miasma, he saw logic and reason as laughable charades, a trick of the light where the true lineaments of reality were picked out in the blackness outside time, beyond space, against life.

All he knew was emptied, the brilliance of human science snuffed out like that matchstick, eclipsed in an instant by the mere being of this thing, this cloud of inky dreams that wore the world like a suit. It was too big to see until someone or something—in this case, Quiroga—interrupted its bleak radiance to let a form be perceived, like a hand casting a shadow in the sunshine.

Maddox's every hope died, shriveling like salted worms before this revelation, yet for all its grandeur, for all its scale, the size of it shrinking his aspirations and emotions to the dimensions of an atom... He realized that all this was just one layer.

He knew that he would never experience joy again, and that the vast witness which had broken him was simply the first letter of an alphabet of ideas, the least word of which would crush human history. He caught a glimpse of a cosmos which was written in that language, endless epics to nullity and paeans to the death of order.

*

His emergence from the catatonia of horror was gradual. He realized he was sobbing, that he'd soiled himself, that he'd fallen from his chair.

Next he realized that James was there.

"Ward! Ward, Christ, what happened?"

Bubbling through the thick mucus of his hysteria, Maddox's voice shifted gradually to laughter. "Not Christ! Not Christ!"

"Ward, we need to get you to a doctor..."

"*Get off me!*" he cried, shoving his aide away. He pushed himself back up to a sitting position and wiped his face, first with his hands, then with a handful of tissues taken from James.

"What happened?"

"I had... it was..." James handed him a bottle of Evian water, which he gratefully guzzled before pouring half of it on his face. "I don't know what happened."

"Okay. Okay. Let's get you cleaned up," James said quietly. "We'll get you a change of clothes, get you to the hotel, tell everyone you've got the flu..."

"Where's my phone?" Ward asked. Then he froze.

His phone had become an impromptu paperweight, holding down a torn-out sheet of notebook paper.

Dr. M.
I will call you tomorrow at 10:30 AM sharp to discuss the payment of my one million dollars. Thank you for your generosity.
-Q.

"That motherfucker," Maddox whispered.

"What?" James was cleaning.

Maddox straightened himself up and tried to recall some of his old dignity, tried to put on the weary charade of being confident and in control. "Go get the clothes, yes. I'll, um, I'll need a full change. I need... well, you know."

"Sure," James said.

"I'm going to stay here with the door closed. Please let it be known that I don't wish to be disturbed. Tell people I'm ill."

"You clearly are," James replied.

"Clearly," the professor replied, staring at his phone as James made himself scarce. Then he picked it up and called a number he'd memorized two months previous.

"Hello," he said. "This is Dr. Ward Maddox."

"Yes?" said the voice on the other end.

"I..." He racked his rattled brain for the exact phrase he'd been taught. "I'm enquiring about tickets to the opera."

"I beg your pardon?"

"Can you tell me what number this is?"

The voice on the other end recited the number he'd dialed.

"Ah. I have called you in error," Dr. Maddox said woodenly. It seemed inane, like a child's game of spies.

"No troubles," he heard in reply, which he'd been taught meant "Someone will be in touch later this evening."

*

That night, a knock at Maddox's door summoned the man to peek out from his hotel room, shivering. Glory looked at him dispassionately.

"Hello?" he said.

"It's about those opera tickets," she said.

He unlocked the door. "His name is Quiroga," he said, withdrawing quickly back to his cup of hot tea. "Mat... Mateus Quiroga. He has a church. I think that's his real name."

"Uh huh." She knew better than to take names at face value. "Why don't you start at the top?" He seemed smaller than he had onstage. Pale and trembling, he looked... Yes, the word she'd use was 'haunted.'

"Certainly, yes, sure... Um, can I get you anything, M-Ms...?"

"You can call me 'Kitty,' and I'm fine. How about you? You... all right?"

"I am a blob of protoplasm in an inherently absurd universe," he said, "And earlier this afternoon I had my face forcefully ground into that fact."

There was a silence.

"I'm sorry," he said at last.

"You're sure this Quiroga guy is a genuine operator?" Glory asked.

Maddox shuddered. "Positive. The things I saw last time, the... the other proof... it wasn't like this." He took a sip of his tea. "Not like this at all."

"Was there any kind of tangible...?"

"No, but he had a *book*," Maddox said, and a change came over his face. His attitude towards his guest suddenly shifted, changing to suspicion and a sneer. "Your *people* are always very concerned about the *books*, now aren't they?"

"Not my end of things," she said, very cool and flat.

He glared. She looked back, impassive as a stone at the bottom of the sea. Finally, he sighed.

"You're *certain* this guy used paranormal powers on you?" she persisted.

"*Yes*, I told you. He's going to c-contact me tomorrow at 10:30 AM *sharp*."

"Outstanding. We'll take it from here, Dr. Maddox. You don't have to ever worry about Mr. Quiroga again."

"I don't want to do this any more," Maddox said, and just as he'd gone from frightened to pugnacious, his mood now shifted to something vulnerable and dejected.

All things considered, Glory had liked it best when he was cross and imperious. "Dr. Maddox..." she said.

"I don't want to make the million dollar challenge and have to see these things," he said, sounding like something between a querulous old man and a sad little boy. "I don't want to know and be... this way."

She frowned briefly, then moved closer and put a hand on his shoulder. "Look, Ward," she said. "You... You're the best thing we've found for getting these guys to out themselves, getting them to let their guard down."

"Can't someone else do it?" he asked.

"You know no one's as good as you. It's not just the money, it's the..." She searched for a way to phrase it other than, 'you're such an arrogant prick.' "You're the big time," she said at last. "You represent everything they aren't allowed to have, respect and admiration and legitimacy."

"Those things are all empty," Maddox whispered.

"They still want 'em though. They think they're owed the, what, the awe of us mere mortals. So you're catnip. They can't, they won't let you be. And that's a *good* thing," she said, trying to lie to him through her grip, trying to convince him that she believed what she was saying. "When they come after you, we can catch them. I mean, who knows what this Quiroga guy has done already?"

He didn't answer and didn't meet her eye. Eventually, she stood to go.

"Do you really think, after this, I'll be able to put on that performance again? To deny the might of Cthulhu after it has been made manifest in my eyes, in my *mind*?"

"The might of *what*?" she said sharply.

"Cthulhu," he repeated. "The beginning. Cthulhu."

"Get some sleep," she said. "As for what you say, who cares if you believe it? No one ever asked you to. You're the great disbeliever, right?"

She was almost out the door when he asked, "Can I watch you kill him?"

"You know that's not how this works," she said.

The door opened, and closed, leaving him alone again.

Service
by Lynnea Glasser

You minimize your presence. Body pressed flat against the wall, neutral smile, head slightly bowed—the affectations of a good servant. Master Harkin has already finished the dregs of his tea, while Master Bennett squints through his glasses at the newspaper, food untouched. You stare at them both. Harkin is simultaneously stroking his beard and wiping crumbs from his vest, no doubt appreciating his own efficiency. Bennett has forgone his vest again, but he at least keeps his face trimmed. He takes his glasses off and wipes them, the fifth time this morning. He's nervous about something. Harkin's idling at the table means he's composing another lecture, which, if you're quiet enough, he won't unleash on you. They're always on the same tired subjects—the hidden edges of reality, the secrets to finding the unknowable, the dangers beyond space and time. It's all just a bunch of self-indulgent rambling, but you're paid enough to feign interest.

Of course, feigning too much interest sets off Bennett's nerves. He'll accuse Harkin of reckless indiscretion, of being too free with secrets, as if you cared about their work, retained their pointless lectures, or had the bad sense to subject anyone else to that inanity. You almost wish you could get that point across to them, but you doubt they'd believe—or even understand—the sentiment. You wish, too, not for the first time, that you didn't have to stand over them and watch them eat their breakfasts on cracked china and tattered table runners. Bennett's ancestral cliffside house is unsustainably large. While the glut of sold-off furniture leaves you with less to keep clean, they've refused to hire on replacement help, or call for repairs, or even purchase anything they deem non-essential. The result is a slowly deteriorating, grossly unfashionable shell of former opulence. You are just here biding your time, saving what you can for the day when, inevitably, you will have to leave and find even more unsavory work.

Bennett reaches for a pen and begins circling numbers in the newspaper. Getting a daily paper out here, so far from civilization, is one of the few luxuries they afford themselves these days. You wonder if that's what the silver has been going towards. Harkin rests his elbows against the table—forcing it to wobble—as a smirk spreads across his face while he watches his partner's absent-mindedness. You're less keen about such antics. The man will forget his hunger now and remember it later, and then you'll be the one who has to fix it. Better to deal with it now.

You clear your throat and broach the subject. "Sir, would you..."

Bennett jumps with a sharp gasp, "Oh, Tabitha!" He gives a half-grin then quickly tucks the newspaper beneath his arm.

Harkin leans back, waiting for the situation to play out.

You take a deep breath and do your best to finish strong, "... would you perhaps prefer something else?"

Bennett insistently waves off the suggestion. "How thoughtful! No, I'm fine. Just lost in thought." He makes a show of eating some toast. "Since you're here, I suppose I should mention—" He clears his throat and continues, "We're expecting a shipment. Please take care of it, will you?" Then he hunches over definitively and starts on his eggs, while doing his best to keep the newspaper from slipping.

You give a small curtsy. "Of course."

Harkin stands and stretches lazily. "It's a shipment of mercury, so be careful."

Bennett adjusts the newspaper and scowls at the air.

Harkin over-casually shrugs. "Only because it's toxic. I'm not telling her what it's for."

Bennett mutters into his toast, "She should be careful with it no matter what it was, if she were any good."

You stiffen, hold your breath, and do your best not to draw attention to yourself.

Harkin walks over to his partner, yanks out the newspaper and then opens it wide, angled just exactly for you to see it best.

You politely avert your eyes, glancing about the room. Which is too bad, because now you've noticed that the flowered wallpaper is starting to peel again, just in the corners. You'll have to fix that later.

Harkin points at your gaze. "See that? She looked away. She knows her place."

Bennett runs a hand to his temple, pushing back his glasses. "She does a fine job with what she's assigned, but we should not be so cavalier as to trust her overmuch, is all."

Harkin folds the paper, silently refusing the argument.

Bennett waves it off. "Just... Never mind. We'll talk about it later." He stands and leaves, half his breakfast finished. Hopefully that's enough that he doesn't ring for you later. You hear the second story floorboards creak. Apparently he's going to pout in his bedroom.

Harkin casually turns to you as if he were just continuing the conversation from his first sentence, "Anyway, be sure to pay and tip the man."

As if you weren't right there during all of that. As if you weren't always one lost argument from being thrown out. As if you actually cared what they did in their lab, what they did with the newspapers, what they did in their rooms. One day you'll leave, you'll find something better.

Until then, you curtsy. "Of course."

Harkin buttons his cuffs as he continues on, "One other thing, now that Bennett's gone. We're expecting guests. Please prepare the spare rooms."

Well, that's some damn short notice. You hide your surprise with a deeper curtsy, along with the expected, "Of course," which is your third, "Of course," in a row. You fidget with a snag in your woolen overcoat. That phrase feels like the extent of your permitted vocabulary sometimes.

Harkin strolls out down the hall—probably to pompously stare at very important things in his smoke-stained study—when the implication of the request sinks in. Prepare for a visitor? They trust someone enough to bring to their lab? Must be someone special.

The last threat of guests to entertain was a year ago, and that fellow was delayed indefinitely because he had been tainted by a Watcher. At least, that was the explanation Bennett gave, back when he actually trusted you. He'd gesture grandly about at the shelves of unopened books, at the stacks of unperturbed maps. "We're trying to sneak a peak without being noticed. But how do you do that when Watchers are everywhere?" You'd smiled, nodded, continued about your work. Books, used or not, still gathered their dust, and keeping busy gave you an obvious way to excuse yourself.

Questions showed interest, and interest made them feel that conversing with you had merit, which it didn't. Not because you didn't have your own thoughts, but because they were always dismissed, or laughably wrong, or else correct enough that they suspected you of unsavory help. It was never worth it, even back when they were cordial enough to speak with you on the topic.

You look over the remains of the breakfast, and eat a few pieces of toast yourself before carrying the plates back into the kitchen. As you scrub them clean and place them to dry, you start thinking ahead. You'll have to prepare all three guest rooms, just to be sure, in case one of them proves unsatisfactory, and in case Harkin or Bennett decides to temporarily abstain from the master bedroom out of some sense of decency. That means several sets of fresh sheets. Laundry. You look around the kitchen—grease coating the fading walls, blackened stove soot collecting on the floor, remnants of spilled foods sticking to shelves—and sigh. You had been hoping to use the day to clean your station, but there's always some demand or another that pulls you away.

It's just as you finish placing the last plate that the doorbell rings. You hike your skirt to answer a bit faster, but even with your haste, the doorbell rings a second time just as you open it. Outside stands a drowsy workman with clothes as greasy, sooty, and sticky as your kitchen. You try not to visibly curl your lip at the reminder of how much worse things could be than living here. The workman simply points to several already-unloaded gallon-sized casks laid out in the mud. Technically, that mud should have been a paved driveway, if properly cared for. The nearby ocean is always breezing in more sand to cover it up, and the morning drizzle washes it out further, but still, the man should have had more thought.

You eye him sideways for the shoddy job. He's your class. He could have waited for you to open the door, to unload them inside and saved you the trouble of having to clean up after them. But either he didn't care or he didn't realize. You sigh and pay, and he leaves without even offering to carry them further.

As the truck drives away, you make a small effort towards pulling the casks into the foyer, but they're much heavier than they look, so you abandon them. That makes sense, on reflection. Ultimately, their transport is no concern of yours, since you're not allowed down to the lab yourself. You wonder what the workman would have thought of that place, if he had been allowed to deliver them to their final destination. Apathy? Fear? Pity? Maybe pity for you. Maybe he'd have invited you to take a ride back with him to town, urged you to get a new job.

Apathy be damned, how could he leave a lady in such an improper situation?

Of course, even if you went back with him, your savings wouldn't last you that long, and what jobs are there for women? Cooking, child-rearing, and washing. You need letters of recommendation for the first two, which you'll never get, and washing is impossibly miserable. Then there's wifery, which is just a combination of all the worst parts. There are just no options out there. You're not sure what you're going to do when this job dries up, but you know you've got to ride it out as long as possible.

The upstairs floorboards creak. The two of them come out of hiding now that the stranger has left. They thank you for dealing with the delivery man, doing their best to pretend that it was dignity, and not caution, that had kept them from answering the door. Of course, you indulge them. They carry every cask inside and lock the door before starting the longer trips carrying the casks down the stairs together. This strategy leaves behind rings of mud on the bare wooden paneling of the foyer, and for once, you're thankful that they have gotten rid of that entryway rug. The mess will be easier to tidy up.

You tie your hair back and bring out a rag, kneeling to take care of the mess while it's still wet. From down here, you can see the grime caked into the engraved floor molding all along the walls. You do your best to ignore it. You can't allow yourself to be drawn into even more ancillary cleaning tasks before completing the more pressing matters. There are so many old, tattered, tarnishing pieces of this house that it's all you can manage to just keep it in the state it's in. Perfection is an impossible goal.

You refocus on the floors. There's one muddy scuff mark that's giving you trouble. You eventually give up when you remember that the mark was actually from the grandfather clock that they had stripped for parts a year ago, and gave you the same trouble back then too. Well, certainly it is not worth your time a second year in a row. As you stand up, you hear splashing, scraping, and the creaking slam of their lead-lined door, followed by a faint, rhythmic chanting. There's no doubting what the workman would have thought about that. Are you so resigned, so desperate, that you are willing to put up with what should really be intolerable? Or is it actually not so bad, and you've just had the time to get used to it?

You sigh as you rinse out the rag. You really shouldn't delay that laundry any longer, washing being a full-day task, and most of the morning already gone. You start the fire and mix the soap water for the tub, then pull all the sheets. It's not long until you're stirring the whole mix in a rolling boil. The steam alone would bring a sweat, but the manual effort makes the task insufferable. Your sweat dampens several layers of clothing, and even your thick underarm pads are pushed to their limit. You wish you could roll up your sleeves or hike up your skirt, but you've got the scars to show what happens when there's a splash.

Finally, the water turns dark enough that you feel satisfied, so you put out the coals and hang up the pieces. It's once it's all done that the true fullness of your misery sets in. Your hair clumps, your clothes stick, and your hands swell and crack. It is the most vile, disgusting feeling you could possibly conjure. You can't imagine doing this all day in some massive laundry house. You'd be dead within a week. You already need a break. You need a walk along the ocean.

It's a godsend. The breeze dries and cools, the sharp-smelling surf burns away the overly-sweet detergent, and the rhythm of the waves helps you slow your breath. The haze is just starting to recede, some birds cawing gently, and you watch as waves tumble over each other, new waves crashing before old waves can pull back all the way. And you, perched up on this cliff, just get to sit up here and watch it all.

This is why you don't leave. This is the thing that makes all the madness worth it. So beautiful, so peaceful, so wholly absorbing. You take the time to just sit there and enjoy it for much longer than you should. It's too bad for the professors that they're too anxious about the ocean to go near it anymore. You look back at the house. Such a large arrangement of bricks and wood and paint and cloth, but from this distance, and especially compared to the ocean, it is just so tiny, so minuscule. Perhaps that is why they dislike the view so much. It gives too much perspective.

You take off the hair tie and shake your head out, enjoying the feeling of an extra breeze closer to your scalp. The day is getting late, and you still have so many other things you should be doing. The dusting, the sweeping, the polishing, the lunches, the dinners. You maybe could have even gotten the kitchen cleaned, if you hadn't taken such a long break. You sigh. There is always more work to do.

You trudge through the day, staving off the chaos of dirt and disorder, and it's not until sunset that you remember about the ironing. It is actually the kind of task that should be put off until the next day, but they didn't give you enough notice to do the job properly, now did they? Should you bring it up to them, ask them to be more considerate next time? No, there wouldn't be much point, considering how infrequently they even have guests. Better not to make a fuss. Better to suffer in silence.

After all, making a fuss is why all the rest of the staff were let go. They were brazen enough to complain about the constant secrecy, the increasingly strange demands, the wild accusations. They also smelt financial troubles, as suddenly more and more household niceties were branded as too expensive. How much longer until you're similarly categorized as too expensive? There's a reason you're banking your pay in your pillow.

You beat the bugs out of the sheets, pull them in, and start the iron heating. As you wait, you think ahead towards what you can catch up on tomorrow, until you figure you've waited enough. You wrap the handle with a small rag, test its metal with a drop of spit, and start running it over the large, flat cloth, leaving a trail of clean, smooth beauty. More and more passes. The heat bleeds through the hand rag, even with how often you stop to re-wrap it. Already cracked and dry, your hands start to blister. You pause to roll up your sleeves and once again re-wrap the cloth. Your back cramps, your hair sticks, your clothes cling insufferably yet again. There's no way you could do this all day. Maybe if you had to become a washerwoman, they'd let you do the folding. That would be nice.

You finish the final sheet, and gently fold it—a perfectly crisp stack of white, the only thing in the entire house that you can make so clean and so beautiful. It is such a small thing, to be sure, but you do enjoy that sense of accomplishment, despite all the pain and suffering. You dress the beds before finally turning in yourself. You stare up at the slowly crumbling ceiling before finally falling asleep.

You dream of beautiful places, friendly people, and the kind of rest that you deserve.

You are awoken by a light, fast knocking. You open your eyes and do your best to focus... Clothing, getting dressed, becoming presentable. This takes altogether too many layers, too many intricacies before you are considered sociably decent. Your mind unfogs. Could that really be their visitor at barely dawn? The rapping continues, perfectly rhythmic, as you scurry down the hallway to meet it. Harkin bounds down from the upstairs, all flourishing smiles and confident professionalism. His beard is trimmed, his vest embroidered, his smile large and wide. He waits for you to open the door, gently rocking up and down.

You open it, revealing a woman. White skin, covered in dark purple taffeta and lace, heels to gloves, with two dark black bags that match. Her taxi is already driving off in the distance. But all of that fades into insignificance when you look at her face: unnaturally beautiful, unnaturally smooth. Not a single wrinkle over her entire face. Not even as she speaks. "Well, what a pleasure!

How I have been looking forward to this." She smiles wider than seems possible. You take a step back. You should run.

There is clearly something very wrong.

You look over to Harkin, but he just keeps on stupidly grinning. "How fantastic of you to join us, Doctor Tilden! I do so look forward to our working together."

What? Can he not see her skin?

You hear the creaking of stairs. Bennett is coming down. Good. He will know better, and he'll deal with the creature, and then you'll all be safe. He approaches—still missing a vest—but he's playing with a cravat as though threatening to actually tie one for once. He catches note of the woman's face and... and... gives his own pleasant smile. He bows slightly. "Oh, you've arrived already? I'm looking forward to getting started."

This. This can't be. Neither of them notice anything? Should you run? Shout for the taxi? You back up against the wood paneling in the hallway.

She just smiles more widely still, and offers Bennett a large carpet bag with a breezy, "I'm eager as well. Would you carry in the equipment?"

He clutches it close. "Of course! I can't wait for all the pieces to be together at last."

She turns to Harkin. "And maybe you could help me with my personal effects?"

His face falters a bit, but he recovers quickly. "Oh, well, I think Tabitha could help you better with that..."

She shoves the bag into his arms and winks at you. "But think it through. Won't she need to be starting breakfast?"

She moves soundlessly through the foyer and into the receiving room, where she sits like a perfectly normal human being on one of the overstuffed, faded couches. Harkin and Bennett join her, opting instead to more sensibly lean against opposite ends of the oaken mantelpiece. They begin the most inane discussions about nothing: how nice it must be, living close to the ocean, and yes, it's nice so far from the city, unless oh, did she miss the city?

You keep your expression neutral as you excuse yourself to the kitchen.

Finally alone, you weigh your options. Should you leave? Just go out the back door, run to the nearest house or town? Maybe you could at least get your money from your room first—or would that raise suspicion? Or, would you instead do what was expected of you, prepare their breakfast, leave them to their business, keep your job? Leaving seems like it should be obvious... but then the doubt creeps in.

Maybe the smoothness is natural. Maybe it is some beauty treatment. Maybe you will get into town, and people will laugh at the silly country maid who didn't realize that smooth skin was possible with enough money. They will taunt you, "Just like a lady to think that wrinkles would be worth a pact with the devil." The professors did not see anything amiss. And wouldn't they know better than anyone else? Isn't that their area of expertise? You are clearly overreacting.

So you make the breakfast, serving it on the nicest, most intact plates you can find. You draw back the plush curtains of the dining room, and do your best not to wince at the brine-stained glass. Then you stand back and watch over them, just like you are supposed to do. None of them even touch their meals.

"It is too early for me," excuses Harkin.

"Actually, I had already eaten," excuses Tilden.

Bennett is too busy talking to eat, all about mirrors and lights and measurements and contractions. He's pouring out all the things he's been silently guarding for years. Tilden gives encouraging nods while Harkin fidgets. And all the while, you do not take your eyes off her beautiful, unnatural face.

It's not until Bennett gets to talking about gates and keys that Harkin finally clears his throat to interrupt, with an obviously-strained smile. "Perhaps Tabitha could help Doctor Tilden to her room?" His smile loosens as he continues. "After all, I'm sure she'd appreciate the chance to get settled in."

You politely bow, and gesture towards the hallway that leads to the second-floor stairs. The smooth woman glances at your outstretched hand and arches an eyebrow. You straighten yourself, and hide the hands away, painfully aware of how worn, how damaged, how common they must look.

She narrows her eyes at Harkin. "Certainly, I would appreciate having a small rest before we start." She pushes in her own chair and follows you out.

From behind, you can hear Harkin give a long sigh as Bennett launches into the topic with renewed vigor.

As you lead her on, your nerves start to get the better of you. The carved banisters press in on you, and then once you've reached the top, your lack of exits feels particularly predictive. But you shove those thoughts down, keep walking, open the best guest room, and let her inside. She waves you in with her, glances back out, and then turns back to you.

"I have a question, now that we're alone. How do you feel about these two? Are they dangerous? Paranoid? Into anything... unnatural?"

Well, that's direct. Is their work actually dangerous? Or just strange? Maybe on the border. And anything "unnatural" is of a more mundane nature than you suspect she'd be interested in.

She picks up on your hesitation and jumps in to clarify. "I'm not asking you to betray their trust. I just want to know who I'm dealing with. People in this field tend to go mad, and I've learned to check." She smiles. Too disarmingly. Too smoothly.

You assure her that they are merely eccentric.

She sits down on the bed, making wrinkles of your perfect sheets, as she appreciatively runs her hands against them. "And what of you? How are you doing?" She cocks her head. "I noticed the hands."

You mumble out an excuse about cleaning, to which she rolls her eyes.

"Woman's work, right?" She pats the bed next to her.

You pause and look at the door. It's reassuring that it's still open. You could run, if you needed to. So you take a steadying breath and follow the suggestion.

Tilden leans in close, "If you had an opportunity to leave—a real one, for a better position, would you take it?" Her face rearranges into a wrinkle-free frown of concern, "They seem on the edge. You seem too good to be stuck, and I could use a new assistant."

You look about the guest room, silently counting everything absent. The rugs, paintings, vases, pictures, extra linens, all sold off or destroyed. The remaining pieces of furniture—the lush down bed and solid wardrobe of embellished mahogany—are just remnants from the house's glory days that they don't actually care for, just can't be bothered to either replace or outfit properly. To them, you're a similar relic. They'll either pitch you out, or keep you until you rot. You need to leave. Although, even admitting that you need to leave... Would leaving with her be an even worse mistake? Probably, although it's not like you have options. Maybe you should take whatever you can get while you still can.

"Yes," you breathe out, with a sudden lightness. You feel... excited about this decision? Yes. Excited.

She smiles. "Excellent! Now, I'll want you to join us down below, so you can get used to the sort of work we'll be doing." She puts a hand on your shoulder, and the decision solidifies. You've finally been given a chance to be free, and you're going to take it.

The floorboards out in the hallway give a warning creak, and then Harkin knocks on the open door while exclaiming, "We're ready to start, if you are!"

She laughs. "Well then how about we all go down to the lab?"

Harkin stiffens in polite surprise. "Wait, all?"

She nods calmly. "Of course. Having a fourth will afford us faster results."

His smile falls. "But the Watchers..."

She flounces her hand. "Oh, I'd think that if she were a Watcher, we'd all be dead already. We need her help. Simple as that."

He lowers his eyes, and grudgingly leads the way down both sets of stairs into the lab.

It's been a while since you were in there last, and you gasp at the sight. Things have changed. All their old brass instruments, glass beakers, slides, log books, and their solid and liquid chemical containers have been shoved into a corner, with many of the pieces looking to be damaged or leaking. The majority of the space has been ceded to an enormous sandstone trough filled with dark black liquid and sealed with a flat glass surface.

Bennett is affixing curious metal prongs to the glass. The walls themselves they've painted with indecipherable dark red symbols that blur your vision when you look at them too long.

Bennett startles at your presence, but calms quickly. "Ah well, it's going to be done soon enough! You should witness it."

Tilden bristles at this, but says nothing.

Harkin glares at Bennett. Apparently he had been hoping for a more hostile response from his more cautious partner.

Tilden swoops by your side and whispers, "I know it looks odd, but that's a measuring device, and the symbols, like the lead and sandstone, are just extra protection against interference. It's really quite all right, if a bit messy."

She gives you an encouraging grin, and you give the best return that you can manage.

Bennett rubs his hands together as he exclaims gleefully, "We're about to do it, to see behind the veil!"

Harkin snaps back, "If we haven't ruined it at the last minute, that is."

You do your best to shrink away. You consider offering to leave, but a thought strikes you—what if they don't let you leave? You might be considered a leak. Would they restrain you if tried? You decide not to try. You want to be here, after all.

Tilden puts a steadying hand on your shoulder while she turns to address Harkin sharply, "Now, I didn't agree to lend you my mirrors just so that you could go mistreating our willing assistant. We should stop dawdling and get started."

Harkin scowls, but dutifully closes the lead-lined door.

Bennett chimes in, almost singing, "I've already prepared the sulphur lamps!"

Tilden guides you to boxes of photographic slides. "You will replace these each time we take a measurement. Simple enough, yes?" She points at the mirrors. "And Harkin and I will be ensuring that the alignments are correct every time we measure."

Harkin makes no response as he starts inserting mirrors into the prongs.

Bennett talks on. "How do you measure accurately when they are always bending geometry?" He laughs. "By experimenting in secret!" He unloads a box of candles. "Today we shall discover the true reality of the ether, and they cannot stop it!"

Harkin puts a hand to his temple and says, "We should not tempt them, even with such protections."

But Bennett is too caught up to be dismayed.

Tilden moves in to give you one last bit of encouragement. "I'm glad you're here. Imagine if I were here by myself."

Bennett lights the sulphur lamp. "Well, I have good news, we're ready to begin! First measurement!" Tilden raises the lamp hood, the mirrors light up, the photographic plate takes a print, and she closes the hood. You remove the plate, and before you can replace it, the two men move to your side, clamoring for the results. Tilden waits patiently at her station as the men jostle.

"Insignificant?" spits out Harkin.

Bennett lays a trembling hand against him. "We can't expect to get it on the first go. We have to try all the angles."

Tilden sighs. "I'd prefer to take several measurements in every direction before we get all excited. Gentlemen?"

The two men rotate the entire glass apparatus against the mercury base, correct the mirrors, and the four of you take another measurement.

"Still negative?" Bennett mumbles, melancholy creeping in.

Harkin descends into sullen silence, and not even Tilden's assurances stave off the othering feeling.

Your decision solidifies even more. You can't wait to leave them and their stupid accusations behind. They go through it again and again, rotating the glass, measuring in finer and finer increments. Even Tilden slips into quiet acceptance. You shrink apologetically into the corner of abandoned equipment, giving up your station. Thankfully, Tilden doesn't press you about it, just moves in to take over for you.

As another aligning candle burns out, Harkin moves to replace it, droops into his shoulders, then dashes the candle to the floor. "Even here, they interfere! How can we learn anything? What did we do wrong?"

Tilden moves a few cautious steps towards him. "The setup was perfect. We did nothing wrong."

Bennett offers a resigned sigh. "There is no shame in a negative result. We shouldn't have been surprised, given the history."

Harkin's eyes fix straight past you, and he insists, "No. It is interference. I know it." He circles the device towards you. "Their gaze pierces the protections. They watch us even now."

Bennett frowns. "That can't be. We have the runes, the wall-to-wall lead, and absolute secrecy. What more could we do?"

Harkin nods, then pauses, mumbling, "Sacrifices..." He clears his throat and repeats more clearly, "Sacrifices." He clenches his jaw. "We didn't offer up a distraction. We should draw their attention elsewhere."

Tilden tilts her perfectly smooth head. "Do you know what it is that you're suggesting? You'd condemn yourself. Would you really give yourself up quite so easily?"

Harkin closes his eyes. "Yes. Whatever it takes to fight them."

Bennett's eyes dart about at the protective runes. "What... what exactly are you suggesting?" he ventures cautiously.

You all know what he's suggesting. Your mind starts calculating. Could you outrun him? Could you fight him? Grab a nearby blunt object? Or would that struggle just prolong your suffering?

Harkin shrugs in reply. "I thought I was clear. Blood." He points at you, just to finalize his meaning.

The world dims around you. You should run now. You should have run hundreds of times before. Whose fault is it that you've stayed until it got this bad? So weak, so foolish.

Bennett refuses to look up. "It might not even work, and consider the price. You... You'd be stained. I'm... I'm just not sure." Ah, he's not even concerned about you, but then why should he break habit now?

Harkin walks over to Bennett and pulls him into a deep, heavy embrace. "I know. I know. But it's the only way. I have to take this risk."

Tilden gives you a surreptitious nod and moves between them and you. At least she's here, she's on your side. Can she protect you? Save you?

Tilden clears her throat. "Well, I agree it's worth a shot, but a traditional sacrifice requires a circle of people, so you'll need a second, and I volunteer. Bennett can do the measurements by himself, I'm sure." Harkin eyes her, but she throws her hands up innocently. "I'm just trying to be helpful! Come now, we shouldn't hesitate or our resolve may falter." She sidles over and grabs your arm with a reassuring squeeze.

Harkin steels his face in determination. "You're right—we should move quickly. To the ocean, closer to their home."

She nods vigorously. "Yes, wherever you think is best." She waves off Bennett with a "Good luck!"

He doesn't acknowledge, just mechanically attends to the equipment.

Tilden guides you along, and you follow. Bennett closes the lead door after you. Harkin launches into an undirected lecture about his self-sacrifice for the greater good while Tilden offers congratulatory platitudes and soon, you three reach the cliffs. Harkin pants from the postulating and the climb. He looks around sheepishly. "Well, I suppose... I suppose this is where we should be starting..." He pats his vest. "I... Perhaps I should have brought a knife."

Tilden raises her perfect eyebrow. "I'm sure any rock will do."

He nods and sets to looking for one.

She fixes you with a glare, demanding your full attention. She smiles wide, then wider, until the skin on her face draws itself back like a curtain. Underneath is an impossibly folded mess of black sinews. You startle, gasp, kneel. Too late, you realize that your instincts were right. Why didn't you trust them? Why didn't you run? Satisfied at having made the appropriate impression on you, she resets her skin, the sheets overlapping and merging back over her nose. She cocks her head over her shoulder in one last questioning glance: *Would you prefer to leave with me?*

So that's what it means to leave with her—become a thing like that. Harkin has found his rock, and he's on his way, mouth open, saying something or other. What alternative do you have? You nod in the affirmative.

Tilden grins. "Perfect." She shoots out her hand, palms Harkin's head, and digs through his skull with her fingertips. She twirls the arm, and his body unravels. The death feels so trivial that your mind already starts to put his life behind you. Will someone like him even be missed? She sighs apologetically at you. "A paltry sacrifice, but necessary." She offers out her clean hand, and pulls you up into an embrace. Other appendages click as they unfurl from out of her taffeta. She scales you down the cliff, skitters across the sand and into the ocean. The appendages wrap tighter around you as she rushes you through the surf, faster and faster. The water heats from the speed and pounds against you, a cleansing boil.

The pain spreads from your damaged hands to the rest of your body. All over, your skin cracks and peels, your deeper flesh swells and blisters. You try to scream, but the water fills your lungs... and then... then the water cleans away the pain, the impurity of such a meaningless emotion. The water seeps into you, out of you, becomes part of you, soothes you. Then you are being pulled and stretched out impossibly thin, across all of eternity. You see it all. Galactic fortresses made from bent time and captured light. Stars dying, worlds reclaimed. Clouds of blood, seas of tentacles, tornadoes of ash, and mountains of chitin. You see beyond to the infinite dreamer in its restless slumber.

You turn back to look at the multitude of lives that you could have been, each more miserable and useless than the last, always ending with death and rot. You take those wasted lives, take all those disgusting possibilities, bleach them white, and flatten them into one single sheet of beautiful perfection. The thing that will be your new life. Then you finally are allowed to see him: your true master, the devourer waiting to return. He accepts you, and you are made to feel the full truth, joy, and purpose of your decision. In that moment, you know that you will never want anything else ever again. Your body is set back where it was before, out on the cliffs, out next to the ocean. Tilden sits next to you and waits, bubbling in anticipation. She is eager to show you the work you will be assisting her with.

It takes some time before you attempt to dig yourself out of the wet sand. The new appendages click as you expand and contract them. You touch your face, and are surprised to find human skin, human wrinkles. Were you cheated?

She laughs. "You know what to do."

Oh yes. Yes, you do.

You smash through the lead door, smear the wall-painted symbols. They never had any power over your kind, not really, but the idea of such a power existing must be punished. You wrap Bennett up in your writhing mass. The screams are distant, those of a lesser kind. He apologizes, appeals to your humanity. You drag him over the apparatus, press his body against the glass, smash it through, immerse his body into the black. Drown him in his hubris. It is over quickly. You touch your face. Smooth. Perfect.

Tilden gestures at a lit candle. "Would you?" she asks. You take it from her and curtsy. "Of course." You drop the candle into the box of photographic plates. They catch quickly, and you delight in watching the fire clean away the last of their arrogance. You slither back from the growing flames and concentrate on preparing yourself to leave. Body twisted into human shape, appendages tucked away, even the illusion of clothing—the affectations of a good Watcher. Tilden gives you an approving smile and leads you back up the stairs. There is always more work to do.

The Star that is Not a Star
(The Statement of Natasha Klein, April 1996)
by Lucy Brady

And the third angel sounded, and there fell a great star from heaven, burning as it were a lamp, and it fell upon the third part of the rivers, and upon the fountains of waters; And the name of the star is called Wormwood: and the third part of the waters became wormwood; and many men died of the waters, because they were made bitter.
– Revelation 8:10-11

Before I moved to Uppsala, a snow as late as April seemed a strange thing. Here they fall even as the buds of spring are contemplating their first flowering. Yet it is not simply my childhood in Cologne that makes this seem perverse to me. Recalling more recent events, I'm filled with a sense of things out of joint, a profound wrongness in the substance of the world, whenever I sense the warmth of spring in the air but feel the prickle of snowflakes on my skin.

The end of all things is a subject we seldom think of in earnest. When we do, it is as a mere fancy, a willing invocation of sublime terror, safe in the confines of an immutable cosmos. It is only when one finds oneself too long in the contemplation of strange ideas that the inconceivable starts to become possible, even inevitable. In such a state of mind, obscure conclusions become logical deductions, and miscellaneous scraps of data suddenly emerge to verify them. It is this state of mind that I sought to understand when I began studying for a doctorate in psychology at Uppsala University in the autumn of 1988.

My thesis concerned the spread of Millenarian philosophies amongst fringe religious movements of the 20th century. In a Post Judaeo-Christian Universe, the Millennium no longer holds the same monolithic quality it did for those in centuries past. A rounded number is a convenient focal point, but for many it is little more than that: a numerological unit of little symbolic value. More creative spirits have determined the coming of the apocalypse from asteroids, Neolithic architecture, oblique weather patterns, and perplexing statistical abstractions from the writings of long dead scholars. Such people seem to think little of the nuclear conflagration that has loomed over much of this last century, as if the idea of a man made apocalypse seems somehow absurd. Many things seemed absurd to me when I first began to ask these questions. Nevertheless, in the time I spent in contact with strange ideas, and the curious truths they have brought to light, my interest in the field has become something more than academic.

In four short years, the Millennium will be upon us, but it fills me with no fear. For me, the end has already come. Indeed, it has been with us from the beginning. We do not await the end of time, but merely the end of matter, for matter is not nearly as material as we would care to imagine. My studies have taught me this, and it is from what I have learned that I still feel a chill when the days grow bright and long, and the snows of winter still prickle my skin.

*

Chernobyl. In the Ukrainian tongue, the word means Wormwood, *Artemisia Absinthium*. It proliferates in vast tangled forests around the region of Pripyat (that doomed metropolis) and the nuclear facility that bears its name. In the scriptures, it is synonymous with bitterness, and lends its name to an avenging angel who looms large as an omen of destruction in the writings of St. John. During the events of that fateful spring in 1986, its name was to take on a new dimension. Chernobyl would henceforth become an international shorthand for disaster, and would epitomise those final, fraught days of the decaying Soviet Union.

I was just twenty four at the time, working for the communications wing of the Swedish security services in Stockholm. I had graduated from Hannover the previous year, studying European languages with a minor in psychology, and was now serving an internship as a translator. I would witness first hand the unease that pervaded the office when reports began to emerge of the abnormal levels of radiation detected in the skies over the Baltic, and of sinister activities in the east. Yet while my colleagues muttered nervously of 'fallout', and monitored the morass of incoming reports from our Western Allies, my task was a very different one.

I was given a list of terms, and assigned to monitor the police radio channels, taking record of whenever these occurred, and noting down their different combinations. The list was a curious assortment of items, comprising mainly electrical equipment. Though no engineer, I recognised some components as the transmitters and amplifiers involved in radio telescope apparatus, as well as some surprisingly sophisticated data processing computer systems. In addition, some of the terms described wholly unrelated things, with far more to do with biology than engineering, and even a few suggestive allusions to skin lesions.

Separated off from my team, I spent those strange few days in a small, dark room on the second floor of Telecommunications Building One. If other junior employees like me found themselves cut off from the team in this way, assigned to similar tasks, I do not know. In the service, respect for secrecy is a virtue, and it was clear that measures were in place to see that we did not compare notes. Sat before the dusty radio-lab unit, listening through cracked leather headphones, the voices would reach me across the airwaves, hundreds of them. 'Chatter', they called it, disconnected fragments from dozens of encrypted networks, security teams in close co-operation from different departments, broadcasting from police cars, border offices, airports, and military stations, not one of them aware of my furtive interceptions. My knowledge of languages came in useful, as transmissions were drawn from places beyond our borders – Berlin, Paris, London, Rome, Kiev, Moscow. I translated and dutifully noted all that I could, trying as best I might to draw meaning from the endless stream of information.

In my list there was also a scattering of names. None was distinctive enough to link to any known person or organisation but for one, which came up more than any other. Whoever this was, they were clearly heavily implicated in these events. That name was Fabienne Rozarte, known colloquially as 'The Frenchman'.

My shifts were changed, switching to a nocturnal vigil that left me alone with the voices throughout the darkest hours of the night. Though I would achieve an almost intimate knowledge of some of the personnel I tracked, this Fabienne Rozarte would remain a mystery to me. On what was to be the final morning of that paranoid vigil, curiosity and frustration drove me to ask Commander Rasmussen directly just who was this mysterious Rozarte? With an unexpected smile, he confessed that he did not know, and nor did certain of his correspondents in the Stasi, in whose custody the unfortunate Frenchman now languished.

It seemed that several days earlier, they had apprehended Rozarte attempting to cross into West Berlin, bearing his inscrutable cargo – items of electrical equipment, the names of which had now become unsettlingly familiar to me. He had with him, they discovered, an array of false travel documents, and tickets bound first for Copenhagen, then Stockholm. Yet what had most excited their suspicion was a map found in his possession. It showed a relief of the countryside surrounding the city of Pripyat, with a number of sites marked in pen between the city and the Chernobyl facility to the south. It was clear that subterfuge was suspected, a terrorist plot connected with the events emerging from behind the Iron curtain. Yet what plot could necessitate the improbable array of equipment he harboured, or what he sought to do with it in Sweden, none could say.

On the 28th of April, news of the disaster finally broke. With fears that this was in fact some attack now dispelled, our task was complete. It was 9am on that bright spring morning when my exhausted colleagues and I strode out onto the roof of the building to take the air. For many of us this was the end of a shift after a long night, and the sunlight, though welcome, was painful to our strained eyes. We shared cigarettes, and as we talked, a light snow began to fall, and with it an uneasy silence as we wondered what the snow might be bringing down with it. I remember clearly how some nervously stubbed out cigarettes and hurried back inside, whilst others merely chuckled and drew up their hoods. Next to me, a junior assistant was telling a colleague how, when the Americans had made their first speculative tests of the atomic bomb, there were some who believed that it would bring about a chain reaction, atom destabilising atom, until the entire earth was unmade.

*

It seemed that neither the true identity of Rozarte, nor the nature of his bizarre mission, would ever be established. The manner of his subsequent disappearance was also something the East German authorities kept to themselves. The episode was soon forgotten as all eyes turned from Berlin to Chernobyl, and thence to Moscow. In the wake of that morning after the last night in the radio tower, I spent much of my time watching the events unfold on television. I remember seeing strange things: vast armies of soldiers and construction crews in gas masks, rallies of newly vindicated anti-nuclear activists on city streets, Ban Ki-moon descending into the Ukraine by helicopter. I even recall curious scenes of remote controlled robots braving the intense radiation to gather carbon rods flung from the reactor core in the explosion. I remember finding them rather endearing.

The years would pass and the days of Gorbachev, *Glasnost*, and *Perestroika* would throw open the Russian empire, and expose the weight of corruption that had been its downfall. The world would learn of the failings at the Chernobyl plant, and the irresponsible experiments that had proven so disastrous. With no cause to suspect a plot, none was sought.

My own work was filed away unresolved, but by then I no longer cared. My internship concluded, I resumed my studies, having recently taken an interest in the psychology surrounding fringe religious organisations. Professional courtesy required me to forget much of what I had seen and heard during that time. Indeed, I would almost have done so were it not for a chance discovery of a clipping from *The Washington Post* – re-printed in the European Journal of Parapsychology – that would herald the beginning of a wholly different journey.

This information came to me when I was reading through a collection of newspaper reports, which comprised the earliest materials in my research. They consisted of investigative reports from

New York based journals of the early 1970s, whose methodologies in many ways mirrored my own.

These proved an uncommonly fruitful resource, as they seem to have coincided with an important moment in the history of the New Age movement in America. After two decades, large sections of the movement were imploding, as a wave of disillusionment saw many of the more established organisations beginning to fragment. With this came a mass exodus of former devotees, leaving California for New York. These individuals, older and jaded by their experiences, were often easily persuaded to talk. This had generated a considerable body of scholarship, which would set the foundations for my own research several years later.

It was by then 1989, and I was attempting to track down certain high profile figures behind the Peoples Temple Agricultural Project, which would later be known as the infamous 'Jonestown' cult. A recurrent theme in the membership of such societies was the frequency with which they switched between different groups and ideologies, seldom acknowledging their apparent contradictions. No one group seemed to hold a unique appeal, and many were hard to distinguish from one another. It seemed, for those involved in these fringe societies – or cults, for want of a better word – it was the condition of membership within a countercultural movement, more than any of the group's teachings, that held the main attraction. Tracing the membership history for someone involved in the movement for any period of time was thus to unravel an interconnected sequence of very similar organisations, all imploding or otherwise disbanding within a few years of one another.

It was only as I was tracking one individual in particular, as part of a case study, that I came across a society of believers that stood apart from the counterculture milieu. They called themselves the Venangalian Society, and what I could find of their history was as distinctive as it was scant. They boasted a history dating back some four hundred years, but for much of that time, it had owed its preservation to just one ancient family of Heidelberg: the Von Gruensteins. In truth though, it was the last of that line, one Frederick Von Gruenstein, then living in the US, who was responsible for its sudden revival in the early 1950s, and the form it was to take.

The journalists who had uncovered so many of the earliest revelations of these cult activities were able to unearth no more than a dozen ex-Venangalians in their investigations. Of that number, only about half were able to say much of any value. A decade or more of drugs and indoctrination had left only scarce memories of what had come before. All but one of those reached for interview, I noted, were in their thirties or forties. Being so young at the time, many only in their early twenties and even their teens, their knowledge of Venangalian doctrine was restricted by the rigid system of induction and graduation upon which the group operated. Thus, their knowledge was often limited to only the most basic rudiments of the group's philosophies. Yet from what I could gather, their preoccupations were with a kind of Pan-European Renaissance of occult knowledge, with some mention of UFOs and dubious 'Blood sciences', all combined with a staunch anti-Soviet message.

I would have to go closer to the source to uncover more, and that summer I spent several months as a visiting scholar at the New York State University. There I passed many hours plundering libraries and newspaper archives, poring over crumbling journals and reams of microfiche. The search was not an easy one, and it would be a lie to say my other investigations did not suffer as a result. Nevertheless, as I read on, a more definite picture began to emerge.

With the death of Frederick in 1961, the society fell into obscurity, many of its adherents flocking to the nascent Church of Scientology and other such movements. Yet it was said that one of the central figures of that group had carried on the Venangalian message when all else had forsaken the cause. His name was Henri Valentin, but during his time with the society, Von Gruenstein would bestow upon him a new name. For seven years he would thus be known as *Astroluminus Rozarte*.

That name, of curious Greek origin, filled me with a shock of recognition. The mysteries of that strange few days in 1986 at the radio-desk in Stockholm came back to me once more. It had been suggested that the Fabienne Rozarte apprehended in East Berlin had been a terrorist, operating toward some strange occult agenda. If there were indeed some link between Henri Valentin and the 'Rozarte' whom the authorities held in custody – especially if the investigation had been conducted in secret – then I may have been the first person to have made it. Overnight, the focus of my research altered dramatically, my excitement dampened only by a growing unease at where such researches might take me.

Diffuse as they were, the Venangalian doctrines held a striking consistency that hinted of undeniably sophisticated ideas. They dealt mainly with spiritual concerns, promoting a message of primordial purity and man's advancement towards this ideal, in a manner not far from Gnosticism. Yet where Gnostics saw their end in God, the Venangalians spoke only of *the light*. Their other central tenets were similarly borrowed from other faiths. The most common of these were *Spirit Flight*, a Shamanic concept common to pagans of America and Northern Europe, and *Compound Flesh*, which alluded to a particular notion of soul and identity, broadly analogous with that of Buddhism.

The ultimate fate of Rozarte was unclear, but it seemed that with the death of Von Gruenstein, he had reverted to his original name of Henri Valentin, and moved to his native France. There was a rumour however, hinted at in a number of interviews with his former peers, that when he did so, he took with him a substantial remnant of the Von Gruenstein fortune. This, it was said, had been granted for the continuation of the various physical and chemical experiments that the two had together conducted in secret in the cellars of Von Gruenstein's New England mansion. Yet if there were any truth in these later suggestions, none wished to come forward to venture any further information.

On learning of this later detail, I intended initially to travel to Paris, and there seek out any census data pertaining to immigration in the 1950s and early 1960s. My plans were redirected with the arrival of a letter from Berlin. I had been in correspondence with an old friend from university named Dieter Metz, who now pursued a career as a lawyer, and to whom I had lately confided the nature of my researches. The letter I received from him contained a clipping from the newsletter of the Gallerie Bassenge auction house dated June 1967. It concerned the sale of a number of works of art and literature. It had not been an especially notable auction, selling off the belongings of a deceased collector for the benefit of his debtors. Comments were kept brief, but two items were underlined. One was a manuscript, a rare treatise on metaphysics written around 1610 by one Joseph van Angelus of Prague. The second, a large print illustration depicting a model of the universe, was dated a year earlier. Among those listed as attending was one Henri Valentin.

The name, like the apparent connection between Venangalian and 'van Angelus', was undeniable, and provided us with the first clues as to Valentin's life in Europe. As it happened, despite bidding extensively on both items, he won only the diagram. The book went to a private collector named Heinrich Von Minct. For his part, Valentin spent over 22,000 Marks. I now understood what had become of the last of the Von Gruenstein fortune.

I journeyed to Berlin the following month, and spent the length of my stay in the apartment of my old friend, in Neukölln. None of the staff at the Galerie Bassenge from the time of the auction were likely to still be working for the gallery. Yet their archives retained many of those listings, expertly assembled by the resident researcher, Dr. Meyerhold. Though brief, the records supplied crucial insights into Josephus van Angelus. They recounted how in 1598 he had travelled from his native Holland to visit the court of Emperor Rudolf II, and there petition his patronage; how he had distributed no more than a dozen copies of his metaphysical treatise to select recipients across Europe; and how in 1612, he had shared the fate of countless alchemists and sorcerers who had come before him, meeting his end by fiery self-immolation in his own laboratory.

The listing for the diagram was shorter, suggesting only its apparent provenance, and comparing it, stylistically at least, to the engravings of Robert Fludd and Theodorus de Bry. Its decorative embellishments of architectural details and heraldic animal imagery suggested imperial allegiances. Yet the document also displayed a small photograph, from which I could make out a few details. It consisted of a series of concentric circles, often intersecting in the manner of an Euler diagram, and a handful of oblique labels referencing *Gott, die Teufel, Himmel, Hölle, Ebene Erstellt,* and *Jenseitsreich.* These last two, 'Created Plain', and 'Beyond-Realm', indicated, the listing said, ideas absent from any other writings of the time.

No information about the buyers was kept on record beyond their names, but while this meant Valentin's identity remained a mystery, I had only to ask our guide where I might find the other individual I sought. At noon the following day, after a perfunctory phone call, Metz and I presented ourselves at the Charlottenburg residence of Heinrich Von Minct. We were met at the door by a neatly presented woman in her mid twenties, who introduced herself as Dorothea von Minct, the niece of the late collector, whose death had come the previous November following a bout of pneumonia.

Our disappointment must have been visible as, offering coffee, she suggested she might be able to help. She explained that she had taken leave of her studies of Art History at Oxford in order to set her reclusive uncle's affairs in order. This included making a catalogue of the countless treasures of art and literature collected over the years. The magnitude of this task became immediately apparent as we walked through once airy corridors, now all but impassable for the mass of items crowding the walls and floors. We were led to a sitting room at the centre of the great, silent house. She confessed that even after a year's labour the task was still scarcely begun. Something in her manner suggested that the strain may have begun to affect her. Her speech was eloquent but somewhat erratic, and she demonstrated an aversion to some of the articles which had come into her uncle's possession towards the end of his life, taking odd turnings to avoid passing through certain rooms. Even so, she heard our queries into the Van Angelus book, and asked us to come back in a week, when she would try and present us with the item.

With little more to occupy my stay in Berlin, I spent my time in galleries and bars, imbibing the culture of that newly re-united city. Berlin in the autumn of 1989 was the most exciting place in the world to be, and I welcomed the chance to visit, and there break from my studies. One afternoon, Metz and I took a walk upon the Teufelsberg hill, and in the waning light of that day in early autumn, we studied the cityscape from that vantage point. Moving south from the Reichstag and the Fernsehturm tower, we both found our gazes alighting on a gloomy concrete building on Ruschestraße, where the East German security services still held sway, and where the mysterious Fabienne Rozarte was last seen alive. As we stared, we shared our thoughts on what truths, what unassailable secrets they held beyond our grasp. While we looked, a cold wind blew up, and the dying light of day drew long shadows pointing off towards the east.

*

A week later we arrived again at the door of Dorothea Von Minct. She greeted us with all the charm and geniality of before, but there was something evidently different about her this time around. Her face bore a distinct tiredness, and her voice was cracked, betraying a kind of nervous exhaustion that belied her immaculate make up and dress. We were ushered in and told of her discoveries.

Her search had not been a failure, yet even so, the news was not good. In 1976, over a decade after Von Minct had acquired it at auction, the book had been stolen. Some little investigation into her uncle's personal effects uncovered a folder of documents concerning the police investigation that followed. Henri Valentin had been an immediate suspect, but it was soon discovered that he had at this point been dead for more than two years. A visit to his grave at Montparnasse Cemetery soon confirmed this. Records from the report indicated that his 'son' was mentioned by several of his acquaintances, but they were unable to confirm either his name or whereabouts, and so he could not be approached for question.

These same effects also brought to light a letter, addressed but not sent, to a fellow collector in Bremen. It seemed that with the theft of the book his interest in matters of the occult had transformed from a passing artistic curiosity to an obsession. The letter was brief, evidently part of a longer correspondence:

I've not been able to track down a copy since the robbery all those years ago. I had no idea of its rarity when I bought it at auction, but it seems that it may already have been the last in existence. In the last thirty years, every extant copy was either stolen, destroyed, or otherwise made to disappear in a ruthlessly systematic campaign to suppress its secrets. Yet in the researches I've made, and my own memories of its contents, I think I have come to the heart of it. Like so many of those old alchemical texts, it hides its meaning behind a screen of elaborate sentiments and oblique, fantastical imagery. Yet while many were an exercise in moral philosophy toward some quasi-spiritual truth, I suspect Van Angelus to be concealing something altogether more literal.

The idea they come back to time and again, and the one I find most troubling, is what they call 'transcendence'. Philosophers throughout history have spoken of transcending the material world, often in search of learning or spiritual ecstasy. But Van Angelus seems to go further. The book speaks of it as a literal journey, one from which none return. I first suspected madness or death to be the truth of this 'enlightenment'. To them, the journey is one of body and spirit, and leaving this world for one beyond, which they call Jenseitsreich.

They're doing something, Valentin (if he lives) or one of his degenerate cronies, and if anything is to be done then it must be done soon. This 'Transcendence' alone is not the end point in Van Angelus's philosophy. There is something more. This is going to sound absurd, but things I've come across in my researches point to this year as the one when Joseph Van Angelus comes back to us. There are those alleged to have made this 'spirit flight', this 'transcendence', and returned to tell of it, and their names are Simon Magus, Zoroaster, and Hermes Trismegisthus! Yet if Van Angelus is Earthbound once more, then it shall be as no less than a high priest of ruin.

It all revolves around that star, and a damned thing it is! A star beyond the material universe, beyond space and time and all that is made by God. 'The star that is not a star.' A light that existed before creation, and by whose rays they may guide themselves on their dread 'spirit flight', and thereby gain insight equal to God's. I don't profess to know what it truly is, but there are all manner of perverse theories. Van Angelus professes that it is not evil, only that it is inimical to life in the created universe, and thus names it Apsynthion *– Wormwood, the epitome of all that is bitter and terrible, do you understand? If that is not evil, then evil does not exist, and if that is so, then was this last* *century not an evil one? For my part, I believe the star to be that which inspired the earliest primordial myths of that first brightest son of God, found to be imperfect and struck down. I shan't invoke his name here.*

I think I now also have some insight into how this 'ritual' shall transpire. They speak a lot of mirrors – mirrors that can reflect things not only in our world, but in the worlds beyond. Like so much else, it seemed a metaphor, with mathematics or alchemy as the likely candidate, but I now suspect otherwise. Whatever the case, the intention is thus: to set ablaze a beacon by which the traveller can guide their spirit flight by re-creating the Star of Apsynthion here on earth.

If there is any chance of making your trip to Berlin any sooner, I would gladly help make arrangements. There is a lot I dare not convey in writing, as I trust so few people these days. It is only with such urgency that I do so now.

Sincerely,

Heinrich Von Minct

This letter was dated April 19th, 1986.

We sat in the dark, echoing drawing room of the Von Minct estate while the letter was read, and after it was done, we lapsed into an uneasy silence. It was only the rain that began pounding the high windows to the south, reducing the view of the unkempt gardens to a white-green blur, that wakened us from our reverie. We made our plans to return to the city. On leaving, we implored Dorothea to return to Oxford, Metz suggesting a trusted archivist and conservator who might continue the work of sorting the collections in her absence. She entrusted the letter to me with undisguised relief, and said she would write to me at once with anything else her searches turned up, but confessed that she was not hopeful of much. In his final years, her uncle had become increasingly furtive, and seldom made his thoughts known.

On the plane back, I read the letter again, and studied a facsimile of the diagram that the auction house staff had kindly granted me. Looking closely, I saw a shape which I had not noticed before, but which the blown up version now made clear. It was a geometric eight-pointed star, and bore the name *Apsynthion*. I stared at it for several minutes, my gaze only broken when the lights dimmed and the plane began to ascend. As I drifted off to sleep, I looked out of my window, and beheld the light of Jupiter just beyond the wing tip.

*

With the trail so abruptly cut short, I returned to Uppsala, and there resumed my other researches. Yet I found myself unable to keep the matter long from my thoughts. With no more material evidence to back up my hypotheses, I often found myself pondering what thinkers of the past had done when confronted with great, implacable secrets. The change had evidently affected my thoughts more than I knew, for in those months, I found myself beginning to dream. I dreamed of New York, of the former cultists and the strange lives that had led them there. I dreamed of those weeks in 1986 when I had spent so long in the company of disembodied voices. I dreamed of Rozarte and the face my unconscious had assigned him. Most of all, I dreamed of fire.

It was as I reflected on this strange state, one evening in January 1990, that I turned on my television and switched to a broadcast that would once more bring me back to Berlin. Shaky footage showed a street at night. I realised this was live. The street was filled with people, young people mostly, in heavy winter coats, standing in groups or walking back and forth beneath the glow of spotlights. Many were talking amongst themselves, their faces anxious, determined, angry. Over the general din came the sound of chanting. Lined up before a looming concrete structure were police in riot gear, outnumbered but as defiant as the crowd themselves. It was then that I recognised the street, Ruschestraße, and began to have some inkling of what I was seeing.

Three months before, the world had seen the great wall descend while the authorities simply looked on, acknowledging the peaceful victory of the protestors, that final joyous celebration of unity. But tonight the mood was far darker, the people gathered with a wholly different agenda.

The target of their attention was the gloomy concrete edifice which served as headquarters for the Stasi. Recognising the impending upheaval, the personnel stationed there had taken a drastic decision, and had turned upon their archives in a great purge of all classified documents. In doing so, they hoped to conceal their many crimes of intimidation, espionage, torture and other abuses conducted in the Stasi's four decade existence. The crowd had other ideas. Pushing the guards aside, they stormed the building in force. Their goal was not destruction, but preservation, and they would see to it that nothing more was lost to the shredders. I muted my television, but continued to watch the ensuing events as I dialled the number for Berlin, and waited for Metz to pick up.

I planned to go to Berlin at once, but Metz persuaded me otherwise. He would instead exploit his position as a lawyer to involve himself in the subsequent investigation of those plundered documents, and write back to me of his findings. I am still endlessly grateful for his assistance. Though saved, the archives were vast, and for aggrieved relatives of individuals lost within them, the task of negotiating the files would take years. Ours, however, was a comparatively simple task. We had the benefit of knowing exactly when and how our man had come into the charge of the Stasi, providing vital clues to his whereabouts. Even so, our search could not be done quickly in an office turned upside down, and it took considerable time and persuasion on Metz's part to render everything he could.

The wait tested my patience to the limits as I considered what other avenues of discovery we might be able to pursue. The Soviet Union itself, or whatever it became, may too open its archives, and reveal its hidden history. God only knows what secrets may lie buried there, lost within boundless vaults, unknown even to their curators. Under reams of letters, manuscripts, copy sheets, microfilm, audiotape and video, resting like uranium in a concrete shell, losing none of its potency for all its years lost.

Four months of searching turned up only two documents pertaining to Rozarte, or Fabienne Valentin, or whatever his true identity. The first was a record of his arrest, telling me little more than I had already inferred. He had been picked up at the checkpoint in possession of his strange cargo, and held in custody, about which he maintained his staunch silence to the last. It did however enlighten me as to what his fate had been. Within two months of his arrest, Fabienne Rozarte was dead, radiation poisoning as the suspected cause. While he had been almost healthy when first discovered, his condition had soon deteriorated, organs and vital functions failing in rapid succession as the latent effects of the radiation were realised. It also seems that his silence was not completely total. Before he died, he lay in a delirious trance, and there uttered his last, strange words. The nurse at his bedside had only passing French, but was able to record the following in her notes:

The forest, distant [...] The head, vast, like a great projection hovering. Exposed flesh, skinless, hideous. Light, that expression of madness. The face in the beam, it was him. His soul was gone [...] Failed, incomplete [...] Only seconds before we had to use the earthing rod [...] as if the ground was boiling from below. Then it was gone. Nothing.

This was not all that the Stasi were able to discover, however. Following the death of their suspect, they had written to colleagues within the KGB with furtive entreaties. Their reply constituted the second major document Metz was able to turn up. It was a facsimile of a letter seized from one of the soldiers who had been present at the time of the vast cleanup operation at Chernobyl, and read as follows:

We spent many days in the hills and forests around Pripyat and the facility itself. We have come across countless small hamlets and lonely dwellers in tiny shacks. This is their home, so many refuse to move, even though we stress the dangers of staying. One group we met seem wholly unlike the others. They did not seem to be local, so their attachment to the place is striking. Their accents were varied, but their manner of speech suggested all were educated, and likely came from Moscow or Kiev. Not that they spoke much. It was clear they had been there for some time, in tents and primitive shelters. They were greatly irradiated, and many were so far gone they could barely speak or stand. Clearly they had been near to the facility at the time of the explosion, as they sported great weals and burns. One, a blind heavyset man called Boris, appeared to be a leader, but when questioned, seemed always to defer to 'The Frenchman'. This Frenchman was absent, presumably dead like so many of their group. Boris did not say. Like many, he was clearly deranged by radiation, paired with the terrible conditions in which they lived. They rambled endlessly, speaking of hideous things. Their main preoccupation was what they described as the apparition of a 'great misshapen head' that manifested for only a few moments before being 'earthed'.

That afternoon, they took Captain Nikolai Pronin to the scene where this event purportedly took place. Here, we discovered a structure, long since disused, which had once served as an external site connected to the facility. Inside there was evidence of a fire, and a scattering of damaged electrical equipment. It seemed that at the time of the fire, they had been re-routing electricity from the grid to power some unknown device, now either destroyed or dismantled.

My colleague, Andreas, spoke ruefully of the ILYA XIII footage, which we had viewed with equal confusion the previous week. For this remark, he was sternly reprimanded by Pronin.

*

Today is April 12th, 1996.

Secrets that possess a certain magnitude seem to have their own affinity with one another. A kind of potent magnetism that they each possess. This was a notion I borrowed from an individual I encountered in my researches, and I can't deny that it seems to have some weight to it. Like magnets, they can drift about indefinitely, without a pull beyond a certain range. But once they come close enough, recognition is inevitable, and they are inexorably drawn together. Likewise, they also possess the power to repel certain others, so that it can seem like there is only one course by which these secrets can be uncovered. This is why the search for such things seems at once so tantalising, and yet so galling, and few can follow it without succumbing to fanaticism or madness.

Likewise, I believe there are certain places on this Earth to which secrets are drawn by some supernatural force. Among them are the shrine of Delphi, the pit of Gehenna in Palestine, the mountains of Tibet, the Scottish Border Country, and the great forests of Northern Sweden, where I believe Fabienne Rozarte was destined before the radiation claimed him. Here, the fabric of reality is at its thinnest, and wondrous things may happen. They are often remote places, but whether absence of humanity gives them strength, or if it is their very potency that drives off human occupation, I cannot say. I believe Chernobyl is such a place, and was named in honour of the star that grants it power. Or perhaps it was the place that named the star. Perhaps it was here that all the first of that genus Artemisia came into the world. Only those earliest Scythian mystics who inhabited that place knew the truth. Yet it hardly matters. All things exist in similitude.

It has been six years since my trip to Berlin. The tenth anniversary of that terrible few days in 1986 is now approaching. Neither Metz nor I was ever able to unearth anything more from the old DDR archives. These few tantalising fragments are all that remained of the Rozarte case. But where the authorities had left off, I vowed to continue. My academic research has fallen apart, but I do not regret this. I am on the cusp of something altogether more profound. The ILYA XIII footage never resurfaced. I know this for I have read of the destruction of the archive in which it was once held. No room for old, tainted things in this new Russia! But through endeavours which have cost me dearly in both time and mental energies – endeavours I do not care to speak of – I have learned what it is, and what it contained.

ILYA XIII was the nickname for an MF-3 model robot of German design. Bearing the name of a figure of ancient Slavic folklore, ILYA XIII was one of the unsung heroes of the liquidation campaign to control the extent of the disaster at Chernobyl. The MF-3s were sent into the most dangerous parts of the facility, and there collected contaminated debris for safe disposal. Like so many of those robots, they were never recovered. Within only a few hours at the site, their circuitry degraded, and one by one they went haywire or broke down. ILYA XIII was no exception, but its story does not end there.

It was as the MF-3 advanced into one of the innermost sections of the site, close to where the reactor core lay buried under air-dropped concrete, that the footage was recorded. Its progress was monitored by its human controller, to whom the robot was connected by video link. The footage, it is said, was already marred by static, but the film was still clear enough to see what followed. The camera appears to pan suddenly upwards, and then gradually fall back, and it was supposed that the robot had fallen into an underground chamber through a crack in the floor. What came next, however, is so singular that it can be attributed to no known error of video data transmission. The feed falls into darkness, a crisp unbroken darkness, free even of the static interference that marred the earlier footage. Then shifting light suffuses the screen, scintillating in shades and patterns that resemble no earthly phenomenon.

It is often said that one can see strange things in static, or hear voices in the howling of the wind, and it is only human to suppose such things. Then it is only reasonable that this curious quirk of human perception was what caused the operator to believe he saw, in amidst the chaos of light and colour, shapes – features – of unmistakably biological character. The controller later confided that he owes his sanity to the simple fact that the footage was not accompanied with sound. At the end of its three second duration, the screen fills with static as the link is severed, but not before the image disappears, suffused with a burning bright light that seems to melt the lens.

Whatever it was that happened, the world may never truly understand. The site was entombed in a vast concrete sarcophagus to contain its evil conflagration from releasing its poison into the world. But this is of no consequence. I know what happened, and this knowledge comes in part from what I have read, and in part from what I have dreamed. The course of these revelations has left me strangely attuned to such things, and the intuition it has given me has filled in blanks which would otherwise be left unfilled.

The 'ritual', which Von Minct described and my own esoteric researches have confirmed, was a spiritual exercise intended to put the agent of its undertaking in a state of heightened spiritual sensitivity, whereupon their soul becomes a mirror of the *Apsynthion,* the star of Artemisia. From that, the voyager to unknown depths may be brought home to the physical realm that gave them birth. I believe that through his curious scientific endeavours, Fabienne Rozarte sought to make physical manifest of this. But his attempt was ill timed, or perhaps contributed in some way to what became. For at the instant of its enactment, the ritual light was replaced by a far more perfect analogue for what the Artemisia Star truly is: the very unmaking of time and space. A vision of the beginning, and of the end. So ends his story.

But what of my dreams? They come in many forms, but I believe the message is the same. One in particular occurs more than any other. In it, I am surrounded by trees. They reach up high, but their branches are bare, and through them I see a cold white sky overhead. The forest is vast, but there is space between the trees, and far off I can see endless columns of soldiers, their uniforms grey, so that they appear like great throngs of ghosts marching to places unknown. There is no sound but my own breathing. I walk slowly, the path being clear, and I need not hurry as I seem to know exactly where it is I am going. It is then that I usually see him. He appears as an indistinct shadow, coming from between the trees far off. I often take him for a human, though I make no attempt to hail him. There is no need, our meeting is destined in this place. I stand in the glade, the pale light rendering all in an uncanny clarity. He emerges from the trees, the treads of his tracked feet leaving long trails in the carpet of grey dust and fallen leaves that coats the forest floor.

We approach each other, and as I draw near I extend my hand and place it upon the articulated camera arm which answers for a head. I look into the green and red lights, and the dark lenses that are his eyes, and know he recognises me as I do him. The mind he now bears is far in advance of the primitive sensory system which we had given him. I ask him "ILYA XIII, what wonders have you beheld?", yet even as I do, I know that he will never be able to say, as I will never be able to understand. No human, born with the subjective senses of this world can truly comprehend the wonders that reside beyond the universe. Only the objective mind of a machine is destined for such a gift.

The moment passes, as it always does, and I am distracted. I hear a rumble, whose depth and clarity I can hardly comprehend. Looking up, I see a great black plume of smoke above the tree line, incalculably vast, and looming with a grandeur more terrible than any earthly mountain. Blood turns to battery acid in my veins, as the sight of it fills me with a fear for much more than my life (for who can fear for their life when the very atomic structure of their being is at stake?) I want to look away, but I am transfixed, as a pinprick of light emerges from the impenetrable blackness of the cloud. Steadily it grows, and I can see that is not the sun. It is too close. And with this realisation, I understand it is a malign intelligence, an indomitable will that can never die no matter how many aeons it survives. A wind picks up, a warm wind, blowing from the east. It reminds me that I am still here. I then feel a prickle on my skin, and see droplets of water, melting from the snowflakes that fall on my exposed flesh, dropping their microscopic payloads of irradiated material – chemical memories of an end yet to come.

August Lokken
by Yma Johnson

August Lokken assumed his brother visited whores, the sad, ever-forgettable women who serviced penniless fisherman from the dilapidated houses near the docks. Olaf was a hard, salt-scarred sixty-two, and August could not imagine any decent woman letting his younger brother show up in the middle of the night and leave before daybreak.

Over the last few months, Olaf had taken to leaving the darkened cabin after the night had settled in. He staggered back in without explanation as dawn bloomed across the Olympic peninsula. If Olaf happened to wake August, he pressed his face into the couch, pretending to sleep even as the smell of burnt plastic and rotted fish crowded him. He had only questioned Olaf once about the disappearances. His brother had fixed him with a glare so full of metal and rage that he'd shrank backwards on his bed and tucked himself into the shadows. Hands trembling, he'd drifted into a tangled sleep peopled with disembodied legs, shoeless feet, and suicide skies.

One morning, Olaf flung open the door, shattering the cabin's yellow warmth with the chilled Pacific wind. Pebbles of rain cracked against the roof as he shook August awake, then slapped on the light. "I know you're not sleeping, brother." Olaf's voice was saturated with mucous and cement.

August had, in fact, been sleeping. He gasped, and shoved his face into the blanket, shielding himself from the smell. "Turn the damn light off, now!" His shout was muffled by the bedding.

Olaf cut the lights and walked in slow, deliberate steps past the rickety wooden dinette to the television. His mud-colored galoshes squeaked across the wooden floor. He turned on the TV, speeding past infomercials, and early-morning prayer shows preaching the fanned flames of hell and the blood of Christ. Finally, he settled on a dead channel, and turned the volume down until static was sucked into silence. He dragged a chair across the floor to the edge of the couch.

August was still half-asleep, and the slow creep of something he refused to identify as fear fogged his senses. He stared at his brother, watched as he reached into the front pocket of his frayed flannel shirt. Olaf tugged out a pack of Pall Malls and offered one. August shook his head.

Olaf's fingers were ridged and thick from hauling fishing nets. He lit the cigarette and inhaled. "Do you want to know where I've been?" he asked, blowing his words through smoke and the deep wetness in his lungs.

August said nothing. His questions, his curiosity, had been washed from existence with the morning rain. Olaf turned away, as though he hadn't expected an answer, and gazed out the window that faced the sea. Their cabin was high on the mountain, and curtains of water obscured the arrival of dawn. Storm and sea were indistinguishable. August watched his brother's wrinkled face ripple in the gray light. Tufts of maniacal white hair struck out every which way. Cigarette smoke haloed him, then melted into the moist air, mixing with the stench of God's forgotten.

"One night soon you'll come with me." Olaf nodded to himself. "Yes, you'll come."

Molly, August's cat, howled a long, low, desolate howl before leaping from behind the couch. She inched towards Olaf, then froze with one paw extended. Her back arched, fur on end like she'd been struck by lightning.

"Eh, there now, Biscuit."

"Don't call her that," August said.

Olaf looked at Molly without smiling, his bright blue eyes glittering with malevolence. He bent over slowly, stretching his open palm towards the cat. The cigarette hovered a few inches from her flattened ears. "Why so nasty? Come here and give us a kiss."

The flickering glow from the dead channel fractured the attack. Molly lunged at Olaf's arm, in a riot of claws, screaming, and teeth. Then the cat fled to the back of the cabin like she was on fire. August stared in open-mouthed horror.

Olaf didn't jerk or cry out. He leaned back in the chair, and took a final puff from the cigarette before stubbing it out in the ashtray on the floor next to him. He lifted his arm slowly through the flickering shadows and looked at it like it belonged to someone else. There was blood—a lot of blood, so much that it dripped on the floor. "That Biscuit." Olaf pressed his hand to his mouth then pulled it away, leaving a layer of blood on his lips. "She doesn't seem to like me much."

*

Two nights later, Olaf shook August awake. Still half-asleep, he obediently stumbled to his brother's rusted out pick-up. A whisper of moonlight vanished behind a cloud bank, and he shivered. They were ready to pull out when Olaf jumped from the cab and disappeared into the shed. He emerged a moment later, hefting two five-gallon pails full of fishing bait in each hand, and set them in the truck bed.

"I don't really want to go fishing." Fear thickened August's words with the round, Norwegian vowels of his childhood. He started again. "I don't want to go—"

"You don't know what you want," Olaf snapped. He glared at his brother, the faintest smile tracing the edges of his lips. Gravel slowly crunched as they pulled away from the cabin. August felt his world lurch, a boat cut free of its moorings in storm-tossed seas. "We're not going fishing."

Olaf rolled down his window. Cold, pine-scented air rushed through the truck as they wound down the mountain towards the open sea. August looked out his window in time to see a shooting star burn up and flicker out. Something very beautiful and far away had just died. Death, he thought, was everywhere, but only on the rarest occasions was it beautiful.

*

Death followed Olaf like a loyal friend. It always had, leaving a graveyard in his wake. It seemed like something or someone was always sick, dying, or dead in his brother's presence. A litter of foxes in the forest. A doe mangled by a mountain lion, who instead of devouring it, mysteriously left its prey to bleed to death. As a child, Olaf had watched the neighbor's cat twitch and foam at the mouth with detached interest.

One young summer, he and his brother had been fishing beneath slate skies off the pier in Hammond Bay. August had seen the body first—a bloated woman belched up by the sea and wedged between two rocks so she moved slightly with each inland pulse of the waves. The veins in her eyes had burst, turning them into crimson balls, and her hands were curved claws. Ten-year-old August ran screaming to where his parents and a few friends were setting smørrebrød topped with salmon and boiled egg onto paper plates. The howl made his mother leap to her feet. Sliced fish tumbled onto the sand as she plunged towards him, terrified. She was the first adult at the shoreline where, Olaf, an odd smile on his face, had stayed behind to stroke the woman's hair. The last thing August remembered about that day was his mother dragging his brother to a spot several yards away from the dead woman, and alternately forcing his hands into the ocean, and then scouring them with sand so hard she nearly took flesh off the bones. All the while, she shrieked and cursed at him in Norwegian.

That same night, August had woken slick with sweat in a ghost-crowded room of formless dreams. His body had trembled in the moonlight as he'd peeled off his damp pajamas. He stumbled over a toy, and Olaf stirred. At first he'd thought Olaf was awake, because one eye was open, but his brother's breathing was steady in the room's half-light. The younger boy was still asleep, one dead, blue eye watching August as he quick-hopped into dry pajama pants, then scampered into the hallway. He pulled his robe around him and headed to the sanctuary of his parent's room. Sometimes they let him snuggle between their warm bodies.

"You didn't see how he looked at me." Mommy's voice was thick with despair, and the tone made him stop in the hallway. Their bedroom door was slightly ajar, and he could see them propped on pillows, with the moon looming through their window. Mommy looked old, dabbing at her red cheeks with a tissue.

"It's just high spirits, Grethe." Daddy's face was motionless, and August knew his father was afraid.

"It's not!" Her shriek startled both August and her husband. She lowered her voice. "It's not high spirits, and you know it. There's something wrong with him." She began sobbing. "The way he looked at me when I made him stop touching that... corpse." She shuddered and shook her head. "He was angry. Enraged." Her voice dropped down to a whisper. "His eyes... It was like he had no soul."

*

Olaf's elbow startled August from the memories. A freshly opened pint of Kentucky's Best was tilted towards him. His brother turned the radio to an oldies station. Peggy Lee's velvet voice floated through the cab, recalling fire, destruction, and the flavor of disappointment. August took a large swallow, gagged, and handed it back. His brother held up the bottle, singing along with macabre enthusiasm.

Olaf yanked a Pall Mall from the pack with his yellow teeth, lit it, and coughed until he hacked a wad of mucous out the window. August shook his head, and for a moment annoyance and disgust chased out fear. The oozing uneasiness flooded right back as Olaf turned off the main road and into a narrow two-track path, densely lined with old-growth pines. Branches slapped the cab, and the truck pitched and jerked. Even with the brights on, it was tough to see what was ahead. Where the hell were they going?

As if sensing the question, Olaf said, "We'll be there in five minutes." He bit down on the cigarette, and folded his face into a grimace as he twisted the top off the whiskey, and offered the bottle again. August swallowed a large mouthful, and was still fighting the burn as the song changed to something more upbeat.

Olaf shoved the bottle back between his legs, turned the radio up high, and sang. He grabbed August's hand, and tried to swing it back and forth in time to the music. The truck bounced hard, with deep squeaks. Low-hanging branches slapped the windshield, whacking it, then sliding down the side of the truck. Each noise tore another thread out of August's fraying nerves. He was jerked against the seat belt. The dashboard light tinted his brother's face with a patina of green, and the truck's motion yanked his head from side to side.

Olaf cackled, grabbed August's hand, and tried to swing it around like they were dancing. August snatched it back into his lap. Olaf flicked his cigarette butt out the window, drained the last of the whiskey and, with magician's grace, produced a second bottle from inside his coat.

At this point, August was fighting a full blown panic attack, suppressing the urge to leap from the truck and run, and keep on running until his future became the past.

"You're no fun!" Olaf shouted over the music. He threw his head back and laughed, then shoved his face towards August.

"Watch where you're going!" August yelled.

Olaf turned the radio off. The unexpected silence was oddly disquieting. "We're here, brother."

Here was a desolate clearing in the heart of Olympic National Park. Olaf stopped the car, humming to himself. August turned on the lanterns while Olaf dragged the pails from the truck bed. He handed one to August and pointed to a steep, unmarked trail. They half-skidded, half-walked down the mountain, kicking rocks loose as they wound their way towards the beach.

"*Are* we going fishing?" August asked.

His brother stopped abruptly and smiled. He propped his chin on the flashlight, illuminating iron eyes. His head appeared suspended in the blackness. "Sort of."

Something in those two simple words made August's mind run towards—then dance away from—the possibility that his brother might be insane. Before he could cage it, the question flew out like a startled bird. "Are you going crazy?"

Olaf stopped again on the path, and turned around. He held the light under his chin again. "Maybe." He paused then added in a taunting tone. "God knows it would be a short trip." He threw his head back, and laughed.

*

Being in the woods with Olaf always reminded August of the suicide. It had been the same twisted summer as the drowned woman. The brothers had been playing hide and seek or kick the can. He couldn't remember which now. His brother had vanished among the towering evergreens while August searched with the quiet focus of a determined hunter. He spotted his brother's yellow shirt through the foliage, and ran towards him, skidding to a breathless stop to shout, with jubilant triumph, "You're it!"

Then he saw the hanged man, and crumpled to the forest floor. Olaf was whacking its legs with a stick, making it sway like a ghastly piñata. Although August must have seen the man's face, in both nightmares and waking memory he saw only from the knees down. Purplish flesh was stained brown from where man had soiled himself when his neck snapped. One shoeless foot had been liberated from a blue tennis shoe by pre-death convulsions.

From that day forward, August's childhood had collapsed. His life grayed into a seamless catacomb peopled with ghosts, disembodied legs, and shoeless, liver-colored feet. At night he sat up in bed, board straight and screaming, still asleep but with eyes wide open. He refused to speak, ate little, couldn't attend school, and became hysterical whenever Olaf got close to him. He refused to sleep in a bedroom with Olaf, who was moved to a guest room. In the fevered grip of desperation, his parents enlisted a cadre of devout, gray-haired spinsters to pray at the house every night. They spoke in hushed, apologetic tones, and comforted his mother. Her heartbreak and emotional disintegration quickened with each passing day.

Over time the nightmares slipped away, and some months later August was himself again, more or less. He clambered from bed one ordinary morning, and in the hallway mirror he glimpsed a knife-thin child, rib bones stretching his chest. His mother and father were in the kitchen having breakfast. He asked, in a slow whisper, if he could also have pannekaken with raspberry jelly. It was the only time he ever saw his father cry.

*

At the edge of the beach, beneath the moon, August watched clouds roll over the swelling Pacific. This coast was tortured with prehistoric rock formations, thrusting skyward out of fathomless history. Olaf held the lantern high and stepped onto the boat. He motioned for August to move towards him. August did not, acutely aware of the sand beneath his boots. Its solidity was infinitely preferable to boarding the boat. He turned from the ocean to the mountains, longing for his cabin's yellow light.

"Get in." A blast of wind off the ocean whipped Olaf's hair into a turbulent crown, and he glared down at August.

"I think not," he replied, Norway heavy in his voice. "Time to go home." It was a plea, masquerading as a command.

The brothers stared at each other, motionless. Cruelty, terror, and coercion hung in the stillness between them, swinging like a body from a noose.

"Get in."

Over the years, August had charted many a course of action, only to be snatched helplessly into his brother's current again and again. It was an ocean blank of possibilities. He shifted beneath the bullet-black eyes, and stepped into the boat. Olaf smiled his riptide smile, and powered up the motor.

The Lokkens had lived by—and off—the sea for centuries. In fjord-side villages at first, and then the Washington coastline, on the hammered Juan de Fuca Strait. From the shores of two continents, they had navigated beneath a wide canopy of constellations, following salmon and halibut. Fear of unexpected storms, mechanical failure, drowning, and open water hid just beneath the surface for every fisherman. This night, his fear of his brother attached itself to all his other fears.

The boat jolted over the black ocean. August licked briny spray from his lips, watching Olaf's back as he opened the throttle, launching them through the silence towards uninhabited islands. The man pulled the half-finished pint of Kentucky's Best from inside his jacket pocket, unscrewed the cap with one hand, and swallowed a slow mouthful. He offered the bottle, and August sidestepped the bait pail full of guts and skin to get to it.

"Why don't you tell me what the bait is for?" August said.

Olaf smiled, put a finger to his lips, and motioned for the bottle back. "Soon. We're almost there."

"Almost where?"

Olaf pointed towards an angry, upward blast of granite that locals called the Screaming Head. The name seemed like a stretch during the day, but at night, under a clear moon, an open mouth choking on sea water emerged. Panic began as a tingling in August's scalp and moved down to the flesh on his forehead, before rolling over him in black waves.

"Brother!"

August snapped his head around to look into Olaf's grinning face.

"You got wasps in your stomach?" He was hunched over the wheel, his shoulders shaking with laughter.

A swell of fury broke over August. He was enraged at being mocked, enraged about being dragged to the Screaming Head, enraged at being swept out to sea on another one of Olaf's grim adventures.

"Hey now. I was just playing a bit." Olaf's smile settled into a slash beneath iron eyes. "No need to look at me like that."

The boat bumped shore. August, already off balance, nearly fell over.

"Steady now, brother." Olaf dropped anchor then hopped into the inky shallows. "Hand me the buckets."

August grabbed the lantern with one hand and picked up the pail with the other. Olaf splashed towards the shore, set down the first pail, and returned for the second. The tingling in August's forehead turned to a throb, and against every instinct for self-preservation, he descended into the ocean and waded towards shore.

"Pull up a chair," Olaf said cheerfully, motioning to a large rock next to him. "She'll be here any minute now."

August looked at the sand, the coiling waves, the endless skies. There was no sign of another boat. He turned uneasily to the shadow-filled rocks behind them. "She? What sort of woman–?" He stopped, gawping as a muffled green light appeared beneath the water, near the boat. It expanded, becoming a bubbling circle ten feet wide, distinct in color and texture from the surrounding water.

"There!" Olaf grabbed his brother's arm and squeezed tightly, his voice hoarse with excitement. "There she is!" He leaped to his feet, flipped the top off a bucket, and snatched a strange looking piece of fish from the gore. He held it out in front of him, guts dripping on the sand, vibrating with anticipation. The stench of fish and burnt plastic engulfed the shore—and something came out of the water.

It was six feet long. The bottom half of its body was covered in muddy brown and green scales. It lay close to the edge of the water, and white foam brushed over the edges of a fan-like tail. The top half looked like a human torso, except for layered gill slits where ribs would be. The skin was gray and rubbery. Four webbed, clawed fingers poked from bony arms. Its skull looked tender, like a newborn's. It was mostly bald, except for occasional thin black strands somewhere between tentacles and hair, that moved on their own. Its lidless black eyes covered half its face.

August was too terrified to scream.

"This," said Olaf with quiet awe, "is Sheila." He tossed a chunk of gray flesh to her, which landed on the sand. She made a noise like water running through a sewer and delicately picked it up.

"Holy Father in Heaven," sputtered August. He watched her fin undulate in time to the ocean's ebb and flow. "What in God's name?"

Sheila opened her mouth to reveal four parallel sets of blade-sharp teeth. She nibbled on the fish with surprising tenderness and made strange gurgles. August could only assume they were expressions of pleasure.

"It's a havfine, brother. A mermaid. The legends are real." He leaned towards August with undisguised menace. "You mustn't tell."

"Olaf Lokken, by my soul." August's teeth were gritted. "You'll go to hell for consorting with a creature such as this!"

"I'm going to hell anyway." Olaf slid a blood stained hand into the bucket of chum. "May as well take a friend."

"I'm leaving."

"No." He tossed another piece of fish. "We stay until dawn. She likes long visits."

August rushed towards the boat, then froze. Sheila was staring at him. A few of her cranial tentacles pulsed in slow motion around her shoulders. "She—" He shuddered. "This thing is... an *abomination*."

"Don't talk like that." Olaf's tone was cold and threatening as he stepped close. "Sheila—"

"Sheila be damned."

The creature stopped nibbling. It fixed its bottomless, onyx eyes on the brothers, then tore the fish in half with its claws, and resumed eating.

August's terror was so complete that his words could scarcely be recognized as English. "You're a nasty piece of work, and I—"

"Shut up." Olaf shoved his hand into the bucket, splashing blood onto the rocks.

"Stop feeding it!" shouted August.

Olaf tossed the fish, staring defiantly at his older brother. "Can't you see she's hungry?"

"I said stop it!"

The creature opened its mouth wide, and bit something that looked like a finger off a chunk of flesh.

"What are you feeding it?" August croaked.

"Oh, different things," Olaf said. He was clearly reveling in the moment.

August snatched the lid off the second bucket and held the lantern up to see Molly's decapitated head floating in a bloody soup of fingers, organs, and feline and human body parts. He choked, and vomit exploded out onto the sand. He hunched over as he gasped, shaking, breathing hard, trying to grab hold of something that still made sense. He heard a plop on the sand as Olaf tossed another piece of meat to Sheila.

"Molly!" He moaned, sobbing now. "Poor Molly!"

"I think you mean Biscuit. You know, I never liked that cat."

A lifetime of rage and fear roared through August. He leaped onto his brother, who fell backwards, hard. Olaf's head struck the rocks, and his eyes rolled up so that only the whites were visible. Straddling him, August grabbed a fist sized rock. He paused for a moment, then screamed and smashed the rock into Olaf's face, over and over again. He stopped at last, and a wet, slapping noise emerged from the fright and silence that followed.

Sheila! The creature was flopping its tail with grotesque awkwardness, using its bony fingers to drag itself further inland.

It reached the pail, pulled out a piece of gray meat, and bit deep. Blood ran down its chin as it ate, eyeing him suspiciously.

The havfine chewed and watched, watched and chewed. August snatched the lanterns and rose to his feet carefully, desperate to avoid startling or, worse yet, angering the thing. It ate human flesh. He grabbed the lantern, and sloshed backwards through the surf towards the boat. He took the widest arc possible, never looking away from the creature. It flop-dragged its way towards Olaf's corpse, then leaned on the body for support, gill slits spasming from the exertion of moving over dry land. It licked a bit of blood from Olaf's head.

August felt a ripple in the sand beneath his boots. He turned frantically towards the boat's ladder, and almost lost his balance, clawing at the air with his free hand. If the ocean doused his lantern, he would be alone with the thing. The ripple beneath his feet became heat, and the ocean started to bubble all around him. His eyes stung, watering at the familiar overpowering stench of rotted fish and plastic. The ocean about him bubbled black, then swirling green, aglow with a sourceless light.

He stood in the center of the green froth, a blinking madman with blood crusted fingernails. Sheila was dragging Olaf's corpse towards the ocean in coiling, unholy jerks. Panic swept through him like a virus, and he tried to run through the water. His breathing was ragged, like a broken bellows, and he could hear himself making inhuman, insane sounds in his fear.

Something clawed his leg, jerking him off balance. He screamed, thrashing and flailing, towards the boat ladder. The world spun. Salt water rushed into his mouth and nose, choking him. He beat at the green water with both hands, the lantern bobbing into blackness. In the phosphorescent green light he could see heads— an ocean of grey, amphibian heads surrounding him, all hollow eyes, writhing tentacles, and riotous teeth. They swam toward him like eels, soundless in the roiling sea. The green light reflected off their eyes so that they glowed, mirroring smoke and ocean spray.

Wake My Lord
by M. S. Swift

Jez pointed toward the window, his eyes vacant. "Twisted lumps of driftwood rise from the sands. Their pitted forms clutch at the dusk like frozen dancers. The sunset falls across the sea, its gleam shatters on the shifting water. I see it now."

Sasha turned and threw a caustic look in my direction.

Jez continued, half-rising from the bed. "Soon enough, fire dances, conjuring faces from the driftwood. Beyond lies a nothingness so intense I feel it burn. You wake, my Lord, as a blankness so vivid that everything else – this fire, the marsh, the trees – are leached of all colour." He turned and looked into me. "All is ashen. It is you, Lord, coiling around me, coiling through ground and sky until they crumble away into the boundless depths of nothingness."

Sasha moved toward him, making soothing sounds, but he stood and began to shiver and paw at himself.

"Your presence is a blank flame burning through everything. I am your candle; feed upon this flesh, this slime. Receive this life, rise within me, and on the searing rush of your being, plough me through this world until all is shattered into the empty endlessness, Lord."

Sasha manoeuvred him back onto the bed. "What the hell is he going on about, Tom?

She had rung me first thing, concerned about him. She knew we'd met up, and wanted to know what drugs he had been on. I knew that she didn't believe my denials. I hadn't hung round when I had dropped him back on the previous evening, just knocked and then slipped off, leaving him at the door. I couldn't have faced her reaction – I'd needed to rest. She sounded so worried on the phone that I'd agreed to come back round. When I arrived, Jez was staggering around their one bedroom flat, feverish and muttering to himself in a more poetic fashion than usual.

Once Sasha had settled him to sleep, I told her about the previous day, and the camp we had found on the beach adjoining the Dee marshes.

*

I had met Jez in the late afternoon, once his workfare programme was done for the day. It always put him in a foul mood, maintaining the beaches along the Dee estuary with other jobless young men. I had a fresh stash of weed with me however, and we rolled one as we walked downriver. The tide had turned, and twilight had settled. Auburn skies defined the shaded Welsh mountains rising across the river. The low light fell across smooth boulders, coaxing rich colour from the rock, and lay molten in the motionless pools. It gilded the tracks of water curving across the mud flats, and the broad, sweeping waves skimming the sand.

The drug worked its magic. As the sun glowed stridently beyond the rippling silhouette of the Welsh hills, the boulders around us became seals waiting for the tide, and giant faces slumped from the clay cliffs to our left. The dark line of the marshes came into view, along with pale forms stretching across the shore. As we drew nearer, they settled into huge chunks of driftwood positioned in a circle on the last of the beach. In their centre, an upended rowing boat was wedged at an angle into the sand. A tatty tarpaulin draped over the hull formed a make-shift tent. Ash smouldering in the fire-pit and a pan dumped close by suggested that the place was both inhabited and beyond the reach of the waters then sweeping around the pebbles studding the sand.

We could hear the voice of the waves and the cries of birds as we passed into that circle. Each lump of driftwood had been positioned so that knotted remnants of roots or branches spread against the sky like a range of sheer mountains. Once within, the wood resembled a huge, abstract flower resting on the sands. It was the adornments hanging from the spears of wood that suggested that this was more than an eco-art project. Jez noticed them first. Small rodents suspended by thin strips of seaweed. Some were fresh, others sagged with decay. There were other things moving softly in the breeze – a dead gull, its huge beak scraping against the wood, and shards of bone, some with flesh attached. If it hadn't been for the autumn chill, the place would have been infested with flies. Even through the comfortable bubble of the cannabis, it was unsettling.

And then the man stood among the marsh reeds. He was some distance away, and I don't know if he saw us at first. We could hear him dragging something through the mud. The idea that he was dragging a body played across my mind. Neither of us moved as the tall, thin figure picked his way through the marsh. When he broke onto the sands, there was a moment of silence as he stood staring manically at us. In turn, we made out the patch over one eye, the loose, fraying clothes, the hair and beard as tangled as the bare boughs of winter.

"Help me then," he whined, in a rather shrill, cracked voice. His sunken eye scanned us both, and I felt it lock onto me. He chewed at his lip, and raised his right foot to rest against his left thigh. For a moment, I felt rooted to the spot, and then we were both heaving at a cold, slippery bulk half-sunk in the mud. He stood back, jabbering away at the approaching sea whilst the pair of us floundered. We might have been wrestling an eel from the depths. Eventually we heaved a heap of stinking blubber onto the sand, and dragged it into the circle of driftwood. It was a dead cow, its back legs missing and a mess of coiling meat spilling from its rear end.

The pair of us stood back, breathing heavily. It was nearly dark now. The rising wind and the constant lapping of water disturbed the stillness.

When he spoke again, his voice was refined. "What is wrong?"

"It's a dead cow," Jez replied. "It can make you ill."

"It's skin, gristle, bone," the old man snapped back. "Just like us. We are no more than this, surely?" There was a pause as he fixed his eye upon first Jez and then me. "Besides, it is a gift, another one."

"Gift?" I said.

He knelt and began stroking the crusted hide of the creature before looking up again. "A gift. From the Goddess."

"Sure it is, mate," Jez muttered.

"This river, the waters, they are sacred to her," he went on. "I knew as soon as I returned."

Jez began again, but fell silent as the old man reached out, caught at his elbow and spoke in earnest.

"I first met her many years ago. She fired within me, like a bolt of energy. I was jolted upright from meditation, my limbs crackling with unseen fire. It was at once profound, joyous, and visceral. I saw, smiling within my mind, the Goddess, wreathed in a garland of flowers. A light spilled from her, animating a kaleidoscope of images that gently rotated beneath her face – it seemed everything on earth rose like waves from her radiance only to fall back into her blessed glare. I had finally awoken. For a long time I lived among fellow devotees, but now I have been sent back to the lands of my birth."

He stared at us, then parted the tarpaulin. He indicated a large log covered with a sheet. When I dragged it from under the boat, he removed the covering and held it up. "See, the God sleeps within the shining void of her being."

I used my lighter to illuminate the image of a Hindu god sleeping beneath waves, a lotus rising from his belly to flower above the waters.

"He sleeps within her light, and his dreams flower within her endless luminescence." The old man indicated an array of figures amongst the petals, and pointed to a many-armed figure. "He moves through the dreams like one walking through a meadow – the dreamer within the dream."

"What has any of this got to do with dead cows?" Jez asked.

"Everything, everywhere, is dream. We are dreams, flickering across primal reality. Unless of course, you think we are only gristle, bagged around bone."

Jez and I looked at each other, enjoying the ravings.

The old man indicated the trunk. "This is the means by which we can experience our true nature, see beyond fleeting illusion."

He turned and flung a couple of logs onto the smouldering fire, and blew until flames danced under the twilight. We finished the spliff and examined the box. It was a tree trunk, some five or six feet long and three wide. It was worn smooth, save for knots that opened like eyes across the wood. Either end was shattered, suggesting the tree had fallen naturally. The lid that rested on the top was a thin slab of light brown wood. Small fragments of white stone had been pushed into its surface in ornate, concentric circles. The crudity of the design suggested that the tramp had performed this decoration himself.

"I was drawn here, where the river is alive." He indicated the shore with an expansive gesture. "She sent me the wood, to build the camp."

"How do you know that the river is sacred, that your goddess sends you gifts?" I found myself asking.

"The world stretches and fades," the old man replied, apparently by way of explanation. "The glare of eternity burns through before something arrives on the tide, a gift, sent to me across her divine waters."

I asked him why.

"It is time. The Lord who dreams our reality stirs, ready to awaken. When he does, all will be embraced within him as he experiences the undivided unity of her reality." His voice was filled with conviction as he moved away from the fire. "She sent this box, this vessel, to enable us to wake from the dream before it collapses back into him. I have experienced the trace of the divine harboured within us. She is the spirit of each and the source of all, and I shall wake into her blissful presence forever!"

He paused. "As I have a meal to prepare, you must leave me – unless you wish to awaken into the joy that never wanes..."

"How can that thing–" Jez started.

I could tell he wanted to believe the old man. I said that we should go, but the old man moved to his box, and wordlessly shoved back the lid. Whilst the smooth exterior glowed in the firelight, its knots peering through the gloom, the hollow centre was in shadow. I had the strange impression that the lid of a tomb had been shoved aside, revealing a rent plunged deep into the ground.

The shrieks of sea birds clamoured above the rushing waves. An arc of stars stretched around the sky, but that shadowed interior was blank. Before Jez could step in, I advanced and plunged my hands down. For a moment, my hands seemed to reach into nothingness. I should have been touching wood, but there was nothing. A dry whisper, like leaves shifting against each other in autumn passed around me. Again and again it came until I was suspended in a different world. The camp and the wider beach seemed displaced, shifting with a life of their own whilst I reached into blank endlessness. That space felt strangely light, as if I would be weightless if I slipped wholly in. It was a calming experience, yet something made me flinch back. The flames fluttered around us. Shadows slipped and slid through the circling driftwood, and the wrinkled knots blinked along the beached head of the log.

Jez leaned over and then folded himself in, his leather jacket creaking. I expected him to plummet into a hole, but his fingers dragged the lid shut after himself.

The old man turned upriver, and lifted his eye-patch. The fire cracked and the waters rushed ever nearer. I could hear the creak of Jez's jacket and his voice muttering, until the old man began to intone deep sounds. His mouth moved slowly, as if he kneaded the utterances into the air.

I felt a growing unease, imagining Jez clamped in the darkness. It seemed to me that a disturbance awoke around us – everything shivered and rippled, like reflections on water. Sand shifted underfoot. The driftwood circle contorted, its undulating shadows and golden wood twisting and stabbing through the firelight. The dead things stretched until they vanished before reappearing, splintering into fragments and shrinking away again. Nothing was fixed.

The old man muttered on into the darkness, even when the lump of cow shivered and heaved, its flesh fluttering. It did not bother him that the mouth pawed at the sand or the eye-lids shifted over empty sockets. I found that I could not move. It was as if I was suspended amid strong winds or a great wave that I couldn't push against. I could neither look away nor even blink as the dead bulk contorted and stretched. Jez's voice called. It seemed far away now, as if a long distance down the beach. The old man turned, and although I was stuck, he seemed to melt through the unquiet air with ease, his gaping eye the only constant.

I seem detached from the memories now, like I was removed from the experience, but I swear that the driftwood clambered around him as he walked, a sea of spikes and shards over which he towered until he reached the box and pushed back the lid.

A blank space gaped within. The fluttering fire illuminated great, scaled eyes along the side, and wriggling limbs at each end. Finding myself able to move again, I forced myself to the box and glanced down. The roughly hacked sides of the trunk vanished into blackness. The old man looked at me through his good eye. It seemed something glimmered in that other hole in his face.

Jez's voice came again. He still seemed far from us. The driftwood circle continued to reel on the periphery of my vision, rearranging itself into an array of patterns as I plunged my arms down. Again there was nothing. I was suspended between this world and the other gaping below. I looked up. The carcass twisted and heaved beside the fire, the flesh partly slipped from several, upraised ribs, gristle slimed between them.

The old man kneeled down. Something definitely glinted in the depths of his ruptured eye. My hand fleetingly encountered something cold and sticky. I flinched, and would have drawn back if the old man hadn't reached in as well. Following his lead, I pushed down and felt a hand meet mine. Together we drew Jez from the depths. He was curled, foetal, dank and cold to the touch. He stank of seaweed. I supported him as the old man wrapped the sheet around him, and smiled down into the static face. It seemed his empty socket was angled over Jez's mouth. I couldn't be sure, but something may have dropped from that hole onto the upturned lips.

It took a while for Jez to register where he was. When he did, he nodded once at the old man and turned to me, his face manic. "Did you feel him? He is wonderful..."

I muttered a reply.

"Did you give yourself to him? I opened myself, allowed him to mark me." The words tumbled from Jez's mouth. "I sensed what he was waking to..."

The disturbance under the earth and sky had settled by this point, and I could move freely again. The flames seemed to have died down, and the light fluttered gently across the driftwood. The tide was just feet away now, and I wanted to leave that place. The stoned feeling of earlier was replaced by groggy unease. The old man said nothing as I slowly guided Jez away from his camp.

*

I stumbled to a halt.

Sasha had listened wordlessly. Occasionally she glanced over at Jez who shifted on the bed. Outside, it was bright. The sunlight fell through the large windows of their second storey flat and burst from the mirror propped on the table, lightening the cluttered room. She said nothing at first, her face a mixture of disbelief and disapproval.

"Definitely tripping," she finally managed.

I insisted that we had taken nothing except a couple of joints, and that we had accepted nothing from the tramp.

"Well, if that's all true, why did Jez get into that box thing?" She sounded exasperatated.

"Lots of reasons. He was pissed off with workfare. I think he secretly liked all the weird stuff, the dead things, the occult. Maybe he was thinking it might inspire that demo he hasn't recorded yet."

She nodded. She was used to Jez. It was her tree surgery business – and woodwork on the side – which kept them going.

"I think he was intrigued by the old man's comments on his Goddess," I added. "He wanted to explore something you're into."

"Well, if weed and that weird old man have messed with his head, I'll try and settle him down again," she said.

She consulted one of her books on witchcraft, before clearing a space on the table. She filled a bowl with water and left it in the sunlight. I watched dust motes settle and drift across the glinting surface.

"Sit up, Jez, and focus on this bowl of water," Sasha said. "See the sunlight reflecting from it. Try and still your mind, make it as calm as the surface of the water. As I invoke the goddess, try and attune yourself to the living universe, to the beauty of the trees, the waves, the starlight, the moon emerging from the clouds."

Jez didn't stir as she lit a joss stick. Incense swirled from the holder as she raised it, and calling out to guardian spirits, moved in a circle, releasing sweet bursts of scent in her wake.

"The universe is cracked," Jez said, from the bed. "All is awry. The old man's eye opens into nothingness. He masks a nothingness so intense it burns, so vast it gathers us in its depths. It is the separation from that void which terrifies. To be part of it is ecstasy."

"Okay, honey, there's too much of this negative talk now. Come on, let your mind rest in the light." Sasha's voice was soothing.

"You don't see it," he replied. "It shines, burning behind the world. He will awaken among us and lead us there."

Returning to the table, she straightened and raised her arms, her hands curling into semi-circular shapes. As she called out to a goddess of sea and shore and sky, her eye caught mine, and I glanced toward the water in the bowl. The sun's reflection pierced the water, and the dust drifting across the surface vanished in its glare. Sasha raised a chant of praise to her goddess, and in the corner of my eye she seemed to straighten and grow taller.

And then I knew that the sunlit room with its clutter of books and clothes and music was an illusion. It seemed faded and stretched over a space that opened behind it. I clutched at the table, suddenly conscious of a shadow staining the floor beneath the bed. The room rippled – a reflection across waves – and a gap opened where the bed had been. There was a moment where all distorted before settling back, save that Jez had gone.

*

There was no way that Jez could have slipped past us. Besides, the chain remained on the door and there was no other means out.

"Jez said that the world is cracked. Well, I think he's right, it is, and he's fallen through..." I said. We had dutifully searched the flat, and then the building as a whole. Sasha made a non-committal sound. "He's at the beach," I went on. "I can't explain how, but I know that he's there."

It was overcast, with a wind driving in from the west, by the time we parked up. The sun was setting behind thick coils of cloud, and the beach was deserted. The tide had turned, its multitude of voices merging with the far shriek of the gulls.

We hurried along, and the circle of driftwood soon came into view through the twilight. Smoke rose, and fabric hung from a pole now planted in the sand.

"This place stinks," Sasha said. "Can't you smell it? Really? I can from here. That's usually a sign to leave somewhere well alone."

We reached the circle of wood. A squatting figure stirred a pot suspended over the fire. It was the old man. He stood, patch in place, impassively watching us through his good eye.

"What have you done to him?" Sasha called.

"He has woken from the dream of existence," the old man shouted back, his face creasing into a joyless smile. The place *did* smell, now that Sasha had pointed it out. It took me a while to realise that the fabric flapping against the branch driven into the sand was shreds of cow hide, that the shapeless lump planted on top was the head, and that fragments of its bones glistened on the wood.

"I'll wake you from the dream of existence if you carry on like that," Sasha said, striding into the camp. I trailed after. It felt like the ground shifted beneath me – as if we stood on soft sand.

"He is awake, we are the dream. He is with the God who lies dreaming all of this, all of us, into existence. He will return to us, urging us to wake and behold the Great Goddess, the Absolute Reality..." The old man pointed toward the cow's head. "All shall return to the Great Mother."

Sasha was bristling with anger, ready to snatch at the thin figure.

"We can try and lure him back to sleep again, or we could waken from our illusions and join him," the old man said, swaying lightly, a strange smile flickering across his face.

Sasha shook her head in disbelief, and pointed at the trunk that still lay on the sand. "Is that the thing he got in?"

The waves were forging their path toward us now, and birds swirled on the strengthening wind.

"It was a gift," the old man said again.

She shoved at the lid and flung it onto the sand, leaving a gaping space beneath. She paused over the darkness. There was such intensity about it that the beach and the sky seemed to fade.

"The world is splintered, the blankness burns," I found myself saying.

"It's a hole dug into the sand," Sasha muttered, before shouting Jez's name.

"He answers," the old man said. "He calls the dreamer into the dream!"

She reached down into the ground. A faint voice sounded, barely distinct from the sound of the approaching waters or the moan of the wind. And then she was dragging at a shape from the box.

"Leave him to complete the awakening," the old man called.

The wind harried the ridges of softer sand and birds shrieked on the wing as Sasha scooped a slick, shivering mass from the hole. She staggered, demanding help. I hesitated, thinking it was a mass of slime clinging to her arms. When it groaned I knew that it was him, and I grabbed at his torso, helping drag him from darkness.

The wind hissed across the out-riding water, scything droplets aloft. I stepped away as Sasha hugged at her boyfriend. He pulled away from her clasp and stood, vacant, facing into the west.

"I can feel him approaching," Jez said clearly. "I feel the earth shaking as his feet hasten to us."

On and on the wind came. It raked through the water and streamed toward the fragile cluster of lights along the coast. It snatched Sasha's questions, tore at the grass in the marsh and set the trees writhing, until she too turned seaward. Even through the twilight, the rain clouds that gathered over the sea were dark – a wall of nothingness stretching from the deep, up into the endless sky. The distant birds whipping in circular patterns were pale streaks lashing through the gloom.

"I woke, I saw him, the Lord who sleeps beneath the waves of life," Jez screamed into the wind, anxious that we should understand him.

"The land is aglow, raising its inward flame to the awakening Lord," the old man cried back, pointing to an ambient light above the cliffs.

"It's the moon rising," Sasha called. She looked at me, gesturing that we should get Jez back to the car. However he had slipped behind us to heave frantically at the boat, trying to overturn it. Sasha implored Jez to leave, but the old man whooped excitedly and helped to haul the boat over.

"He parts sea and sky," Jez shrieked, before the two of them dragged the derelict craft toward the sea. The moon pierced the clouds behind us, shedding light across the waves and angling into the gloom. Its light was caught by the rain over the sea, creating the illusion of a vast hulk rising to stretch through the sky. The two men boarded their boat. We followed. Sasha was determined to drag Jez away from the approaching waves, but the old man batted at us, screaming that his lord had awoken.

When the moon broke fully from cloud, Jez reached toward the radiance reflected from the vapour, and the old man lifted his eye patch, allowing the light to fall inside his head. We both tried to haul at Jez, but the wind was frantic, and he leaned forward, intent upon that light. Sasha dropped away, and when I again looked out to sea, I backed off.

The moonlight caught among the clouds had intensified until it seemed to fall upon a substantial force twisting and coiling and lurching toward the shore. The two men appeared rapt, but I found myself walking backwards in dread. It would have been a tornado, except that it swelled through sky and sea in every direction. I had never seen anything like it. I couldn't work out if it expanded, uncoiling itself through the moonlight, or if it was a rent cracked through the world that swallowed the light. Either way, the two men on the static boat were silhouetted, straining against the wind, arms upheld in surrender.

The air shifted, rippling against the wind as Sasha and I passed back between the driftwood. The ground shuddered beneath us and the waves churned angrily. I saw solid things – the beach itself, stones, the boat the men were on – heave and stretch, before rippling across a power that surfaced beneath them. The trees on the cliff behind us contorted, grasses bristled and thrust themselves from the sand, and even the fire simmered with latent hostility. Sasha was somewhere behind me and may not have seen that boat shudder and rise, buoying as if at sea, before drifting into that featureless light. I watched its progress until it was lost against the glare.

That was the moment I knew that whatever bore down on us possessed awareness, and was intent upon its actions. Closer it came, splintering the clouds overhead. Soon it would swallow the driftwood and blank out the moon, and we two would also collapse into its depths.

And then I heard Sasha's voice. I turned to find that she had dragged the log upright and stood examining it.

"This is a beautiful piece of wood," she said. Words tumbled from her. "This was once an oak, growing under the sky, roots digging deep into the mountain side, leaves whispering above running, living waters, I can see them now, a grove of oak trees, there's a spring here, and the mountain above..."

She stepped into the log, and raised her voice into a chant. I couldn't make out her words, but I imagined myself sinking down into the ground, breaking into a web of fibres nudging their way through soil. Yet her words could not repel the force that ploughed through the ground and swallowed the sky. The space around our camp shimmered like sands beneath the fiercest sun of summer. It surfaced among the driftwood, swelling through the cratered contours, contorting them, stretching them into long, rippling shapes that lurched into its nothingness.

The fire leapt among the ashes, its final flames pulsing before they too were swallowed. Nothing was real. The strings of bone, the staff with the head, all fractured and dispersed like ink in water. Overhead, the moonlight fissured. There was a final brief blooming of light, and then the orb itself was gone, absorbed within the blankness that writhed and expanded everywhere.

There was no time for fear when it fell across me. There was a brief convulsion as bone and gristle jolted and sprang free, but the pain was fleeting. A burning anticipation fired within, searing the pulse and silencing the senses, laying me bare before a light of profound clarity and nothing else was.

*

A voice called across the emptiness. It might have been the void itself.

"Mountains rise from the spreading sea, soft skies host the moon and stars, their light reaches across the shore, settling across rocks, reflecting from the water curving across the mud flats and the broad, sweeping waves skimming the sand."

Shadowed waves creased through the light.

"Leaves cluster on the bough and shiver in the breeze, sun's fire is cupped within their green weave."

The words awoke a hunger within me, and as silence fell, forms emerged as if through mist. When the voice sounded again, I recognised it as Sasha's. Her figure took shape from the nothingness. She stood within the trunk looking out upon an unfamiliar landscape. Water flowed between boulders heaped at her feet, oak leaves thrust overhead into a pallid light. Her face was expressionless, and she looked into the distance. I felt that only she was real. Everything around her – the wind whistling across the rocks, the water rattling through the stones, the shivering leaves, the sunlight – they were all expressions of her.

The sense of weightlessness diminished, and I felt myself slump heavily. I was aware that my body ached and each breath gasped when it detached from the encircling void, yet I remained cocooned from the pain amid a sensation of expansive warmth. She repeated her initial words, and my body stood as if on a hill in fog. Vague shapes stretched through the featureless surround, growing in definition, until a lifeless tree appeared. Thin branches splayed through the blankness, glistening in her radiance until it became the old man breaking free.

He walked with his arms outstretched toward her. "My lady," he called. "My lady intones the words that awaken the dream of life. Sing, Goddess, lure him back into sleep, sing of the manifold lives that rise from your fastness, source of all, soul of each..."

"Call out to your Lord," her voice intoned. "Remind him of his dreams. Let him fashion a world in which he may be enthroned within the heart of all."

The old man raised a leg and rested his foot against one knee, and began to chant sonorous mantras.

Clustering leaves and rushing waters expanded around her until it seemed landscape after landscape flowed from her, spilling around us out into the void. A lightness of spirit propelled me to circle the old man and Sasha. I called joyously until the remnants of a boat burst from what remained of the gloom, and the lean figure of Jez struggled into definition. He emerged from the nothingness as the familiar backdrop of sea, shore and sky slowly solidified around us. Sasha looked out to sea impassively as Jez ran over, his eyes stretched wide, mouth hanging open. He gave no sign of recognition when he skipped over the ashes of the fire and threw himself against the tree trunk.

*

My mind has fallen away from them, Sasha standing motionless, the old man laying the remnants of the cow before her, Jez resting at the trunk. I soar beyond the ache and drag of the body into the remnants of the sunset scoring the horizon and the moonlight tracing the shifting waves through the night. Their beauty burns vividly within me. I sense the unseen fire dancing within all. It rolls everywhere – the circling driftwood, the sea sighing against the sand, the birds that call in the distance. Its searing presence coils my body around the circle, it courses through my voice and ploughs me beyond the driftwood into the marsh.

When my body fails, I lie in the mud, absorbed in the spread of the stars overhead. I feel no fear when the old man and Jez emerge from the night, eyes unshuttered, faces like masks that slump from their heads. When the old man scrapes at a shred of skin hanging from my leg with a clam shell, the pain is distant, even when he slips his mouth around it, nuzzling and gnawing until he snaps it away. When they drag me through the sharp grasses and the mud, I howl in delight. The blood that sprays from me is drunk by the tide, and I feel its drag back to the deeps. I sense the spread of roots and the shiver of leaves as I am heaved among the driftwood. As the two men gibber and circle, I float within the power that swells through all of us.

It is when Jez lunges with a sharp splinter of wood, jabbing into my face, and the old man spits a droplet of gristle into the wound that the eye finally beholds. In an eruption of blinding light, I am unknotted from the world. Blissful waves bear me beyond their voices and away from the body that they wrap in cow hide to haul before Sasha, whose hands curve into crescent shapes as she whispers, "Dream, my Lord."

The body that was mine is forced into the trunk, and the lid pushed into place. Darkness does not fall around me, for I am looking into the boundlessness burning behind the spread of water and the stretch of shore. The static lady, the men now tearing at their own flesh, the trunk on the sand, all grow smaller as I rush into shining nothingness. Their figures become specks of glistening dust and the earth and sky flicker only faintly behind me as I shatter, hungrily and joyously, into burning, radiant endlessness.

Puddles
by Thord D. Hedengren

"You've been here before, Mr. Morgan."

It was Gerrard Morgan's third visit to the faculty committee's conference room. Once had been for a party, and he'd enjoyed it. The other time, like this one, it had been a summons. No sense trying to pretend he didn't know what they were talking about.

"Yes, sir," Gerrard said, trying to look unfazed. "When I had problems."

"With alcohol, as I remember it," said the chairman. He was an older gentleman, one of those passed-over professors who ended up at private schools instead. He wore that role very convincingly.

"Those are behind me now, sir." That wasn't entirely true, not anymore. This whole affair had led Gerrard to revisit his relationship with the bottle. It wasn't as bad as it had once been, but it was still bad enough that he'd had to steady his nerves (and his hands) this morning with a shot of vodka. He wore the functional boozer's part just as well as the chairman wore his tweed vests though, so he didn't think they could tell.

"I'm sure, I'm sure," said the chairman. "Why don't you tell us what happened, Mr. Morgan?"

*

Gerrard *had* been drinking that evening, but not much. He didn't see that it mattered. No sense in getting into more trouble than he already was. There was nothing hinting that any of his students had noticed it.

The camp had been great up to that point. The A team were great swimmers, obviously rejoicing in the chance to go on a pretend competition. The state finals weren't until next year, but preparation was key. He always took his teams on excursions like this. The B team weren't as happy, mostly because they lost every race. Although there was a competition at the camp for them as well, Gerrard felt for them and their inability to muster the necessary enthusiasm. Who likes to be first in the failures' competition? He did what he could for them, and so they got some extra time lakeside.

He'd brought his classes here for years, ever since the archeologists had decided to pack up and leave, as the army had before them. The barracks, worn as they were, served well enough for a couple of days of swimming in the calm lake. Plus it was cheap, which was something that the school appreciated. Gerrard preferred lakes to pools. Swimming wasn't about controlled measures. The kids were competing, sure, but the whole purpose of learning to swim was so that you wouldn't drown.

That hadn't worked out this time though. The screams still woke him in the night, summoning up all his old demons.

*

"After that it's all a blur, really. Everything happened so fast. The girl was dead when I got there, and the other kids were obviously stunned. I administered CPR, but there wasn't anything to be done for her. The ambulance took her away."

"Horrible, horrible," said the chairman, and cleared his throat. "And the other kids, Mr. Morgan?"

"Shocked. They couldn't understand how this could've happened. I shielded them from the whole scene as best I could, of course, but they saw enough. It wasn't until the ambulance arrived that I could get them away."

"How could this happen?" That was the principal, Anne-Karin Anderssen. Gerrard clearly heard the accusation in her voice, and he didn't blame her for it.

"I'm not sure, honestly," he said. "I've been taking the teams to the camp for years, you know that. There's never been a problem. There are no currents or anything in the lake, no rocks to hurt the kids jumping in, and, well, there's nothing."

"The child, was she a good swimmer?" asked the chairman.

"She was. They all were, that's why they got to go."

"Where were you?" asked the principal.

"Preparing the campfire. I'd just gone in to fetch some things."

"Wait a minute," interrupted the chairman. "The kids were alone by the lake? In the water?"

Gerrard paused. They were. They *always* were. He always gave the kids leeway. It used to be because he wanted a drink, but more recently, it had been a matter of knowing nothing could happen. He obviously didn't know that anymore.

"Mr. Morgan?"

"Sorry, sir. Yes, they were, but just for a moment. As I said before, we've been coming to the lake and the camp for years and years. There's nothing dangerous there."

"Except the lake and the water, for that poor girl," said the principal. There was more acid in her voice than in a chemistry lab.

*

The dreams were vivid. Gerrard was struggling to get out of shallow water, not much more than a puddle. He woke up sweaty, frozen in fear of whatever was hiding beyond the veil of dreams. It was taking him longer and longer to start moving again every morning. Sleep not only eluded him, it proved outright impossible to find without alcoholic assistance.

The phone rang, but he didn't pick up. Voicemail was full too, angry parents and PTA representatives demanding his resignation. He hadn't done anything wrong, as far as he could tell. Just a horrible accident, a girl drowned, downright horrible, and that was that. Except it wasn't—not for him, not for her family, and not for any of her friends. He could still see her strangely watery eyes staring at him as he tried to breathe life into her, almost as if there'd been a glimmer of sentience deep inside them.

His mobile phone started ringing. That number was secret, a burner phone he'd only told the school board about.

"Hello?"

"Mr. Morgan? This is Detective Johnson. Would you please answer the door."

"The police?"

"Yes, Mr. Morgan. The police."

"Okay."

Gerrard opened the door feeling both dazed and buzzed. He was in the same T-shirt and tracksuit pants that he'd worn yesterday, and the day before that. Perhaps he smelled bad—he wasn't sure—but at least he didn't smell of booze. That was the beauty of vodka, it barely smelled of anything when combined with mixers. Had he added something last night? Maybe.

The doorway let in sunlight, which stung.

"Mr. Morgan? Detective Amanda Jones." Detective Jones held up her badge.

He made a show of looking at it, but honestly, the only thing he could see in the sudden brightness was the detective's silhouette, and the shape of someone else standing on the gangway behind her. Probably another cop.

"May I come in?"

Gerrard coughed, and finally caught his bearings. "Let's talk in the sun." Suddenly, he felt ashamed of the state of his dreary apartment. Also, there were the vodka bottles. That never looked good, however understandable they might be in a situation like this. The detective nodded, and he closed the door carefully behind him.

"Did we wake you, Mr. Morgan?"

"I was slumbering. Sorry, detective."

"Having trouble sleeping."

"Yeah."

"It happens. Guilt." Her voice was matter of fact.

"I didn't do anything wrong. It was an accident, a horrible freak accident."

"So they say, yes. That's not why I'm here."

"It's not?"

"No. Mr. Morgan, do you know anyone who'd like to hurt you?"

Gerrard didn't know what to say. For a moment, he just stared at her. She seemed agreeable, despite her short hair and stern face. Then he burst out laughing, unable to help himself.

The detective actually smiled. It was a small one, but a smile nonetheless. "That bad or that good?"

"Well. The school board's pretty pissed off, but I don't think they'd want to hurt me. Principal... No. Sorry." He composed himself. "There are parents screaming for blood, but that's about it. I'm a gym teacher. It's not a profession where you make a lot of enemies. Not even among the fat kids."

"That's what I thought," said the detective. "Some of the threats are pretty intense though, and there's excrement as well, so we're taking it seriously."

"Wait. Excrement?"

"Blood, tissue, hair. That sort of thing. Oh, and wet letters. That puzzled us for some time. Can you think of any reason for the threats to be wet, other than the obvious one?"

"The obvious one being that the kid drowned?"

"Yes."

"Then no."

"The threats were sent to your school, Mr. Morgan. We understand that your home address is secret."

"All the teachers' addresses are."

"And you're confident that this holds true in your case?"

"I can't see why not."

"Good, then I think we're done. Unless there's something else?" She handed him her card.

"No, no. Thanks for stopping by, detective."

It didn't occur to him until after she'd left that perhaps some of the numerous, and quite vocal, threats on his answering machine could've helped the investigation. By then he'd opened a brand new bottle of vodka. Any lingering concerns were washed away by its innards.

*

Two days later, Gerrard was slumped down behind his desk. He shared an office with three other teachers, but they weren't there. For a moment, he wondered whether their absence was because of his presence, or if they just had better things to do. He decided not to dwell on that question.

There was a box of letters, all open, on his desk. The threats, sent back from the police department. He read one at random. A pissed off anonymous parent felt that Gerrard was unfit to watch his or her kids, and that he should go hang himself. He shrugged, and tried another one. It was more of the same, but spelled incorrectly this time.

He pushed the box to the side and hid his face in his hands. He felt sick, but he wasn't sure whether it was because he was back at work, or because of the lack of vodka in his system.

A quick knock on the open door made him sit upright, much as his sergeant had made him react when he was in the military. The knock was familiar. Principal Anderssen.

"Sleeping on the job, Morgan?" There was no kindness in her voice, nothing playful at all. Just malice.

"No, Principal, just taking a moment."

"You've been reading your fan-mail then?"

"Something like that. Nutters."

"Can you blame them?"

"I can." He couldn't.

"Well, I can't, Morgan. You shouldn't be here."

"I don't need more time, I'm good."

"That's not what I meant," she said, and left.

She might have been right, but Gerrard had no intention of quitting a job that had been all right for so long. Besides, word traveled fast. He'd have to move far away to get a similar position elsewhere, one where they wouldn't immediately know what happened. If such a place could even exist, nowadays.

He glared at the closed door. "Fuck you, I'm staying."

*

The noise from the pool area was soothing. Kids were laughing, water splashed, and everything was as it should be. It even smelled right. However, Gerrard felt like there was something out of place, perhaps because it was his first swim class since the accident—or because he hadn't had a drink yet.

He decided it was probably the latter. He grabbed his coffee and went over to the infants' pool, where his backpack was. He poured some vodka into his cup, careful that nobody could see, and sat to soak his feet. It was warm, the infants' pool, and pleasant. He splashed his feet, looked at the kids doing their drills, and closed his eyes for a second.

When he opened them again, something was in the water, something that hadn't been there a moment before. It was looking at him from the tiles at the bottom of the pool. It wouldn't come into focus, and he couldn't really see what it was. For a horrifying moment, he saw watery eyes beyond, staring at him, through him, into someplace else. He froze, blinked, and the eyes were gone.

"Are you all right?" asked a distant voice.

Gerrard nodded. "I'm OK, John. Do another lap, then hit the showers."

His heart wouldn't slow down, and he had the unshakeable feeling that the eyes were still observing him, somewhere that he couldn't see them.

*

The scream echoed through the gym. Gerrard was there in a moment.

"Stand back, all of you!" he barked, as the kids gathered closer around Emma. She was a petite thing, and she looked very young and scared as she lay there on the floor, squirming and trying not to cry.

"What happened?" he asked, but he could already tell. A weight, dropped on her foot, a heavy one at that—Emma was trying to build muscle to compete with the A team—and it didn't look good.

She was sobbing quietly, trying very hard not to release the full waterworks. Most kids believed that you had to be strong in front of your team mates.

"Fetch me a bucket of ice," Gerrard said, and John hopped to it. He was the teacher's pet here, useful. "Sam, you call the nurse. Clarice, get the stretcher from the back."

"Is it broken?" asked John, returning with the bucket of ice.

"I don't think so," said Gerrard, knowing full well that it probably was, in at least a few places. Lots of small bones in the foot. Easily hurt. "The nurse'll know more. You take it easy, Emma, it'll be all right." He made an impromptu ice-pack with a towel, placing it on the angry area. "You hold on to this now," he said. With some help from John, he got Emma on the stretcher, just in time for the nurse to arrive with his assistant, tut-tutting at it all.

"And where were you, Mr. Morgan?" the nurse asked him, not hiding the sarcasm in his voice.

"He was right here," John said, glaring. "Sir."

"Enough," Gerrard said. "I'll see you later, Emma. Don't worry. The rest of you, dismissed."

Damn shame, he thought, as everyone piled out of the room, the nurse and his assistant carrying Emma on the stretcher. Bad timing, too.

He bent over to pick up the bucket of ice, and found himself paralyzed. Watery eyes looked at him, over him, through him, from the bottom of the bucket. They were getting closer. Engulfing him.

It took every bit of strength he could muster to pull away, and when he did, he was dripping sweat. He couldn't help himself from taking another stupid peek, but the eyes were gone, and the ice had turned to water.

*

Gerrard was afraid to go home. His dreams were too real, too weird, too horrifying. Not wanting to sleep, he'd decided to avoid it altogether. It was his third day of mere slumbers, and it was starting to show. A lot. He excused himself from the afternoon class, left John in charge with a substitute teacher who was only really checking her phone, and headed for the bar.

"Closing time, son," the elderly bartender said, much later. A nice fellow. "Get some sleep."

Gerrard nodded, and left a good tip.

The walk home was sobering, and it brought thoughts that he didn't want. Ones that suggested he was going mad, that he needed help, maybe a shrink. Booze wasn't helping anymore, and if he didn't do something soon, he'd be forced to take a leave of absence, which wouldn't work out. The principal really had it out for him, more than ever after Emma's accident with the weights. Any chance the bitch got, she'd take. He couldn't even blame her anymore.

He stepped into a back alley to relieve himself. Vodka was better than beer, not so much pissing to be done. The thought cheered him up. He remembered that there was some left at home, by the bed. Surely that'd help him get some rest.

"I really need to sleep," he said to himself, feeling like a cliché from a bad movie.

Maybe I'm just stressed out, tired from all this shit. Maybe things aren't so bad.

He looked at the piss forming a puddle by the wall, moving towards his right foot. Bile welled in his throat as he stared into watery eyes, huge and all-encompassing. They stared at him from the yellow urine, seeing him, seeing through him, seeing beyond everything, heralding the end. They were drawing him down with them, to another place where everything was soul-splinteringly wrong.

Gerrard fell backwards, smashing his head on a trash can. The last thought his broken mind could muster, before he passed out, was that at least he'd get some sleep.

*

Bobby Sanderson was a quiet kid, never making much fuss in class. He was an adequate swimmer, but not even remotely close to being fit for any of the competing teams. He just took the swimming class because you had to take something, and Bobby liked to be in the water.

"My son almost drowned!" Bobby's mother, Cassandra, was not quiet. She was quite the opposite, and annoyingly so. This wasn't the first time Gerrard had needed to speak with her, but it was by far the most serious.

"And where were you, Mr. Morgan?" asked Principal Anderssen.

To call Gerrard's office crowded would have been a significant understatement.

"I was there," he said. His nails were driving into the flesh of his cramped fists, his anger threatening to boil over. "Bobby was fine."

"He nearly drowned!" said Cassandra. "Tell him, Bobby."

"Well," said Bobby, looking at his shoes, clearly wanting to be anywhere but there. "I hurt myself, and then I was under the water. It was scary. I couldn't breathe."

"There you have it!"

"Bobby," said the principal. "What happened next?"

"John helped me, ma'am."

"Where was Mr. Morgan, Bobby?"

"I don't know."

"Where you even by the pool, Morgan?" demanded Cassandra.

"Yes, Mrs. Sanderson."

Cassandra turned her back to Gerrard in the most obvious show of power that he could imagine. "Principal Anderssen," she said. "I'm going to make a formal request with the Teacher's Association, but I'll say this to you right now. I want him gone. He's not reliable. He's already caused one tragic death. How many more will die or hurt themselves before this man's fired? He should be happy no one's pressing charges."

"What really happened, Bobby?" asked Gerrard.

"Don't you *dare* talk to my son!"

"Bobby?"

The boy looked very young and very scared. He couldn't take his eyes off his shoes.

Principal Anderssen reached out a finger and lifted his face. "Bobby, is what you told us the truth?"

"You won't get in trouble," said Gerrard.

"How dare you!" screeched Cassandra.

"No," whispered Bobby. "Mom! I don't want them to fire Mr. Morgan! He's a nice guy."

A nice guy? That's a first from a student.

"So you didn't nearly drown?" asked the principal.

"No."

Principal Anderssen stood up, sighing heavily. She glared at Gerrard for a moment, clearly disappointed, and then turned to Cassandra. "You have some explaining to do, Mrs. Sanderson. My office. Now."

Gerrard wasn't invited to join them. It didn't matter. Poor Bobby, with that devious monster as a mother.

He stayed late, just sitting there in his chair, thinking. He'd dodged a bullet, but there would be more. Or maybe not—maybe it was just this nutcase, and when her scheme came out, then everyone would back off. Leave him alone. The more he thought about it, the better the prospect seemed. There was hope again.

A nice guy. Poor Bobby. But a nice guy, huh? He smiled, for what felt like the first time in ages.

The vodka bottle in his drawer was untouched when he finally locked up for the night.

*

It was a pleasant evening for a walk, warm under the cloudy sky. Gerrard skipped the bus, enjoying the walk and his newfound sense of hope.

It was getting warmer, and more humid. A little peculiar perhaps, but it beat freezing. The streets were empty, and he was in no hurry. He considered ordering in, perhaps even catching a movie on the way home. It had been a while since he'd considered such pleasures. He smiled, and almost loathed himself when he began to hum a tune.

A light drizzle started. It was warm and encompassing, and it didn't bother him. It was even nice, walking in the rain. He hummed the few lyrics from *Singing in the Rain* that he remembered, but they quickly became repetitive. Perhaps he should watch the movie when he made it home. It would be on one of the streaming services. He could at least download the song. If it hadn't been raining, he'd have done that on his phone, right now.

The rain was getting harder and warmer, making it hard to breathe. Like his vacation to Thailand, which had been in the monsoon season. The walk had become a lot less pleasant. He stopped humming, started sweating instead. It felt like someone was watching him, but when he turned, he couldn't see anyone. Suddenly the darkness was scary. He stepped up his pace.

The rain was pouring now, and it was really warm. Still not actually hot, but as warm as any rain he'd ever encountered. As warm as the pool back at school.

Watery eyes were suddenly in front of him, staring, glaring. They were huge, vast shapes made up of smaller eyes, which were in turn made of yet smaller eyes. They saw him, all of them, saw around him, saw through him. They blinked as one. Gerrard froze. He tried to breathe, but his lungs were drinking the warm rain, as if he had opened his mouth underwater. It felt right at first, for a moment, but then everything broke. Reality distorted. He found that he could see beyond the mortal realm, beyond everything. The being was so old, so terrifying, so incomprehensible, that Gerrard didn't know whether he was screaming, or dreaming, or going insane, or all of the above. The watery eyes were welcoming him, drawing him near, away from everything.

The being engulfed him, wrapping him in majestic tentacles, drowning him in a sea of eyes, and he—and they—could see all truth and all secrets. For a moment, it was calm, right. It made sense. Then there was only agonizing darkness, and the peculiar sound of a mind shattering.

*

"What have we got here?" Amanda asked.

"Coroner's on the way, ma'am. Multiple stab wounds, but from a scorcher or something. It's pretty weird."

Detective Jones passed the police tape to huddle by the victim. It took her a moment to recognize him. "This is Morgan, the gym teacher."

"You know him, ma'am?"

"No, just of him. Gerrard Morgan. There were death threats made against him after that kid drowned at swim camp a few weeks ago."

"Oh, yeah. Might be the motive then?"

"Possibly."

Jones looked around. It was a quiet street, but someone might have seen or heard something. "Canvas the area, will you?"

"Yes, ma'am." The officer turned to leave.

"Hey," Amanda said. "Did it rain last night?"

"Just a little bit after dark, I think."

"That's what I thought. The body's wet. Soaked."

"Huh. Yeah, it is. Weird, right?"

"Yes. Weird..."

The officer left to organize a canvas, but Amanda didn't take much of it in. *Who'd want to kill this guy?* He'd been stabbed, many times, by something that must've been very hot to make scorched holes in his body like this. Had he caught fire and then been doused? Was that why he was wet? She looked around, but the street was dry enough, just a few puddles here and there where the water had no other place to go. She stood, wanting to walk away, but something drew her back.

"There's something with his eyes," she muttered, making a mental note to tell the coroner. She leant close to see for herself. The eyes were a watery, dark abyss, and in their depth, something stared back at her, through her and her very being.

She froze in place for a second, and then straightened. *That was weird*, she thought, and rubbed her eyes. When she left for the precinct, she felt as if there was something following her, looking at her from below. As if the puddles in the street had eyes.

Sometimes, the Void Stares Back
by Marc Reichardt

Glerg. The bubble popped through the black rubber flaps of the sink drain. They were small and triangular, and made me think of some toothy maw belching after a meaty mouthful. The bubble was followed by the kind of bass shudder that signaled deeper problems. I wondered if the pipes could know pain or relief. I heard a surging noise, and realized that the water droplets were scurrying around the sink. That gave me a moment of panic, as I thought about everything that might get ruined by a real backup—one I somehow couldn't control by simply turning off the tap.

It was all too easy to imagine the backup building up on its own, pouring out from the drain. The low light above me shone on nothingness in the drain's depths. Darkness seeped from it, as if it were the shadows which were backing up, to soon engulf the room. Then there was another low rattle. Something was still moving down there. I thought briefly about the landlord, but decided he'd have me committed long before he stopped to check the P-trap.

I stood back from the sink and sighed, and glanced from side to side, being careful not to move my head. Deep down, I think I was hoping that someone else might appear in my one-bedroom apartment to give me the answer to a question that I'm not sure I was even really asking. It was just a clogged sink. But I knew there was more.

There had to be.

The little tug behind my ear told me it was watching me again. I knew it was. If I looked back for it, there would be nothing but my drab furniture and the fake wood-paneled walls. But it was there.

The drain gurgled in response, and I looked into it again. A glistening form roiled from one side to the other, now catching the light. The aged filament in the bulb overhead seemed to sing to the clog, reassuring it that all of the worn elements of my home were joined in its fight against me. This always happened past midnight, when there was no hope of finding anyone to assist with a real problem. I told myself it was just gas shifting around, making it look like an eel had crawled up my sink pipe and was curling around the blades of the disposal. I considered flipping the switch and listening to the shrieks of whatever it was, but I suddenly didn't want to disturb the silence. Besides, the old house was on the outskirts of Coldwater—so far removed from anywhere eels could have come from that it wouldn't even make a good 'alligators in the sewers' story. It would just be me ranting about phantoms and shadows.

I realized that I'd only noticed the clog when I had woken up —again—in the middle of the night. Out here in the sticks there were hardly ever noises loud enough to notice, much less wake me from a dead sleep. But even though I told myself it was a mystery, I knew what it really was. I'd been dreaming of the Toad again. I could never sleep for long after his arrival.

I began making some coffee. The hissing and burbling of the machine took over from the now-silent drain, and its elusive denizens. Caffeine would keep me up for the rest of the night, but I wouldn't be sleeping anyway. Besides, it wasn't that I had discovered that the sink was clogged. I hadn't been running water into it. I had simply gone to gaze into the drain, because that's where they were. An urge had driven me. They... called to me. I wasn't sure if they were even connected with the Toad.

I sank down onto the couch, rough polyester against my bare skin. It was the perfect material for my cat, Mike, to sink his claws into and shred. He wasn't around at the moment, probably sleeping like any other intelligent being. I leaned back and closed my eyes, knowing that the vivid image of the Toad against the blackness of my eyelids would keep me awake.

It was huge. Or did it appear that way because I was so close to it? I'd started dreaming about it shortly after my arrival in Coldwater, a few weeks before Christmas. I was covering the agriculture/enviro beat for the local daily. There wasn't much going on in January, so I ended up spending most of my time wandering the limits of the county. At this time of year, it was resolutely white or gray. Mostly gray. I'd taken the job because I'd felt a need to escape my stifling rut, to find something. Or perhaps nothing. What better place to find that but in rural America? So I had come out here to the gray (and white) and had found something. Or it had found me.

Unlike the county, the Toad was black—a deep black that made me wonder how I could see it in such fine detail, all the wrinkles and warts. It stared at me with huge, bulbous eyes that were somehow blacker than the rest of it, pits so deep I felt like I was staring into outer space, or the deepest holes on Earth.

Given the period, I hadn't really made contact with people around town, and I hardly knew anyone in the office. Satellite reception was intermittent because of all the snow we'd been getting, but I didn't have anyone to contact anyway. I avoided the TV because I'd started seeing images in the background that resembled the thing. Life had become a bit of a cocoon, but such were the trials of the lonely reporter, or so I'd been told. Still, the lack of sleep was beginning to tell.

After the first couple weeks, I'd started shouting back when I awoke. What did it want? Why was it there? Why me?! But all that did was scare the cat, since there was no one else in the old house to hear me. The landlord never seemed to visit, and the unit that took up the other half of the tiny building seemed to be empty. There were never any noises from the bolted door in my living room, which I assumed led there. But the Toad never moved, or made a sound. It just sat there, staring at me. The sounds came later.

From the drain.

*

I was standing over the sink again, waiting for the motion to start. I didn't know why having creatures in my sink fascinated me so much. They definitely were creatures, too. It wasn't just a hair-and-grease clog or whatever else usually stopped up a drain. They were in there. They moved and hissed. I wasn't sure whether the noise was a vocalization, like a snake's, or came from their motion in and through and around the warren that was the house's ancient plumbing. I just had to wait, and I would hear it.

I looked up at the window. Light was slowly seeping into the world from somewhere behind the omnipresent cloud cover. The ground was still covered with snow, ice, and the gray slush of traffic. A broken mirror of the dolorous sky. No one was moving out there yet. Winter will do that, even in a farm community, but I did wonder if there was something else at work too. My muted reporter's instincts slowly pushed me forward, and I decided to make contact with a local for the first time in days. I ran the risk of having them think I was crazy, but perhaps that was better than only me thinking I was crazy.

I dressed, and walked out into the bitter air. The temperature hadn't risen above freezing for some days. Weeks, maybe. The wind was steady, although I never really heard it inside the house. My car was encased in snow. There didn't seem to be any point in trying to dig it out, given the equally buried driveway. My nearest neighbor was a gas station about a half mile down the road. Otherwise, there was nothing but fallow fields in either direction until you entered the city proper.

So I set out for the light I could see at the station, knowing they were open all night. Thankfully the road was both decently plowed and unoccupied, so I walked in the westbound lane. The only thing I had to dodge was a delivery truck, heading for the big dairy on the other side of town.

Originally, I'd felt like I'd emerged from my cocoon because it was getting lighter. Now that I was actually outside, that light was getting more and more distant. Had I misread the time? Was it actually evening and moving toward night? I shook my head. Cabin fever. I was just confusing myself. Still, I looked from side to side, trying to find some clue that would tell me that it was actually morning, and that I wasn't completely lost in time. Nothing came to me, but it did start snowing again in heavy, wet flakes.

Eventually, I stepped into the lights of the gas station—overhead strips for the lot, another near the door, the "Open" sign glowing in scarlet and azure neon. The snow highlighted the various bubbles of light as if they were solid walls, domains that kept the shadows at bay, if you were allowed to enter. I took the chance, stepped into the one by the door, and walked inside.

The light in the store was different than it had been the last time I was here, some random number of weeks ago. It was yellow now, like the one above my sink. It made the colorful tiers of candy and magazines seem fuzzy, like a watercolor with more water than paint. I couldn't see any lights in the coolers along the back wall. Bottles of beer, soda, and juice lurked in the shadows. The young woman who had always been behind the counter whenever I'd stopped by before was still there—small, wan, bundled in a white button-down shirt and a handmade rose-colored sweater. Her straight brown hair and thin face held not a hint of welcome or expectation. Maybe she was finishing a night shift.

I grabbed a small bag of chips from a rack. I wasn't even a bit hungry for them, though I couldn't quite remember the last time I'd eaten. I stepped to the counter and laid them down, digging in my pocket for the little bit of cash I had on me. I smiled, probably a diffident effort, and asked, "Lights change? Out of fluorescents?"

Her hands worked the register by themselves while she looked at me, eyes half-lidded and expressionless. "No. It's always been like this. Cheaper." Her voice was as flat as a test pattern, as indistinct as everything else in there.

I nodded, took the chips and my change, and turned to the door. When I reached it, I turned my head back toward her. "Uh, this may sound weird, but what time is it? I'm pretty sure it was morning when I woke up." I attempted the smile again. "I've been working some odd hours."

She looked to me, face unchanged. "It's morning. Early. Morning."

I nodded and tried to laugh in response, as if she had just said something obvious to the idiot guy who walked here in a subzero snowstorm. I pushed into the outside, and the dome of light was even more prominent now that the snow had begun falling harder. It was darker than it had been, and as I walked beyond the reach of the lights, I realized that what she'd said meant that it still could have been the middle of the night. The house wasn't visible in the darkness, but I stepped into the road anyway.

*

I was standing in my living room in my underwear, with a rolled-up copy of my employer's drivel in my hand. Sweat was streaming down my back, and meandering across my face as well. The flies were swarming, and I was on the hunt.

I had no idea where the flies could have come from in the dead of winter. It's not like I kept any real food around, as my fridge was a ghost town of aged condiments. And the heat! I hadn't touched the thermostat since I'd moved in, and couldn't remember ever having felt the need to. But here I was, crouched under the dim light of the overhead bulb and its cloth shade, watching the flies circle it and occasionally dive past my head. Their shadows danced around the room—vague visions of encircling drones. I waited for one of them to light on the small table next to the couch, and watched it sitting there. It rubbed its forelegs together and slowly raised its wings, as if preparing a plot. I took one small step forward and snapped my wrist. The newspaper smacked to the tabletop, and the fly's crushed body dropped to the floor. I nodded in satisfaction, and examined my weapon. The insect was smeared across it, like the trails of a dozen others that I'd finished in the last hour. I jumped into the air and swung the paper at the light, rattling the shade and scattering the small swarm. If I could bring them to my level, it might go faster. Sweat trickled into my eyes and I blinked it away, looking for another target.

I told myself that I was doing this so I could sleep, to simply get the insects out of my space, but I knew there was something more. There was an urge. It was testing my limits, observing—in this trivial manner—how willing I'd be to serve. I tracked one of the flies to the kitchen sink, slowing my pace as I closed in. I could see it sitting on the edge of the sink, forelegs rubbing. It turned and regarded me with its faceted eyes. It was watching even as I advanced toward it, paper exterminator at the ready. Its eyes stared into mine, just like the ones in my mind. It knew me. It understood the base urges, the wants, the drive. It knew what purpose it served.

I lunged forward and swung. The crack of the paper echoed from the bare walls, indicating the removal of another foe. The drain rumbled and I eyed it, waiting for some kind of real reaction from the spawn. That's what the drain-things were, I now knew. Spawn. Of the Toad. They were his creatures. They existed to serve him. Was it a biological thing? Or did they simply serve the power of its mind, its presence, the message across the ether that spoke of power, that swept aside all material and sensory satisfaction in the name of the darkness? Is that what I'd been seeking? The deprivation?

The spawn curled across the mouth of the drain again, black rubber teeth flexing in its wake... Or were they *its* teeth? Did it feel the extermination of the flies, or did it feel me? Sweat from my face dripped into the sink, and it retreated. The heat was getting worse. I dropped the paper and staggered to the bathroom. The light in there was similar, a plain incandescent bulb fixed to the ceiling. It activated with a pull chain that shivered in the heat like a mirage. I grabbed it, filled the tiny room with dingy lemon, and turned on the shower. The pipes growled with air pockets as water sprayed out. It was lukewarm, which was fine. I was only interested in getting some of the sweat off, and escaping the swamp that my apartment had become.

I stepped into the shower and shut the frosted glass door, the light of the bulb receding as I slid under the cascade. I stood, eyes closed—thankfully without imagery—for several minutes before the first rumble came from below me. I could see the flicker of shining black pass by the drain as the spawn wormed its way through the pipes and beyond. It was as if there were no boundaries beneath the floor of the house, and the structure itself was the prison. It certainly felt that way to me.

The bathroom light hissed, fizzled, and went out. The darkness was impenetrable, but I just let the water keep running. I could stumble my way around the tiny room and then back to the light of the living room. Strangely, I couldn't see the glow from the latter, either. I felt the water coursing down my leg and into the drain as I stood there, motionless. The stream was a coherent whole, not spraying anywhere else. It followed the path of my flesh to the grate. Soon it felt heavy. I still couldn't see anything, but I could imagine the spawn slithering up the stream of water, slowly enwrapping my leg as it searched for... what? A way in? A place to feed? My hand hovered over my leg, afraid to touch what might be slime twisted around it, afraid to confirm the physical nature of something that still might be a product of isolation in a new place. I closed my eyes and the Toad was there, the barest hint of yellow teeth now showing from its engorged lips.

I wasn't alone. It was there with me.

*

I was lying in my bed, still naked and wet from the shower, but no longer sweating. The heat had been localized in the living room. I couldn't hear or see the flies anymore, either. Light outside streamed in through the small window of my bedroom, but only of the vaguest sort, like moonlight behind the clouds. I lay there waiting for something to happen, something to change. I could feel my eyes closing, but mostly out of simple fatigue. My mind was still racing with thoughts of what had been happening to me. When I did close my eyes, the Toad was there. Watching. Waiting. I watched, in turn, for some kind of reaction, but still the only change from weeks previous was the slightly curled lip. The black abyssal eyes remained motionless over the pale maize of the fangs.

I got up, and headed to the door in my living room, the one that led to the other apartment. I released the bolt on my side and tried to open it. Common sense warned me that I'd be stopped by the bolt on the other occupant's side. Somehow though, I was completely unsurprised when the door drifted open.

A blast of cold air greeted me. I looked up to see a caved-in roof, a gaping tear which allowed a dim moonbeam to shine through. Tracing the path of the light, I saw a massive hole that took up the entirety of the space. It looked as though a meteorite had struck, and dragged the other apartment down into a crevasse. The splintered ends of wooden crossbeams and remains of a concrete foundation formed a jagged edge around the rim of the pit, but I could see nothing further. I briefly thought about how I could have rented the good half of the house without noticing this and then dismissed it. It didn't matter.

I stepped to the edge of the cavity, drawn to it. The night was very cold, but I wasn't really affected. The sides of the hole were ragged, as if dug out by a giant animal, clashing with my meteorite theory. Shrugging, I stepped out onto what felt like a steady beam. Once secure, I lowered myself to an outcropping of rock and earth, and began picking my way down. It required climbing in some spots, but just delicate walking in others. There was no sign of snow or ice despite the open sky far above me.

I don't know how much time it took until I reached the bottom. There was a cavern of blackness to my right. Like the drain. That's where they were. I walked toward it, hesitating at the edge. My eyes wouldn't adjust to the almost tangible darkness. I would be entering their world. Maybe I already had. I walked in.

The passage narrowed and widened randomly, as if formed by things of uncertain size or shape. I was certain it had been formed. This was no more natural than the septic tank under my apartment. This was done by the spawn. That fact didn't dissuade me from walking right into it, because I knew that I was supposed to. I stopped for a moment, and closed my eyes. The Toad didn't appear, which just meant that I needed to find him. Needed to. That was what this was about.

A faint light was slowly fading into existence up ahead. I kept walking, and soon noticed shaped stone under my feet. The light, a dim gray that apparently radiated from everywhere, became stronger. I approached a wide room. There were concave paths running in all directions, as if to control fluid that might spill out across the simple limestone floor. Most of those fluid paths led to circular openings in the distant walls, coming from the dais that rose up before me.

The central block was a rectangle of black stone, accessed by ramps. Upon it sat an enormous, gelatinous egg. The jelly was mostly transparent, but there were small, twisting shapes running through it like veins. A black form quivered inside the egg, a larva easily over 10 feet in length, and its movements made the whole shape pulsate.

Arrayed in front of the dais were a half dozen squat urns, carved out of that same black stone in the shape of the Toad. Clawed feet emerged from the base of each, the mouths extended forward to present an opening, impassive eyes peeking over the rear edge. They were inscribed in red with some kind of language that I couldn't identify. I knelt to look at one, trying to figure out what culture or pattern it might be, but with no luck. The letters themselves seemed to pulsate when the egg did, glowing alternately brighter and dimmer. As if the urn was breathing. Black eyes bulged from the rear of the stone pot, staring into me. The inside of the mouth was pure darkness.

Glerg.

The shape inside the egg shifted, and the whole jellied mass quaked in response. The darkness inside the urn I was examining bubbled, and then erupted. A mass emerged, like a dribbling of black candle wax in motion. It thrust up from the urn and stretched out toward the ceiling. I fell to the floor, half-crawling backwards, and saw that all of the rest had the same shapes winding toward the ceiling. They were like long tentacles of tar, spiraling, rippling and bubbling like an oil gusher in slow motion. They reached toward some unknown point in the darkness of the ceiling then, in unison, all plunged to the floor in front of their respective pots and collapsed with a loud squelching noise. It was all too similar to the sounds that had been emerging from my sink for the past few weeks. They had become masses of black ichor, each the size of a small car, bubbling like simmering water. Four of them immediately flowed into the concave channels, spilling over the edges like thick gravy, and slid away into the tunnels around the chamber. Two remained, including the one in front of me.

I sat, mesmerized, as it extruded pseudopods from one side or another. Finally a large one projected toward me. I watched the slime peel back as a ring of irregular, ochre fangs poked out in my direction. They could have been anything from shark's teeth to lion's fangs. They had varying lengths and thicknesses. The orifice opened and closed rapidly, as if scenting the air. It made no sound, writhing and chomping in total silence. At the same time, smaller tentacles erupted from elsewhere in the mass. They too displayed rings of smaller teeth as they hovered around, perhaps searching for targets to clamp onto.

I sat paralyzed, watching the spawn, until motion from the other side of the room caught my eye. The girl from the gas station walked into the chamber, still dressed in her rose-colored sweater, shirt, and plain slacks. The blank expression on her face hadn't changed. She completely ignored me and approached the other spawn, which had also sent forth an array of fanged mouths. Mechanically, she stripped out of her clothes. Her skin was pale and showed a latticework of veins not unlike the egg. She knelt before the creature, eyes closed. I looked to my own skin, to see how far I'd gone.

The spawn before her eased its largest maw forwards. The girl had begun writhing, matching the spawn's silent motion. She extended her head toward it, chin thrust forward in apparent yearning. This was the answer. It was right. But she opened her eyes at the last moment, and gave a little cry of fear when she saw how close the thing was.

Immediately, the tendril clamped down on the top of her skull. The rest of its mouths shot forward and latched on to various parts of her body, teeth sinking into thighs and arms. She shrieked in agony as it drew her into its form. Blood streamed everywhere. The pair writhed in concert as she disappeared under the cloud of its shape. It still pulsated with her motion, and I could hear her howls from within it as it devoured her. The last sign of her existence was a knee, just discernible through the black slime, before the whole mass settled into a large pool, fanged mouths and girl subsumed in its bulk. It flowed into one of the channels, and departed.

The egg quivered, the sound of its movement surprisingly loud in the near-empty hall. The small network of arteries rearranged themselves under its surface. I sat there, feeling nothing, aware of the symmetry of it all. The Toad. His spawn. The nameless girl's failure. I would... succeed. Succeed at finding the truth behind the malaise that had become my existence? Was that engagement or surrender?

The spawn in front of me shifted its mass, encircling me. Its smaller mouths waved around the periphery of my vision. The main protrusion came toward me, biting slowly in anticipation. Its teeth were spattered in dried blood. I realized the mistake she had made. She had not given herself to the Toad. She'd fought for some meaning in the last moments of her existence. But I was past that point. The darkness was a comfort.

I stared into the ring of teeth, and calmly put my head forward. I watched as the ichor flowed over the teeth and the opening became nothing but gelatinous blackness. It encircled my head and my shoulders, and flowed around me. The Toad entered my vision in the blackness and, finally, smiled fully. There was nothing, and I had found it.

Beyond the Shore
by Lynne Hardy

In her dreams, there was always a beach. Its sands whispered to her, the insignificant grains jostling and shoving each other in their desperate bid to outrun the ceaseless breeze. The light on the water was so bright that it blinded her, forcing her to direct her gaze towards the apparently endless crescent of coastline along which she walked. There were no gulls to cry plaintively. The lapping of the waves and the rasping susurration of the sand were her only company on her stroll beside the restless sea.

Some would have thought the beach a lonely place to dream, a nightmare rather than a comfort. That would have been a mistake. Here, alone, she could escape from the world, with its two-faced people and their incessant murmurings. Only here was there any peace for her, which was why she loved it more than life itself.

*

It began when she was a small child, an only child, full of life and excitement at the world around her, with lots of small and equally eager friends. One day she fell ill, a sore throat and a sore head. This was worrying to her parents, but not excessively so – after all, she'd spent virtually the entire day running about in the sunshine, singing and shouting for all she was worth.

The fever came that night, fierce and unremitting. She vaguely recalled her mother's tearful face. Her father carried her to the cottage hospital for help. She was a rigid, unresponsive doll clasped tightly in his arms. After that, she remembered nothing, not for the longest time. But when she woke, much to the delight of doctors, nurses, and parents, the voices were there too.

They whispered to her, silently, constantly, whenever someone else was around. At first, they told her many wonderful things: people's hopes and dreams, their joys and expectations. Although it was a little strange, she soon became used to the window into people's lives the voices gave her. Being so young, she frequently had no real understanding of what it was they talked about, but it was nice all the same.

Of course, there were times when, all innocence, she made pronouncements based on what the whisperers told her. For a while, people thought it was rather sweet; a terribly staid and serious six-year old speaking to them with a voice and understanding beyond her years, in words that sounded exactly like ones they would have chosen. That particular realisation – that the voices did indeed belong to the people she was with, that they sounded so much like them because they came from within them – didn't dawn on her until she was much, much older.

After a while though, the novelty began to wear off. People tutted that she'd spent all of her time with adults since her illness. It would do her the world of good to be with others of her own age. Perhaps – understandably, they grudgingly admitted – her mother was mollycoddling her. Keeping her indoors out of fear that she might become sick again. It was turning her into a little old woman long before her time.

These sounded like plausible explanations, over tea and cake at the local mothers' meetings. After all, what did they have to fear from a slightly eccentric little girl? However, those unflinching brown eyes and her habit of cocking her head ever so slightly to the right as if she was listening to something (or someone) *were* odd. She began to make people feel deeply uncomfortable whenever she was around. Although she was always pleasant, those around her faced a growing dread. One day, her insight might see beyond their carefully constructed facades to all the lies and petty jealousies lurking beneath. And that would never do.

So she found herself pushed away by the grown-ups who had fawned over her. Where once they petted her like a little lamb for her amusing precociousness, now they encouraged her to be with their children instead. The problem with trying to play with the other boys and girls though, was that her friends had moved on. She had been ill for a very long time, almost a year in fact.

Her peers now looked at her with suspicion. It felt as if they *knew* that she could hear what their voices said about them, while the adults only suspected it. Younger children also watched her warily. They were unsure of what to make of her and what she knew about them. Naturally, she was too much of a baby still for the older ones to even consider her worth the bother. But she tried, for her parents' sake and the sake of their friends, to be a good little girl and do as she was told.

*

The voices began to change as she got older – slowly at first, but inexorably, like the oncoming tide. They were no longer heart-warming and comforting to her in her loneliness, but colder, crueller. They became all about the guilt, the lies, the fears that people did their best to hide, from each other and from themselves. The good things were swallowed up by the darkness. Finally, all the voices did was show her how ugly the world was, how twisted and bitter and revolting people's everyday existence could be.

At first people gave her a little leeway. "She was very poorly, after all, you know – did it do some permanent damage to her mind, d'you think?" But soon they just dismissed her as a spiteful, nasty girl, determined to ruin everything she could. There were always questions. Why did she have to do that? Did she not like other people to be happy? Was she jealous? Why did she have to be so cruel? Why did she have to lie?

But, of course, they weren't lies. They were the truth, whether people wanted to acknowledge it or not. She could see it in their eyes whenever the syllables dripped from her mouth. Even as they proclaimed her words to be poison, they wanted to know how she knew their darkest secrets, their deepest fears and loathings. To ask would mean exposure however, and that had to be avoided at all costs. So easy to blame a child, one you've labelled as a trouble maker, a liar through and through. Much easier than facing your own imperfections or letting others see your weaknesses.

She learned, eventually, to keep her mouth shut, to keep her thoughts to herself. To avoid people whenever she could. It was almost impossible at school, though. She was taunted and bullied by everyone around her, staff and pupils alike. It formed a constant litany, the sly comments, the "accidental" kicks, the stolen pens and pencils, the hundred other small but carefully targeted indignities. Her reputation, which everywhere preceded her, ensured that when she complained to her parents or her teachers, she was called a tattle-tail, a snitch. She was the lowest of the low, one whose vicious lies were a pathetic attempt to pass the blame for her own inadequacies onto all of those "nice" children. Because butter wouldn't melt, obviously.

So she took the only option that was left to her and retreated ever further. She fled into her own world, a world of books and stories and wronged princesses who were eventually rescued from their subjugation and torment by powerful, mysterious princes who punished everyone who had ever harmed their one, true love. She knew it wasn't real, that there was no happily ever after. That didn't stop her from longing for it, for someone who understood. Someone who didn't look at her with fear and trepidation the way her parents did. The way everyone did.

She often cried herself to sleep. She wished the nice voices, the kind voices that spoke of warmth and friendship and happiness, would come back to keep her company once more. She missed them so much. That was when the dreams began, and she first escaped to the never-ending crescent of sand and the oh-too-bright sea beyond. Her place of release from the burden of knowing other people's thoughts.

Her subconscious mind's idea of what embodied the perfect hideaway confused her at first. It wasn't as if she'd ever been to the seaside. Her father didn't hold with such things as holidays. Day trips were usually to the zoo, or some dusty museum staffed by fossils almost as old as the ones they exhibited. And yet, there it was, perfectly formed in her mind's eye – golden, warm, and utterly devoid of anyone but herself. For the first time in more than a decade, she felt relaxed, at peace.

Actually, thinking back, it wasn't perfectly formed – at least, not at first. There had been a haziness at the edge of her perception, a sense that her remembrance of it was somehow incomplete. And that was the truly odd thing about it all, really. It genuinely did feel as if she had been there before. Try as she might, she couldn't quite figure out how or when.

It didn't matter. What did matter was that she now had somewhere to escape to that was hers and hers alone. At the beach, no-one blamed her for their deceit, no-one was afraid of her and what she might know. She didn't have to pretend to be what she wasn't. She could dig her toes into the fine, pale sand and feel the sun penetrate and warm her soul to its very core.

Miraculously, she began to come out of her shell, to smile again after so many years of bitter, sullen looks. Her parents were relieved in some small measure. Perhaps it had just been a phase that she'd been going through.

*

When the war came, her family had to move to a new town. Her mother didn't want to go, but her father insisted that his new job was important work. That they all had to do their bit. Everyone had to make sacrifices in a time of crisis, and this would do very nicely as theirs.

The voice that came from her father was suddenly overblown with its own self-worth. Before, it had always been full of bluff and bluster, yet riddled with doubt and insecurity. Now, it was positively gleeful at the misery and carnage that had given it such a sense of grandeur and importance. So it told her all sorts of interesting things that it really shouldn't have. It so wanted someone to know just how wonderful it was, even if it was only her.

It was just as well her father knew to hold his real tongue. He would have been dragged up for very spectacularly failing to keep secrets despite the War Office's strictest advice. She fantasised briefly about becoming a spy. She could leak what she knew to some handsome and ever-so grateful foreign agent. He would sweep her off her feet and take her on whirlwind adventures across the globe. But she had no idea where she would find such a person, so quickly abandoned the idea as a bad job. Somehow, she very much doubted that handsome spies hung around at the corner shop, waiting for femmes fatales to whisper sweet classified information into their perfect ears.

Before the world had lost all reason, she'd learned to almost completely block out the general background murmurings that came from large numbers of people. But the bombings, the shortages, the unrelenting gloom chipped away at her mental barriers until she couldn't ignore it anymore. She had to get away, or it was going to drive her mad.

Fortunately, there was a war on. The source of her increased misery – and even her wonderful dreams had become desperate moments snatched between air raids – was also the source of her escape. So she volunteered, to get away from the town and its factories. She found herself far away in the fields, knee-deep in muck, digging for victory like thousands of others (without being the least bit like them at all).

Work – hard, physical toil – made her tired, so tired that sleep came easily. It was deep, perfect sleep where she could walk along the beach, the horizon always just another footfall away, alone and happy. Because everyone else was working so hard, breaking their backs to keep food on people's tables, their voices only seemed to be able to complain about the little, inconsequential things. Blisters and splinters and aches and pains and mud.

It wasn't all plain-sailing. Trivial jealousies and rivalries often arose, their voices clustering around her. Then, they were all but shouting in their fractiousness, stridently declaring how it just wasn't fair – whatever "it" happened to be this time. She just worked all the harder, taking on the dirtiest of jobs that the pretty little missies didn't want to disarrange their curls over. Yes, it meant that some of them thought that she was standoffish. Others put it down to shyness. Quite a few didn't care either way.

All she wanted was to work and sleep, work and sleep. The repetitive movements of shovelling this, hammering that provided the rhythm of her waking life. At night, the lap, lap, lap of the waves was music to her slumbering ears.

She had the chance to go to a beach, a real one, during her time on the farm. She couldn't bring herself to take the trip. She was too afraid that what she saw wouldn't match what she experienced every night, and that it might somehow tarnish her dreams. It just wasn't worth the risk of losing the one thing that meant anything to her.

*

And then, all of a sudden, the war was over. The years had passed by so quickly, in drudgery and blissful release, that she had somehow completely lost track of all time. She was sad to leave the farm, with its isolation and its endless, mindless tasks. It had kept her from thinking, from feeling, from dealing with other people's apparently endless hypocrisy. She had no desire to go home, but she was no longer needed or wanted. So back to her parents she went, and tried hard to keep the world at arm's length.

To her dismay, she no longer had the strength to blot out the massed voices that greeted her return. They surrounded her, beating themselves against her, refusing to go away and leave her alone. The communal spirit that had existed withered away as the rationing went on and on. The voices were furious that they had given so much, lost so much, been promised so much, and still there was not a brighter day. There was no end in sight. All that was left was misery and despair.

At first, she tried to find gainful employment, but there were so many demobbed soldiers wanting jobs that young women just couldn't get a look-in. Her father flatly refused to let her work in a pub. "No daughter of mine!" had been the start of that particular argument. Her erratic schooling had not shaped her into good secretarial material.

She slept more, demoralised and isolated, afraid to leave her dreams for the impotent anger of the waking world. At first, her parents were content to put it down to sheer exhaustion. Like everyone else, they'd heard the rumours. Girls being used as virtual slave labour, fed on scraps. Life in conditions that were worse than those for animals.

But as time wore on, they began to recognise this young woman who only came down from her room for meals. She was an even more exaggerated form of the moody, lethargic child they'd hoped had been banished all those years before. Her mother worried. Her father – no longer important, seething at a world that had failed to recognise his steadfast service – grew increasingly impatient.

They pretended that nothing was happening. Her father had his reputation to maintain. Appearances had to be kept up, for everyone's sake. When she was found by a local policeman, wandering and confused, apparently sleepwalking, everyone agreed that something had to be done. She had been indulged for far too long. It was time she snapped herself out of this malaise and started behaving like the adult she was.

When a good, stern talking-to failed, they sent her to see learned men in white coats. They were all very nice, very reassuring when she went in to see them. At least, they tried to be. Their voices whispered spitefully about what they actually thought of her – a selfish, spoiled child who refused to grow up.

Despite all of their prodding and poking, the doctors couldn't quite figure out what was wrong. It wasn't hysteria, they were fairly certain of that, but there were several other things that it could be. Some were interested that she had suffered from catatonia as a child as part of her bout of sleepy sickness. Others pooh-poohed the notion that the two events were at all connected. They decided that it was probably depression, pure and simple, and they had just the cure for that.

She wasn't thrilled by the idea of someone passing an electrical current through her brain. The voices wouldn't leave her alone any more though, and her sleep had become so disturbed that she couldn't make it to the beach for respite. Any attempt to close her eyes during the day, even for a few seconds, was rudely interrupted by pinches and slaps from the overzealous staff. At night, she lay awake and stared at the ceiling, wishing she was dead, crying like a child again for her lost paradise. She had been left with no choice, no choice at all.

The difference in the voices when she arrived for her first treatment was both remarkable and unnerving. The anger and the hate were gone, replaced by a whimpering terror that she had never known before. It felt as if they were scared that she was going to leave them all alone in the darkness, with no one to hear them.

"Serves you right," she whispered back defiantly. "Perhaps if you hadn't made my life so miserable, I wouldn't be here now, having to even contemplate this. My life could have been normal. I could have been normal and happy. So spare me from your wheedling insincerities. You've only yourselves to blame."

The hospital was not a welcoming place. Its harsh, bright lighting hurt her eyes. It reminded her of her lost sun, forcing her to choke back a sob that garnered her a very odd look from the nurse. The overpowering aroma of disinfectant couldn't quite mask the scent of dread that permeated the walls and floor. The stench settled in the back of her throat, constricting it even further.

She'd wanted her mother to come with her, but her father had forbidden it. He claimed it would be too much for Mother, who was – as she well knew – rather delicate herself. She knew nothing of the sort. They just didn't want to be there so that they wouldn't have to admit their shame. Officially, she'd gone on holiday to the countryside to recuperate from a long illness. More lies. It made her sick. It had to stop.

They settled her into her room, measured her vital signs, and told her to relax in a patently obvious triumph of hope over weary experience. Later, they came and took her down to the theatre. The lights in the ceiling whipped past above her head, her eyes blinded by the glare. She closed them and begged to see the sand, to hear the waves, but there was only the creak of the trolley and the squeak of the orderlies' shoes on the clinically sterile floor.

The nurses, stiff and starched in their prim uniforms, gathered around her, ready to hold her down. The voices said nothing, but she knew that they were listening for her to say something to them, to reassure them. She had no intention of doing so, not on her life or theirs. They could go to hell after what they'd done to her.

The doctor swabbed her temples with something damp, and nodded to the waiting nurses, who grabbed her arms and legs. She couldn't see what was behind her, but she could hear the sharp clicks of what sounded like switches and buttons being toyed with. She felt a growing sense of panic, a realisation that this was all some terrible mistake. There was no getting away from it now, however.

"You should have listened to us," the voices hissed, triumphant but petrified. "We did try to warn you."

She felt something pressed against her head. Then, as when she had fallen asleep all those years before and they had all feared that she would never wake, everything stopped. There was only darkness and silence.

*

"And how do you feel, young lady?"

She looked at the doctor beside her bed, her forehead creasing slightly. "I have a little bit of a headache, Doctor, and I feel slightly sick. Is that normal?"

He nodded, seemingly very pleased with her answer. "Oh, yes, my dear. Perfectly normal. Tell me, what do you remember?"

She crinkled her brow even further. After a few seconds, she shrugged. "It might be easier if I told you what I don't recall."

He laughed, a forced, brittle sound that gave her the impression of being far too well rehearsed. "But how can you tell me what it is if you don't remember it?"

The crease reappeared. "I don't remember when I came here. I don't really remember why I came, only that I needed help. There's something..." She paused, then shook her head. "No, I'm sure it's not important."

The Doctor smiled and checked the woman's records. She had now completed a full course of twenty treatments, and the staff considered her demeanour markedly improved. She had stopped constantly attempting to sleep. She bore no ill-will against the doctors, although if she'd recalled anything of what she'd undergone, she would have done. She had become such a very well-behaved patient.

"I wouldn't worry too much about the amnesia." The Doctor smiled, and scribbled onto her sheet. "If it's important, it will come back to you eventually. While there is some long term memory loss related to the period before treatment commences, the benefits far outweigh that minor inconvenience."

"Oh, good. Thank you, Doctor. Can I go home now, please?"

"In a few days, my dear, when we know you're steady on your feet again."

As he left the room, he turned to look at her. Despite her apparently contented smile, he had noticed the slight look of panic in her eyes at the mention that she might remember what she had lost. He dismissed his observation, unable to fathom why such a thing might be frightening.

*

Her parents were more than a little apprehensive about their daughter's return, but she seemed genuinely happy to be home. Here was the daughter they remembered from thirty years ago, before the illness. While it lasted, it was good. They were a family again, fervently making up for all that lost time. Her father even insisted on taking them all to the seaside for candyfloss and some bracing fresh air. She discovered the noise of the amusement arcades, the slightly decayed air of decadence coated with a thin layer of stone-cold chip fat. She couldn't explain why, but the fact that she could gaze out over the waves as far as she could see almost broke her heart.

It was shortly after the trip that the whispers started again. At first, she just asked if her parents had said something that she hadn't quite caught. Then the haunted, hunted look began to creep back into her eyes. She gained a new nervous tick of wafting at her right ear as if trying to drive away an annoying, buzzing insect. The smiles and laughter slowly vanished, replaced by sullen silence and bouts of staring off into the distance, lost in a daydream.

They sent her back to the hospital. The doctors shook their heads and admitted that she was not the only one whose symptoms had reoccurred. Their cure was not as perfect as they had at first believed. But, they stated confidently, the treatment worked before so it would undoubtedly work again. And so it did – each and every time she went back over the next few years. But the gap between visits grew steadily less and less, and her depressions grew deeper and deeper. New tics appeared, and she began to scream in terror every time she woke.

When she tried to throw herself from a pier into the dark waters below, everyone decided that enough was enough. She had to be locked away for her own safety. They gave her drugs to keep her calm, make her docile. She didn't mind, not really. The voices were hard to hear through the soft, fuzzy buzzing in her head, and the cocktail of narcotics helped her sleep.

Sleep, of course, meant the beach. Her beach. The pale, rustling sand that went on forever. The frothy white edges of the great, rolling waves that she couldn't quite see. The golden, warming sun burnt through her, scorching out the fear, the pain and the loneliness. And so she found her peace again, and smiled at them when they came with their needles and their pills. She didn't fight them. She didn't want to. They were giving her everything she needed, instead of taking it away, jolt by useless jolt.

It was bliss.

The only problem was that she kept waking up again. Even though her mind was almost permanently shrouded in a drug-induced fog, there was still a part of it that was capable of plotting, of planning how to get exactly what it needed. A little self control, a little painful but necessary self denial now, and she could sleep forever.

*

They found her one morning, her eyes wide open, staring at the light fitting in the ceiling with a crooked smile on her rigid face. There were enquiries made as to how she had managed to obtain enough tablets to be able to overdose. Staff were quickly and quietly moved to other facilities to avoid a scandal. There were lessons learned, her devastated but strangely relieved parents were assured. They nodded at the soothing words. It would never do to challenge the omnipotence of the white-clad gods of medicine. Life went on without her.

*

She was not alone on the beach any more. The whispering that she had always thought was the sand was actually the voices of a host of other dreamers. They had walked the beach invisibly beside her, present but unseen until now, year after year. Their every step had been matched to hers, just shifted slightly to one side of her awareness. She wasn't sure she liked it. She'd come here to get away from people, not to be surrounded by them.

The sun was in the wrong place as well. It no longer glared at her from above the water, but glowered over the dunes. Its incandescent fury forced her to turn her gaze beyond the shore. For the first time in a long time, she could see across the waves. For the first time in a long time, she remembered.

She had been here before, as a child, back when she and all the others – those who walked beside her now in their own sleepy reveries – had first been ill. She recognised their faces, even though nearly thirty-five years had passed. They had been her friends once before. They would be so again.

She also recognised the corpses floating in the waves. Their putrefying bodies bobbed up and down with the swell, arms outstretched towards the island that loomed on the horizon. They reached desperately for it, but it was eternally beyond their grasp. They had been weak. They had not dreamed deeply enough. They had perished, becoming inconvenient flotsam and jetsam. A warning to the faithless of the fate that awaited them.

She recognised the outlines of the buildings on the island, too. They were carved from a greenish stone that she instinctively knew could be found nowhere on the earth she'd left behind. Even at this distance, the sheer scale was breath-taking. She longed to walk amongst the impossible streets and twisted, nightmarish statues that were waiting to welcome her home. The waves had stopped her once before. They would not do so again.

No, it hadn't been the waves, had it? The time had not been right. The song had stopped. Those who were strong, who belonged, had been sent away to watch for the day when the island rose again. And now there it was, dripping and glistening, so close that she could almost touch it. She would not fail this time. Today, she would join with those who slept below, those whose song wrapped itself around her, burrowing into her and through her like the burning sun.

She strode, unafraid, into the waves, brushing the corpses to one side, wading deeper and deeper into the grey-green water, raising her voice to join the ancient hymn that called her on.

Bleak Mathematics
by Brian Fatah Steele

It all started in a hovel on Route 44 called The Green Room. I stood outside my car, smoking, watching the band load gear inside. The Green Room was one of those dive bars that had somehow managed to evade being condemned for decades, and numerous bands wanted to play there simply because other bands had played there. I never understood that, especially since the place was a notorious shithole. The sound was bad, the lighting was worse, and their beer selection hadn't changed since the 1980s. Unfortunately, a booming punk act wanted it as their stop in northeast Ohio, and that meant I was covering the show.

I eyed the pink highlights in the drummer's teased black hair and snorted at the idea of this band being "punk" anything. I didn't mind their music, but I had a hard time swallowing their genre labeling. Whatever. I wasn't here to critique, only to snap some photos and then report.

"Kirchner!" The voice came from the other side of the car.

I turned to see a younger man weaving his way towards me, and swore. I'd hoped Alternative Report wasn't going to bother sending anyone, but if they had to, I'd *really* hoped it wouldn't be Joel Barrows. So much for that.

"I see Alt-M-App managed to get you here," said Barrows with a big grin. "Good to see you out at a show."

I wrestled with the urge to punch my former coworker repeatedly in the face. "Yes, you and I, here at the luxurious Green Room."

Barrows frowned. "Dude, this place has history."

I flicked out my cigarette and walked away from him, the desire to punch him growing.

The Green Room was basically one big square, the stage at one end and the bar at the other. Closer to the bar end, slightly raised up, was a sound board where a guy who looked like Paul Bunyan's little brother swayed back and forth drunkenly, fiddling with a mixer. Off to one side were an office, a storage room, and what the staff laughingly called restrooms. The brown plastic paneling, perpetually sticky tile floor, and broken drop ceiling completed the ambience.

I ordered a vodka tonic—it tasted mostly like lighter fluid— and sat by the bar. Barrows sat beside me, and agonized over the meager beer selection. A monumental effort of will allowed me to keep my mouth shut. I couldn't fathom why he was sitting there, other than trying to provoke me. You don't poke the guy whose job you stole.

"So, how do you like working for Alt-M-App?" he asked, grimacing down at his cheap domestic beer. "Is it much different than Alternative Report?"

I turned and looked at him, ready to rip in, but he looked genuinely interested. It had been six months since I'd been let go from the magazine. My editor had decided she could use my somewhat lax expense reports as justification for firing me. The very same expense reports I'd been handing in for twelve years. Then she had given her baby brother the job. I wondered how much he knew at the time. I wondered how much he knew now.

"Alt-M-App doesn't pay as much, but I have a lot more freedom," I said. "Basically it's all freelance, unless I sign up for a certain assignment. I can do anything from concerts to album reviews to interviews to photo ops to editorials. They were actually pretty happy to get me."

"Well, that's... good," replied Barrows, still looking at his beer.

I couldn't help it, I had to get something in. "Best of all, no expense reports."

He groaned. "Man, I am so sorry! I had no idea Jessica had done that, I swear. Yeah, I wanted a job at Alternative Report, but not like that. No one takes me seriously now there, either. That's why I'm asking about Alt-M-App. If I quit to go work for them, maybe you can get your old job back."

I honestly didn't know what to say. I hadn't expected this turn of events. Here, I'd been hating him for six months. I mulled it over as the band began sound check. Alt-M-App wasn't the best, but it was okay. It was one of those multi-media platform things the kids loved these days, plus the app was making more money with every download. But I had given twelve years to that magazine. Go back to Alternative Report?

"Thanks, Barrows, but no. Not after what your sister pulled. Alt-M-App might still be getting its legs, along with me, but this is where I'm at now."

He started to say something, but the band kicked in and the crowd started cheering. "I'll talk to you after the show!" he shouted in my ear.

I nodded as I got out my phone to take photos and notes.

The show went down pretty much as I expected. Lots of power chords and repetitive choruses. The two hundred or so fans in attendance seemed to enjoy it, and I made sure to note that. I can be a pretentious music snob, but I understand that some things appeal to other people. I'm not entirely sure why, but I begrudgingly accept it.

The crowd filtered its way outside and I found myself by my car. Barrows had said he wanted to talk again, so I waited. I started to grow impatient as more cars disappeared from the parking lot. I was just getting ready to leave myself when he finally appeared. He looked a little disheveled, but I didn't comment.

"Sorry, I got a little wrapped up in something," he said. I lit up a cigarette and motioned for him to continue. "Listen, I get your decision, but I still feel bad. I figure I could help you. Like, quietly."

I squinted at him and took another puff. "How so?"

"Alternative Report gets press releases that maybe Alt-M-App doesn't. Upcoming shows, albums, merch, I dunno. I might be able to pass some of that along to you."

"I'm pretty connected, Barrows. I've been doing this for over a decade. Besides the albums – which would be illegal and get you fired – what could you give me?"

A small smile pulled at his mouth. "Bleak Mathematics."

"What?"

"Exactly. They're gonna be in Cleveland in two months, sometime at the end of May, but nobody knows the exact date or location yet. The most secretive underground band ever, with the most loyal, die-hard followers. I don't care about this emocore crap from tonight, I came to talk to a Bleak Mathematics fan."

Now I was officially intrigued.

"Where did you hear about them?"

"Whispers at concerts, rumors on message boards. I've only put together bits and pieces. They're a touring band only. Never recorded a single song. They never play actual music venues. No idea who the members are or how many, and no idea what type of music they play. Their fans are like a cult, zealous and secretive, but I managed to find out they're coming here in two months."

I nodded, feeling my own smile on my face. "Okay, I'm in."

*

Barrows wasn't lying when he said Bleak Mathematics and its fans were secretive. After a few basic online searches revealed nothing, I figured the kid was lying to me. No band in the 21st century has zero online presence. I dropped it for a day and worried about writing up my article about the concert, including selecting the best two photos from the dozens I had taken. Once that had all been sent out, I thought about jumping into a piece I was considering. I wanted to explore the influence of British Shoegaze rock from the '90s on current American Indie trends. I couldn't stop thinking about Barrows' mysterious band, though.

He had mentioned something about message boards, so I logged into one that I knew to be frequented by opinionated egotists such as myself. Most of the threads bemoaned the death of rock music, the commercialization of song writing, arguments on genre, or their Great Satan the RIAA. It took a while until I actually found a thread about bands.

The search function on the message board only worked if the key words were in the thread's title, so that didn't snag me any luck, but I found some promising leads. Under *Obscure Bands,* I found a number of users discussing post-rock, performance punk, psychobilly, and more. Even I hadn't heard of some of the acts mentioned, and I assumed some of them had to be unsigned. A user named Shoggoth1 brought up Bleak Mathematics, eliciting responses from two users. His post said that no other band could "hope to replicate the sheer sonic dreamscape" of their music.

The first user to reply, ZoSoEvermore, said he had heard of the group and asked several questions: What kind of music did they play? Why didn't they record anything? Did Shoggoth1 know if they were gonna be in Houston anytime soon? Didn't they have a damn website?

The second reply, from DagonsGirl92, simply told Shoggoth1 to stop talking about them.

He did. I scoured the site, but could find no more mention of the band. Or, for that matter, any more posts from either Shoggoth1 or Dagonsgirl92.

Knowing that Barrows hadn't tried to play me, I was able to set the topic aside and write my Shoegaze article. It took a few days, but I got it sent off, secure in the knowledge that I now had a tidy sum in my bank account. I had another concert coming up in a few days where I'd most likely see Barrows, so I wanted to jump back into our cryptic band. Unfortunately, I didn't find much more. Just a few lines here and there in passing, the band name on some list or at the very most, someone asking, *who are these guys?*

*

It had been a week since I'd last seen Barrows. I couldn't believe I was actually excited to talk to him. The show was at The Outpost, a much nicer establishment, and I was standing right outside the door, smoking in the cold. The snow had melted into a wet mess, but the wind was still biting. I could have easily waited inside with a nice hefeweizen draft, but for some reason I was eager to talk to him as soon as he arrived.

Everything I had been planning on saying to him dried in my mouth when he came around the corner. He looked as if he hadn't eaten since I'd last seen him, and like someone had beaten him with a brick this morning. The big smile he gave me didn't help at all.

"Hey, Kirchner, I was hoping I'd see you here."

"What the hell happened to you?"

He looked honestly confused for a moment. "Huh? Oh, rough week. Let's get a beer."

I followed him inside, not sure what to say. If he didn't want to talk about it, I wouldn't push. It wasn't like we were close or anything. We both sat at the bar, ordered, and waited for the other to talk first. Finally I broached the subject of Bleak Mathematics and what little I had been able to track down. Barrows nodded, as if expecting my progress.

"Yep, that's about as far as I got initially. And that's about as far as anybody is gonna get without help from an actual fan. It's so weird. It really is a cult."

I sipped my beer and gave him a sidelong glance. "So what else is there?"

"Symbols, code words, stuff I don't even know yet."

"Why? To what end? They're just a rock band. Why all the mystique?"

"Maybe because they are just a rock band? Or because they're Satanists or terrorists or disenfranchised art students? I dunno. But they take it all insanely seriously, and so do their fans."

I shook my head. "The industry gets weirder every year. So what are some of the symbols or codes?"

Barrows gulped down the rest of his beer and ordered another. "I don't know any of the symbols yet, but I've got two of the codes. The first is 'Fhtagn' and the second..."

"Wait, what did you just say?"

He snagged a bar napkin and wrote it down in big block letters with a pen. I stared at the nonsense word, trying to pronounce it the way he had. To me it was just six letters that shouldn't go together.

"What is this?"

"Well, it has some great significance to the band and its fans," he said, between chugs of beer. "I'm also under the impression that if Bleak Mathematics had an actual album, this would be the title."

I went to ask him another question, but the band started up. I had been so engaged in conversation, I hadn't noticed the place filling up. It was an indie-folk band tonight, pleasant enough, if somewhat boring. I went to yell something to Barrows but he held up a hand. Beneath 'Fhtagn' he wrote 'Kadath Known.' I looked at him, eyebrows raised, but he just shrugged.

"Second code," he yelled, before picking up his small digital camera and wandering off into the crowd.

I rubbed my temples, then folded the napkin and slid it into my pocket. The show progressed as I expected it to. I took my notes and shot a bunch of pictures. Overall, it was a decent performance. Afterwards, I waited for Barrows, but I never saw him. Finally realizing he must have left before me, I grumbled my way to the car and went home.

*

The next two weeks passed, and I worked on my usual assignments, along with looking into Bleak Mathematics as much as I could. I searched for the codes Barrows had given me, but all I kept coming up with were results that led me back to some long dead horror author. I tried variations on the spellings, but that got me nothing. Could the band members themselves just be major fans of this Lovecraft person? There was quite a bit about him online – pretty popular for a guy who died in 1937. I researched him, and even read some of his stories. Not really my thing, but I could see how this would appeal to a conclave of other fans.

I decided to switch gears, and forego music message boards in favor of Lovecraft sites. This took me longer since I was far less familiar with them, but after a while I found some of the more obscure ones. Taking a cue from the other users, I gave myself the handle *REanim8or*, hoping it would allow me to blend in. I went right for the thread titled "Fhtagn." It was a password protected thread. On a hunch, I entered in "kadathknown."

I was shocked to see how many users were interacting inside, easily over fifty. I didn't even type anything, I was so busy trying to scribble down some of the information I was seeing on the screen. Tour dates, song titles, band members, strange things. Bleak Mathematics had been touring for over two years and had hit every major city in the continental United States at least once. They'd be in Cleveland on May 28th, but I couldn't seem to find where. "Kadath Known" was actually the title of the first song in their set, along with others like "Lurk on the Threshold No More" and

"Her Thousand Young." The song "Blind Idiot God" seemed to be a favorite. There was a lot of talk about the final song, but no one mentioned its name. More interesting, I thought, was mention of the band members themselves. Zann, Pickman, and the Wilcox twins. The fans spoke of them reverently, about how they were the "heralds of the dream." There was a lot more of that kind of hyperbole, and given the song titles, I assumed Bleak Mathematics to be some type of heavy Prog-rock act.

I was still taking down notes when a message screen popped up from one of the site administrators. A Yog-Simon wanted to know if I planned on interacting in the thread or just loitering. I replied that I was just a little intimidated. He then asked for the second password. Unsure what else to do, I gave him "lurkonthethresholdnomore." I was instantly bounced out of the thread, and my IP address was blocked from the site.

Mildly pissy at all these fans and their secrecy concerning a damn tribute band, I still got what I needed to know. I'd undoubtedly see Barrows in a few days, and we'd compare notes then. We still had about a month to go before Bleak Mathematics would be in Cleveland, and then we'd see what all the damn fuss was about.

*

Klub Khameleon isn't the biggest venue by far, but it's one of my favorites. It's got a comfortable atmosphere, decent booze selection, and really hot bartenders. I've always enjoyed watching shows here, even when it was some singer-songwriter darling like the opening artist. After I endured yet another song about a breakup, she gave way to a neo-rock group that I always enjoyed immensely, although I was surprised they seemed to be trying to fit all seven members on the small stage.

I was trying to keep my mind off of the fact that Barrows hadn't shown up. I knew all the other possible local correspondents from Alternative Report, so it wasn't like his sister had sent someone else. That he just wouldn't bother showing up seemed unlikely. I took another swig of my beer, wondering why I was so worried about it.

The headlining band was finally starting up when I left my place at the bar. I'd invested in a top of the line Smartphone back when I was still with the magazine, one with the best built in camera on the market. It made my job now a hell of a lot easier. I worked my way through the crowd, snapping pictures of the band in action, until I got to the other side of the room. Climbing up on a bench against the wall, I was taking a few more shots when something pulled at me from the bar. I can't describe it. It was instinctual, primal, hardwired into that lizard part in my brain. I felt it drop in my gut. It ripped my eyes away from the stage and back across the length of the room.

Over by the door, near the end of the bar, someone stood there staring back at me. Me, just me. I blinked, and realized it was Barrows. But something was wrong with him, something... incorrect. Where before he looked beaten, now he looked broken. And blackened. I felt my testicles clench up so hard they hurt. No one around him seemed to notice his presence as he stared at me. Without thinking, I pulled up my phone and snapped a picture. Glancing back, he'd vanished.

When I looked down at my camera, he was as real on my screen as the bottles behind him.

*

Another week went by before I got the phone call I had been waiting for.

"Kirchner."

"Hey, Jessica."

"Listen, I know for a fact you've been in contact with my brother, so..."

"I never said I wasn't."

"What? Oh. Well, he's disappeared. And if you have any idea why, I want to hear about it now."

I sighed. "Your brother and I were working on a story together, and I'm worried he may have gotten too deep into it."

"You're music journalists. What, did you do too much acid with some psychedelic band?"

I explained everything, from the beginning, to the point I was at now. Jessica only interrupted once, to make me say the word *Fhtagn* again. Once I was done, she sat there in silence.

Finally, I said, "So?"

"You are so full of shit, Aaron Kirchner."

"I told you exactly what happened! Joel came to me. I'd never heard of them."

"Joel looks up to you for some stupid reason, and you sent him on a snipe hunt."

"Fine, Jessica. Call the cops. I'll tell them the same thing I told you."

"I will! You'll be hearing from them and my attorney!"

She hung up, and I stared at my phone in frustration. One more thing to deal with.

But I never did hear from the cops.

*

I downloaded the picture of Barrows to my desktop. Examining it didn't help me, it just made me feel sick. This wasn't some ghost, some trick of the light, like I had hoped it had been. He was physically there, in the room. I could see reflections of him off of two of the bottles. I don't know how that could be, given his physical state. His elbows were bent *backwards*, and his neck was stretched at the wrong angle. It looked like blood was seeping out of his eyes, ears, and mouth – blood that was far too dark. His jaw looked broken and cracked off to the left, while his skin was mottled a dark purplish-black. I don't know how I recognized him from so far away. I don't know what made me look at him. I don't know what made no one else look at him.

The search for answers about Bleak Mathematics continued. When I couldn't find out about the band, I began to find out about the fans. Everything came back to the author H.P. Lovecraft. The usernames, the song titles, the codes. I began to suspect the symbols that Barrows had been seeking were also in the fiction as well. The Yellow Sigil, The Elder Sign, The Necronomicon Seal. When I wasn't working on pieces for Alt-M-App, I was becoming an expert in all things Lovecraftian. I was determined to unravel the mystery of Bleak Mathematics and find my way to their show on the 28th.

A number of things began to pop out at me. Numerous times in his stories, Lovecraft spoke of places and things utilizing Non-Euclidian geometry, sometimes to great extents and potency. I wondered if perhaps this was the inspiration behind the band's name. I also came across a fan site that seriously discussed the existence of the so-called "Great Old Ones." One theory put forth, with much acclaim from readers, stated that these great alien gods had no true form, but were actually complex algorithms that simply took the shape of tentacle monsters or what have you when they manifested in our universe. I couldn't get over the sincerity with which the author spoke on the matter.

Perhaps too much time was being devoted to this side project because thoughts of it began to spill into my dreams. I didn't recall much of them, but they were not pleasant. I awoke twice, gasping for air and clawing at my sheets. I know in at least one, Barrows' uneven, leaking face was trying to whisper something to me.

*

Two weeks were left until the show and I still had no idea where Bleak Mathematics was playing. Through some poking around on message boards, Lovecraft research, and pure deduction, I came up with the notion that wherever the band would be playing, not only was it not going to be a traditional setting, but it would be marked with the Necronomicon Seal to alert fans. Unfortunately, Cleveland was too big a city to be driving around, hoping to find a single building with an arcane symbol spray painted on the front.

I was sitting at a table in The Amethyst Ballroom, a delicately named venue for a place that loved to host heavier acts. A metal-core band was ready to go on for a crowd of mosh-happy teenagers. I would be taking photos from the rear this time. There was a small patio off to the side, and I was wondering if I had enough time for a cigarette when I felt a tap on my shoulder.

"Kirchner."

I was shocked to see Jessica Barrows at a show. She hadn't bothered going out herself since the early days of Alternate Report. She had any number of personnel she could've sent out to cover this show, even with her brother MIA. I firmly reminded myself that statuesque brunette or not, she'd knifed me in the back.

"You're not here for the show, you're here to see me."

"Wow, it's like you're a journalist or something," she replied with a smirk.

I picked up my drink and headed towards the patio as the band kicked in. They were the opening act—popular, but I would still have time to snap pictures later. She followed me out of the venue, glancing around. The cement slab had two picnic tables bolted down and nine foot tall, privacy-insulated chain-link fence around three sides. We were alone, except for a teenage couple moments away from having sex on the other table. I ignored them, lit up a cigarette, and turned to my old boss.

"Where's your attorney?"

Jessica made a face. "You were right, I was wrong, okay? Are you happy to hear that?"

I was more shocked than happy, and said as much. "What made you change your mind?"

"Joel left all his stuff. I had one of my techie interns hack the password on his laptop. Everything you said was right there in his files."

"Haven't you reported him missing to the cops?"

She leaned back against the fence and played with the strap on her purse. "I did, but they're only mildly interested. He's a single adult male who works for a music magazine. They figure he's absconded to Europe and is doing coke off a supermodel's ass with the lead singer of some random band. I'm worried as his big sister rather than as his boss."

I nodded and took another puff. I could see why the cops might react that way, erroneous as it may be. They didn't know Barrows, and they didn't know the full scope of the situation.

"Did you look into the Bleak Mathematics stuff," I asked her.

"Yeah, I did." Her features went hard. "At first I thought it was crap, but I kept digging. Aaron, these people are insane. Do you think they're insane enough to hurt Joel for having looked into them?"

I dropped my spent cigarette to the ground and crushed it under the toe of my shoe. Then I finished the last of my beer, and chucked the plastic cup into the garbage can. The teenagers hadn't stopped making out. The girl looked ready to orgasm right there, the way her boyfriend was kissing her neck. Ah, to be young again. Innocent. I peered up at the black sky, all the stars extinguished by the light pollution of the city. No help for me there, just pointless, decayed darkness.

"Yeah," I replied finally. "Yeah, I think the fans could've done something to him."

*

It was the easiest answer I had to give her. It was also possibly true. I didn't necessarily believe it, but Jessica didn't need to know that. I didn't know what I believed. She stayed with me through the remainder of the show, partially because she wanted to talk more, and partially, I believe, because she wanted to see how I covered it for Alt-M-App. Afterwards, in the parking lot, she made me promise to keep her in the loop concerning any new information I discovered about Bleak Mathematics, their fans or the upcoming show, while she would do the same. I agreed, dubious that she would live up to the bargain.

I tried to keep working, on both my regular assignments and the Bleak Mathematics mystery, but my sleep was growing more troubled by the day. When I wasn't plagued by insomnia, sleep was erratic, and often filled with nightmares. Those nightmares were remarkably consistent, and found me elsewhere, a location that I can only assume was birthed from the imagination of Lovecraft's prose. I had forced myself to consume it too greedily in search of the elusive band.

The dream was massive in scope, slabs of grey stone cut from a mountain creating a labyrinthine system of hallways, caverns, dungeons, and temples. Like many dreams, logic did not apply there. No map could apply reason to even any single room of that place, let alone its overall design. Some spaces had ceilings, but most opened up onto a deep darkness similar to the one I'd gazed at during that last concert. But somehow I knew this sky was different. More alive. The knowledge weighed heavily on me, the same way each step I took in that delusional construct hacked away at whatever mental tranquility I'd ever possessed.

These sojourns into the city of aberration were bad, but at least the city was abandoned—except when it wasn't. I couldn't tell you how often, but every now and again, I'd turn a corner or take a few steps up into a temple, and feel Barrows behind me. I always knew it was him. Although I could never quite see him, I could see enough. Elbows broken backwards, jaw cracked to the side, ribs crushed inward, mottled skin, and leaking black blood everywhere. I could see enough in my periphery, in the gloom. He always stood right behind my shoulder whispering, always whispering. He would tell me about the dream that we were in and how it was *His* dream, whoever 'He' was. According to Barrows, His dream was a gift, a muse sent to inspire. Such art! Such tributes! But one did not partake of such divine stimuli without engaging in one's own creative endeavors. No, only those who would share His dream would see it, so that it may be forever growing until the stars were right.

He said many of these kinds of things, babbling about dreams and artists and "His Will" and other things I don't totally remember. He also spoke of what happened if you didn't join in this dream, or couldn't. From what I could piece together, Barrow himself was an example.

"This is the best your mind can fathom of The Home," Barrows' voice sputtered in my ear. "Each little corner a different dimension, each plane operating on a different frequency. Can you imagine what that does to a human body? It should be obliterated instantly, but He won't allow that. It won't allow that! Oh no, we serve as we are needed, to ensure the dream propagates."

Awake, I tried not to think about the nightmares. I was caffeine-fueled and working on articles already days behind, but it was hard to put them aside. A large part of me just wanted to forget I had ever heard of Bleak Mathematics and ignore Jessica's texts. There was still a good chance we'd never find out where they were playing on the 28th. Still, I couldn't deny that there was a need in me to actually see this band play and understand what it was about their music.

One of Barrows' statements from my nightmares continued to haunt me. "One day, everyone on this planet will either create for the dream, or have succumbed to the dream."

*

Jessica continued to text me every day, usually with nothing new to add. My masochistic streak increased as I returned to Lovecraft's fiction, telling myself that there might be clues among the tales. I knew that all I was doing was further fracturing my already fragile psyche. I was aware of the damage I was inflicting on myself, and of all my pent up stress, guilt, and resentment, but somehow knowing didn't matter.

On the 25th, I got a call from Jessica. I don't know how she did it, but she tracked down a source that gave up the location of the concert. Some old warehouse near the Cuyahoga River, starting at ten o'clock on the 28th. For some reason, all the terror that had been charging through me settled. It was going to happen, and I'd have some kind of answers, whatever they may be. I agreed to meet her at four, far in advance, to scope out the building and anyone coming near it. Something told me plans wouldn't unfold as nicely as she thought.

*

Nor did they. Between a mild emergency at Alternative Report and traffic backed up because of a Cleveland Indians game, we didn't get to the spot until after six. Jessica and I were both confident we had found the place, due to the size of it and the two large vans parked off to the side. Still, we waited out front and watched. I had yet to spy any symbols marking it as the designated location.

"Do you think he'll be in there?" Jessica asked, making me jump.

I had been ruminating on what the band was going to be like. Was it all about the subject matter to the fans, or did the band hold some type of sway as well? After these past two months, would I leave disappointed or enlightened? Probably a bit of both. But as I looked over at Jessica Barrows' face, here only seeking her missing brother, I couldn't tell her the truth I felt deep in my gut. I couldn't tell her that I believed her brother, body and soul, had been taken from the earth to a cold, shattered hell. No.

"Hopefully," I said, and patted her hand awkwardly.

We waited for another hour, and were starting to get restless when we began noticing more people arriving, cars pulling up around us. We took that as a good sign, but Jessica noted that no one was getting out. I thought that was weird too, until I recalled the symbol. She wanted to get out and stretch her legs, but I convinced her not to. More cars kept parking in the area, yet still no one got out. At eight o'clock, a young man came out and hung a square banner outside the warehouse. All black with no text, it simply displayed the Necronomicon Seal in white. Like an alarm had been sounded, all the people in the vicinity began to disembark from their vehicles.

Jessica gave me a look and clearly mouthed *"What the fuck?"* as we followed suit. I was fascinated, and studied the fans of Bleak Mathematics while we made our way up toward the entrance. It was a sampling of everyone, men and women, all ages, races, backgrounds, everything. I tried to wrap my head around the Asian girl with a green Mohawk in an animated conversation with an older man wearing a tweed blazer. At least we wouldn't stick out.

The guy at the door was of average height, but as thick around as a car tire, with arms the size of my legs. As physically imposing as he was, that wasn't what gave me pause. His head was as bald as a baby's butt, and wide-set eyes bulged in his face above a flat nose and thick lips. I'd never seen such a slackjaw in my life, nor ears that stuck out quite that much. To say this unfortunate looking individual was ugly would've been an understatement, but worse, there was something about his features that pulled at my memory.

"Twenty bucks," he said.

"What?" I stammered.

"Twenty bucks to get in, pal. Let's go, there's a line."

I paid, and stumbled into the warehouse. I was more than a little disturbed to see what appeared to be the door guy's four brothers wandering the space with shirts that read "Security" on their backs. I tried to put it out of my mind, and take stock of the so-called "venue." The building was equipped with restrooms, but that was about it. No bar, no merch table, not even a soundboard. The stage looked to be assembled by roadies, or maybe by the band themselves. Behind it, tacked to the wall, was another variation of the Necronomicon Seal, along with four other smaller symbols in the corners that I had never seen before.

People kept pouring in, mostly excited, but speaking in hushed tones. Some looked like soccer moms, some like teenage goths. I felt a bit more at ease when I realized that a number of them were wearing Lovecraft tee-shirts, and one even had a lime green Cthulhu toboggan on his head. I started to let myself believe this was just some silly tribute band after all.

"I still haven't seen Joel, have you?" Jessica looked amped up, ready to start screaming accusations and punching people.

"Listen, there's still time. If need be, you can take photos of fans during the show, and then follow up afterwards. There's no point in getting kicked out now."

She nodded and bit her lip. I hoped she could contain herself until the end. At that point, I'd help her on whatever fruitless pursuit she wanted, but I needed this now. As that thought crossed my mind, what passed as house lights went off, leaving only the stage illuminated. Everyone assembled went silent and turned to the front.

We watched as four people climbed onto the stage and I was surprised by the normalcy of their appearance. They were all quite attractive, probably in their early twenties. They took positions with their respective instruments. A sturdily built lad with a shaved head and goatee sat behind the drums, and introduced himself as Clive Pickman. A pretty boy with long black locks holding a guitar announced himself as Gabriel Zann. Off to the other side, a slender fellow with a bit of scruff and a bass introduced himself as Edmund Wilcox before nodding to the final member. A young willowy blonde woman, pale with big blue eyes, stood in the center before a keyboard and another mic, scanning the crowd with an expression that I can only describe as regal. I found myself holding my breath, waiting for words to fall from her lips, for her decree to be heard.

Finally, "And I'm Emily Wilcox. We're Bleak Mathematics."

The stage erupted into music. It was electrifying, beautiful, and brilliant. Layered and structured in the manner of classical composition, in the way many post-rock songs are. Heartfelt and dark, it built upon itself, growing into something that felt bigger than just a piece of music.

Then Emily Wilcox began to sing.

I knew there were words, words I recognized, but somehow they didn't register. Her voice went beyond them, affecting something deeper than a cognitive level. Her brother's voice joined in, and sensation began to take hold of me. It was inside me, it was all of me, the music was gestalt. There was no longer a warehouse, no fans surrounding me, only those impossible angles in the distance and that undulating darkness above. And something else, something beyond measurement or definition. I could feel it beneath me yet also around every corner, waiting, watching, caressing the shadows with delicate, elongated appendages. It wasn't patient, because it had no sense of time. It wasn't evil, because it had no sense of morality. It wasn't hungry, because it had no need to feed. It simply *wanted.*

The music slowed, ebbed, and Emily Wilcox's voice reached out. "Do you dream for more? This next one is called... Nights in Carcosa."

Perhaps some did seek more from the band, but we weren't here to satiate our desires or our dreams. As the music suffused me, taking me back again to that battered kingdom I had only previously visited in the sweat-soaked sheets of nightmare, I understood that the band served its own function. The second song of the night played into the third, fourth, fifth, and the music of Bleak Mathematics continued to strip me down, layer by layer, to my most primal aspect. That's what the music was, a soundtrack to a dream. *Its* dream.

The concert continued, although I'm not sure how much of it I was coherent or conscious for. I awoke on the floor, my body aching. At first I was more than a little disoriented, not sure where I was. It took me a moment to recall where I might be, especially because the warehouse was now completely empty. The lights were on again, but everyone was gone, including the band, their roadies, and their equipment. And Jessica.

I pulled myself up and stumbled around, looking for any indication of where they might have gone. I figured Jessica had followed some of the fans outside, trying to track down leads on her brother, but I was pretty pissed at her for leaving me face down on a concert floor. Spinning around, I almost ran right into a teenage girl.

"Oh, wow! I'm sorry," I said, still trying to get my bearings.

"No worries, everybody's like that after their first time. Well, the ones who make it," she said.

I stopped and looked at her. Short, very attractive. with blonde hair and green eyes. She looked vaguely familiar. Her top was showing off quite a bit of her cleavage, but I was more concerned with the smirk on her face and what she had just said.

"What did you mean by that second part?"

"Some people don't make it. Like that woman you brought with you, the one you were with at The Amethyst Ballroom a couple of weeks back."

I squinted at the girl and it hit me. "You were the chick making out on the picnic table!"

She smiled. "Yep. Your friend wasn't ready for this. Neither was her brother, who may have been if he'd just taken the time— like you did. You did, and you were accepted into the dream. You can be useful."

"What happened to Jessica? What happened to Joel?" I barked, grabbing the girl's arm.

The girl pulled out of my hold and slapped me. "You might be useful, but we are *all* expendable. I'm here to tell you what your job is. Write about the show tonight. Write it up like any other show article, but of course, as a Bleak Mathematics show. All the secrets and puzzles, the journey and dreams, the fans and the music. Send it here for proofing before you send it to your editor."

She handed me a card with nothing but an email address before walking away. I stared at it blankly, my mind still not processing. At the door, she turned back.

"You're one of us now, remember that. Oh, and the band left you a set list by where the stage was. They thought that might help you write the article, since this was your first time."

I nodded dumbly, still staring down at the card.

The girl sighed. "Just so you know, it's at the end of the show when those found unworthy are taken. Just look at the last song."

My head came up, but she had disappeared through the doors. Slipping the card into my pocket, I walked over to where the stage had been. A number of the fluorescent bulbs had been broken out, but there was still enough light to see the single piece of paper lying on the ground. Plain lined notebook paper, a shoeprint on the back. Twelve song titles were scribbled out in black magic marker, just like untold numbers of other set lists.

I stood there and stared at the last title for a long time before leaving. I had to hike a few blocks before I could find a cab. Jessica had driven.

I don't dream about Barrows anymore. Maybe it's because it's like the girl said, I'm one of them now. That doesn't make me feel any better. I haven't written the article yet, I've written this instead. I wish she hadn't told me about that last song title.

"Descend Home To R'lyeh."

Father of Dread
by Matthew Chabin

No one knew what possessed them to do it. An unusually powerful spirit of iconoclasm, perhaps. Maybe they'd hoped to purge the land of idols yet still mitigate the world's outrage—unlike when the Taliban dynamited the Buddhas at Hajarazat. Still, it is hard to imagine how sane men, capable of all the necessary calculations, could have arrived at such a "solution."

The great Sphinx of Giza was twenty thousand tons of sandstone megaliths. It was extracted, intact, by the most exacting and expensive stratagems, and placed upon a massive iron float. This was then ferried for more than a hundred miles down the Nile, requiring constant dredging, and causing frequent, deadly mishaps. Finally, it was towed out beyond the breakers at Raz El-bar, only to be cut loose and left to drift away. To do all this in a time of war, with limited resources and the world falling down around them... It was one of the maddest undertakings in the history of the human species. And yet they did it.

Then, when the pride of the pharaohs was a vanishing speck on the waves, when the engineers had been dismissed, when the baffled soldiers had been debriefed and sent back to the front, the planners of the feat, those inscrutable midwives, took cyanide and put pistols under their chins—both measures in tandem—and spoke no more. No one knew why they did that, either.

The Sphinx, once delivered, moved steadily west. It was seen from the island of Crete, from the shores of Tripoli and Tunis. Past Malta and Mallorca it drifted apace, and like a key guided by an unseen hand, found its way to the Strait of Gibraltar. On a night when the waves tilted blackly against the coastline, and crimson lightning lanced the cadaverous skies, this progeny of the ancient world slipped through into the cold, heaving wilds of the Atlantic.

The Australians attempted a recovery, but were thwarted by a sudden squall. The Russians tried for it, and lost two of their ships and fifty-nine men in a terrible, freak collision. Bad weather and bad luck attended it like grim handmaidens, and in the turmoil of those years the errant beast of Giza ceased to be a *cause célèbre* and became instead a baleful sign of the times.

Mariners told stories—how it lingered over the graves of the *Titanic* and the *Athenian Venture,* as if hunting the souls of the dead. How it dwelt among strange currents and mysterious swells and eerie, subaqueous glows. How it was notoriously *hard to sneak up on.* How, even at a distance, its dead gaze tended to settle upon the lookout, and how that man who first spied it was changed by his misfortune, troubled in his sleep, anxious in his work. A good bet to meet with a bad end.

At length, the Sphinx became what it must have been to its conscripted builders and wretched supplicants of old. A monster. A dire and unaccountable *thing*, rampant upon the earth.

*

The more he tried not to check, the more Walter became convinced that the man loitering in the hall beneath the yellowed tympanum of the Resurrection was looking at him.

True, the light was bad, at least for a reading room. The green lamps in their vine-shaped Art Nouveau sconces hummed and flickered on a pinched current, and the high cupola windows admitted only a wan, leaden daylight. It was also true that Walter was prone to misread visual cues. Just the other day he'd been parking his car in the dim catacombs under the Woolworth Building and had mistaken—if only for an instant—a standard poodle in the neighboring Cadillac for an old woman grinning fox-fangs at him. It had given him a serious jolt (not just that such a thing could *be*, that that it could be out *driving around*). Other people in the same situation might have laughed, but Walter didn't. His history, in conjunction with certain recent developments, made laughter quite out of the question.

In any case, he *was* being watched. The gaunt, elderly gent wore a herringbone vest, with an overcoat draped about his shoulders like a cape, and was definitely watching him. He held a tabloid newspaper in his lap, but his eyes kept creeping up from the page, and with a sly angling of the head their gaze consistently tacked to Walter. There was something intense, something unhealthy about that gaze. Walter wasn't sure, but he thought the faint, brittle clicks he heard from all the way across the room were the man's teeth grinding.

Walter looked the other way and saw with some relief that Maureen had returned. He got up and walked over to the help-desk. She was a comely young woman, with a glass eye, a stylish bob, and a wry manner. She looked up and smiled. "Mr. Church?"

"Maureen. How'd we do with that list?"

She placed a stack of books in paper sleeves on the counter in front of him, an index card with a list of titles taped to the top. "All but one," she intoned gravely. "That one's checked out, and—" her library voice dropped even lower—"and between you and me, Mr. Church, I hear the Department of Homeland Security is after it. Section 215 of the Patriot Act. Don't worry, I kept your name off the query list."

He adjusted his glasses and scanned the card, tapping pensively with his index finger.

"Of course they don't tell us *why* they want it. There's a rumor—" her voice cut to a whisper—"that *OBL* had a copy on him when they, you know..." She made a subtle shooting gesture, and rolled her good eye. The glass one stared straight ahead. "They're worried about codes. Mad Arabs bombing the subways—"

"I say, Maureen..."

"Hmn?"

"Do you see the man sitting in the hall back there, your eleven-thirty, on the bench?"

She craned her neck. "Yes?"

"Do you suppose he's... all right?"

She looked again. "Has he been there for long?"

"Well, he seems to be—"

"Oh, there he goes."

Walter looked. The man was walking down the hall, tapping about him with a long cane and drawing glances from a group of uniformed grade-schoolers coming the other way.

"My God," said Maureen. "Have you seen this?"

"Hmn?" He looked down at the newspaper she'd turned around for his inspection. The headline read "Five Arrested in Plot to Dynamite Ancient Treasure," and surmounted an image, familiar by now, of a dark silhouette against the Manhattan skyline.

*

At Battery Park, three months and seventeen days ago, Walter had been standing with a crowd of several thousand, pressed against the rail with a front-row view of the harbor. He'd seen it emerge from the dense fog that lay on the water, immense and impassive, blackened by the sea, gliding along on its iron bed beneath screaming throngs of birds. A gasp went through the crowd and a few starkly isolated shouts rang out as the great beast of Giza came fully into view. Six thousand miles it had traveled, dreaming upon the illimitable deep. Walter had the unnerving impression that it was looking right at him.

The harbor masters were ready and had sent tugs to guide its passage, but their exertions did little to persuade twenty thousand tons of limestone-freighted inertia. Of its own volition, it headed toward the mouth of the Hudson and finally came to rest about a thousand yards off Governor's island. From Walter's vantage, it skulked about the fog-dimmed skirts of Lady Liberty like some bastard offspring, come to ransom its legacy. A helicopter circled above it. Walter began to feel dizzy. He turned and shouldered his way through the crowd.

As days went by he found himself increasingly taken with the strange, brute charisma of the thing. In this he was not alone. Almost immediately, "tourists" started coming by the boat-load, boarding the iron platform with ladders, ropes, ramps, whatever they could use. Some of these immediately stripped naked and crawled fawningly over its outstretched paws, or kissed the stone, or feigned suckling at its flanks, encouraging others to take pictures. Others tagged it with spray-paint, or chiseled souvenir fragments to keep or to sell. Still others tried to scale the limestone shelves, carious and slick with sea-grime as they were. Many fell and shattered their bones, or banged off the lip of a barge and were drowned. This toll continued until one morning at dawn, when a squadron of harbor police took the platform and beat the pilgrims back into their boats. From then on a regular guard of men in riot gear stood ready to discourage further encroachment. A semblance of normalcy returned.

Walter's approach was rather the opposite of the enthusiasts'. It was distance, not closeness, that he sought. The distance to comprehend the breadth of circumstances, the space to discover the truth. That, he believed, had always been humanity's best response to plague, to calamity, to war and genocide. It still was. The best way to shake the irrational feeling that he, Walter Church, at fifty-two, was living in somebody's nightmare.

*

Joey Church dangled his legs over the stage in the Rockaway High auditorium. Long, curly hair veiled his face. He was 16 and good-looking, with a leading role in the school play—a play ostensibly written by Joey Church. He had his grades locked up for the semester, and visions of being the next Edward Norton or Robert Downey. He didn't give a fishtailed fuck about some 5,000 year-old piece of crap rotting in the harbor. Joey Church was the real deal, the Sphinx of Rockaway High!

"Okay, people bring it in." Ms. Ortega rapped her clipboard and settled in a swirl of skirts and perfume on the stage next to Joey, a little close for his liking. He'd considered her hot at one point—like, *really* hot—but recently her bohemian style and gypsy camp manners had struck him more like sloppy affectation. A lot of things were disappointing him lately, though he mostly kept these sour impressions to himself. Apart from his sister and maybe Fox Creasy, there was no one he felt like confiding in.

"We open exactly one week from tonight," said Ms. Ortega, "and some of you still don't have your lines down. That makes my brain bleed and hallucinate little green gnomes eating you alive, but I know it's no use calling you out here. You know who you are, you know what to do." A few guilty groans and murmurs answered her. "Get it done!"

"Mea-culpa, Ms. O, mea-culpa!" wailed Clay Widerski, swooning dramatically. Fox jiggled his wrist over Clay, and Joey screwed up his lips to keep from grinning.

"Now, a few of you have asked to have your lines cut down. Normally I'd just give you a straight answer, like *no*, or *hell no*, but since the playwright is sitting right here on his gifted little tuchus..." She jabbed a painted nail at Joey. There were some appreciative chuckles and a knowing smirk from his sister. "I guess he's your daddy. Mr. Church, you have those chops under review?"

"Yes, ma'am."

"I need your ruling by tomorrow. Please be kind to your fellow thespians, some of those lines are pretty ornate. But keep the Book of the Dead stuff. I'll murder you if you chuck that. 'Kay. Questions? No? Get out. Go home and practice."

Joey was popular with the drama kids, but not in general. The only time he liked attention was when he was on stage. If he'd known his father's batshit script would actually win the contest and become the school's fall production, he might have turned in his own work instead, the one about the Garden of Eden reality show. Now here he was, playing the Sphinx in some kind of baroque, schizoid cross between Oedipus and the Wizard of Oz. Which was cool. Sort of.

Better than clomping around in cowboy boots singing about corn, or watching Clay Widerski's Puck OD on fairy dust, anyway. On the other hand, some of the dreams he'd been having made him feel like a stranger to himself. They weren't just the usual 'fuck, what's my line?' dreams, but not exactly screaming nightmares either. More like *really* dark, immoral fantasies.

His backpack was in the first or second row of seats, he was sure—but now he didn't see it. He walked along, scanning the rows, and jumped when Fox Creasy slapped him on the back.

"Hey! Whoa, you okay?"

"Fine, why?"

"You look a little... I don't know... Still in character."

"Na." He smiled. "I'm all right. What's up, we rollin'?"

"Yeah, well... Me and Allie was gonna catch a cab over to Forest Park, check out those sculptures she's been on about."

"Naw yo, I can't. Promised Moms I'd pick up the dry cleaning. They close in two hours."

"Oh right. Then..."

There was a pregnant pause, and Joey realized he'd declined a non-invitation.

"Ay, Joey, son, you know me an' Allie been spendin' time an' shit. I hope that's okay wit' you, cuz, you know I'd never disrespect her or nothin' right?"

"Naw, naw it's cool yo, just be good, y'know, don't get lost out there."

"Naw, f'sure, we'll be careful. I'll have her home by ten."

"*Ten?*"

Fox frowned. "What... like eight?"

Joey held the glare for a good three seconds before Fox saw a crack and they both broke into laughs. "Shit, son."

"Fuck outa here, man."

They slapped hands and Fox retreated quickly down the aisle. Allison was waiting at the door, and blew Joey a kiss. Then they were gone, and Joey stood in the empty auditorium. He looked to his left. As if by magic his backpack was there, second seat in, practically under his nose. He shook his head as he shouldered it. *Fox and Allie, huh.* He figured he ought to be happy—who did he trust more than Fox? Just felt kind of weird.

He was almost to the door when something made him look back. The auditorium was empty—it looked empty, it *felt* empty. But something had just rippled the curtains. He felt like he had dreamed this moment, like he was dreaming it right now.

He shrugged off the shiver that ran down his neck, re-slung his bag and banged through the door. *Fuck it!*

*

Walter's fellowship had finally dried up almost six weeks ago. The university had lost interest when his work took a turn into what they politely referred to as "more speculative territory." Now from his tiny garret in Upper Manhattan, he worked on borrowed time and borrowed money, with all the English tenacity his father had bequeathed him. He wanted to see the thing through and make his mark. At fifty-two it felt like a losing prospect.

Still, 'if you can fill the unforgiving minute'...

It was Friday, his day of rest, his day to stop off at The Cloisters to tarry amongst the herb gardens and translated monasteries of his beloved Europe, his intellectual Eden. Usually he meditated on the Unicorn Tapestries, those marvelous minglings of pagan and Christian heritage. Today he found himself in a different gallery contemplating an illumination, *The Procession of the Flagellants* from the Duke of Berry's *Belles Heures*. The men in this delicate rendering wore wide-brimmed, black hats and white gowns that clung precariously to their hips. They walked in stately ranks, two abreast. Two in the foreground were on hands and knees, receiving lashes from two others in masks of white cloth.

Walter marveled, first at the hand that could do this, second at the rather blatant homo-eroticism—one of the men was whipping himself with one hand and caressing himself the other—and finally that an act of self-debasement should be rendered with such superlative grace. He felt a kinship with these men, who in their time, in their peculiar folly, had also believed their efforts were holding up the heavens, holding back the darkness.

Of course the real scene must have been somewhat less picturesque: naked fanatics beating themselves bloody in the street. More like Goya had painted it. His eyes drifted up to the anguilliform dragon, either swimming in the barred abstract of sky or else impaled on one of the cross standards. The latter would imply a horrible blasphemy, would it not? The fiend crucified in place of Christ?

Walter felt ill. The room turned about him, and the venerable air of the place grew musty and close, like a tomb. The next thing he knew he was out in the corridor, vomiting against the wall. People murmured, and a guard's radio crackled. Shamefaced and retching, Walter went for the first exit he saw, and staggered out onto a stone landing overlooking a river. The river, once called the Hudson, was now called something else—some terrible name he couldn't remember, couldn't pronounce. "Oh *God!*" he groaned, mopping his sweaty face. He wished that he could vomit it *all*, get it out of him, this muck of accumulated knowledge, this tired, unclean store.

He looked again. There was no sanctuary. The sky was a leprous purple and red. Every saturated cloud was an evil, floating brain. The river was a lamentable afterbirth. It drained away in the shadow of the Jersey Palisades, which Walter understood to now be serving as execution grounds.

*

"Yo, your pops is a fuckin' genius, yo."

It was a cold, blustery afternoon and Canarsie Pier was almost deserted, just the way they liked it. The three of them had taken over a bench, looking out over the water and passing a bottle of citrus Mad Dog. The sauce was just a tune-up for the real road show, due to start any minute now. In an hour they wouldn't even remember they'd drunk it.

"Fuckin' genius," Fox repeated, leafing through the pages of the script. "Kinda fucked up, though. Like that part where the Sphinx marries Ed to his mother, and his father comes back from the dead. That's pretty fuckin' seven-thirty, yo, but I like it. Like Shakespeare on shrooms, yo!"

"Yeah, whatever," muttered Joey. "You didn't have to live with him."

"What's he like?" asked Allie. "You never talk about him."

Allison was Joey's step-sister. Her own father was a jolly Puerto Rican stevedore who lived in the Bayview Projects, just ten minutes walk away. Dark skin and crystal-blue eyes made her a fetching study in contrasts, no less so than her Catholic faith and penchant for boys and drugs. Joey was not especially tough, but he'd decided at a young age that he was willing to go to prison for her sake. Most guys understood this and acted accordingly.

"Jo-ey," she said. "Jo-jo. You at home, bro? Those caps kickin' in?"

He looked at her. "Huh?"

"I asked you what your old man is like."

"Oh... Professicus? Maximum Over-choad? I don't know, just imagine growing up in the London Natural History Museum." He tipped his bottle, took a swig. "With weekends at the circus."

"Fuckin' shrooms taste like garbage," muttered Fox, picking at his teeth. "Give me some skeezies, yo."

Joey took the bag of Skittles, placed one in his open hand. "One." He placed another. "Two." He reached into the bag and placed a third—"Three"—then hit Fox's hand from below and sent the candy flying. "Fuck outa here."

"Oh, you fuckin' gloryhole cunt-mugger..." Fox's punches hooked into Joey's back and shoulder as he laughed.

"Here, bitch, take 'em." He shoved the candy into Fox's hands and winged a hook of his own.

"Okay-okay," said Allie, "the English history part I get, I mean I know that part. Tell us about the circus."

Joey sighed, looking up the shoreline. The wind riffled the cordgrass and made the salt flats shimmer with fanning textures of light. The marshes were dying here, a little more every year. No one knew why. For some reason he thought of that thing floating in the adjacent harbor, like a big rotting tooth. That thing he didn't give a fuck about. *That* one. Was that what his father's loopy play was about? Some kind of whack-job fuckin' allegory? He hoped it was something like that, and not...

"The circus," he said after a long silence, "was him going through my mint-condition Alien vs. Predator comics with a red fuckin' sharpie, saying he's finally figured it out, the reason for the Holocaust." He looked over and met their blank stares. "That's right. The Holocaust. The one in Europe. You probably thought it was Hitler's fault, huh?" He shook his head. "Batman and fuckin' Predator."

Fox burst out laughing. Allie looked sad.

"He's nuts," continued Joey. "He spent a whole year in a loony-bin. That's why Moms got custody. Oh, and he cheated on her with his research assistant. Brian."

"Fuck!" shouted Fox, belting it over the water like a war cry, and Allie gave in to a sad mirth as she stroked her stepbrother's back.

"Goddamn, I'm *feelin'* it," said Fox. "Yous feelin' it?"

"Mmn," Allie said.

"Lil' bit," said Joey.

"Come on, let's run through it." Fox leapt up, brandishing the script. "You're the Sphinx. Daddy's takin' a dirt nap. Momma, wassup wit' *dat ass?*" He pulled Allie off the bench and she laughed, slapping his hands away. "Sphinx, your line."

"Naw, you two go ahead," said Joey. "I'm gonna sit for a minute."

Fox shrugged and followed Allie over to the rail. The sun was going down in a red bath to the west, and the bay made a rippling, blood-purple backdrop to their rehearsal. The mushrooms were *indeed* kicking in. His body felt like a thing apart, a suit of crawling, alien armor, a busy android housing his brain. The edges of his vision unraveled and re-knit with seamless fluidity, and Fox had Allie in his arms and Joey knew it was just the scene playing out, but...

It was as if he had two minds, the one frightened of the other, frightened at the anger, the resentment, the *jealousy* that flowed up from secret, poisoned wells and flooded his entire body. The wind in the trees became a throaty roar and the hassocks bristled like great hogs in rut. He watched his best friend kiss his sister, not a stage kiss, a real kiss. She was *letting* him.

And somehow these two minds, one of rage, one of terror, abided within him like sun and moon behind an impassive face of stone. A face that gave nothing away. A face that could look for five thousand years upon the wretched fate of the world and never. Once. Blink.

*

"I used to be afraid I was losing my mind."

Dr. Edison—a tidy, owlish man with a goatee, silvering hair, and a habit of chewing his nails in session—did not reply. He smoothed his notepaper and waited, as if for something more noteworthy.

"Take these pills, for instance." Walter reached into his jacket and produced a bottle with his name on it. He set it on the table between them. "You hear that?"

"Hear... That?"

"Exactly. Quiet as a choir of church mice."

Edison's forehead wrinkled.

"At night I can hear them crawling around in there. Oh yes. If I hold it by my ear, I can almost count them by the..." He skittered his fingers on the tabletop. "Or if I hold it up to the light, I can see their shadows, crawling up the sides. *Open* it... they're just lying there. Little blue pills, looking so very innocent. And I take one, I do. I tell myself that the one I take will make the others settle down and behave."

"I see."

"Do you?" Walter was quiet for a moment, stroking his chin. Then he reached into his pocket. Edison tensed, ever so slightly. "Doctor, have a look at this, will you?" He took out a newspaper and spread it on the table. Pointing to an article in the lower left-hand corner, he read aloud, "'City Breaks Ground on Audacious New Building, Purpose Unknown'. Did you hear about this? They killed three people at the opening ceremony. Volunteers, they said. Clubbed them like fish, right in front of the cameras, cut their throats and mixed their blood with the mortar. Now does that not seem a tad... atavistic to you?"

"It upsets you?"

Walter sighed. "For once, Doctor, please consider that my reaction may be immaterial. It only occurs to me that we didn't use to do these things. Or rather we *did*, a very, very long time ago, and now our sensibilities are in regress." He leaned back and rubbed his eyes as Edison jotted a note. "I used to be afraid I was losing my mind, Doctor, but now I fear it's much worse than that."

Edison glanced at his watch.

"Yes, I know." Walter rose and gathered his things, the pills, the newspaper.

"We might try you on a different medication, perhaps—"

"Doctor, pardon me, but how did you come by that painting?"

Edison turned to look at the enormous oil behind his chair. "Oh? You know, I don't remember. Do you like it?"

It showed a medieval hall, an ape-like creature seated at a table lit with candles, wearing a crown, devouring the naked corpse of a man.

*

A rain of cherry blossoms (pink confetti) fell over the courtyard, covering scattered weapons and fallen soldiers. This was the final scene, the aftermath of a great battle. In the background, an imposing replica of the Lincoln Memorial glowered blindly. Its gouged eyes wept blood, and King Laius slumped at Lincoln's knees, awaiting his resurrection. There was a shout, a puff of smoke, and Joey entered stage left in headdress, beard, wings, and pendulant, jeweled breasts. (The arts department had outdone themselves). The groan of metal horns and the beat of drums sounded from the speakers. The house lights went dark and black-lights flooded the stage, making the set glow and drip neon color. Gods and surviving mortals alike reeled in awe.

(He wanted to be away. Everything about this was fake and ridiculous and he wished he really could strangle his *fellow thespians*. Especially this motherfucker. Right. Here.)

"Daughter of Orthus, Father of Destiny, take us into your house. You have made us victorious. Now make us one flesh. Marry us!"

"Oedipus, behold thy mother." *My fuckin' sister, you fuckin'—* "Would you tread upon the laws of heaven and earth? Look how these divinities and powers hide their eyes for shame at thy brazen words."

"These gods and powers are hypocrites unrivaled, born of incest, every one!" The gods staggered and groaned. "This woman is my mother, aye, and mother to us all. Shall the star of Heaven lack her consort? I say again, marry us!"

(*Marry you? I'll fuckin' rip your—*) "Answer my riddle, and be you wed. Answer false, and be you *dead*."

A seeping tide of green light crept over the stage, and hidden fans stirred the banners. "Agreed. Ask."

"I," intoned Joey, his voice reverberant through the speakers, "am your first enemy and your last friend. Know me, I make you. Forget me, I unmake you. I am in your hand, but look, I surround you. What is my name?"

The king looked down at his sword, at the field, at his slain father. "Your name..."—the living and the immortal host leaned in to hear—"... is Death."

(*No. Death is only...*)

"Step forth and be married."

King Oedipus (Fox Creasy) took Queen Jacosta (Allison Santiago) in his arms and kissed her fiercely. "Mazel tov!" shouted a dead soldier (Clay Widerski), and everyone laughed, Fox, Allison, the gods, even Ms. Ortega in the front row.

All but one.

*

Walter sat on the pier at Liberty State Park, sipping black tea with cane sugar and watching a fiery, orange dawn break over the Manhattan skyline. For the moment he was content. If he could separate the world and its troubles from his troubled perception of the world, then he could take his problems with him when he went. He just had to take things in stride, and focus.

He took the last drink of tea. A cold, damp wind was blowing off the water and he turned his collar up as he walked to the edge of the pier. The Sphinx had drifted considerably in the last few days, further into the mouth of the old Hudson. This, the easternmost pier by the old CRR train shed in Liberty State Park, was the closest point of landward approach. At less than a hundred yards, it was also the closest Walter had been to it, close enough to hear the racket of the birds and read some of the graffiti that covered its lower flanks (had he been able to bring himself to read that junk, that was). Two harbor police were manning the barge, one pissing over the side while the other pointed his finger at Walter and mimed shooting him.

Walter paid them no mind.

He stepped behind a brace of coin-operated binoculars, fed his quarters through the slot, and stooped to look. The shutter clattered open and he saw before him a frozen waste, with snaking ribbons of ice blown by the constant wind. The Sphinx was exactly the same size, but now icebound, minus the guards, and bearded with hoary icicles. Behind it the metropolis that had once been Lower Manhattan was going down under a mountainous glacier. The skyscrapers gathered in its embrace like broken toys, tipping into one another, their steel girders distended like burst ribs through the failing concrete. Behind the incessant scrolling blast all was still, all except one moving shadow, a black thing with long, jointed legs climbing the white ruin of the Chrysler Building. Walter thought of the pill bottle on his table at home, and what strange seeds an ocean of time would bring to hideous flower.

He straightened and blinked into the sun. The position of the Sphinx was the same, exactly, so perhaps what the binos showed was not the future, but a radically different *now*. Was it possible that two such parallel realities could mingle? Could the madness of a single man be the conduit for their association? But that would mean he wasn't mad, would it not? Oh, he was feeling confused again.

He walked back to the bench and sat down, lightheaded, missing his tea. He took out his map and marked the position of the binoculars. He took out his morning paper and scanned the headlines. The border-closing ceremony at the Lincoln Tunnel had turned violent (three dead, twenty injured), several landmarks had been rechristened with names he didn't dare read, even in his head, and there was an editorial calling for a number of prominent people to be arrested and chemically mummified. The weatherman predicted snow by the end of the week.

"Mr. Church?"

"Mm. Yes?"

"Can I have a word please?"

Walter glanced up at the elderly woman in the droopy cotton hat and aviator glasses sitting next to him. "I'm sorry, do I know you?"

"Not exactly. You may have seen me around. You can call me Terri."

He looked again more carefully. There was something familiar about her, the gaunt frame and bushy eyebrows. Her jaw moved, and her teeth clashed loudly in her mouth. "From the library!"

"That's right. I was hoping this little chat wouldn't be necessary, but you're very persistent."

"I'm sorry," said Walter, "but you were... dressed differently last time."

"I change," she said. "Frequently, and in any way I can. It keeps me on the outskirts, out of his dreams, more or less."

"I'm sorry, I'm not sure I underst—"

"Mr. Church, time may be extremely short. What would it take to convince you to forget this whole thing and go back to your old studies?"

"My... Well, you see—"

"What if I told you it could save your life, your sanity? What if I told you that forgetting certain things you may have noticed is absolutely your only hope?"

Walter could think of no reply.

The woman, Terri, removed her glasses, and the tiny pinpoint pupils of her eyes bored into his. "Take it from someone who knows, Mr. Church, someone who's been around. That thing on the water isn't just a statue—it's the ark of his dreams. How many people meet those eyes every day? A thousand? More? The sensible ones feel a shiver and look away. But you don't have the shiver gene. You look back, you take notice. You become *involved*. He's dreaming of you, Mr. Church, dreaming *through* you. He can reach right through your heart and touch the ones you love. Perhaps he already has."

"What are you talking about?" snapped Walter. "Who's dreaming about me? Who the fucking bloody hell sent you? What do you know?"

"I *know*!" she said, with such sudden ferocity that Walter drew back a little. "I know well enough not to speak that name! I know how dangerous this conversation is, for both of—" Her whole body jerked and went rigid, her eyes rolled up into her head, and her jaw worked frantically. The clash of teeth was so loud it sounded like she was chewing rocks. This spell lasted for several seconds and then she slumped out of it, took a breath, and put on her glasses as if nothing had happened.

"Our obsessions take us far afield," she said, gaining her feet and letting her folding cane deploy. "When, Mr. Church, was the last time you checked in on your son? Joey, is it?" She walked quickly away, tapping around her and muttering something that might have been a prayer.

*

"Have you seen him?"

"Hell yes! I was in the bathroom and I came out of the stall and—swear to God—there was this face in the mirror!"

"Nu-uh!"

"I don't know how to describe it. It was—"

"Hey," said Joey. The girls, one dressed as the Delphic Oracle, the other as the cat goddess Bastet, stopped talking and looked at him. "What's that about?"

"Oh," said the Oracle, "we're talking about the Sphinx! It's totally going around. Bethany saw it, and Clay saw it, and now this loopy bitch here she says she saw it too."

"I did see it! It was *so* tripped out!"

"They say you only see it for a second, and it changes your whole perspective."

"Have *you* seen the Sphinx, Joey?" Bastet's tone was suggestive. The girls tittered.

"No," said Joey in a cold, flat voice, and their smiles dropped away. He got up and walked out of the greenroom. There was a bathroom right next door, but it was full of geeks, and he wanted solitude. He walked the length of the hall and turned into the deserted east wing of the school. *Ol' Fox Creasy, he's a foxy one. (Shut up) Think he's foxed his way into her crease yet? (Who is that?) Have his foxy red rocket in her by the end of the month, whad'ya wanna bet?* He grabbed his hair in fists and squeezed. *(Shut the fuck* up, *you're not me!)*

The boys' room was empty, dark. He flipped the switch and the lights flickered on. On the mirror above the sink some wit had scrawled *FAG* in black marker, with an arrow pointing up, and above that, a pharaoh's headdress with beard, lopsided tits, and outlined eyes framing his reflection. They even knew how tall he was. His stage makeup—a pale base, blue lipstick, and imitation kohl darkening his eyes—made him look like a painted corpse, a zombie clown fleshing out the crude cartoon. He skinned back his blue lips and grinned at himself, then hit the water and started splashing his face.

Remember three years ago? 'Member vodka summer, home-alone summer? How you two played? Do you remember what it felt like to put your hand down her pants, how she shivered, how she looked at you? You're just gonna let her forget?

"Ooagoddamyou!" He left the water running as he banged into the stall and fumbled with his zipper. His cock sprang up, hard as a steel rivet, and found his wet hand. He swallowed and breathed, remembering that day, drawing his whole self from that memory, *there, no sister by blood*, the words a mantra, *no sister just... just... Allie!* He whispered her name as he came, splattering the toilet wall. He opened his eyes and a rich, narcotic blast of endorphins and guilt rolled through him. He snatched some toilet paper and cleaned himself up.

He stepped out of the stall and grimaced at his slinking, ghoulish reflection, the half-washed makeup smeared down his face. How could he have let this happen? More than anything he hated and feared the stigma of his father's madness, the trace of it *in him*, the knowledge that he was likely genetically marked. And yet here he was, courting it, taking it to the ball, acting out his father's artfully scripted insanity. *Wanting* his sister. *Hating* his best friend. But what, then? He would drop out, quit, go away. Everyone would think he was batshit, that he'd caught the family bug, but fuck it, let them. He'd be saving the best part of himself.

"Joey."

He spun around. He was alone. The voice had come from the hall. *Not* in his head, he was sure.

"Joooe-ey."

He opened the door and peered out. The hallway was empty, but what was that? He started walking. *Something,* way, way down at the southeast end, was going around the corner. He quickened his pace, almost running to the end of the hall. He turned the corner and saw the door to the gym was open. It was dark inside. He stepped through the door. (*Get out of there!*) "Hello?" (*Don't speak to it!*) "Someone in here?" (*Run!*)

The face, the pale, oval face with the placid smile and sparkling black eyes, floated out of the darkness at midcourt. At first it was just a face, but as he walked to it—his heart knocking in his chest, his breath coming in shallow little sips—the rest began to take shape. That smile of perfect serenity, that doting, generous mien... "Joey," it said, with a voice like dribbled honey. "Let's have a word, shall we?"

*

Walter's TV dinner tasted bad tonight. Worse than usual, as if it had been thawed, left to turn, and then re-frozen to seal in that little gift of decay. He stopped eating halfway through, pressed the 'mute' button on nightly news, and picked up the telephone. It had been so long. He couldn't remember the number until his thumb was on the keypad and then he knew it by touch. The little code of sequential beeps unlocked something in him, a dark room painted in sad shadows where he had spent far too much time already.

As he waited for her to answer, his tired gaze took in the room. Cold radiator, bookshelf, liquor cabinet with French and Latin volumes crammed between the bottles, old Singer sewing table he used as a writing desk. These things were the same. That was something. The TV was showing a handheld shot of a home interior, cluttered and rundown, zooming in on a blood-soaked sofa, with the caption "Horror at Red Hook." It seemed the news was positively chock-full of horrors these days.

"Hello?"

"Amanda. It's, um… it's Walt."

"Walter. Hi. Is everything okay?"

The words stuck in his throat. He shook his head.

"Walter?"

"Fine," he blurted. "I just, um… Well I know this is bit how-do-you-do and out-of-the-blue, but… I was wondering how Joseph is doing?"

"Oh. He's fine. He wanted me to thank you for the play."

"The play?"

"The one you sent him to use. *Father of Destiny*, or something like that? He told me the school is actually putting it on."

"I'm afraid I don't… Are you sure that was the message?"

"You don't remember? He told me you said it was the best thing you've ever written."

"Wh—ah—when… Ah, Amanda, when did I give him this… *play?*"

"July? August? I'm sorry, Walter, I don't remember. But they're opening tonight. I can't make it, I have to work. But you should go if you have the time."

"I will," he said. "I certainly will."

"I'm sorry, Walter, I have to go."

"Not at all, I—" But the click told him she was gone.

Walter glanced over at his pill bottle. Silent, for now. He unmuted the news. Apparently there'd been a string of disappearances along the East River. Mysterious drownings. No bodies.

He watched a cockroach preen its antenna under the radiator.

Like an intruder through an unlocked window, a terrible, icy premonition crept in through the back of his mind. He knew in that moment that something dreadful had happened—was happening—was *about to happen.*

"He can reach right through your heart and touch the ones you love."

He got up and walked out the door, leaving the TV on, heading for the stairs. His car was parked three blocks away, and by the time he reached the street he was running.

*

Opening night at Rockaway High, and the audience had been promised "something unique." So far, *The Father of Destiny* had delivered. There'd been laughs, shrieks, cheers, a few indignant walkouts (all the better to weed out the lames), but Ms. Ortega, watching from the balcony, hadn't counted a single yawn. The scene where Oedipus rescued his mother from the house of the dead—by weighing his heart against a feather and matching wits with a baboon—had been a great sell, really drawing them in. They had that blissfully mesmerized look that audiences get when a show really starts to score. Their eyes were drinking in the story, primed for the big showdown with Laius on the steps of the Lincoln Memorial. It was like bringing a dream to life, cast in living flesh, and for once she had no regrets about her career. At least a small part of her wanted to track down Joey Church at the after-party and jump his precocious bones.

If Joey, brooding in the darkness backstage in full Sphinx regalia, looked like death, it might have been assumed that he was just getting into character.

*

It was just Joey and Allison now. The rest of the spare cast had been drafted into one of the armies. She wore a shimmering gown of blue gossamer and pearls, selected to make her eyes pop in the black light. It gave her a fierce, numinous beauty, she knew. She

195

was pacing the wing, pricking her thumbs with her fingernails and mouthing her lines. Joey's eyes followed her, the only part of him that moved.

"Where is my mother? Summon her!"

Fox's command from the stage meant her big scene with him and Laius was coming up. Suddenly she ran to where Joey was standing and hooked him round the neck. She nuzzled his shoulder, mindful of his makeup, and whispered, "I love you, Joe. Thanks for being so cool, brother." She started to go for her entrance, but his hand shot out and caught her wrist. "Eh? Joey, wha—"

"Don't go out there," he hissed, his eyes brimming with sudden intensity.

"What, what are you—"

"*Please,* Allie! The play, it—it—it's bad! Th—there are secret lines my father wrote... Allie, it doesn't end how you think it does!"

"Hey. HEY! Joey, let... GO!"

"Please, don't go. I can't stop it if you do! I love you Allie, please, we can go, we can leave right now and be together, we can—"

"Hey... Crazy *fucker,* let go!"

His grip faltered and she snatched her hand back. For a moment she saw the deep pain in his eyes, but only for a moment, before it hardened into a flat, nothing gaze. A dead gaze. She shrank from it and practically ran for the light of the stage and Fox's outstretched hand.

The scene unfolded with crackling aplomb. Allie was rattled at first, but managed to find her stride within a few lines. Once or twice she glanced back at the wing and thought she saw her brother back there—his eyes at least, glimmering in the shadows. The battle raged around her and she was Jocasta again, her passions torn between her husband and her son, and anxious moreover for that part of her that defied them both, the secret, smuggled heart of a woman. And then it was over. Laius lay dead. Oedipus Fox, victorious, drew her close and kissed her in front of gods and men and left her breathless and dazed.

The drums and the metal horns sounded and the theater went dark. All eyes looked to the wing. Allie Jocasta looked.

And her mind broke in two.

For what now took the stage, with heavy thump and shuffling drag, aglow and ghastly in the cold blue light? What taxidermist's nightmare, what unnatural abuse of form, what desecration of life, what dread ancient now cast its shadow on the audience and fixed them in their screaming shock? What now addressed the bloodless face of the king with a voice that blew the speakers out and sent a wave of despairing groans through the onlookers?

"Speak!"

"D—Daughter of Orthus," sputtered the king, helpless to stop the words from forming. "Father... t—take us... m—make us... marry us!"

"Answer my riddle."

The eyes of the king refused, pleaded, begged to be reprieved, but he had no power to refuse what was written, and trembling he replied, "Ask."

"What is my name?"

"Your name..." whispered the un-made king, tears streaming down his face, "is Death."

"No. I am one who dreams a million leagues below death. Death is only the beginning. You will see. I will show you. You are mine!" It reached for them, took hold of them, and they screamed louder than all the rest, if not as long.

*

Walter got out in front of Rockaway High auditorium, leaving his car to idle in the street. People in disheveled eveningwear were trickling out of the entrance like poisoned bees from a rock. They tripped over their own feet, searched the ground with blasted vacuity, or tilted strange grins to the starless sky. One dusky woman in voluminous skirts looked up at Walter as he hurried past, her scooped-out eye-sockets weeping blood.

He fought his way through the door, down the dark hallway full of gibbering, reeling, reaching forms, and threw open the auditorium doors. The air was thick, syrupy with death, full of mutters and groans and half-articulate lamentations. What remained of the audience rolled and swayed in the murk of the reflected stage lights. A man traced invisible signs in the air, a woman clawed at her naked breasts while a mass of tentacles wriggled from her mouth, a teenage girl held up a toddler with a broken neck like an offering... All of these were but shadows, poor stewards to the towering horror of the stage.

"*Joseph!*" he screamed over the woeful din. "*Son!*"

It heard. It looked up from its abominable labors and turned its gore-slathered face to him. It pawed the ruined bodies. "Father!" it said in a voice dredged from the gutters of Hell. "Behold your work!"

"No, no, no—" chanted Walter, the last and only word he would ever know or speak again. "No, no, no—"

"Father, I am born!"

"No..."

"Sehk noth l'tak'gn!"

"No..."

"Behold your son!"

He Sees You in His Dreams
by Samuel Morningstar

My new therapist was young and pretty, but her office was a dive. The college diploma on her wall looked like it had been printed off a computer. It was the only decoration on the blue, peeling walls. We were sitting on cold metal folding chairs. "And how long have these nightmares been plaguing you, Mr. Hewlett?" she asked, from across a very plain table.

"Nine months," I answered. "Ever since..."

"What?" the therapist prompted.

She was court appointed, which probably explained the cheap sparseness of the office. The last thing I wanted to be doing was talking to a therapist, but I couldn't get disability without someone signing off that I was mentally unfit to work. I'd forgotten her name two seconds after she'd told it to me, but she resembled Betty from the old *Archie* comics, right down to the ponytail. She was my third therapist in as many weeks, and I was determined to give her the same amount of information I'd given the last two.

"I can't." I swallowed hard. "Talk about it."

"Mr. Hewlett," Betty said, in what she probably thought was a no-nonsense tone. Her voice was too squeaky for any authority figure. "You describe symptoms which are textbook Post Traumatic Stress Disorder. Almost *too* textbook, if you catch my drift." She picked up a manila folder, opened it, and leafed through. "The problem is, there's no precipitating trauma in your chart. Interviews with your co-workers indicate everything seemed fine until one day you just stopped coming in to work. No family or friends that you'll tell us about. No police reports. There's no corroborating evidence that you've suffered any kind of trauma that would cause PTSD. Unless you can give me something more than vague nightmares, I'm going to have to recommend denial of your claim. You can appeal with a judge if you want, but I wouldn't be optimistic."

Damn. For a second, I considered getting up and leaving. But my savings were just about gone. When my father had died a couple of years ago, I'd inherited his house and a stack of unpaid bills. He'd been more of a drinker than a worker. Selling his house and car, I'd ended up with about twenty grand after paying off his debts. I'd been living off it ever since I quit my job, but even being frugal I could see the end of my green coming. I'd heard getting disability for mental issues was easier than for physical problems, but so far that wasn't bearing out.

Fuck it. It wasn't fair to blow Betty's little mind with my story, but I hadn't chosen this path. She'd never believe me, but if she wanted evidence I was mentally unstable...

"Fine," I said. "You remember those disappearances last year? Those girls?"

"Yes," she said, carefully.

"I saw the last one. I don't remember much, just flashes, but I was there when she was taken. I saw what happened to her." I was staring into Betty's widening blue eyes.

Six girls had vanished off the face of the earth, one every Saturday night for a month and a half. It had made national headlines. All were sixteen to nineteen years old, from good Kansas families. No history of drug abuse. No run-ins with the law. No threatening correspondence. Nothing linking the girls except their ages.

There had been no ransom letters, no communications of any kind. They'd all been presumed dead.

And then one day they were back. They claimed the whole thing had been a high school prank, that they'd had no idea people would cause such a fuss. It was flimsy, but the media bought it. No one questioned if they had actually known each other before the "prank." The girls claimed they'd wanted to draw attention to the way people freak out over young white girls going missing. If it had been six black or Hispanic girls, it might not have even been reported in the news. The "prank" sparked media debate about prejudice, and the girls were praised for their demonstration of inequality.

Again it was flimsy, but it calmed things down. Within a week, the media had moved on to other stories, and the Kansas prank was forgotten.

"Mr. Hewlett," Betty said, slowly, enunciating every syllable. "What exactly are you telling me here? Are you insinuating those girls weren't playing a joke, but were kidnapped and somehow rescued?"

"Rescued?" I laughed harshly. "There ain't no coming back from where those poor things went."

"What do you mean?"

"He dreams." I wasn't *trying* to be cryptic, but it was all I had. "But not like you and I dream. His dreams affect the world. That's why I can't sleep, why the nightmares terrify me so much."

"You're not making sense, Mr. Hewlett," Betty said, leaning away from me. "Why haven't you gone to the police? Have you been threatened? Are you afraid for your life?"

"My life? Honey, I'm afraid for my soul."

She closed my file with a long sigh. "I think we need to try an alternate form of communication here."

"What do you mean?"

"Close your eyes," she said, standing up.

"I'm not sure I'm comfortable being hypnotized."

"I'm not hypnotizing you. This will only take a second."

I closed my eyes. I could hear her come around the table, high heels clicking on the tiled floor. She gently took hold of my right wrist. Given her tanned, all-American girl appearance, I'd have expected her hands to be warm, but they were ice. I heard the clinking of metal behind me.

Before I could stop to wonder what she was doing, she'd grabbed my other wrist and slapped hard metal around both of them. A dual click I'd heard a million times on cop shows told me I'd just been handcuffed.

I opened my eyes and tried to twist around to look at her. "What the hell are you doing?"

Betty stalked back around the table, all trace of the mousy girl I'd been talking to gone. She reached down by the side of the table, rummaged in her purse, and retrieved a tiny pistol. "Just makes a small pop when you fire, unlike larger guns. Most people don't register it as a gunshot and ignore it. But just in case I need more subtle persuasion..." Another rummage in her purse produced a small leather bag, from which she extracted several scalpels.

"Who the fuck are you? What do you want from me?" I yelled.

"Your story," she said, retaking her seat across from me. Her voice was no longer high pitched, but low and husky, like an old Hollywood film seductress. "Without all the nonsense." There was something odd in her eyes, but I couldn't nail down exactly what it was. It seemed as if her eyes were reflecting some light from behind me, but my back was to a blank wall. "Let me make my position perfectly clear, Mr. Hewlett. Your life means nothing. Whether you live or die today is of no consequence to me. Your story is the only thing you have that I value. You will tell it easily or painfully, but I *will* get what I want. There is no one else in this building to hear you scream."

I thought about testing the theory, but she was probably right. Hell, in this neighborhood, screams and gunshots weren't uncommon. No one would react even if they *did* hear. We were in a small three-story building in a run-down part of downtown Kansas City. The area had been hopping in the 1940s, but was now mostly boarded up. When I'd arrived, I'd put it down to the Disability Office being cheapskates. I hadn't seen a soul upon entering. Betty had been waiting patiently in the basement room we now occupied.

"Who *are* you?" I asked again. "Some kind of government agent?"

"I'm the person who is losing patience with you." She picked up one of the scalpels and began toying with it.

I didn't need any more prompting.

I told her my story.

*

I knew there was something wrong with Jeff Klein the minute I laid eyes on him. I was working in the rental office at the Shelby Klein Ford dealership in Overland Park at the time. I sat there for eight hours a day renting cars to people with their vehicles in the shop. Boring. Klein was tall and built, if a bit puffy in the middle. An aging jock. He spent a great deal of his time at the dealership telling stories about how he almost got picked out of college to play for the Kansas City Chiefs. His family owned the dealership—another fact one learned about the man within moments of meeting him. He was a church-goer, liked to fish and camp in the summer, and hunt in the fall. The kind of man I'd usually dismiss as being a typical redneck blow-hard. But sometimes he'd walk by and the short hairs on the back of my neck and arms would stand up. I won't say he had "bad vibes" or any such New Age nonsense, but I was always damned glad when he went upstairs and stayed in his office. The other members of the Klein family that I'd met struck me the same way—creepy in some indefinable way.

It didn't take long to find out my instincts had been correct. I'd become friendly with Rex, one of the Service Advisors. He often wandered down to the rental office when he wasn't busy, and we ate lunch together in the employee break room. We had a shared passion for crime and serial killer stories.

"Looks like this will be our last burrito together, compadre," Rex said one day.

"Oh?" I said, raising an eyebrow, Spock-like.

"Got hired on at Molle down the street. You oughta consider putting in for a transfer yourself. Get away from the bad mojo here."

This surprised me. I'd never shared my feelings about Klein to anyone and hadn't realized anyone felt the same as me. I asked him to explain.

Rex scratched his graying beard. He looked around cautiously. We were alone in the break room. The flat screen in the corner was on, but the volume was low. A game show contestant was jumping up and down like a crazy woman. Without the sound, she could have been in either agony or ecstasy based on her expression.

"How much do you know about the Shelby and Klein families?" he asked.

"Not much," I admitted. I knew the dealership had been founded by two high school buddies, Ron Shelby and Rick Klein.

Their pictures were on the wall outside my office and I often heard the sales staff telling customers the inspiring story of the small car repair the boys had started out of the Shelby barn in the small town of Salina, Kansas. They'd worked hard and now they owned dealerships throughout the state. Both men were now in their seventies and retired, leaving the company in the capable hands of their respective sons, Jeff Klein and Cooper Shelby.

"Their rags-to-riches story is bullshit," Rex said, his voice low and careful. His eyes kept darting to the door, as if expecting someone to come barging in any second. "Both families are loaded and have been for decades. They own tons of farmland out in Salina, and live in big plantation houses. They're both part of some damned cult."

This surprised me. Jeff kept a Holy Bible on his desk, and was always telling people what the Good Book said.

"Smoke and mirrors, Al," Rex said. "They know how to say and do all the right things, but everybody in Salina knows on certain nights you gonna hear crap like a voodoo ritual gone crazy coming from those houses."

"You're saying they're secretly devil worshipers?" I'd read hundreds of crime books on actual cults, and they all used love and light as the lure. True Satanic cults were as rare as hen's teeth.

"Something like that," Rex said.

The television fuzzed loudly and we both jumped. The game show came back on after a second.

"You scared they're going to recruit you?" I asked, only half-kidding.

"No, their shit's generational. You have to be born into it, from what I hear. No, I'm getting out because of those girls." He nodded towards the television, which was now showing a commercial for the evening news, promising an update on the missing high-school girls at ten.

"You think they have something to do with it?"

Rex ducked his head down. "I thought the names sounded familiar, so I looked 'em up in the Service records. All three of those girls have been in the dealership with their families in the last two months."

A cold prickle wormed its way up my spine. That had to be a coincidence, didn't it?

"They're being chosen," Rex said, finishing up his burrito and wadding up the wrapper. "I don't know for what and I don't *want* to know. I got a girl starting high school in the fall, and I don't want her coming around here."

True to his word, he was gone the next day. I wasn't really too friendly with any of the other staff, so I spent most my time in my office. Summer was slow for service rentals, so I had more time than usual. Rex's story kept bugging me though, so I decided to debunk it. The easiest part should have been the first—ascertaining the origins of the Shelby/Klein fortunes. Turns out, old Rex had been correct. Both families had owned land around Salina since before Kansas had officially become a state in 1861. Salina had been founded in 1858, but neither family was mentioned until around 1860. They could have been homesteading out in the boonies for years before any official records came into being, though. Both families had constructed huge plantation style homes miles from town and had invested heavily in the railroads that came through, transforming Salina first into a cow town, then into a wheat-producing empire once the cattle trade had moved west. The first lie exposed.

Another week went by and a fifth girl disappeared. By now, the story had been picked up by the national news and was running on CNN every hour. Manhunts were being organized. The latest girl's name was Trisha Howard.

I recognized her.

I didn't want to believe it when I first saw her picture being flashed on the television screen in the customer waiting room. There was a Starbucks machine in there that I pilfered several times a day for a steaming cup. I nearly spilled scalding coffee all over myself getting back to my office. Hart didn't like employees looking up previous rentals, so they archived records older than a month, but fate was with me.

Rupert Howard had rented a compact from me one month prior. I remembered Trisha had been with him. She'd sat in the corner while her dad and I did the paperwork, staring at her cell phone. She hadn't struck me as being any different from a hundred teenagers that I passed on the street every day.

Only she was now gone.

Rex was two for two.

I was frantic. Should I call the police? I only had Rex's word that the other girls had been in the dealership. What if he'd been wrong? More than once, I picked up my phone to call the local hotline, but eventually put the receiver back down. I just didn't know what to say.

So, I returned to researching the Shelby/Klein families. There wasn't much, but I ended up thumbing through the Salina Gazette archives. They'd scanned every paper from 1901 to the present and put them online. Nothing much on the Shelby/Kleins, but during the summer of 1915—exactly one hundred years earlier—I found something that nearly sent me running in terror from my computer.

Six girls had disappeared in 1915, one a week for six weeks. They'd never been found. A short blurb on the disappearances mentioned one of the girls had briefly worked at the Shelby house as a maid. The Shelby family had generously offered a reward for her safe return.

It was there, in black and white on my computer screen.

Six girls, one a week, in 1915.

And now, five girls had disappeared, one a week, in 2015.

Five girls.

That meant one more to go.

*

It took me two days to work up the nerve to call my boss. I knew what I had to do, what I felt I was *meant* to do. It was Wednesday night when I finally called. I told my boss I was bed-ridden, running a fever, and needed a couple of days to recover. He hemmed and hawed a bit, but in the end he gave me the time off. I had plenty of sick time coming. I hadn't requested a day off since I started with the company. It was just a pain in his butt to send somebody else to replace me. Nobody else wanted to work at Shelby because it was considered a dead end if you aspired to move up in the Hart company.

So, on Thursday morning—two days before the final girl's disappearance would take place—I packed up an overnight bag, got into my 2002 Dodge Intrepid, and drove the three hours to Salina, KS. I was oddly calm the entire trip. I should have been terrified out of my mind, but I drove in a Zen trance. I had no real plan besides check into a hotel and then drive by the Shelby and Klein homes and see if anything looked suspicious. Tons of crime writers talked about the role synchronicity played in their investigations, the right information jumping out at just the right time. Maybe that would happen to me. Honestly, I mostly hoped I wasn't about to make a damned fool out of myself.

I checked into the Angus Inn around noon. I'd prepared a full cover story for what I was doing in Salina, but the geriatric in threadbare overalls behind the counter couldn't have been less interested in me. His eyes were glued to a ball game blasting from the small lobby's flat screen. I could have handed him Monopoly money and he wouldn't have noticed. Strangely, I thought I heard the old man mutter, "He sees *you* in his dreams," as I was walking out the door. I turned, but he was staring almost catatonic at the television.

I glanced down at my key.

Room 23. Bottom floor.

I wanted a quick nap. It was nearly a hundred degrees outside and it had been a long drive. We were in the dog days of summer, and I was covered in sweat.

They were waiting for me in my room. I didn't see them. I opened the door and they had me surrounded. A rough voice in the cool darkness of the room ordered me to keep silent. Heart pounding, I did as they asked. A cloth bag that smelled like oats was shoved over my head and I was hustled out and tossed unceremoniously into a car. I was appalled at the audacity of the kidnapping. Granted, my room was opposite the street and faced a lush forest, but this was still a bold move.

My recollection gets a bit fuzzy here. We drove for quite some time before stopping. I was pulled out of the car and frog-marched into a big, echoing space with what felt like an earth floor. The smell inside was sickening, a sulfuric vomit-and-rotten-egg odor that had me gagging from the moment I came inside. Something deep inside me started to scream. My legs buckled. I was pushed down into a chair, and tied tightly with coarse rope. Satisfied I couldn't escape, my unseen kidnappers left, shutting the doors behind. I heard the soft thump of a board being put into place to bar the doors.

Darkness. Stench. It was unbearably hot. I could hear the low hum of an electric heater somewhere in the room, and a noise like something breathing. It was labored and rhythmic, like someone on one of those electric lung machines.

I don't know how long I stayed in there. Seemed like hours. For a while, being tied up made my muscles spasm painfully, but eventually everything settled into a pleasant numbness that I knew was dangerous. I tried wiggling, but the men had done an exceptional job at binding me. Even if I *could* have moved though, I'm not sure I would have. I was almost paralyzed with fear. How could I have been so stupid as to come down here? I rented cars for a living, for Christ's sake! I was no crime reporter.

Luckily, the bag over my head cut down on the smell somewhat. I must have dozed off, because I started violently when the bag was finally ripped off. I blinked several times trying to get my eyes to focus.

I was indeed in a barn. Jeff Klein was in front of me, scowling.

He'd lit a small gas lamp and hung it from a ceiling hook. In the flickering light, I could see what appeared to be a four foot tall egg at the far end of the barn. Someone had draped a beige tarp over it. The breathing sounds (and wretched smell) were coming from the egg. It might have been a trick of the light, but it was almost like the egg was expanding and contracting with every breath. Tall electric heaters were placed on all four sides. From the brightness of the orange glow coming from the machines, they were cranked to the max.

"Getting ready to hatch," Klein said, following my gaze. "Saturday night, with any luck."

"How did you—" I started, but he waved me off.

He closed his eyes and shook his head slowly. "You did your damned research in *my* building, Alan, through *my* servers. I know everything that everyone does on a computer in my company. But that was only the icing on the cake. I knew you were coming because *He* showed me."

"He?"

"Cthulhu."

"Ka..." I struggled with the odd name.

"Don't bother," Klein said. "I could describe him, but you'd only see a hideous monster, not the beautiful god that he truly is."

I had no response to this. He was apparently crazy and—as Rex had surmised—deep in some sort of cult.

"I don't pretend to understand the metaphysics of it," Klein went on. "He lies dead, but dreaming, somewhere out in the deep Pacific. He dreams, but not like we do. You ever felt a deep anxiety without knowing why, a dread you just couldn't put a name to?"

I had to admit that I had indeed. Sometimes, it felt like dread was the only emotion I was capable of feeling, but there was no reason for it. I grew up in a decent lower middle class home. Normal childhood. No traumas or scarring events growing up. But I was indeed anxious. I constantly felt as if something was creeping up behind me, but when I turned to look it wasn't there.

"That's how most people interpret his dreaming influence," Klein said. "They've been brainwashed into believing that God should be human, should come in a form that's familiar. But to those of us who understand the call, that dread turns to anticipation, anxiety into excitement. This ain't no pretend bearded guy on a throne who sits in the clouds. When the stars are right, Cthulhu *will* rise and all the petty human nonsense will be washed away in orgies of blood. No more civilizations. We'll get to be primal again, fucking and killing and running free with wild abandon. Like we were meant to be before some damned fools domesticated us."

"You're crazy." Lame, I know, but it was all I could get out.

Klein threw back his head and roared his laughter. "You'll get to see proof in just a day or so." He jerked a thumb back at the tarp-covered egg. "This was brought from R'lyeh, *His* sunken city. Part of it comes to the surface every now and then. Others who have heard the call retrieved it and brought it to Africa. My family went to great trouble and expense to fetch them here."

Despite my terror, I was intrigued by his delusions. "What is it?"

"Shubbah Wraith." Klein pronounced the words carefully. "They're some of the rarest of the rare. A queen only lays six eggs at a time, and it takes a hundred years for them to hatch if they're kept warm. They're beautiful when they first come out, all soft and squishy, like a jellyfish and an octopus got tossed into a blender."

"What about the girls?" I asked, taking a deep breath. "Where are you keeping them?"

"Oh, they're just fine." Klein's smile was wide and insane. "Better than fine, in fact. They'll get returned to their families a little after the sixth hatches. Takes a bit of an adjustment period for them to learn to think like a human being."

"What the hell are you talking about?"

Klein reached back over to pull the bag back over my head. "You'll see. I already got the last one picked out. Real cute girl. Good family. She'll serve us well."

Before I could say anything else, Klein extinguished the lamp and left the barn, thumping the board back in place.

Once again, I was left to the hot, stinking darkness and the weird breathing. Only now, I had horrible images in my head of a tentacled monstrosity getting ready to push its way out of the egg only a few feet away.

*

"And that's my story," I said, exhausted from the telling.

Betty was looking at me with a mixture of skepticism and thoughtfulness. "So, how did you escape?"

"Escape?" I laughed feebly. "I didn't. I don't remember anything clearly after that conversation with Klein. I woke up at home, in my own bed on Sunday morning. I got up Monday morning for work and had a panic attack. I couldn't leave the house for nearly a month. A friend brought me groceries. Every time I tried to sleep I'd have terrible nightmares. Even coming here was a struggle. I see flashes every now and then of that weekend. I see them dragging in that poor girl, unlucky number six. And I have a dim memory of the creature that came out of that egg. But I want to run when I think about it. The girl is dead, and so are the others."

"The girls came home, Mr. Hewlett," she said. "It was on the news."

"I don't care!" I yelled at her. "I can't explain it, but I *know* they're dead."

"Are you sure you didn't just hallucinate this whole thing?"

"I worried about that for a while," I admitted. "My credit card statement didn't show a charge from the Angus Inn and when I called, a woman said she had no record of me ever having made a reservation there."

"Well, there you go," she said. "Perhaps you saw a horror movie on television and freaked out. It happens."

I shook my head slowly. "My car."

"What about it?"

"I keep track of my mileage. I have to pay attention to mileage for my job, so it's a habit. Sunday morning, it had 350 more miles on it than it had the week before. I only drive about 5 miles a day. Salina is about 170 miles away. I went there and came back. No doubt about it."

Betty sat back and nodded, seemingly satisfied with my answer.

"So, you going to tell me who you work for and why I'm handcuffed? Is the government investigating this cult?"

She laughed. "The United States government was founded by those who'd heard the call."

I froze in terror, my face growing hot. "Wait, you're... one of... *them?*"

She ignored my question. She leaned in close to my face. "Tell me about your nightmares," she purred.

My heart rate sped up. I gasped for air. My eyes darted from her face to the gun she'd laid down on the table. It didn't seem so frightening now, compared to the monsters she was in league with. I struggled to remember the name she'd told me when I'd first came in. I'd been too lost in my own misery to pay attention. It suddenly seemed very important.

"Tell me," she repeated, in a more commanding tone. "Your nightmares."

I decided to oblige her. "I keep dreaming I'm in a palace. The architecture is weird—gigantic in places, with odd angles. I'm taking care of all these children. They're mine, but not all of them are human. Some of them have tentacles, others are so strange I can't even describe them."

Betty smiled, showing perfect white teeth. I blinked. Suddenly, she looked much younger than I'd originally thought, barely out of high school.

And then it clicked. I'd stayed away from my television, but even casual viewing brought up the disappearances.

She was the last girl who'd vanished. I'd seen her picture—one of her smiling happily during a family picnic—a dozen times before all six girls had magically reappeared. I'd seen her in the barn. I'd been too panicked to pay attention to her face. All I'd seen then was blonde hair.

"The mistake they made in 1915 was not returning the girls to their families. Almost caused a panic." Betty stood up and began unbuttoning her blouse.

"What are you doing?"

"You passed out shortly after I was born," she said. "Your poor little human mind couldn't take what it was seeing. They brought that girl in, Candace, and laid her down for me, drugged so she wouldn't fight. You screamed enough for you and her both. It was the absorption process that finally made you pass out. I consumed her totally—hair, skin, skeleton, internal organs, every delicious, succulent inch of her. It's how I *became* her. It took a few days to integrate her memories and personality. By then, they'd released you, and sent you home in a blank stupor."

She pulled her blouse and bra off, revealing a tight, tanned body and perky breasts I'd normally have been in total lust over.

"I don't understand."

"I *ordered* them to release you." Betty or Candace or whatever her unholy name was licked her lips lasciviously. "My sisters can give birth to all sorts of wonderful creatures, but I am a *Queen*. The first to be born in thousands of years. Only *I* can give birth to more Wraith eggs." She pulled down her suit pants and panties in one smooth move. Tanned, shapely legs. Shaved "V" between them. It would have been a dream come true, except for the strange lights moving behind her eyes, revealing her terrible inhumanness.

My bladder gave way, hot wetness spreading all over my jeans. The stink of urine filled the room.

She laughed. "You did the same thing when I leapt on the girl." She straddled me and laid a soft feathery kiss on my lips. Despite the horror of the situation, I felt my body responding, growing hard and hot at her touch. "The Dread Lord has chosen you to be my consort. You should be honored. Your seed will be the damnation of the human race. No one knows when the stars will be right for our Lord to rise. Until then, we'll make sure he has plenty of beautiful children to greet him when he finally ascends."

"But... Why did you let me go? Why this subterfuge? Why did you let me be tortured for the last nine months?"

"Because it's fun, for one thing," Betty teased. "And I had to make sure your mind was going to snap back. You bent, but didn't break. Most people in your situation would have gone mad. But you, you've managed to hold onto your sanity. You've proven yourself worthy to be the father of the reborn race of Shubbah Wraiths."

As she reached for the zipper on my pants, I began to scream. She silenced me with a deep kiss, but that scream will echo in my head for the rest of my life.

Short as it may be.

Isophase Light
by Daniel Marc Chant

Lighthouses tended to be lonely places, but the one at Wolf Rock was especially noted for its air of desolation. Close enough to the mainland to be reached by causeway at low tide, it could lay no claim to being particularly inaccessible. Yet there was something about it that played on the mind, inducing melancholy in even the heartiest of souls. It had been decommissioned after nearly two hundred years of service, but even before then, few keepers had willingly taken a posting there. Those who did had seldom volunteered for a second stint.

"I can see why," Maxwell Blake admitted. He looked through the thick glass window at the top of the lighthouse. Before him, the Atlantic Ocean stretched like a great, grey carpet beneath an equally dull sky. "This place feels like the edge of the world."

"Which," said Professor Bracken-Holmes, "is precisely why I persuaded the University to purchase it for an observatory." The old scientist joined Maxwell at the window. "The nearest town of any size is fifty miles away. No light pollution to spoil our view of the heavens."

"Assuming we ever actually get a view of the heavens."

"If the weather forecast is to be believed, come nightfall the clouds will have moved on." There was a disconcerting click as the professor made an effort to straighten his back. For just a moment, he looked impossibly frail. "You must be patient, my boy. Though it seems much longer, we have been on this rock barely a week. We knew before we got here that the weather would not be kind to us."

"I'm not complaining, Professor."

"Which is why I chose you for my assistant. Any of your colleagues would be screaming to be let off this rock by now." The professor smiled warmly at him. "If I had a dozen more students like you, dear boy, I could transform our understanding of celestial mechanics. I would go to my grave knowing my life hadn't been wasted after all."

"And how has it been wasted?" Maxwell demanded. "You've made countless contributions. It was one of your books that got me interested in the subject."

"I wrote it fifty years ago! Around the time of the last of my 'countless' contributions. Astronomy has changed almost beyond recognition. It used to be that a cheap telescope and a great deal of patience were all that was required. Now it's all Big Science, vast devices dissecting creation like some wretched lab rat. They've taken the ghost from the machine, Blake, little realising that without the ghost there *is* no machine." The Professor removed his spectacles and rubbed wearily at his eyes. "Forgive me. I should not have ranted so. I'm an old man whose dreams have never quite come to fruition."

"But they will! We'll find this comet of yours, exactly where you predicted it. That will prove beyond doubt that you've been right all along."

Professor Bracken-Holmes put his glasses back on. "It will, won't it?" He patted Maxwell on the back. "You're right. The game is not yet over. Tonight I pave the way to rewriting every astronomy textbook in the world!"

*

The weather forecast proved more accurate than Professor Bracken-Holmes had dared hope. Standing on the balcony that ringed the top of the lighthouse, he gazed happily at the sky above Wolf Rock. It resembled one of Pollock's action paintings, light scattered across black velvet. The sight made him feel both humble and godlike at the same time.

Blake pushed a jack plug into a socket, and a hum confirmed that the last bit of machinery was now up and running. "It's all yours, Professor."

"Thank you. You'd better get back to your studies. I'll call you when I find anything interesting." The Professor frowned at the equipment cluttering the balcony. Each piece was attached to his 24-inch reflecting telescope, controlling or gathering data from it and its many sensors. He waited patiently as Blake went back inside and descended the stone stairs. As soon as the boy was out of sight, he turned his attention to the telescope.

If he'd had a mind to, he could have used one of Maxwell's infernal machines to point the telescope at the spot in the sky that interested him. He wasn't about to let a device rob him of that pleasure though. Peering into the eyepiece, he adjusted the focus until the stars were well-defined points of light. Then he gently moved the telescope upwards and to the right until he had the W that formed the constellation of Cassiopeia in his sights.

A little to the left of it, he hoped to find his comet. If it was where he'd predicted, it would be a stunning confirmation of his theory of celestial mechanics.

Wishing his hands didn't shake so much, he fought to move the telescope with the precision he needed. He rubbed at his arthritic fingers to get blood flowing through them, and as he did so, he noticed something strange in Cassiopeia. One of the stars twinkled ferociously, like a ballroom glitter ball.

As the professor tried to make sense of what he was seeing, the star suddenly bloomed, throwing out shards of light in all directions. For a moment, it filled the telescope's entire field of vision. Then it seemed to implode, shrinking rapidly until it was only slightly larger than the other stars.

"A nova!" he cried excitedly.

He heard footsteps, and then Maxwell Blake's voice. "What is it, Professor? Did you say something about a nova?"

The professor looked up to find Blake standing in the doorway.

"Out of the way." He hurried past his pupil to the concrete block which had once held the tower's rotating lamp. Now it was cluttered with charts and books. "Where are the damned things?"

"Can I help, Professor?" Blake was at his side.

"My charts and almanacs. The ones I told you to make sure were here. Where are they?"

Blake grabbed a small pile of books and slid them towards the professor. "Here are the almanacs, and over there are your charts."

"Blast these hands! You'll have to open the books and unroll the charts for me. Quick! I need all the data we can find on Cassiopeia."

As quickly as he could manage, Blake found the data the Professor was after and placed it all within easy reach of the old man. The professor looked through it twice before announcing, "It's not mentioned anywhere. It's something new."

"You said it was a nova?"

"Yes, but it can't be. An exploding star wouldn't dissipate that quickly."

"Then what is it?"

"Something new – some phenomenon that has never been seen before. I hope those machines of yours are faithfully recording everything, Blake. Their data may well gain us both the Nobel prize."

"May I have a look, Professor?"

"No, you may not!" The professor was taken aback by his own tone of voice. He hadn't meant to bark at the boy. He made a deliberate effort to sound calm. "Once I am done, the telescope is all yours. In the meantime, I would consider it a great favour if you were to fetch a couple of notebooks and act as my scribe. Will you do that for me?"

"Of course, Professor."

"Rest assured, if this discovery is as momentous as I believe it to be, I will ensure you have your share of the glory."

As Blake dashed downstairs to scrape up some notebooks, the professor hurried back to his telescope. He was greatly relieved to find the strange star still there. All his life he'd waited for a moment like this.

"Now I'll be remembered," he muttered. "And not just for a handful of out-of-date volumes that no one reads any more."

He adjusted the telescope to bring the mysterious object into the centre of his view. As he did so, it dimmed abruptly.

"No!" he cried, afraid that the object was about to disappear completely. "Damn you!"

As if responding to his exclamation, the object flared once

more. It should have dazzled him, yet he was able to gaze upon it without so much as blinking. If any light could be said to be cold, this was it.

"Impossible," the professor told himself, thinking about how quickly the object had ballooned. Unless it was within the home galaxy – and he felt sure it wasn't – it must have expanded at close to the speed of light. Not even the most violent of supernova explosions could achieve that.

The object receded and seemed to pull the surrounding stars towards it, as if the very fabric of space was being warped. Again, the professor could only think of one word to describe what he was seeing. "Impossible."

What came next was even more impossible. Pulses of light and dark rippled from the object, an outpouring of colours – unnatural, unappealing hues that reminded him of gangrene. They radiated from the object, twisting into vortices. A feeling of nausea rose within him, giving way to terror.

"The universe is being poisoned!" he cried out, forgetting that his protégé was downstairs. "That thing is a tumour! Do you understand me, Blake? Creation is dying. It is the end of everything!"

*

Maxwell Blake looked up from Kepler's *Astronomia Nova*. Was that Professor Bracken-Holmes he'd just heard? It was hard to tell over the sound of the wind and the rain.

He briefly considered going to investigate, but decided to stay put. His armchair was one of the lighthouse's few luxuries, and the room was warming up nicely, thanks to the paraffin heater he had running. It would take more than a vague unease to lure him into the dank and draughty stairwell.

His watch told him it was just past ten o'clock, which meant he had been reading for a solid three hours. No wonder his eyes felt tired. His neck ached, too. Perhaps he should climb into bed and read until he fell asleep. What else was there to do with no television and the weather making it impossible to work?

There it was again! This time, there was no doubt that it was the professor.

"Damn it!" Nursing a sense of injustice, Maxwell put aside Kepler and got to his feet. *Better go see what's troubling the old man.* A wooden door kept his room sealed. As soon as he opened it, he was hit by a blast of cold air that made him shiver and cuss.

He hurriedly stepped out onto the stairs and closed the door behind him.

"Poison!" The old man's voice was coming from below.

Maxwell hurried down the stairs and knocked on the professor's door. "Professor? Are you okay?"

"Evil! Darkness! Damnation!"

Half-convinced his mentor had gone mad, he pushed open the door and peered in. Unlike his own room, the professor's had a fireplace, in which some feeble flames reluctantly burned. The professor had fallen asleep in his armchair, a handful of books on his lap. "Such malevolent light," he cried out, his arms twitching, his head flopping rapidly from side to side. "Wave after wave of hatred!"

"Professor?" Feeling like an intruder, Maxwell tip-toed up to the professor and gently shook his shoulder. "Wake up."

"What?" With a jolt, Professor Bracken-Holmes opened his eyes. "What are you doing, boy? Where are the notebooks I sent you to fetch?"

"Professor, you were dreaming."

"Nonsense! What have you done with my charts?" The professor took a deep breath and looked round. "A dream, you say?"

"Something of a nightmare, by the sound of it."

"I wasn't on the balcony, looking at the stars?"

"Listen to that wind, Professor. You'd be mad to even think about setting foot outside on a night like this."

The professor placed a hand over his heart. "Just a dream! Thank God for that."

"Would you like me to fix you a drink, Professor? Some rum, perhaps?"

"Good lord, no. I just need my bed." The old man suddenly rose, scattering the books on his lap onto the floor. "I'll see you in the morning, Blake."

Clearly somewhat dazed, the professor staggered into his bathroom and closed the door behind him.

Maxwell was bothered by the books on the floor. Books were amongst the most valuable things in the world. They had to be treated accordingly. As he bent down to pick them up, he saw most were standard books he'd read for his degree. One of them, however, was a ruled exercise book with tattered edges.

Intrigued, he opened it and found himself looking at a page of what appeared to be doodles. There were spirals and stick figures, as well as occult symbols and sigils representing signs of the zodiac. Turning the page, he was confronted with symbols he didn't even recognise. Everything was laid out in a way that suggested some sort of logic, without revealing what that logic was. The same symbols occurred over and over throughout the book, but never in the same order.

The professor had hinted at inventing his own mathematical language, and using it to encode his theory of celestial mechanics. Without knowing why he was doing it, Maxwell stuffed the exercise book into his trouser pocket. Then he hastily put the other books in a neat pile on a table and hurried back to his own room.

Lying on his bed, he looked through the exercise book and tried to make sense of the symbols. Their meaning seemed to be almost within his reach, like an overheard conversation in which the words couldn't quite be made out. He was on the verge of conceding defeat when sleep finally claimed him.

*

Maxwell understood the symbols. Taking the purloined exercise book, he went up to the observatory and stepped onto the balcony. The storm had passed, leaving the sky as clear and star-strewn as he could have hoped. Straight ahead, the constellation of Orion the Hunter bestrode the sky. Turning the pages of the exercise book, he found what he was looking for. With a feeling of victory, he discovered symbols on the page correlating to Orion with his belt, sword and shield. Other symbols described the famous Orion Nebula, just south of the belt.

In this dream, the symbols that had defeated him during waking hours became a language he could understand.

He turned to the next page. This one represented Cassiopeia, and something he didn't recognise. It seemed as if it wasn't quite right, somehow. Was it this which had caused Professor Bracken-Holmes to cry out in his sleep?

Eager to find out, he peered into the telescope. The big *W* of Cassiopeia was straight ahead, but he could discern nothing remarkable about it.

Except, maybe... What was that smudge of light? It was faint almost to the point of being invisible, and he wasn't entirely certain his eyes weren't being tricked.

Could it be the comet the professor was searching for?

His heart lurched as the star exploded, filling his eyes with horrid colours that could only exist in dream. Light raced through his optic nerves like electricity and pulled the colours into his brain. Synapses fired with uncontrolled abandon. Maxwell's body was no longer his own. Spasming muscles threw him to the floor, where he twitched and drooled and cried out in terror.

Then, as suddenly as it had begun, the fit vanished. He was on his bed, clutching the exercise book. A bead of sweat rolled down his left temple. He lay still as the pounding of his heart slowly quietened, and his breathing became less ragged.

Outside, the storm was raging. He could hear rain drumming on the window, mighty waves crashing against unyielding rocks, the wind howling mournfully.

Sleep would be impossible amid such a cacophony. He decided to spend the rest of the night studying. He got off the bed, and was about to pick from his selection of books when he heard a scream.

Another scream swiftly followed. And then another. And another.

"Professor!" Maxwell ran down to the professor's room, and burst in.

What he saw made him recoil in horror, fuel for years of nightmares. Professor Bracken-Holmes seemed more animal than human. Crouched on all fours, his eyes red and full of malice, he snarled, mouth foaming like a rabid dog.

"Get out!" he yelled, seeing Maxwell. "Get out before it's too late."

"It was just a dream, Professor."

"You've seen it too, haven't you?" The professor was suddenly on his feet, reeling like a drunk. "We are damned. All of us. The whole bloody universe!"

"Professor. Please! Let me –"

The professor cut him off with a long, anguished howl full of misery and pain.

"These eyes," he said, raising bony fingers to his face. "They have seen things no mortal should ever see. Out! Out, accursed things!"

"No, Professor!" Realising what the old man was trying to do, Maxwell sprang at his mentor and grabbed his hands. Bracken-Holmes was weak, he but had enough fight in him to push Maxwell away.

Rallying, Maxwell came at him again. This time, he managed to get the old man in a bear hug and pin his arms to his side. Although blood oozed from both his eye sockets, the eyes themselves still seemed intact.

"The fires of Hell await us!" the old man screamed. He seemed no longer be aware of his surroundings. Perhaps in his mind he *was* already in Hell. "Evil is coming. It cannot be stopped."

Maxwell wrestled the professor onto the bed, and was eventually able to hold him in place with a dressing-gown belt and some ties from the old man's wardrobe. Although he no longer struggled, he still screamed and cackled, and shouted an occasional obscenity.

*

The ambulance came in the morning, when the storm had abated and the tide was out. As he watched Professor Bracken-Holmes being taken from the lighthouse on a stretcher, Maxwell told a constable about the events of last night.

"It's Wolf Rock," the constable said, when he'd finished taking notes. "It's driven many a man mad. I take it you'll be packing your things and going?"

"No," said Maxwell. "I shall stay and finish the professor's work. I owe him that much at least."

The constable shrugged eloquently, and turned away.

*

With the professor gone, the lighthouse seemed far bigger and emptier than before. As much as he liked and admired the old man, the solitude suited Maxwell just fine. Now he could work at his own pace, according to his own methods.

He put in a call to the University, and informed them that the Professor had been taken ill. After some dispute, he persuaded the department head to let him stay. He was told to expect a replacement for Professor Bracken-Holmes as soon as was feasible, and tried to reassure the head that there was no hurry.

With that out of the way, he decided to spend the rest of the day reading the professor's notes. It was his intention to look for the comet that had obsessed his mentor so utterly it appeared to have broken his mind. Unfortunately, the professor had kept most of what he knew about it to himself, leaving no clue as to where it might appear.

All Maxwell knew for sure was that it had last passed Earth 279 years ago, on its way to swing around the sun. Its trajectory had been measured and recorded by astronomers all over Europe. Their figures tallied to an extraordinary degree.

Using the data thus gathered, classical theories of celestial mechanics had predicted a time and location at which the comet should reappear. But Professor Bracken-Holmes thought otherwise. He had devised his own theories of motion and gravity, and they told him the comet would appear earlier than expected, in a totally different place. If it did as he predicted, and validated his theories, then he would turn hundreds of years of accepted scientific dogma on its head.

Personally, Maxwell thought that the professor was almost certainly wrong. It was notoriously difficult to predict the behaviour of a comet, especially when all one had to go on was centuries-old data. But he had no intention of abandoning the experiment. He was, after all, a scientist. If a hypothesis stood even the remotest chance of being correct, it should be tested. Besides which, while the experiment was in progress, he could stay in the lighthouse and not have to be bothered by his fellow man.

In Professor Bracken-Holmes's room, he gathered up all the papers and books he could find. It took several hours and many journeys to transfer it all to the observatory. Ordinarily, such sustained physical exertion would have taken a toll on him, but once the job was done, he felt far from tired. He was keen to get on.

The first thing he had to do was work out where the professor thought his comet would be that very night. He quickly realised the enormity of his task when he laid out the professor's notebooks on the concrete lamp block. There were seventeen in all, each filled with notes, formulae and odd symbols he didn't recognise. Bracken-Holmes had yet to write up his 'New Theory of Celestial Mechanics', and the notebooks contained his entire thinking on the matter. Maxwell flicked through a few and despaired of ever making head or tail of them.

It doesn't matter, he told himself. *I don't need to understand the theory. All I have to do is find the comet. But how?*

One by one, Maxwell unrolled the professor's star charts and laid them flat upon the lamp block. Some were printed; others had been created by the professor himself. Surely one of them would indicate where the comet should be?

A few hours of careful study of the charts resulted in frustration and disappointment.

"Damn it!" Maxwell stepped away from the charts in disgust. Tomorrow he would go see Professor Bracken-Holmes and demand to be told the information he needed. If the old man refused to reveal his secret, well that was that then. There was no way he could carry on in the dark like this. It would drive him as mad as the professor had become.

The room brightened. Maxwell looked out of the window to see the tail end of a cloud drifting away from the sun. No other clouds followed and the sky was more blue than grey. With luck he'd be able to do some stargazing once the sun was down, but what would be the point?

Maxwell had an idea, and he wondered why he hadn't thought of it before. He rushed down to his room, fired up his PC and was soon on the Internet, looking at the landing page of a search engine.

He clicked on the input box and typed *comet* and the year in which, according to Professor Bracken-Holmes, his target had last appeared. To his satisfaction, the search engine returned several thousand hits on Comet Haldon. Within minutes, he had before him a table showing the comet's progress on its last visit. It was exactly what he needed to calculate where classical mechanics estimated the comet would be at the present time. Now all he had to do was set up the equipment on the viewing platform and wait for nightfall.

*

Wispy clouds drifted lazily across the sky, but thankfully none were near the section of sky that interested Maxwell. It was an hour past sunset, and viewing conditions were well-nigh perfect. He switched on the telescope's direction control and tapped in a set of coordinates. There was a gentle hum as servo-motors turned the telescope to the left and adjusted its angle.

Peering into the telescope and pressing a button, he could see Saturn spring into focus as expected. There were its rings and its largest moon, Titan, along with a smattering of dots – any one of which could be Comet Haldon. He saved a digital photograph of the view and fed it into a nearby laptop. The PC analysed the picture, checking for anything, such as Haldon, that wasn't in its database. Within a minute, it had done its job. *No anomalies found*, said a pop-up on the screen.

Disappointed but not surprised, Maxwell put the telescope into search mode. It began to scan the heavens, taking photographs for the PC to analyse.

Resolved to waiting for several hours, he decided to use the time trying to decipher Professor Bracken-Holmes's notes. The key, he felt, lay in the first strange exercise book he'd seen, with its enigmatic symbols and sigils. In his dream, he had understood the book's contents, but in an intuitive rather than a literal way.

They're written in the language of dreams, he told himself. *I cannot break the code with reason and logic. It must be done by intuition.*

He retired to his room, where the paraffin heater had been burning long enough to make the temperature cosy. After preparing a cup of tea, he settled into his armchair and opened the book on his lap.

Although his gaze was fixed firmly on the symbols, he tried not to think about them except in the most abstract way. He was sure his conscious mind could never make sense of them. He had to let his subconscious do the work. As an undergraduate, he had for a while been a student of transcendental meditation. He put what he'd learnt to good use. The hot tea helped him relax. Once he'd emptied the cup, he emptied his mind, and waited for enlightenment.

*

When the University asked Professor Joshua Wheaton to take Bracken-Holmes's place at the Wolf Rock observatory, he didn't hesitate to say yes. The thought of spending his time in near-solitude with only a fellow academic for company filled him with enthusiasm. In his mind, the lighthouse stood tall and proud, a monument to Victorian engineering, surrounded by clear blue water filled with exotic creatures. At night he would be able to do the thing he loved most – gaze at the wonders and mysteries of creation.

His first glimpse of the lighthouse shattered his dreams.

"See? What did I tell you?" The rustic taxi driver, Gowther, had charged a considerable sum to drive him the thirty odd miles from the nearest village. "This is as ugly a place as any you'll find on God's earth."

Wheaton wasn't about to argue. There was something off about the lighthouse. He couldn't say quite what, except perhaps that it gave off the air of being aeons older than it actually was. Fighting a recalcitrant seat belt, he leaned forward to get a better view of his destination.

The taxi struggled along the narrow coastal road. The car's suspension had shown its limitations back when the road had still been good. Out here, it was the plaything of every pothole and bump it encountered. Wheaton found himself clutching at the dashboard for dear life.

The road ended where the causeway began. "This is as far as I go, Professor." Gowther brought the taxi to a stop with a jolt. "If I drove this old crate onto Wolf Rock, I doubt I'd get her off again. That all right with you?"

"Fine, thank you." Walking across the causeway seemed a safer bet than relying on a car that even its owner was quite happy to call unreliable. After a brief struggle with the clip, he undid his seat belt and hopped out of the car. His only luggage was a small brown suitcase, which he retrieved from the back seat.

"Make sure you ring me as soon as you've had enough of this place," said Gowther.

With a crunch of gears and a stoic nod, the man put the taxi in reverse, and backed off until he came to a spot where the road was wide enough to permit a three point turn.

Suitcase in hand, the professor gazed upon the lighthouse once more, and seriously contemplated taking out his mobile phone to immediately call Gowther back. "No wonder the old man went mad," he muttered, as he steeled himself to cross the causeway.

He reached Wolf Rock without mishap. Turning round, he saw that the tide was coming in. The causeway was being claimed by the sea. If he wanted to bail out, now was the time to do it. He decided to stay.

The lighthouse door was equipped with an old fashioned bell pull. Without really expecting it to work, he tugged at the chain. From within came a clanging.

"Who the devil is that?" called a voice from above. "Is that you, Professor? Has your madness passed?"

Wheaton looked up to find a man looking down at him from a balcony. "Maxwell Blake?"

"And what if I am?"

"I'm Professor Joshua Wheaton."

"Who?"

"Did you not get a phone call from the University? I'm here to replace Professor Bracken-Holmes."

"Bit young to be a professor, aren't you?"

Wheaton sighed. "No younger than Bracken-Holmes was when he became one."

"The door's open. Let yourself in and wait for me downstairs. I'll be there in a few minutes, once I've solved this damned equation." With that, Maxwell stepped back and disappeared from sight.

Although the wooden door was large and its hinges ancient, it swung open readily enough. In a hurry to escape the chill sea breeze, Professor Wheaton stepped quickly indoors and pulled the door shut behind him.

Dropping his suitcase on the stone floor, he looked around and wondered what the hell he had stepped into. Someone had been busy with white paint, covering the circular wall in equations littered with arcane symbols. Some of the scrawls made sense. Others appeared to be pure nonsense. Similarly, many of the symbols were known to him from his studies of the alchemists of yore. They mostly symbolised the houses of the zodiac, the planets and various chemicals. However, there were quite a few he was certain he'd never before encountered.

A wooden staircase spiralled upwards. The wall alongside was further covered in symbols and equations.

"My God!" Wheaton exclaimed.

"What's that?" Blake had suddenly appeared at the top of the stairs, and was running down them with reckless abandon.

Wheaton waited until Blake reached him before answering. "All this," he said. "Bracken-Holmes must have been quite manic before they took him away."

"You think this is his work? Let me show you something." From his back pocket, the man produced a tattered exercise book. "Here. You can keep this. My gift to you."

Warily accepting the book, Wheaton opened it at random. Its contents mirrored the markings on the wall. "What is this? What does it all mean?"

"Only the Professor and I know the answer to that, and neither of us are equipped to explain it. Read the book, but don't try to understand it. Read it and allow yourself to dream." He took a discomfiting step forward. "Look at my eyes, Professor. Tell me what you see."

For the sake of his own safety, Wheaton felt he should humour his colleague, so he looked into the man's eyes. He was disconcerted by what he saw. The pupils were peppered with tiny swirls resembling cotton wool. "Cataracts? You must be nearly blind."

"Blind?" Blake shook his head. "How can I be blind when I have seen further than any man has ever seen?" He pointed at his left eye. "Cataracts, you say? No, my friend. Look closer. You're an astronomer. Surely you know spiral galaxies when you see them?"

To his profound astonishment, Wheaton realised that the cataracts were indeed spirals. "I don't understand."

"They say that when a man dies, the last image he sees is permanently imprinted on his retina."

"But you're not dead."

"Aren't I?"

"You're ill, that's all." Wheaton backed away. "Perhaps the isolation is too much for you. I think it best we leave now."

"Leave? I am on the verge of completing Professor Bracken-Holmes's work. Do you think I could betray him by walking away from this? Look at the walls. Consider the effort I've put into those equations. You may not yet understand what you see, but you must realise it is more than idle scribbles." Blake suddenly became less intense, and chuckled. "All this must seem utterly crazy to you, of course. It would be futile for me to try to explain. Besides, why should you care? You're here to look for the professor's comet."

"Yes. The comet." Wheaton leapt on the chance to change the subject. "You haven't found it?"

"The weather is against me. Give me one clear night and I'll have it."

"Tonight's forecast says the sky will be intermittently clear. Perhaps we'll be lucky."

Blake brightened a little. "Yes. Perhaps."

Wheaton sincerely hoped so. With the tide coming in, any attempt to persuade Blake to leave the lighthouse was best left till the morning. By then he would hopefully have gained the fellow's trust. There was also a chance that now he had company once more, his mania would dissipate and he'd return to sanity.

"I've had a long journey." The professor put his hand over his mouth and yawned. "Not much sleep last night. If I'm to stargaze with you, perhaps I should rest for a while."

"Of course. You can have what was the professor's room. I'll show you up."

In Bracken-Holmes's room, Wheaton slept more readily than he'd expected. In fact, he was asleep almost as soon as his head touched the pillow. When he awoke, he was momentarily startled to find himself surrounded by spirals. His first thought was that he must be dreaming, but then he remembered he was no longer at home, and was lodging in a room with spirals covering the walls.

Outside, the weather was doing its worst. The room's solitary window rattled beneath the onslaught of rain driven almost horizontal by a wind that sounded knowing and malevolent. He pictured an invisible fist pounding relentlessly at the lighthouse.

Rolling out of bed, he slipped into his clothes before switching on the light and checking his watch. It was a few minutes after six. He'd slept far longer than he'd intended.

And in this weather too! he thought. *I must have been more tired than I realised.*

He decided to bathe before facing Blake again, but as he headed towards the bathroom, the wind suddenly dropped and he heard a sound that froze him in his tracks.

It sounded like a scream.

It's nothing, he told himself. *Old buildings are full of strange noises. I shouldn't jump to conclusions.*

He had just convinced himself he had nothing to worry about when the sound of Blake's voice put the matter beyond doubt.

"Get away! Leave me in peace!"

The wind picked up again. Blake was still shouting, but it was impossible to make out his words.

Wheaton cursed himself. Now he was trapped on a remote rock with a maniac until morning. He seriously considered locking himself in the room and waiting until help arrived. But a quick glance at the door revealed extensive woodworm and dry rot. One hard kick would demolish it. He had no choice but to confront Blake and find some way to either calm or subdue the fellow.

Following the man's strident voice, Wheaton made his way up to the observatory deck. Blake stood on the balcony. The door was open, allowing the wind in to play havoc. Books lay scattered on the floor. Charts flapped against the walls like moths seeking an escape.

Blake shook his fist at the sky. "Stop looking at me, damn you! Stop it!"

Wheaton ran to him. He was soaked the moment he stepped onto the balcony. "Blake!" Even though he yelled as loudly as he could, he could barely hear his own voice. "What are you doing?"

"Tell it to stop, Wheaton! Now you're here, it won't stop *staring* so. I can't take any more."

"Tell what to stop?"

"The eye! Up there! Don't tell me you can't see it?"

"There are only clouds. Come inside!"

"There's no hiding from the accursed thing!"

"Come inside!" Wheaton grabbed Blake's shoulders. A sudden squall blew rain into his eyes, leaving him temporarily blinded. As he blinked away the water, he felt the man slip from his grip. "Blake!"

Wiping at his eyes, the professor looked around. There was no sign of anyone else. He turned to peer into the lamp house, but it was empty. With a sick feeling in the pit of his stomach, Professor Wheaton forced himself to look over the balcony.

Blake's body lay ruined and lifeless on the rocks below.

*

The storm finally died about an hour before dawn. Looking out of the window of his room, Wheaton watched as the last few clouds rolled towards the horizon, unveiling a scattering of stars as they went.

"It's now or never!" he told himself. "I have to act fast."

He turned and gazed with some satisfaction at the reams of paper scattered around the floor. Some of the sheets had been torn from Bracken-Holmes's note books. The rest had come from Maxwell Blake's room.

Every sheet was crammed with data – equations, symbols and notes. He'd had to read the whole lot a dozen times over before it made enough sense to allow him to arrange the papers correctly. Once he had done so, the answer he'd been looking for – the answer which had eluded both Bracken-Holmes and Blake – revealed itself to him.

That was when the storm stopped.

There was no time to set out all the equipment on the balcony, but all he needed was the telescope, which he quickly mounted on a sturdy tripod. He pointed it towards the distinctive *W* of Cassiopeia, and then peered into the eyepiece.

As Wheaton's sanity blew away, and his mind disintegrated, he never even uttered a word.

Icebound
by Morris Kenyon

From notes by third officer William Abbott of the Glen Markie
Monday, February 2, 1942

I was asleep when the torpedo struck. The explosion flung me out of my bunk, fetching my head a bang against the bulkhead. I was stunned for several moments, during which time the *Glen Markie*'s deck rapidly listed to a twenty degree angle. Because of the Arctic cold, I was already dressed. I dragged on my sea-boots, grabbed my kitbag, and made my way up to the bridge, struggling into my life-vest as I did so.

Even in that short journey, it was obvious our ship was doomed. Her tilt was getting steeper, and I heard explosions as ice-cold seawater flooded the boiler room. The alarm was ringing fit to wake the dead when I reached the bridge. Captain Melrose was ordering the radio operator to signal an emergency Mayday call.

The Captain pressed the tannoy system. "Abandon ship," he called. His voice was calm, but we both knew it was a desperate situation. This far north, the Arctic Ocean's heart-stopping chill would kill any man in the water within five minutes.

Catching sight of me, Captain Melrose ordered me to supervise lowering the lifeboats. Given the angle of the hull, our port boats were already out of use. The starboard ones dangled over the ocean. Snapping off a quick salute, I hurried out of the bridge and into the freezing air.

Crewmen had already gathered around the lifeboats, and were wrestling with ice-bound davits. I took charge, and soon two boats were filled and lowered. The men rowed away from the ship as quickly as possible, hoping to escape the whirlpool when she finally sank.

Then another, larger, explosion rocked the *Glen Markie*, and I nearly tumbled overboard. I don't know if it was another boiler explosion, or the U-Boat had fired a second torpedo to finish us off. The ship staggered, and her bows started dipping beneath the green waves. Her stern rose, the screw threshing air, not water. Given the ammunition and tanks we were taking to Murmansk, we'd go under within minutes.

I was about to run back for Captain Melrose when, with a creaking roar, the weakened bridge superstructure toppled over. That decided me. I climbed into the last lifeboat, and ordered Petty Officer McCrudden to cast off. The boat slid down the hawsers and splashed into the water. There were thirteen of us in there – an unlucky number, but I had no thought of that at the time.

"Row," I ordered, seizing an oar myself.

We pulled with all our might, desperate to get clear of the wreck. In the distance, I saw the guide lights of the other lifeboats. Finally, after we'd rowed a few hundred yards, the *Glen Markie* took her remaining captive souls down to Davey Jones's Locker. The sound was incredible, like a great groaning roar but far worse.

I tried to steer towards the other boats, but it was dark, and a mist drew down. I lost sight of them. Sudden fogs are not uncommon in the region east of Jan Mayen Island, and as we rowed in their general direction, it felt as if we were enclosed in our own little world.

"Do you think we'll get picked up, sir?" Hughes asked. This was his first Russian convoy, and although he tried to keep the fear from his voice, it still showed through.

I opened my mouth. "The Captain got off a Mayday before..." I couldn't finish. Tears came to my eyes and froze as I thought of my dead companions.

"We'll be all right, lad," McCrudden said reassuringly. "The Navy will be scouring the seas for us." He glanced at me. We didn't have to say anything. It was long odds against surviving in these wastes rather than succumbing to the bone-chilling cold.

The fog closed in, and we were completely isolated. It persisted for the whole of the next day and night. We huddled together, shivering terribly, and ate carefully-rationed hard tack and bully beef. To keep up morale, I had us all sing songs and tell stories. McCrudden was very good, telling us about his pre-war exploits on the Gut, Malta's most notorious street.

On the second day, the fog lifted somewhat. We carefully searched the horizon for any sign of the other boats but saw nothing – we were completely alone. That and the sub-zero cold made our spirits sink to our boots. I had us keep rowing west. It was more for the exercise that anything, as I knew we'd never reach Jan Mayen.

Twilight was falling when an iceberg loomed out of the mist. It was large, about sixty yards tall, and shaped like a church with a spire of ice at one end. Even in the dim light it shone an eerie, iridescent bluish-purple.

"Shall we head there, sir? We could hack off some ice to drink," McCrudden suggested. Although our lifeboat held a cask of water, it wasn't enough. We were all exhausted, from rowing in the cold on insufficient food, so I nodded wearily. We might as well head there as anywhere. Turning the boat's prow, we cautiously rowed towards the berg. It loomed over us as we drew closer, its mysterious glow appearing to come from within. A handy shelf of ice jutted out from the lee side, though. Carefully, so as not to hit any underwater protrusions, we approached.

McCrudden and Hughes leaped out and hauled the lifeboat up onto the ice. The rest of us followed. The shelf was just beneath the pinnacle, and the ice soared up into the air. McCrudden took a hatchet from the boat and hacked off pieces of ice.

"At least we won't die of thirst," he said through chapped lips.

The men milled around the shelf while McCrudden set up the primus stove to boil the ice. Everyone was glad to stretch their legs and escape the boat's narrow confines for a while. At one end of the ledge, a dark crevice opened in the ice wall. For some reason, we all stayed away from that end. Once the water had boiled, McCrudden brewed mugs of strong cocoa to which he added condensed milk, and a splash of brandy. As the kye hit our stomachs, we all felt much better.

However, when the men were distracted, McCrudden drew me to one side. "We can't stay here, sir," he said in a low voice. "Icebergs are unstable. As it melts it'll turn turtle, and pitch us all in the briny."

I nodded. I had some experience of these northern seas from before the war. "You're right, but it's a large berg and I don't think it will do that just yet. And we all need some rest. We'll stay here overnight, catch some zeds, then I'll climb that pinnacle and see if I can see anything." I used to enjoy mountaineering in my youth and looked forward to testing my skills against the ice. "And what's the worst that can happen? We either die here, or on the open sea." Little did I know.

"Don't talk bilge, sir. We'll make it through." Despite his words, McCrudden looked doubtful but he accepted that everyone needed some rest.

We found a sheltered spot out of the wind, rigged up tarpaulins to make a rudimentary shelter, and huddled together for warmth.

Dawn, or the dim grey light that passes for sunrise this far north, found us not much rested. I had been disturbed by strange dreams of being attacked by savage Eskimos, but those images faded as I came to. McCrudden lit the stove and brewed up again.

While he did so, I investigated that fissure at the far end of the ledge. It opened up into an ice-grotto fringed with stalactites. It was no warmer in there, but the ice walls muffled the sound of crashing waves. The sea seemed to be getting rougher. The dim light filtering through the ice gave the grotto an eerie bluish-grey glow, barely light enough to see by. Aware of thousands of tons of ice pressing down from above, I had no intention of lingering. Then, at the far end, I saw what appeared to be a flight of steps leading down into the berg's submerged interior.

Despite a warning voice at the back of my mind, I climbed down the first few steps. They were more regular than I expected, but ice is strange like that. It had to be a natural fissure in the ice, maybe caused when the berg calved from the Arctic ice sheet. All the same, it was odd. Drawing my flashlight, I carried on downwards. As I descended beneath the ocean, the little outside light faded.

My flashlight picked out strange grooves on the steps. They

looked like footprints. That had to be impossible. Surely I was the first human ever to descend this ice-mount. They were most unusual though, and again, I couldn't account for them. Drawn onwards despite myself, I descended into the very heart of the berg. My breath formed wraiths of condensation around me, and I heard ominous creaking and groans as the ice shifted and settled. It was dangerously foolhardy – but what had I to lose? Once we cast off, we'd return to being adrift in an open boat, with an almost zero chance of rescue.

As if lured by forces beyond my power, I carried on down. Every step had those strange tracks. My flashlight splashed sparkles of colour as it played over the icy walls. Down I went, until my way was blocked by a translucent wall of ice. It was completely smooth, like a window pane, and it rose from floor to ceiling. Rubbing it with my mittens, I tried to peer through the glassy ice.

I couldn't be sure, but it seemed as if there was some sort of chamber beyond. Taking off my mitten, I rapped the wall and found it was hollow.

I'd never heard of anything like this before, and my curiosity was piqued. However, the wall was too thick for me to break down, and I couldn't see any way around it. The thought came to me that something had been sealed off behind it. I stood there for a long time, perplexed by the anomaly.

Eventually, I wearily climbed back up the steps. Even so, there was a part of me that didn't want to leave.

Back on the ice-shelf, McCrudden was gazing out to sea. He was muffled up, and even in the short time I'd been away, the sea had become rougher. Whitecaps danced as far as the foggy horizon. Waves crashed against the berg, the force of them making even this mountain of ice shake and tremble.

"Where've you been, sir? We've all been lookin' for you?" His Belfast accent was stronger now.

I told him about what I'd found beneath the ice. "I'd like to check it out further," I added.

"You're one mad Canuck," he said. "We should leave now before this berg turns turtle." All the same, I could tell he was intrigued.

"It's too risky to leave now. We'll go when the sea calms down," I said. For some reason, it felt important that I find out what was on the other side of that ice-wall. It was probably nothing, as the rational part of my mind insisted, but even so, I felt a definite pull.

He looked at me and rubbed his beard thoughtfully. "It shouldn't take too long. But I think we ought to leave right away, sir. I dunno, this berg feels rotten to me."

Normally I would have deferred to McCrudden's experience, but I was in the grip of a strong desire to find out what lay beyond. Somehow, I was certain that not knowing would nag me all my life, however long or short that might be. In the end, apart from one man left to guard the lifeboat and keep an eye open for any shipping, everyone else went with me.

Carefully, we made our way back through the ice-grotto and down the steps. We took several flashlights, ropes, and other items of equipment with us. This time I felt the mountain of ice above us tremble as the sea battered against it. Several of the men looked like they'd rather return to the surface, but none wanted to show fear before their mates.

"This is a bad idea, sir," McCrudden whispered.

I was tempted to agree, but we were now at the ice window.

"Never seen nothing like this," McCrudden said. He sounded uncertain, but he took a hatchet, hefted it and then swung at the ice-wall. It held firm, making a strange, ringing sound. He aimed another, harder blow at it, and the wall shattered into a thousand glassy splinters, leaving just a fringe of icicles at the top. A draft of sub-zero air billowed out. Unlike the clean, odourless Arctic air, I discerned a faint aroma of long-gone spices. Behind me, the men coughed and spluttered.

Taking the lead, I stepped through the opening, my boots crunching over the shards. McCrudden laid a hand on my sleeve.

"No!" he said, but it was too late.

Raising my flashlight, I was shocked by what I saw. Even the men fell silent. We had stepped into a tomb. Lying on a block of ice was a man in an extraordinary state of preservation. He looked to be merely in a trance rather than dead. His eyes were open, the irises a tawny-golden colour. We gathered around, hushed and awed, stilled into silence. Even the most humble seaman knew that it was a remarkable discovery.

The man was tall, well over six foot, yet slender and intelligent looking. He was clean shaven, fair-skinned, and had an aquiline nose. This was no Inuit hunter. He wore a black robe which had strange golden amulets and talismans sewn onto it. A tall, conical hat, also ornamented with gold, added to his height while a bronze wand lay in his hands. By his side was a bronze book with richly decorated covers.

Yet what shocked us the most was that the man looked like me. The resemblance was remarkable. He could have been my younger brother. The biggest differences were the eyes – mine are grey – and that he seemed to be in his late twenties, where I won't see forty again.

"A Viking?" McCrudden wondered. "They roamed the Arctic."

I shook my head. "This is no Viking. I think he is much older, maybe from the Bronze Age." I was excited, even though I knew it was extremely unlikely I'd ever get to tell anyone about my find. "This changes everything we know – Bronze Age Europeans in the Arctic." As I spoke, I wondered how and why this man had been entombed in the ice. This was a deliberate interment, not an accident.

There was a sudden, rumbling screech as the iceberg complained against the buffeting it was getting. That brought us to our senses.

"We should get away now," McCrudden warned.

This time, I had to agree. Wishing I had a camera so I could record my find for posterity, I pocketed the wand and book as some sort of proof. We almost ran up the steps to reach the illusory safety of the ice-shelf. Nobody wanted to be trapped below if the iceberg toppled over. As if being on the surface would have taken us out of harm's way.

The short polar day was ending when we emerged out of the ice-grotto. The waves were much stronger now, and crashed over the ledge. Peering through the gloom we were horrified to find our lifeboat had been washed away, and was drifting fifty yards off. Fifty yards or fifty miles, it was all the same. We had no way of reaching it – we were trapped on that treacherous iceberg. Worse still, there was no sign of the man we'd left behind. If he'd been washed away, he was already dead.

"We should have got away when we had the chance," Hughes wailed.

"Easy, lad," McCrudden said. "What's done is done. And we have more chance of being spotted here than in a little boat." But his reassurance fell on deaf ears.

Hughes and some of the others called for throwing me into the sea. I was forced to draw my pistol to quell them, but their anger was unabated. I couldn't blame them, but ultimately there wasn't much difference between dying in the lifeboat or dying here on the berg.

Besides, I wanted to investigate that body again.

The men huddled out of the killing wind in the grotto. Along with the lifeboat, our camp had been washed away, so there was no warmth. We all knew we'd succumb to exposure within a couple of days. To lift their spirits, I authorized another swallow of brandy apiece.

Once again, I made my way down the steps. The men were glad to see me go. Their boots had damaged the steps, so that it was hard to see the original 'footprints'. When I got to the ice-tomb, I looked again at the body. It was still extremely hard to believe I was looking at a corpse. He looked so alive.

I yawned. It had been a long day, and I was exhausted. I didn't feel like climbing the steps to stay with the hostile men so, despite my superstitious dread, I sat down on the icy floor and closed my eyes.

I awoke some time later with a scream dying in my throat. My nightmare had been vivid, and unlike any I'd had before. Before the images faded from my mind, I focused on what I could recall.

There was something about a bone-white, marble city. Lining its streets were caryatid pillars, the upper parts of which were carven into images of bearded men. Beyond its white walls, I could make out stark peaks. Yet what had made me cry out was the pole star itself.

Somehow, I'd known our doom would come for us when that star set.

Shuddering with fear and cold, I climbed up to the surface. As I ascended, the nightmare fell away. But nothing prepared me for what awaited me at the top. Everyone was gathered around a prone figure.

"Hey! What's happened?" I shouldered my way through the gathering. The answer was immediately obvious. The man, Everson, was dead. His face was deeply cyanosed, and frost crystals had formed on his skin. I guessed that his heart had succumbed to the bitter cold – that and despair – but I'm no doctor, so I couldn't be sure.

The men stirred sluggishly and looked my way. I was surprised that McCrudden hadn't set a watch, but the cold had probably numbed their senses. There was nothing we could do for Everson, so we took the remains outside and dropped them into the ocean. I said a short prayer afterwards. Unsurprisingly, the men were reluctant to return to the grotto and stood outside on the ice-shelf smoking the last of their cigarettes.

McCrudden stood to one side and offered me his lighter. "Where were you?" he asked.

"You know where I was – down in the tomb."

He narrowed his eyes at this. "All that time? And why?"

I noticed he no longer called me 'sir'. "That's right. I fell asleep down there. You may have noticed that the men aren't too happy with me."

He was about to say more when we were disturbed by a small avalanche from the steeple of ice above us. It crashed into the sea, and waves cascaded over the ice-shelf. We stepped back, avoiding the freezing spray. The entire berg shuddered. I wondered if the whole ice mount was about to capsize and hurl us all into the freezing ocean, to join poor Everson. However, it recovered, and resumed its drift.

Once the berg stabilized, McCrudden said nothing more, but he looked at me intently as if trying to read my mind. I'm not sure he liked what he saw in my face, for he turned away and went to rejoin the men.

There wasn't anything I could do, so I returned to the tomb. To save batteries, I switched off my flashlight. I welcomed the darkness as it allowed me to shut out some of my fears. Perhaps I drowsed, for I dreamed of an invading horde of Inuit peoples attacking our walls. Beyond, rivers that once flowed down mountains I knew as Noton and Kadiphonek had turned into glaciers as the climate worsened. The air was almost as cold as that I now breathed beneath the iceberg. My city, Olathoë, was doomed. Above it all, the north star, Polaris, shed its cold light on the scene.

This wouldn't do, I thought. I stood up, my limbs shaking with cold. Delusions like these were the onset of hypothermia. I punched the air several times, trying to work some warmth into my bones. But without food, and in this sub-zero atmosphere, I knew I hadn't long left before I lay down and let deadly cold leach my life away.

Once again, I climbed up to the surface. The Arctic wind blew my strange thoughts away. One by one, the men had begun to die. Some of the survivors had rigged up hooks and lines, and were attempting to fish. When McCrudden saw me coming, he led me to one side. His face was gaunt, his hollow cheeks covered with stubble.

"You should stay with us. You're meant to be leading us."

"There's nothing we can do," I replied. "We'll either be rescued or not."

"Don't give up. One of the other ships must have heard our Mayday." He was clutching at straws, and we both knew it. There were standing orders that no ship break formation, and there was no chance of the Germans sending anyone.

For a few minutes, I watched the men fishing. They sat with their backs to me, ignoring my presence. I beat my arms, trying to restore circulation. There was nothing for me there, so I found a convenient block and sat. Remembering the book I'd taken from the body, I took it from my pocket. Its covers were of bronze, dulled but not corroded.

Opening it, I saw that the pages were fashioned of thin, beaten copper. The incised words were in no alphabet I had ever seen. The letters bore some resemblance to cuneiform, but were more triangular. However, there were simple, raised pictures set within the text. Most of these were very disturbing, especially those showing a giant octopus-headed creature rising from the depths of the sea. Tiny human figures fled from it in panic.

Yet, even though I couldn't read the book, its age and antiquity impressed me, and I felt sure that its contents were of supreme importance. Its loss would be another major blow that the war had struck against the world. Closing it, I felt an overwhelming urge to descend once again to the icy tomb below. There was no reason to resist.

Once back down there, I flashed on my light for a moment, but everything seemed unchanged. It felt peaceful there, away from the shrieking polar wind. The only sound was the creaking and groaning of the iceberg drifting through the seas. It sounded louder than before. I sat down, and again my thoughts drifted away from that terrible place. I knew I was suffering from exposure and hypothermia, but my dreams were better than grim reality.

This time, my fantasies seemed even more realistic than before. Now the world seemed younger and more spring-like. I was with an army of men, and I somehow knew that we had fled a land even further to the north that had become too cold for habitation. We had been sent on ahead of the main mass of our fleeing peoples to cleanse this new land, Lomar, of a race of cannibal ape-men who blocked our advance.

Looking around, I saw my troop was equipped with bronze equipment that glittered in the hot Arctic sun. Bronze swords, breastplates, and richly-adorned helmets gave them a heroic look. Their shields were painted with the symbol of a white tower. I wore a black robe adorned with golden amulets and sigils, however. My squad was crossing a broad plane, and we approached a mountain named Noton. Leading my men, we cautiously explored a thickly wooded river valley. Oaks, beeches and hazels provided welcome shade.

Then giant creatures out of some hellish nightmare swooped down from the vale's sides. They roared their anger and blood-lust at us, revealing mouths filled with canines. They were covered with matted brown hair, their muscular arms long and reaching. Eyes like coals glowed at us. Some swung heavy tree branches. Others flung boulders. Most attacked bare handed though, relying on their claws and teeth. These had to be our cannibal enemies, the Gnophkehs.

My soldiers drew up in two lines, back-to-back, and prepared to defend themselves. Meanwhile, I concentrated hard. A bolt of light, white-hot, erupted from my wand and struck the lead Gnophkeh in the chest. I could smell the burnt hair and meat as the monster was hurled backwards into its fellows. The rest bellowed their fear and rage, but carried on.

Repeatedly, coruscating light burst from my wand. Every time, a giant ape died. Yet this enraged the survivors, and they attacked again and again. In the end, we held off the monsters' assault until the last few survivors turned and fled.

But my squad was also sadly depleted. We couldn't leave their bodies to our cannibal enemies, so we stripped them of their metal, gathered brushwood and then, offering prayers to our gods, I turned my powers onto the pyre and incinerated them. It took the last of my strength, and I staggered, worn-out, with the remains of my army as we pushed along the river bank.

Wakening, I stretched my cold-stiffened limbs and slowly hauled myself to my feet. Where had those crazy images come from? I tried to hold onto those strange names – Lomar, Gnophkehs, what was that about? They didn't seem like the wanderings of a mind slowed by hypothermia.

I heard footsteps coming down. Flicking on my light, I saw McCrudden. He looked worried.

"You'd better come up," he said.

Following him up, I stumbled more than once through exhaustion, hunger and cold. Up top, I saw it was dawn of another day. How long had I been down in that tomb, I wondered? More time than I thought. However, I saw immediately what McCrudden meant. Two more men had died during the night. As on the last occasion, I said the Lord's Prayer over their bodies before consigning their stiff bodies to the deep.

Yet as I said that prayer, I recalled the supplications I'd hallucinated offering to the much older gods of Lomar. It was difficult not to say the words of those very different prayers. They seemed more fitting, somehow.

McCrudden looked hard at me. "You look different. Younger, almost."

I grinned, my lips cracking. "It's the cold. Does wonders for my wrinkles."

"No, that's not it. You're more like that..." He broke off.

A noise cut through the Arctic wind – an engine. We all looked up, scanning the skies for the source of the sound. Breaking through the clouds we saw a four-engine Focke-Wulf Condor bomber. Despite it being an enemy plane, the men cheered and waved their arms. One or two scaled the ice wall at the back of the ledge as if getting closer to the plane would make them more visible. Even McCrudden joined in the enthusiasm.

How could they try to get rescue from the enemy? We were needed here on this iceberg. *Where had that odd thought come from?* The plane crawled through the grey skies like a fly across a ceiling. I concentrated on the sky, not the plane. The clouds were low and heavy with snow, and before the Focke-Wulf reached us, the first flakes began to fall.

The men redoubled their efforts, and despite their frantic waves and yells, the snow fell thicker and heavier. The Focke-Wulf's shape blurred, and then it climbed up into the clouds to rise above the blizzard. Within a minute, it was lost to view and, crucially, it could no longer see us. I leaned against the ice-wall, more tired and drained than I'd ever been in my life. The plane was gone and I was safe. Safe? I wondered at these strange thoughts intruding into my mind.

Hypothermia, exhaustion, hunger and despair can combine to play tricks with the mind, but these thoughts seemed alien, coming from outside of myself. The men slumped, reflecting my own tiredness, but they seemed more distressed and unhappy than I. The sudden blizzard – not unusual at this time of year – drove us all back into the ice-grotto. Yet one man, a young radio operator called Massie, didn't return.

McCrudden swore and, wrapping his scarf firmly around his face, ventured back outside. Not to be outdone, I followed, the cold squall snatching my breath away. Standing on the edge of the shelf, I screwed up my eyes and peered out to sea. The wind ripped a hole in the snowstorm, and briefly we saw Massie's body floating away. If he wasn't already dead, then he would be shortly. There was nothing to be done for him.

McCrudden was downhearted yet curiously, I felt stronger somehow, as if new energy raced through my veins. Back in the grotto, the men were chipping stalactites from the ceiling and sucking on the ice. Their actions were sullen and lacklustre, and I wondered how many would survive the night. Wind howled and shrieked like death-bringing banshees around the entrance. Even so, we heard a deep rumble and splash as another piece of the berg broke off, cascading into the water. The berg shuddered. It could be only a matter of time before the mountain finally broke apart.

Taking some ice for myself, I descended the steps. It felt more relaxed and peaceful down here, in the presence of the aeons-old corpse. I guessed that once the tomb was opened up, the forces of decomposition had set in. The body looked older and more worn. As the dead man aged, he looked more and more like me.

There was no more to do. I killed my light and sat in darkness. I wasn't sure that I would survive the night myself. I expected hypothermia to claim me too but strangely, I felt more lively and powerful than I had for years.

I wasn't sure if I'd closed my eyes, as it made no difference in the pitch darkness. Images filtered into my mind. This time I stood in a stone chamber in a tower overlooking the marble city of Olathoë. It was filled with equipment such as rune-stones, crucibles, and jars of multi-coloured potions, while a crystal ball collected the polar sun's rays. There was an orrery of the solar system which included the dark ninth planet, Yuggoth, on top of a bookcase crammed with heavy volumes. Yet, despite the city's northerly location, the windows were open and a spring breeze rustled the pages of my book. It was a far different place from the storm-tossed iceberg.

Sitting in a heavily carved chair, I frowned with concentration as I studied a bronze-bound book before me. It was one of the treasures that we had saved from the ruins of our former home. Originally it had come from the blue-lit cavern of K'n-yan, deep beneath the Earth's surface. It had been written by a powerful wizard of the prehistoric, immortal people who dwelled there. As well as immortality, that race had strong extra-sensory powers, including telepathy, and they worshipped the bloated toad-God, Tsathoggua.

For years, I had striven to break the code and learn the ancient secrets of K'n-yan. Sometimes I thought I had cracked it, and the secrets of immortality would be laid open to me, but every time the esoteric knowledge slipped from my grasp. More than once, I had laid it aside in frustration.

But today, by comparing certain known sections of the Pnakotic Manuscripts with the bronze book, I realized that all the secrets hidden within were finally opened to me. Feverishly, I read those incantations which had long been concealed from me.

Finally, I was ready. Putting on my robe, I inscribed certain symbols onto the stone floor. The spell was surprisingly short, yet at the end I felt new power flood through me. I felt reinvigorated – invincible even, and laughed out loud in the knowledge that I had cheated death. I was now immortal, and blessed with powers of mental domination. I could control anybody with a weaker mind than mine – and that meant nearly every human being.

However, I needed to test my skills. Laughing, I commanded a slave be brought up to my room. The man quailed before me, as the slaves all had a superstitious dread of my chamber. Pointing to the open window, I commanded him to jump. Unhesitatingly, he leaped to his death. Soon, very soon, I would become the greatest wizard in Lomar and far beyond.

The vision faded as I dragged myself to my feet. The bitter cold had seeped into my bones. I stood before the tomb, my muscles too numb to shiver. What was going on here? Why was I getting these dreams? The dark chamber repelled me, and I flicked on my flashlight so I could locate the steps and escape to the surface.

Something about the cadaver caught my attention, and I turned to look. It had definitely aged, yet it didn't look as if it was decaying. It now looked more like a man of about forty – my age in fact. Against my better judgement, I approached it. It looked almost identical to me. The resemblance was more than uncanny – it was unnatural.

What were the chances of a man who had been dead for millennia looking like my twin? And what were the chances of our ship being torpedoed so that I could be washed up to discover his burial chamber? That went beyond mere coincidence. In that tomb, I could feel the unguessable wheels of cosmic destiny turning. As if I was always fated to have been drawn here – worse, lured here – but for what reason I had no way of knowing.

This time, I fled up the stairs at breakneck speed, desperate to escape from the tainted atmosphere of the sepulchre. Once again, I found I'd been in the corpse's company for longer than I'd intended. It was full dark up above. Even as I reached the grotto, I heard another long rumble and splash as yet another piece of the berg fell away. It couldn't be long before its centre of gravity shifted and the whole mountain collapsed. I needed to work quickly – and where had *that* thought intruded from?

"A couple more have died," McCrudden told me. "I didn't want to disturb you, so I took care of their bodies myself. Strange thing was, they took off their coats and jumped into the sea."

"They probably felt they couldn't take any more," I said. I felt glad it was dark. The clouds blotted out even the dim starlight as McCrudden studied my face.

"Are you all right, sir? You sound... different somehow."

"Fine. It's just this terrible cold. It's getting to us all. How many are left?"

"Only two, sir. Apart from us."

It will not be long then. I shook my head. The hypothermia was making me lose my mind. These invasive thoughts seemed to be taking over. Yet, strangely, I seemed stronger and healthier than I had when we originally washed up on this berg. I felt as if my time was coming.

No, I thought. *I will not lose my mind.* I could tell that I had access to vast realms of power and force just beyond the horizon. *No! Stop it! My name is William Abbott and I am the Third Officer of the* Glen Markie. *I was born in Oshawa, and I learned to sail on Lake Ontario. I have a wife and two daughters and I am just an ordinary man. My time is not coming – unless we are rescued soon, my time is almost over.*

For the first time, I almost welcomed my imminent death, and hoped I would die sane.

But I could not shake the knowledge that my time was almost come again. After the men of Lomar found what I was worshipping in exchange for my immortality, they placed magical bonds on me. The fools discovered my onyx altar to Tsathoggua in the hidden annex of my chambers, and chained my powers.

In vain, I told them how our earliest ancestors discovered it in the deep, black caves of N'Kai far beneath even the blue-lit cavern of K'n-yan. How it gave great powers to those who worshipped and sacrificed in the old ways. How the old ones granted their followers incredible abilities.

But the men of Lomar would not listen, even though I had proved my worth to them many times. They discovered the remains of certain failed experiments hidden in my cellars, and called me abhorrent, an abomination, and a hateful monster. They had ways of truly killing me, immortal though I was, casting my body into a volcano to be utterly destroyed.

But I cheated them. That night, in the cells beneath Olathoë's court, I entered a trance-like state that perfectly feigned death. Unfortunately it fooled everyone, even my fellow devotees of Tsathoggua. In order to avoid fear in the general population, the rulers of Olathoë allowed friends seemingly unconnected with my hidden worship to take my body.

However, they did not know the spells necessary to reawaken me, or even that I was simply entranced. Thinking I was truly dead, they took me to a tomb set high in a glacier on Mount Noton, propitiated the tame gods of Lomar, and sealed me in for what they imagined to be all eternity.

What is this? Had I not been a Catholic and forbidden such action by my faith, I would have taken my own life. The visions were getting worse as they got stronger. What *was* this rubbish about immortal wizards, blasphemous toad-shaped gods from deep beneath the Earth, and foul rites? It wouldn't be long before I, too, was claimed by the cold.

I stepped out of the ice-grotto and looked up at the massive pinnacle above the shelf. The skies had cleared, and the northern stars wheeled around their axis – Polaris, the pole star. The spire looked like a finger pointing directly towards that distant point of light. Suddenly, I felt a potent force surge through me, channelling up through that spire of ice towards that star.

Immediately, the skies erupted into the greatest display of Aurora Borealis, the northern lights, that I'd ever seen. Now I truly understood why the Vikings called them Witch Lights. Greens, reds, blues and pale, ghostly whites shimmered, swirled and danced from horizon to horizon. McCrudden and the remaining two crewmen came out of the ice-grotto's shelter and stared in awe and wonder, their problems forgotten as they watched the spectacle.

I cannot explain what happened next, except to say that I killed those two crewmen. How, I do not know. My incredible need for energy leaped out from me and drained their life-forces dry. I needed their souls to augment my own.

What was this insanity? This was impossible! You cannot kill people just by draining their souls, and I was no sorcerer from Earth's distant past. All the same, I watched as the two men clutched their heads and screamed out with pain and horror as they were squeezed dry to feed me. Their bodies collapsed onto the ice shelf and lay unmoving. One, Todd, fell face upward, his expression one of terrible fear.

As they died, I felt a surge of energy such as I have never felt before. It left me reinvigorated, more powerful. It was as though I was a much younger man, and had just fed well after a session of hard work. Yet it also felt unclean, and I knew this energy came from much less wholesome sources than food. I rubbed my face and even with my heavy gloves off, I couldn't feel any wrinkles. It was the skin of a much younger man.

McCrudden knelt beside the bodies and looked into their faces. I walked over, and he stared up at me. "Your eyes, they've changed."

He drew his clasp-knife from his coat pocket and popped open the blade. It glittered wickedly under those hellish Witch-Lights. The eldritch colours flickered over the metal.

Keeping his eyes fixed on mine, he stood slowly. "It's you. I don't know how or why, but you killed these men. Not just these two but all of them. You're that body from down below. Somehow it's taken you over, sir. You shouldn't have read that book or spent so long with the corpse. Well, you're not getting me – I'll see you in hell first."

He was fast, I'll give him that. Faster than lightning, he lunged at me, intending to bury that blade in my heart. I hadn't reached new immortality yet and I leaped backwards with a cry of alarm. Yet his speed was his undoing. I had fought the Gnophkehs in Lomar. I swung my hip into his, unbalancing him, and he slipped on a patch of smooth ice. The knife skidded away and dropped into the ocean.

McCrudden looked up at me with fear and hatred. "You..." he gasped, trying to rise. I concentrated briefly, and felt a burst of energy as I stole his life-force as well. I had enough. Now I could continue.

With one last, Herculean effort, I thrust the invading thoughts from my mind. McCrudden was right, in his stubborn clarity. It was that long dead wizard entombed below. Somehow, using who-knows-what devilish spells, he had come to life and taken me over. There can be no other explanation.

I will have to deal with him, while I still can. If I still can. However, in case I fail – and given his earlier control of me, that seems quite likely – the world needs to know about the horror we stumbled across in the Arctic wastes. So, while my tenuous control remains, I am writing this message. Partly, it is a warning, and partly, I am putting off the evil hour when I shall have to confront that which lies below. In a moment now, I shall seal this note within the brandy bottle, and cast it into the sea. If it is ever found, please pray for my soul. I go now to venture down one last time, to destroy the wizard's body.

*

Extract from the log of HMS Orford, *February 16th, 1942*
71.86 degrees North, 4.43 degrees East.

Returning from Murmansk, at approximately two hundred and fifty miles east-northeast of Jan Mayen, we found the sole survivor of a shipwreck clinging to the remnants of an ice floe. He was clutching a bronze book, written in no known language. We picked him up and placed him in the sickbay. The book was locked in the

Captain's safe in case it was a German code. Despite suffering from exposure and hypothermia, the young man seemed in good shape. He was, however, unable to tell us his name.

By the time we made it back to Liverpool, we'd lost far more casualties in our sickbay than original prognoses suggested. This should not be considered a reflection on Dr. Jacobson and his team. Their work has been excellent, and their efforts beyond reproach. The man we rescued from the iceberg made a complete physical recovery, but remained unable or unwilling to reveal his name.

When we docked, ambulances were summoned to carry the injured to hospital. However, an air raid occurred during that time. During the confusion, the man slipped his guards and disappeared. Searching the ship, we found the Captain's sentry dead at his post with the safe standing open. The sentry's body was unmarked, but its disturbing expression suggested that he died of fright. The bronze-bound book was the only item missing.

Assuming the man to be a German spy, and the book some sort of new code, we immediately reported his escape to the authorities. To date, we have not had any word of his capture.

*

From the curator of the Aberdeen Maritime Museum,
September, 1948

The bottle containing this message was found washed up on Newburgh beach near Aberdeen last month. The finder, a schoolboy out walking his dog, brought it to the museum. My colleagues consider it fascinating, an important depiction of the tragic extent to which extreme fear, cold and dehydration can affect a man's mind, particularly when coupled with superstitious beliefs.

I agree with them that it would be an astonishing discovery had anything truly had been found inside a chamber deep in an iceberg. If there were ever objects there, those materials must by now be at the bottom of the ocean, deposited as the berg melted.

The original message itself, as rescued from its bottle, lies in the museum's archives. The text above is a completely accurate copy.

After searching War Office records, both in Britain and Canada, nothing more can be ascertained of Third Officer William

Abbott. It is presumed that he perished on the ice, another unsung casualty of the recent War.

HMS Orford picked up a curious wreck survivor from a piece of ice in the region north and east of Jan Mayen Land not long after the date on Third Officer Abbott's account. The salient report is attached above. No sensible person could seriously consider the possibility of this being a survivor from the sinking of the *Glen Markie*.

If I may indulge myself however, I am not so quick to write Third Officer Abbott's account off as the ramblings of a dying mind. Nor, perhaps, am I entirely sensible regarding *HMS Orford's* stranded survivor. The fact of this man's escape into Liverpool's crowded streets makes me very uneasy. I rather wish that the *Orford* had not found that survivor and his book out there on the ice.

Some things are better off staying lost...

Seven Nights in a Sleep Clinic
by Saul Quint

First night

Diary of Julia Bard

My first glimpse of Hadley Hall was through the copse of elms that marked the boundary of the sprawling estate. A dark brick mansion, it was caught in a weak shaft of late afternoon sunlight. The taxi sped me on, across the last hill of the South Downs and past the old gatehouse towards the lovely, stately home. I am optimistic about the week ahead.

It has taken a long time to get my referral to the Hadley sleep clinic, and I'm encouraged about its location. It seems like I've suffered through endless months of failed treatments. The narcolepsy has blighted my life for three years now. Exhaustion, depression, forgetfulness... I no longer know who I am. This lovely place – an oasis of calm – gives me a real hope that I will be cured. Perhaps I can regain something of my old self.

The hall is idyllic. It retains much of its seventeenth century character, and one would never guess that it housed a modern sleep clinic. As the elderly receptionist explained the workings of the place, my eyes cast around its grand entrance hall, falling in turn upon the inglenook fireplace, ancestral portraits, stained glass, and carpeted staircase that spiralled upwards gracefully towards the bedrooms. My own room is a short walk from the top of the stairs. It's a comfortable affair with Victorian furnishings and a modern *en suite* bathroom. Leaded windows overlook the walled gardens to the hall's rear. After unpacking, I sought out the library and selected a novel. Then I returned with it to my room, to await a visit from my consultant. Light rain had begun to fall, misting the twilight. How I hope the doctor will successfully treat my condition. To be free of exhaustion would be a good thing, but to be free of the terrifying dreams would be a wonder. I cannot help but feel I am at the start of an exciting journey.

Taped conversation: Dr C. N. Hallowell and patient Ms. J. Bard [excerpt]

"It's a pleasure to meet you, Miss Bard. Is everything to your satisfaction?"

"You too, Doctor. Julia, please. Yes, it's a beautiful place."

"Good. I'll keep this brief, as you've had a long journey. Forgive me if I'm recording our conversations. It's for the sake of the records, as per your consent form. I just want to give you an idea of what's in store over the next seven nights. Put your mind at rest."

"Thank you. I'm looking forward to it."

"I've looked over your paperwork. No allergies or medical conditions, other than the narcolepsy. No major histories of illness in your family. No somnambulism – sleepwalking... That's all good."

"Just the sleepiness and the nightmares, doctor."

"Call me Clive. Well, I'll leave you alone now. We put the lights out at ten o'clock here, so you've got a couple of hours to relax. A nurse will come to your room at nine thirty and wire you up. There's about thirty wires, I'm afraid, which we'll simply stick onto you, from your eyelids to your feet. These connect to an electroencephalograph. You'll have heard the term EEG before. In addition to these, we'll attach a thermocouple to your nostrils and clip a pulse oximeter to your finger. You'll very quickly get used to them. That's it. This will allow our polysomnographs to monitor your brain activity, eye movements and muscle activity, as well as your respiratory air flow and pulse oximetry –"

"Oximetry?"

"The levels of oxygen in your blood. Overall it's a pretty sophisticated set up which, I hope, will give me plenty of insights into your condition. We'll have a chat every morning to discuss the previous day and night. Otherwise, beyond being wired up, you're free to relax. I suggest you walk if the weather is fine. You should have been shown our library and spa. Make good use of it all. The idea is to relax you as much as possible, so we can do our job."

"It all sounds very exciting, doctor. Clive. Thank you."

Journal of Dr C. N. Hallowell

Miss Julia Bard, age 37, 5'4" tall, 71kg. Came to the sleep lab presenting severe narcolepsy, diagnosed three years previously. She complains of constant tiredness, and is unable to prevent herself from falling asleep during the daytime. She also suffers frequent nightmares. The condition has affected her attention span and both short and long term memories. Her score on the Epworth Sleepiness Test is a highly elevated 23 out of 24, affirming highly excessive daytime sleepiness. Two courses of standard sleep therapy and a course of dexamphetamine have been provided through her local general hospital, but have proved unsuccessful. She appears tired and lethargic, and clearly pays little attention to her personal hygiene and presentation. Her features are drawn – baggy eyes accentuated no doubt by her dark hair and pale complexion – yet she is amiable and clearly keen to find a cure.

Second night

Taped conversation: Dr C. N. Hallowell and patient Ms. J. Bard [excerpt]

"How do you feel the night passed, Julia?"

"Good. I slept soundly."

"No problems with the wires? Got used to them?"

"Yes, I didn't notice them."

"How long do you think it took you to fall asleep after the nurse turned the lights out?"

"Oh, a long time. An hour, perhaps?"

"Why do you think that is?"

"Excitement, I suppose. I was excited to be here. A little nervousness too, I suppose."

"Would it come as a surprise if I were to tell you that you were asleep as soon as the light was turned out?"

"No! Really?"

"It's a common phenomenon. You passed quickly into deep sleep. In fact you spent a good deal of the night in deep sleep. How do you feel this morning?"

"Somewhat slow, as if I've been drugged."

"Despite all that good sleep?"

"Perhaps it's the nightmares."

"Tell me more about those. Can you remember what you dreamed last night?"

"Fairly well. As I was waiting to fall asleep, I began to hear the waves."

"Waves?"

"Yes. My dreams usually begin with them."

"And then?"

"The calling begins."

"Calling?"

"A soft pulse in my ears. It emerges from the waves, as if it was a tidal current, but gradually clarifies into a low pulse, like very bass whale song."

"Why do you refer to it as a calling?"

"Because I know that is what it is. I feel it drawing me to it, and I want to find it, but something is holding me back."

"You mean that you are unable to seek out the source of the calling?"

"Yes. I can sense where in the darkness it emanates from – it's a long way away – but something keeps me pinned to the bed. I can't move."

"Did anything else happen? Or has anything further happened when you've previously had this dream?"

"I have this dream every night. On some occasions I manage to rise from the bed and walk towards the calling. Last night I was able to walk as far as the stairs. I didn't though, did I? I mean physically?"

"No, you didn't sleep walk."

"What do you think it all means, Clive?"

"Clearly it's a repetitive dream you are experiencing when you enter deep sleep. You're spending a relatively large amount of the night in deep sleep, and the EEG indicates that your brain spends a disproportionately high amount of time in this dream. We'll get to the bottom of it."

Journal of Dr C. N. Hallowell

Miss Bard's symptoms are worse than initially suspected, and her case may not be as straightforward as I'd assumed. EEG indicated that she slept for nine hours, awaking naturally at 7.10am. Sleep onset latency was remarkably rapid. She entered NREM1 sleep within one minute of lights out, and REM sleep two minutes later. Subsequently, she went through only three sleep cycles, each of around three hours duration. Sleep spindles and K-complexes indicate that NREM1 and 2 were very brief, but NREM3 deep sleep was long and REM extremely long relative to each cycle. During REM, Miss Bard did not move. The dominance of REM increased from the first to the third cycle, and a gradual lowering of blood oximetry was observed over time, as if the longer she slept, the more engrossed in deep sleep she became. During NREM3 and REM sleep she snored loudly, at times sounding almost batrachian. During our consultation this morning she appeared very detached and dreamy, often showing little understanding of where she was.

Diary of Julia Bard

How exciting this is! I can't help feeling a familiarity with this place, a strong sense of *déjà vu*. Clive seems particularly helpful, and I feel confident that Hadley Hall will help me regain something of my old self. Despite having to retire to my room for several naps during the afternoon, I managed to explore the secluded grounds during breaks in the rain. It is relatively warm for autumn, and at times a little sun shone through the grey clouds. I already feel a good distance from the world at large, protected, cushioned. Nothing else seems to matter.

All the wires! It took a good half hour for the nurse to get them attached to me, and they are so many they seem like the tentacles of some sleeping denizen of the ocean depths. They were no inconvenience, however. It is almost as if I were born to wear them, although it took me what seemed like an age to fall asleep.

When I did, the dream was particularly vivid. The calling was strong, and I responded quickly. The carpet was soft under my bare feet as I rose to answer. I found the strength to leave the building and walked through the moonlit gardens towards the pulsing noise. I could feel the quality of the air change as the moisture built up. At first a thin mist hung in the moonlight, but as I left the gardens for the nearest field it thickened into a silvery fog. Somewhere within it, I knew I should find the steps, and that when I did their presence would be my secret.

Third night

Journal of Dr C. N. Hallowell

Julia slept for ten hours, waking naturally at 8.00am. During sleep she went through only two sleep cycles. Her brain activity remained remarkably high, with heightened oxygen consumption and signs of physical arousal well in excess of those typically observed in REM sleep. Her secretion of acetylcholine was high, indicating considerable neural excitement, and EEG waves were higher than those typical of waking states, indicative of heightened dreaming for a longer duration than on night one. The most plausible interpretation of the EEG data is that she was in an even deeper sleep state than the first night. This is a remarkably rare set of observations.

Taped conversation: Dr C. N. Hallowell and patient Ms. J. Bard [excerpt]

"Well, you've had another good night's sleep, Julia."

"Yes, I feel deeply relaxed."

"You do seem to have been dreaming for an extraordinary amount of time. What can you tell me about that? Did you hear the calling again?"

"Oh, yes. This time it was raining heavily, and the calling came to me from beyond the trails of rainwater on the windowpanes."

"Did you follow it?"

"Yes, I did. The window was stiff with age but I managed to force it open enough to get outside."

"Through the window?"

"Yes. I flew."

"So you were a bird? Or a bat?"

"No, neither. I'm not sure what I was, other than *me*. I felt the same."

"Did you notice your arms or legs?"

"No, it was too dark."

"Where did you fly?"

"Into the mists."

"What did you find in the mists?"

"Nothing, yet."

Diary of Julia Bard

I feel a great improvement already. I slept deeply for much of the afternoon, and otherwise took walks in the gardens. The food here leaves something to be desired. There is far too much of an emphasis on oily fish, which one of the nurses told me was to raise patients' omega three acids and "get your brain used to the idea of relaxing." It seems to me that the place even smells faintly of the sea.

A soft mist has replaced the rains, although in my dreams the two mingled into one. I soon found the stairs, the wisps of mist parting to reveal the damp granite steps leading down into the darkness. I could sense the moisture in the air, and the stone smelled musty, like an old cellar. I felt vividly aware – sharp – as if I had newly awoken. Far from feeling that I was dreaming, it seemed to me that I was recapturing the wakefulness that I'd lost so long ago.

I slowly descended the steps, steadying myself against the wet stone. I must have gone down twenty feet or more before they came to an end. The darkness immediately grew more intense. Soupy. Steadying my breath, I took several cautious steps forward and found myself sloshing through shallow water on a hard floor, breaking a brackish scum that covered the water like a carpet. The place had a strong fishy stink that reminded me of low tide in my hometown's small harbour.

The feeling of *déjà vu* was overwhelming. It seemed not only that I had been here before, but that I was returning to a familiar place.

I emerged in a narrow alleyway, walls of dark, wet stone rising above me to left and right. It was illuminated by a pale green light that emanated from small, silver lamps hung here and there from stone brackets. The silence was overwhelming. What had happened to the calling? The sound of my feet sloshing through the water cut through the stillness and carried well beyond the oppressive walls. I walked for some time, although precisely how long remains unclear. The surfaces of the coarse stone were covered in strange mineral crusts and growths that resembled limpets. In fact, everywhere there was a sense of the oceanic. It felt as if I were on the ocean floor, in some immense sunken city.

I walked for some further time, without turning. The alleyway didn't change. To my left and right, similar alleys opened off of it every fifty feet or so. The relentless similarity was unsettling. In places, some lanterns were broken. The shadows seemed almost tangible where the pale green light no longer fell, as if it were some kind of dark fungus that grew when the lack of light allowed. In these pools of deeper shadow, the strange mineral growths seemed thicker. In places, they jutted from the walls like stalactites in a cave. I walked on, and yet more time passed.

I came to the first features I'd seen since the lanterns. Here and there were small windows in the alley walls. Barely a foot square, unglazed, they opened a little over my head height, revealing shadowy rooms empty of furnishings or signs of life. Like the walls of the alleyway, these were covered with the strange mineral crusts. I peered into every one of them as I passed. They held nothing to break their monotony. How the interiors were accessed, I had no clue. I could just about make out corridors leading further into the darkness, but none of the alleys I'd explored so far offered any means of access.

Then I saw it.

A shadow in the back corner of one of these miserable rooms shifted, emerging into the dim green light that a lantern, above the small window, threw into the room. It was a bulky, humanoid shape. Dim eyes resembling two molluscs in their shells stared at me. The shadowy form shifted momentarily, and took a tentative step towards me as it realised my presence. We stared at each other, silently, perhaps both of us as surprised as each other. Then, just as suddenly as I'd seen it, it was gone – silently receding into the shadows of the passage that lead away from the light and further into the dark interior.

Fourth night

Taped conversation: Dr C. N. Hallowell and patient Ms. J. Bard [excerpt]
"How did you sleep?"

"Wonderfully. I must admit I did take several naps during the day but that didn't stop me from getting a good eight hours last night."

"Your sleep diary indicates that they were more than naps. You slept for six hours during the day, and then ten hours overnight."

"That much?"

"I want to try to combat your daytime sleepiness, Julia. For that reason, I am prescribing a morning dose of a stimulant, commencing this morning. I hope this will keep you awake. Are you happy with that?"

"Yes, of course. I didn't realise I was sleeping quite that much."

"How do you feel otherwise?"

"Good. I feel sharper and more awake, ironically."

"Well, you're certainly not suffering from a sleep deficit. Do try to get more fresh air and exercise."

"I did walk through the grounds several times."

"And the dreams?"

"They were the same as previous nights. I hear the calling, so I walk out of the hall and through the grounds, and the mists thicken. Somewhere within the mists, I find some steps."

"Steps? Where?"

"I'm not sure, it's all so misty. They open up into the darkness beneath my feet, and I descend."

"Is the calling coming from down the stairs?"

"Yes. So I descend, and come across a narrow alleyway between stone buildings of immense size."

"Anywhere you recognise?"

"Well, I can't recall it – it's nowhere one could visit – but it felt very familiar."

"Are you happy to be there, or frightened?"

"Happy, I think."

"Give me some more detail. Or is this just a vague impression?"

"No, it actually seems very clear. I'm happy to be there, as if I'm returning home. There is darkness, a strong fishy smell like a harbour, and a sense of breaking the shallow water that covers the floor as I walk."

"You say it's dark. Is it night?"

"I don't think so. Night doesn't seem to exist there. It's just dark. I can't see anything. All I can do is to feel my way along the walls, which seem rough, like barnacles on the bottom of a boat."

"How long do you feel that you stayed there?"

"An hour or two, perhaps. I don't really have a sense of time. But I don't move fast or walk very far."

"What else do you see?"

"Nothing."

"How does it feel when you get further from the steps? Are you still happy? Or more cautious?"

"I suppose I'm a little nervous. Butterflies in my stomach would be the way to describe it. The silence unnerves me. That and the darkness."

"You say you can't recall the place, but you feel like you recognise it? Could it reflect memories of somewhere from your youth, perhaps?"

"No, not at all. I sense that the walls rise to impossible heights above me, and that the alleys continue relentlessly over vast scales. I can't think of anywhere I've been which could remotely resemble it. It's more of an impression, a sense of overwhelming scale."

Diary of Julia Bard

I feel much more alive now, sharp, observant, energetic. This place is having such a beneficial effect. It is as if my senses have awoken again after a long sleep, and I am eager to engage with the world once more. The day passed all too slowly. I dozed, or watched the dull, drowsy rain sliding down the window leads. When I managed to sleep I heard the calling, but it was faint this time, as if its strange cadences are amplified by the night and muted by day. Exploring the grounds during my daytime dream, I anxiously sought the entrance to the city. A pale sunlight had dispersed the mist, and I could not find the steps. I am impatient to return to the silent, brooding place. The night cannot come too quickly.

When lights out finally came, I fell asleep instantly. I was relieved and happy, sailing on light feet towards the calling, skipping down the stairs to the familiar alleyways. I headed straight back to the windows, sloshing through the scummy water from lantern to lantern, glancing up the invariable side alleys as I passed them. I knew that there was something I needed to find, the source of the calling.

I somehow knew that if I could do this, everything would be clear – the reason for my existence, my purpose, my identity. Yes, finding the source of the calling would restore my entire person. It would finally cure me of my ill health. The city itself was the cure, and Hadley Hall was simply the way to the city.

The windows revealed only silent, empty rooms. I must have passed thirty or so of these invariant openings, yet I saw no movement, no shadowy inhabitants. Time passed in that peculiar silence. On and on went the alleyway. I kept moving in a straight line, fearing to turn in case I would be unable to retrace my steps.

Why did that matter, though? Perhaps remaining in the city would not be so bad. After all, I felt no tiredness nor hunger, and the strange sense of *déjà vu* that was constantly with me was reassuring. I felt the place was safe. I was coming home.

I dimly remembered — or perhaps imagined – those days so long ago when the stone walls were brightly plastered, when the lamps burned fiercely with a golden light, and when the alleys bustled... But with what or whom? That was still unclear. Who were my co-inhabitants who'd made this place lively so many aeons ago? I could glimpse them only in the periphery of my memory, as if time had grown over them like stalactites. They coyly lurked at the edge of my mind, enticing me to excavate them from their geological tomb.

Something shook me out of my thoughts and back into the alleyway. I sensed movement. A shadow had passed briefly through a lantern's pool of light ahead. It was something bulky, its mass disturbing the dim green luminescence, like an underwater current passing over the sea floor. Wisps of shadow intermingled with the light as if some silent breeze had disturbed the dust of ages. I froze as it settled, and the alley returned to its familiar stillness. Something was watching me from the shadows ahead. Who was this? For the first time, I was unnerved. I was still new to the city, and I wasn't ready to engage with one of its denizens. I was a long way from the steps. Perhaps I'd explored enough for a while. I turned on my heels and began to retrace my path, trying now to avoid the pools of green light and letting the shadows disguise my passing.

It didn't help. As I passed each lantern. I stole a quick glance behind me, nervously scanning the alleyway for my observer. Every time I did so it was there, keeping enough distance between us to remain indistinct. I began stopping for several heartbeats each time I turned, but the bulky shadow would stop too, always at the extreme of my vision. I strained my eyes trying to grasp at any detail. It seemed tall – perhaps some ten feet or so – and was otherwise humanoid in shape, if somewhat indistinct. At times, it appeared as if it were wearing some voluminous cloak of shadow that was swaying in a silent wind.

Journal of Dr C. N. Hallowell

Julia slept frequently during the day. Too much. To counter this, I am prescribing 200mg Modafinil daily. She claimed to have taken several walks, but CCTV confirms that she did not leave her sleep room – either she is delusional, or lying. She slept for a full twelve hours. For the first time her sleep was disturbed. A pronounced rise of delta waves indicated a considerable lengthening of NREM stage 3 sleep accompanied by a correspondingly high delta EEG value. During the NREM3 Julia was breathing rapidly, displayed a reddening of facial and chest skin, and sweated profusely. At times she thrashed her limbs and made loud croaking noises. On three occasions her eyes opened to reveal profoundly dilated pupils, although attempts to wake her out of these obviously disturbing dreams failed.

Her memory of vivid dreams is impressive, yet runs counter to our observations. Assuming she is not fabricating these, they are highly detailed, and do not appear to contain people or places common to her life. Nor do they appear to be disturbing, according to her memories [NB: again, she could be delusional or lying]. The apparently endless, labyrinthine alleyways are a notable feature – could they represent the neural pathways of her brain? Or entoptic images from her retina?

Fifth night

Journal of Dr C. N. Hallowell

Julia slept most of the day in her room, leaving it only to eat a light lunch. I have increased her daily dose of Modafinil to 400mg. Nurses report her behaviour as distant, with her eyes dilated and her movement sluggish. She has complained of being cold, despite the acceptable temperature indoors, and in conversation can appear confused. Despite attempts to make her take fresh air and exercise, she is becoming more detached and lethargic each day. She still shows diligence in writing a daily diary, and her infrequent conversation suggests that she is anxious to keep this in detail.

Our overnight polysomnograph observations are worrying. Julia spent almost the entire night in NREM3/REM; I have never experienced such pronounced time spent in a state of deep sleep. Her batrachian snoring has become very loud, and almost continuous. She emits frequent loud croaks as if she is trying to communicate in this animalistic way. Both her pulse and core body temperature drop to dangerously low levels during sleep, and she has begun to exhibit occasional apneas of 5-10 seconds duration. The nurse has noted that Julia's skin becomes extremely wet, too.

Diary of Julia Bard

I have been able to spend almost all of my time exploring the silent city. Hadley Hall has receded into the distance as my eyes become accustomed to the green light and thick shadows. Now I do not need the mists, do not need to seek out the steps. I simply have to think of the city and I am there, as if part of me is always there, waiting for the rest of me to return. It is only when I return to it that I feel whole again.

I have started enjoying the comforting splosh of the rimy water. I walked through it with increasingly bold steps, feeling the growths on the cold stone walls, passing by familiar lanterns. It seemed to take less time to reach the windows. As I passed each one I paused to squint into the gloom.

The rooms were still as devoid of occupants as they ever had been. My eyes must now be more accustomed to the dark however, as I could discern details that had previously escaped me. The interior walls were constructed of a shiny, translucent material, like a marine shell. It glimmered in the pale green light, describing beautiful swirls that had an almost hypnotic effect on me. Each window revealed walls of differing patterns. The greens, greys and whites curved gracefully, like the internal chambers of gastropods on a grand scale. It was as if I was looking at sections cut through vast marine fossils.

Finally, I felt confident enough to turn into an unfamiliar alleyway. It was a good decision. The alleyway soon came to an end, and for the first time I was presented with something new. I had emerged onto a balustraded terrace which ran around all the sides of an immense courtyard or plaza. For the first time I could see an alien sky – a polychromatic luminescence of greens, blues, yellows and pinks which illuminated the plaza and the gigantic buildings that surrounded it. Beyond them, in the far distance, I could see vast towers and minarets on a rocky horizon.

As I leaned forward to peer down into the plaza, I noticed that the stone was dark granite, veined with red. It was intricately carved in low relief to resemble intertwined tentacles. From these, huge eyes stared out in places. The shiny black stone lent a striking realism to these eyes. The veins shot through it added to the impression that the balustrade could have been made from real marine organisms, fossilised aeons ago. Far below, the plaza was lit by a pinkish luminescence, airier than the green to which

I had become accustomed. Small motes, like disturbed sediment, floated everywhere, as if this truly were the ocean floor. The plaza was covered with the same scummy green water as the alleys. In its centre rose some vast, rusty machinery, long since fallen silent, a convoluted mix of towering columns and massive counterweights. It resembled an agglomeration of titanic oil pump stacks. Perhaps the old inhabitants of this place had actually been drilling for oil or some other substance.

Gradually, I went half way around the terrace. Although other alleyways stretched away from it back into the darker green light, I could find no obvious way down onto the plaza. Like the alleys and their small windows, it seemed as if freedom of movement was being restricted deliberately. When I reached the opposite side of the terrace from my starting point, I turned. I gasped in awe, as my eyes fell on the largest thing I'd ever seen. A vast monolith, of the same dark stone, rose thousands of feet into the polychrome sky. It dominated the distant horizon with ominous presence. At its summit, barely visible in the hazy light, I could just discern the glint of what I took to be gigantic doors. They were a point of brilliant bronze, capping the monolith like the beam of a lighthouse. Somehow, I knew the monolith was the source of the calling. I had to find it.

But I was not alone. I had been so preoccupied with the monolith that I had not noticed that my observer had been following me. It now stood in the shadows in the corner of the terrace. I paused for several heartbeats as we stood facing each other. Then it came towards me, silently gliding as if it were a sunset shadow lengthening across the terrace. I could discern no details whatsoever, as if it were comprised of blackness itself. A whispering breeze of darkness.

But it spoke, and I felt its hoarse voice rush past me like the wind.

"You must leave here. Leave, and never return." Its words were rasping, hasty.

"Who are you?" I managed to stutter.

It was already gone.

Taped conversation: Dr C. N. Hallowell and patient Ms. J. Bard [excerpt]

"I must admit that I am concerned, Julia. You're sleeping much of the day, and spending most of the night in deep sleep. The medication is obviously having no effect despite the strong dose. How are you feeling?"

"I feel well, like I'm recovering."

"But you're not. You're sleeping most of the time, despite the medication. You're still dreaming, I presume?"

"Yes. The same dream."

"Any change? Have you explored further?"

"No. I walk further, but things remain the same. Nothing changes."

"When you say you walk further, do you feel you are spending longer exploring the alleyways?"

"Yes, much longer."

"Could you try avoiding this dream for me?"

"Why? I enjoy it."

"I want to establish if you have any control over the dream. Will you try for me?"

Sixth night

Diary of Julia Bard

Clive has asked me to try to avoid the dream, but of course I'm not going to stop exploring the city. Not now that I'm so near to discovering myself again. The calling is still strong when I'm awake, and I know that whatever waits at the top of that monolith wants me to find it, wants me to discover its truth. It wants to heal me. It wants me to wake again.

I know now that the longer I spend exploring the city the more whole I become. It is like exploring my own self. Nothing else is as important.

With the exception of a brief period of wakefulness during which I ate, I have managed to sleep through the day. I was only vaguely aware of the nurse wiring me up for the night. Good. The calling came immediately upon wakefulness, and now my head throbs with it. As soon as I fall into sleep the pain goes, and I am calm once again.

I was immediately back in the alley, but this time I took the first left turn that I came to. My plan was to take a second left turn as soon as I could, and to explore in the opposite direction to which I had gone every time beforehand. This would surely take me closer to the monolith. Perhaps, at the same time, it would allow me to avoid my pursuer, whatever it was. I walked for some time, passing several dozen lanterns. Once again the alleyways presented a relentless repetition of damp walls, pools of green light, and small windows. But then I came across something new, and my heart leapt. The stone bracket holding a lantern had fallen from the wall. This had pulled some of the stone wall away, enlarging the window opening underneath. Although the slimy crusts had overgrown the breach, with a bit of luck the space would be just large enough for me to crawl through.

I would be able to access the interior.

With some effort, I was able to pull myself through into the darkness, dropping down head first onto the room's wet floor. My elbow jarred against something hard, which fell against the stone wall with a sharp, tinny scrape. It was a small brass lantern, intricately wrought, inside which I could see a wick of some rubbery substance. Someone must have come here before. I lifted it by the short iron chain from which it was suspended. As I did so, it lit up with a pale green light that dispersed a little of the blackness of the room, glinting off of its strange, molluscan walls. I would at least have some light to explore the place by.

Cautiously, I continued deeper into the building. The lantern's pale light swung with the movement of my arm, alternately extending into the inky darkness and contracting about my person, like the light of a ship's lantern played on the night sea. Despite holding the source of light, my arm was indistinct. If anything, the green luminescence seemed only to throw my own body more into shadow, at the same time emphasising its bulk. It felt as if my body were not my own, but had become in some way better suited to this place. A short passage led out of the room, deeper into the building's interior, and I slowly edged along it. I came to a second chamber, walled with the same shell-like materials, but as I passed out of the passage, I noticed that this one held something large. I raised and stilled the lantern, playing its light slowly around the centre of the small room.

I immediately felt a cold terror strike through me like a knife. At first I thought I was looking at the tomb of a medieval knight – a thick stone sarcophagus supporting the life sized carving of an armoured figure – but I soon realised that this was no medieval effigy. It was instead a chitinous parody of a human being, some ten feet in length, laid out as if in a morgue. What I'd initially taken to be a chainmail throat-guard hanging from a helmet was in fact a mass of tentacles, dangling from the rubbery mass that passed as the creature's chin and neck. I froze, my eyes straining to discern further detail in the dim light. The thing's exoskeleton was scaly and black, and soaked up my lantern's light like a fathomless void. A singular, lidless eye the size of a dinner plate stared rheumily from the centre of a pustulent face. Two arms, each as thick as tree trunks, terminated in crablike claws, folded amidst the tentacles on the folds of the thing's chest. Long, spindly legs sported similar claws instead of feet.

The thing exuded a sickening sense of power. My stomach turned, yet I was for some time unable to draw my eyes away from the disgusting creature. Mustering what concentration I could, I forced my horrified gaze downwards, away from the thing, to the side of what I'd taken to be its stone sarcophagus. The black stone there was carved in low relief. The flickering light and dark thrown by my lantern animated a sickening scene. It was finally too much for me. I was looking at something carved – by what hand? – aeons ago, but its meaning was clear. A creature similar to that now lying on the stone block was shown standing on some kind of platform. In front of it were several naked human beings, each cowed in an attitude of subservience. Under its foul, crablike legs was another human, crushed almost beyond recognition.

It was all I could do not to scream. I frantically scrambled out of the window and back into the alley. I ran for several minutes, and by the time I paused to catch my breath, I was soaked through from the water I'd splashed through and fallen into during my panic. I tried as best I could to retrace my steps, but in my terrified delirium I must have run up an unfamiliar alleyway. I was lost.

Journal of Dr C. N. Hallowell
Once again Julia spent much of the day sleeping. During her rare periods of wakefulness she remains distant, almost as if sleepwalking. I am concerned with the further decline of her blood oximetry. We connected her to 10cm pressure oxygen for the duration of the night, but it had little effect. She spent the night entirely in NREM3/REM sleep again, this time highly active, flailing her limbs, sweating, eyes often rolling up into her head, repeatedly croaking a gibberish word at loud volume. If I were to attempt to write out the sound, then perhaps "hru-lye-eh" would come close.

Taped conversation: Dr C. N. Hallowell and patient Ms. J. Bard [excerpt]
"Julia, can you try to wake for a few minutes, please? Just to have a short chat?"

"I... Tired. Too much to do."

"Too much to do? Are you dreaming again?"

"I can't find the steps."

"You can't find the way back? You're only dreaming. Just make some effort to wake now."

"The thing is following me again."

"You're only dreaming, Julia. Remember that. What is following you?"

"The shadow."

"Julia? Hello? It's Clive here. Dr Hallowell. You remember?"

"I can't find the steps."

Seventh night

Journal of Dr C. N. Hallowell
Julia's condition has deteriorated considerably. She slept for most of the day, rising only for an hour or so in the evening. During this time she displayed classic somnambulism, failing to respond to any external stimuli. In this period, she locked herself in her room

and wrote what turned out to be her last diary entry. Shortly after this, she fainted, and has subsequently declined further. She takes only shallow breaths through her mouth, with a constant rasp that suggests some fluid build-up in her lungs. Her incidences of apnea have risen to around 50 per hour, and she has become incontinent, releasing an almost constant trickle of dark, viscous urine that has a strong, saline smell. Her systolic blood pressure has fallen below 50, her diastolic below 30. Her skin is very cold to the touch, and has taken on a blue-green colouring. Her sleep is very restless, and between rasping croaks she repeats "I can't find the steps," as well as the strange "hru-lye-eh" croak from the previous day.

Julia has proven unresponsive to physical stimuli as well as to stimulant drugs. At 23.47, we suffered a brief power cut, which lasted seven minutes. EEG monitoring of the patient was re-established at 23.53. At 23.59 she began to slip into coma. An ambulance was called, which collected her at 00.34.

Diary of Julia Bard
The calling was a deception. I am unable leave this place. Am I still dreaming, or is it some new reality? I walked from alleyway to alleyway, searching for the steps, but I know that I will not find them. I have examined the relentless series of windows, wondering if their small size is designed to keep the denizens in, rather than – what? – out. Eventually, I discovered another opportunity for ingress. In a corner of another small plaza, a huge rusting piece of machinery had fallen against one of the walls, tearing a hole. Once again I lit my way with the brass lantern. The pale green light was no longer comforting, but, I realised, a grim necessity. Without it, my movements would be restricted to the lamp-lit alleys.

I entered into a room, as empty and familiar as its twins. A short passage led into a further chamber, and to my horror I saw, in the darkness, another of the hideous creatures lying on its stone tomb. This time I steeled my nerves, edging around the cold walls to a second passage beyond. It led into a further chamber, with yet another of the creatures. I braved one more passage further into the gloomy structure, and encountered yet another creature. The terrible reality of the place then dawned upon me. There would be endless chambers in this place. Countless rooms with countless passages connecting countless creatures, all lying in their silent tombs. Thousands – millions – of these foul, tentacled things, lying still in their silent parody of a city.

The worst realisation of all slowly crept over me. As I stood examining the third creature, I realised that its torso gently rose and fell. It was almost imperceptible, but the thing was alive. It was all I could do to stop from bolting in blind terror. I could barely bring myself to pass the other two creatures as I retraced my steps. The same glacial rise and fall of their chitinous chests confirmed the worst. They were all alive.

My fear got the worst of me as I left that morgue, and I ran across the plaza. I didn't stop until I'd reached the familiarity of another alley, although this one was poorly lit. Catching my breath, I noticed the familiar movement in the shadows. My follower was there.

"Who are you?" I fumbled breathlessly with my lantern, trying to direct its light at the figure, but only picked out the blackness into which it had slipped. I heard it splashing in the slimy water before it spoke.

"A friend. Believe me. Put the lantern down and walk away from the light." There was a sense of urgency in the way the voice hissed out the command. What was it? It certainly didn't sound human. "You'll attract—"

"I can't. I won't be able to see." I pulled the lantern closer to me as if to prevent anyone snatching it away. "Who are you?"

"Can you still try to leave this place, or are you already trapped?"

"I can't find the steps." Terror flooded me as I realised I could not escape.

"Then you are trapped."

"Who are you?"

"Like you, I followed the calling. It lured me here, and I explored – just like you – until I lost the way, and could not leave this place."

"Where are we?"

"I don't know."

"Are we alone here? Are there others like us?"

"I have seen some others. Shadows, like us. Eventually, the place traps everyone who answers the calling."

"Where are they all?"

"Scattered around. The place is vast, perhaps even endless."

"Why have we been lured here?"

It paused for a moment. "I don't know. You've seen the sleeping creatures. They wait."

"For what? What are they?"

"For the awakening. When the bronze doors will open and the one in whose image they were created will rise again."

"I thought they were dead at first. I thought this place was a vast tomb."

"In a way, it is. That is not dead which can eternal lie..."

"Wh—?"

Our conversation was interrupted by a deafening noise from way above us, a horrible, unearthly sound like whale song, if whales sang of madness and death. The pale light from my lantern spluttered and failed. We were plunged into an all-encompassing darkness. The noise pulsated through my body. It was as if gigantic nightmares were swimming miles above my head.

"What is it?" I shouted. The horrible noises were terrifying, and truly alien in nature. "What is it?" I screamed, tears welling in my eyes. There was no reply. I fumbled around, trying to locate my follower by touch, but soon realised I could do nothing further in this impenetrable darkness. I sat, and slowly the silence returned. Now and then I caught dim flickers of light, whispers of sound. "Can you try to wake up?" someone asked. "It's Clive." ... "She's writing in her sleep." But I couldn't awaken. Gradually the lights and sounds faded, and I was alone.

Now there is only one more thing to do. I grope around, and finally locate the steps. They are cold and rough, and cut my hands, but I am past caring. I begin to climb the monolith.

Mykes Reach
by William Couper

The old man slithered out from the side of the building, his eyes intent on her. No one else making their way in seemed to notice him. Fearful, she backed away, ready to run. His strange eyes followed her, their colour impossible to determine. As he edged closer, she became aware of how tall he was. Danger emanated from him in a thick aura, yet she couldn't bring herself to run.

"You've caught Father Polzic's eye," he said. His voice was an enervating rasp.

"Uh... Who?" she asked.

"There are many who want to see what you do. You have their support."

"Who?"

He turned, sliding away down the street and out of view. She was left with the impression of there being something wrong about his body. Parts of it didn't move the way a normal body ought to. She stood in front of the building for several moments, trying to decide what had just happened. She was still in a daze when she walked inside.

"Good morning, Bridget," said Dylan, her supervisor. "You almost didn't make it this morning." His face, too soft to be truly handsome, was set in an expression of mild amusement.

She flashed him an uncertain smile and walked to her cubicle, aware of him watching her the whole way. She adjusted her modest blue skirt, afraid it had ridden up. Though she didn't like him, she couldn't afford to alienate him if she wanted to get anywhere in the company. Looking unkempt would definitely risk alienation.

The printout on her desk was conspicuous enough, but the weird fungi were what caught her eye. Each individual of the cluster was round, black with luminous green and blue swirls breaking up the surface. The colour and size would have been enough to get her attention, but they floated half an inch above the paper.

She moved the paper and they moved too, as if rooted to it. Curious, she tried to slide her finger under the cluster. One of the spheres quivered and sprayed a cloud of spores in her face. She gasped, coughed, and discovered she couldn't stop.

"Hey, are you okay?" asked her friend Paula. "Oh, shit!"

Bridget barely heard the words. She coughed and hacked, trying to get the tickling feeling out of her throat. She was blinded by gritty particles clinging to her eyes, and her tears did nothing to dislodge them. Her breath shuddered through her throat as she gasped.

Someone grabbed her arm and dragged her away from the computer, across the office floor. There was talking, but she couldn't make out the words.

Water hit her in the face, cold and sudden. For a moment she stopped coughing in shock.

"Are you okay?" Dylan asked.

She managed to gasp once, before succumbing to her coughing fit again. Dylan threw more water in her face, until she had to stop him.

"I'm fine! I'm fine!" she spluttered.

After a few minutes of recovery, she looked around and saw she was in the gents' toilets. She turned to him and he shrugged.

"Don't worry," he said, a smile on his soft face. "Nobody's going to get in. What happened?"

"Weird mushroom things on a printout of an account."

He frowned. "Are you sure about that?"

"Pretty sure. I stared at them for long enough."

"Let's take a look at this."

They left the gents' toilets, and went to her desk. Sure enough, the same green and blue mushrooms floated above the bit of paper. The fungi quivered as though excited. She felt like they were waiting for her.

"Well, that's unfortunate," Dylan said, getting too close to her. "I think you might have to go home."

"No," she said, almost panicking. She couldn't afford a day off so soon after starting the new job. During her first week, she'd assessed her co-workers and the management, and determined this was the place she could progress her career. "I'll stay. I can sit somewhere else."

"That's not a good idea." He smiled, almost as if about to laugh. "It's admirable you want to stay and work, but go home. Some arrangements need to be made. It's fine. Get home and relax, come back tomorrow."

The bus back home was empty. Before she really knew it, she was walking up the stairs to her flat. It seemed empty without Donny there, and he wouldn't be home for hours. She plonked her handbag on the sofa and went into the bathroom to wash. Her face still felt strange. The soap and water only made the tingling worse. She washed and scrubbed again, but the unpleasant sensation remained.

Her face was uncomfortably warm when she came out of the bathroom, the skin pink and inflamed. She looked with despair at the mess of the flat. It was the same mess they'd been living in for a couple of years now. She set to work tidying the place.

"Isn't that your supervisor?" Donny asked behind her, making her start.

She looked at the time, and realised she'd been sitting at the laptop for six hours since she'd finished throwing rubbish out. He'd come back home, carrying bags of Indian food, and she hadn't heard him.

She worried about his weight.

Neither of them were thin, but Donny had developed a bulging gut in the last three years. She thought it related to his turning down a promotion to exit office work. The weight seemed to go along with a general scruffier appearance – long, uncombed hair, heavy stubble, old clothes.

He frowned and looked at the time. "Why are you home so early?"

"You wouldn't bloody believe it," she replied.

"I don't believe a lot of what happens at your job." He stopped. "Hang on. Didn't we discuss that?" He pointed to the screen. "I thought we'd agreed no work stuff at home."

She looked at the screen and found she'd clicked onto the company website. Strange, she was sure she'd been on a social network site before talking to him.

When she looked at him again, he looked hurt and confused. "I know you want to get ahead," he said, "but we need time for us."

"Of course I want to get ahead. One of us fucking has to."

"I was burned out. I'm happy where I am."

"You got lazy, Donny. You couldn't be bothered any more. If we want to keep living here, we need to make enough money. You want to stay in the same place, I want to get ahead so that paying for this place isn't going to leave us wiped out every month. Are you ready to help with that?"

He pursed his lips, snatched up the bags of food, went into the kitchen and started to bang about. She shook her head and went back to look at the bank's website.

*

"I don't think you should go in today. You look like you've got a rash or something." Donny was pulling on one of his tatty polo shirts to go with his jeans. She was already wearing her royal blue skirt and cream blouse.

"I can't afford to take another day off. If I want to get anywhere, I'll have to show how dedicated I am. Anyway, I feel fine." Not entirely true.

She felt different. He was right about the rash, it took all her will to stop from scratching constantly. She wasn't about to tell him and give him a reason to argue against her going into work, though. Other than the itchiness, she felt energised and refreshed.

"There's dedication and there's just being irresponsible. What if something's badly wrong with you and you're neglecting your health just to get a couple of extra quid?"

"A little dramatic, don't you think? Some dust in the face isn't going turn into a serious health problem."

He frowned in confusion for a moment, then gave way to worry. "Tell that to the people with asbestos-related lung cancer."

She laughed. "It wasn't anything as bad as bloody asbestos. How many mushrooms have you heard of that produce asbestos?"

"Mushrooms? What the hell happened to you yesterday?"

Unconsciously, she rubbed her arm, and stopped when she realised. Donny didn't comment on it, so she assumed he hadn't noticed. She couldn't meet his hard gaze. "I'm going to work. There's nothing else to discuss. You aren't going to persuade me to stay at home. I'll go nuts."

He pursed his lips. It was easy to guess what he bit back. She was annoyed by his reticence and his insistence she take extra time off from work. Other than his requirement of no work at home he hadn't tried to hold her back from creating a career with the bank.

"Fine," he said, after a long silence.

She scowled at him and finished her morning routine. Her mood worsened when she saw his expression as she left the house.

When she got to the bank's office building, she looked around the entrance and along the street. There was no sign of the strange tramp who had accosted her the day before. All she saw were focused people in formal wear heading into the building. She joined them.

Her desk didn't look too different. There was no evidence of spores, or a piece of paper with fungi growing from it. The cubicle sat open, ready for her. She'd half-thought someone might have cordoned it off.

"I didn't expect to see you today," Dylan said, after she had sat down. He leaned too far into the cubicle, crowding her. She got the feeling he was studying her.

"You said take a day, so I took a day. I feel okay, so I didn't see any point in sitting at home doing nothing but staring at the walls." She tried a smile that didn't want to stay on her face.

"I understand. Weekends are a bloody nightmare for me. Once I've done all my domestic stuff I don't have anything to do. It's worse when you're stuck home on a weekday."

"I almost went nuts yesterday. I didn't have a clue what to do with myself."

"You're in luck then. There's plenty for you to do, including an account you should be extremely interested in. You can't complain about being bored."

He patted her on the shoulder and walked away. Bridget was glad to see him go.

After a just less than appropriate pause, Paula bustled over. Her thighs made an audible 'shushing' sound as she walked.

"If I were you, I'd have milked a couple of days off out of this," she said.

Bridget looked at her with confused affront.

"Oh, come on. You're telling me you didn't sit in front of the TV and stuff yourself?"

"No." She was genuinely confused this hadn't occurred to her, and now struck her as so unpalatable.

"Not even a trip to the shops? You didn't go for a wander on Oxford Street before you went home? Where's the Bridget who started here three months ago?"

It was a good question. She wondered why she would ever have stayed away from contact with work for such a long time. Nothing had been accomplished by her sitting on the company's website, but it'd felt better than meandering through shops looking at things she had no intention of buying. Even a few days ago, she would have gone shopping.

"I suppose I've grown a bit since then. My priorities have changed."

"Bloody hell, what's that supposed to mean?"

"There are things more important than getting drunk or staring at clothes, Paula. It's time to get serious about life, stop messing around and get some focus."

"You sound like one of the managers."

Bridget considered this and shrugged. "I could think of worse people to sound like. They've got their lives together, and their careers are on an upward trajectory."

Paula edged away, her eyes darting first one way and then another, as though looking for a camera or some other evidence this was a practical joke. "Managers like Tim Layton? He's been divorced twice, and he's under police investigation for fraud. Or Calvin Innes, who's probably in the upstairs toilets working on his mountain of coke and hoping there's no consequences from fucking two of the board members' wives?"

"That's all just rumours spread by people jealous of their positions. The fact is they've knuckled under over the years and climbed to the places they deserve to be."

"Yeah, okay. You keep drinking the Kool-Aid, and I'll see you later." Paula wandered back to her desk, with a few uncertain, searching glances.

If Paula was in any doubt, Bridget meant every word. She didn't know why she hadn't come to the conclusion before, but it was clear to her now that in order to get on in the bank, she had to get serious and cut off any extraneous interests. Her conviction wavered as the morning wore on, however. She'd been absolutely certain when she'd spoken to Paula, but it hadn't sounded like her. It looked like she'd unsettled Paula at least, and at worst hurt her feelings.

When it came to lunchtime, Bridget struggled with the urge to stay at her desk and work through, but decided to fight off the feeling. She caught up to Paula leaving the building.

"Oh look, it's the company man," Paula said.

Bridget smiled. "I deserved that. I'm sorry, Paula. I think I'm still weirded out by what happened yesterday."

"What did happen yesterday? You'd only just sat down at your desk when you were choking and coughing."

"Didn't you see the page from that report?"

"What page?"

Bridget stopped walking and studied her friend, who looked genuinely confused. For a moment, she considered asking if Paula had seen the bulbous blue and green fungi floating above the sheet of paper. She stopped herself, fearing a further strange look.

"What about a report?" Paula asked.

"It's nothing. I must have been seeing things, that's all. Don't worry about it. I'm starving. Where are we going to eat?"

Bridget hid her discomfiture for the rest of their journey to the sandwich shop. She kept up with Paula's chatter, while keeping an eye out for the tramp.

Something had changed in her world since yesterday. She didn't know what it was, and she was afraid of it.

*

"Christ, Bridget, I was worried about you," Donny said when she got home. "It's almost ten."

"I wanted to get some work done," she replied.

"You've been doing this for the past two bloody weeks."

"It's got busy with this account. I need to stay on top of things. Staying an extra few hours is the only way I can do that, I told you."

"We'd arranged to go out tonight, Bridget. You agreed to relax a bit."

"From what I remember, *you* agreed to relax a bit. All I did was shrug. I certainly didn't agree to go out."

He sighed and put his hands on his hips. He took a few deep breaths. "Look, I know you want to get ahead at work. That's great. You can't burn yourself out, though. You have to take a break every so often. You used to be able to take time off. And will you stop scratching at your arms like that?"

She dropped her hands away from her forearms. She hadn't even been aware of scratching. Her gaze remained steady and challenging. "You want me to slow down now, when I'm so close to getting a promotion? I've been invited to a corporate event in a few months. That's a huge thing."

"It's not the same as spending some time with your husband, is it?"

"You're invited too."

"That's not what I meant. It's hardly a night out when you're trying to impress your bosses."

"I'm beginning to wonder how much you actually support me, Donny. I've noticed you've been getting more impatient with me recently. Does the chance of me getting on better than you bother you that much?"

"What are you talking about?"

"You're a minimum wage warehouse worker. I'm on the verge of getting a job that will be a huge boost to my pay. I can see how that would threaten your masculinity."

"That doesn't bother me. I want to have time with my wife. I want to have time with my friend."

"You have to be patient, then. There's too much for me to do to just drop it all and go to the pub with you."

"The pub? When was the last time we just went to the pub? When was the last time we went to the pub at all?"

"Whatever. I can't give up the time. It's a waste."

"A waste to spend some time with me for a couple of hours without talking about work?"

"When you put it that way, yes." It was harsh. She knew it was harsh the moment she said it. Donny's expression went through several strange changes, as if he were trying to find the right one to fit, and failed. He frowned, breathed in as though he was going to respond to her, and walked out of the room.

She could go after him, but what would be the point? He obviously didn't want to see her side of the argument. She sat down, opened her laptop, and started typing an email.

*

It was dark when she woke up. Two forty-two, her Smartphone told her. She got out of bed with care until she remembered Donny had gone to stay with friends almost a month ago. Her regret over his decision had faded over the weeks, as it had allowed her to concentrate more on work.

The itching on her forearms was driving her insane. It had been getting worse and worse, even before Donny left. This wasn't the first night the sensation had woken her up in the middle of the night, but it was the first time she had felt a rough lump.

She hurried into the bathroom, turned on the light, and gasped. A blue-green mushroom sat on the bare skin of her forearm.

For several moments she stared at it, unable to comprehend what she was looking at. It looked like several overlapping funnel-shaped objects, with deep gills on the underside – quite unlike the mushroom she'd squashed on her keyboard two months ago. No one in the office had ever spoken of that incident again. It seemed as if no one even remembered it.

Prodding the large fungus, she discovered that it felt solid, and the skin around its base moved. She pulled it and gritted her teeth as a shock of pain sizzled up her arm. She looked through the medicine cabinet and the chest of drawers next to the sink for something to remove the offending thing. Nothing presented itself, so she decided to take the drastic option.

When she gripped the mushroom, it gave way and released watery blue liquid. The liquid dribbled between her fingers, over her arm and onto the floor. She pulled. The pain didn't increase, but remained constant, so she kept pulling. Her hand shook. The mushroom pulled at the skin while coming free. A thin ribbon of blood escaped, where the base of the mushroom broke through her skin. More of the mushroom came free. The pain subsided. Finally, her skin released it with a pop.

In her hand, the mushroom dripped blue liquid and some blood. It left a small but deep hole in her forearm. For a few moments she was frozen, uncomprehending, before she realised she had a nasty open wound on her arm. She got some gauze, antiseptic and tape. There was little blood or pain when she cleaned and dressed her arm.

*

Finishing breakfast, she looked from the phone to her arm. After twenty minutes of indecision, she picked up the phone and made an appointment with the doctor. The rash was something she would have ignored for a while yet, but a mushroom breaking out of it unsettled her too much.

Once she'd made the appointment, she had to rush out of the house. She was running late. Public transport punished her for waiting too long to leave. The bus that might have got her in on time whooshed off ten seconds before she made it to the stop.

As she waited for the next bus, she felt fidgety, restless. She was afraid panic was setting in. She had to get to work as quickly as possible. Not being in work filled her with a kind of overpowering dread she'd never experienced.

More people congregated at the bus stop, only to edge away from her. They eyed her with worry. She was aware of their unsettled gazes and ignored them. There was no room in her mind to worry about what some strangers thought of her. She stared through them, sweeping her gaze over the crowd. Each person turned away, unable to meet her piercing eyes.

The office needed her. It called to her with a beguiling song, mesmerised her. She clutched her handbag, wringing a few dregs of comfort out of it with a death grip until the bus pulled to a stop. No one tried to get on before her, and no one tried to sit next to her. Her agitation subsided as the journey went on, but her fellow passengers still watched with uncertain expressions and furtive conversation.

Enveloping relief greeted her when she got off the bus and walked up to the entrance of her office building. In her peripheral vision, she thought she saw movement at the corner of the building. She turned and saw nothing.

The relief was complete once she was inside. The security guard at the reception desk gave her a strange look as she stood there smiling. With a surge of confidence, she marched to the lift. The office was busy when she got off. Most of her co-workers were in their cubicles, with the exception of Paula. Her computer was on, but she wasn't there.

She wasn't sure what attracted her attention. There was nothing unusual about the email composition screen. From the lift doors, there was no way of telling what was written on it. She bit her lip, unsure what to do, then crept up to the cubicle, and read the partially-written email.

Somehow Paula had found out about a financial impropriety within the bank, and was in the process of informing both a paper and an independent review body.

Bridget walked away from the cubicle and went straight to Dylan's office. She used to avoid his office. There had been a smell there, undercutting his expensive aftershave, that unsettled her. In the past few weeks she had stopped noticing it.

"Dylan, there's something on Paula's computer you might want to take a good look at," she said, before he could greet her.

"What sort of thing?" he asked, a faint smile on his face.

"You'll see. Just wait until I've sat down before talking to her."

"Why would I need to talk to her?"

"Inappropriate private emails on the company's computers."

Dylan raised his eye brows. Even she was surprised at the speed with which she'd answered him. He smiled at her and nodded. She nodded back and walked to her cubicle. She sat and waited for a few minutes before he went over to Paula. There was a brief exchange, and the pair went into his office.

They were in there for twenty minutes. During that time, she saw Dylan speaking on the phone. Paula looked terrified throughout, and shook her head at several points. Before she left the office, Paula, broken and looking at the floor, nodded.

Everyone in the office watched Paula plod out of Dylan's office, but she only looked at Bridget. Bridget shrugged, and went back to work.

*

When she woke up, another disjointed dream of floating without weight somewhere she couldn't comprehend sat in her mind. The whole night had been filled with strange visions of things she'd never imagined before. They left her feeling weird, tempered by the parade of confusion.

She got up and, out of habit, rubbed her arms. To her surprise, for the first time in months, the skin didn't itch. The rash was gone, and her skin was back the natural white it had always been, even down to the occasional dark hairs she needed to get rid of. Even stranger, the wound on her arm was gone, with not even a scar to show it had been there. When she rubbed the area, it felt like it always had, solid and whole.

A new desperation to get to work overwhelmed her. She threw the bedclothes off in her eagerness to get ready and leave the house.

*

"Paula, there are some serious errors in this report. I've made a few notes for you." Bridget dropped the printout onto Paula's desk.

The woman hadn't looked her in the eye for weeks now. She flicked through the pages, mumbling, "I'll get right on it after I've finished this, Bridget."

"You do that. You've got a performance review in a few weeks. You could do with making a good impression after what happened."

Paula grunted something she didn't make out. Bridget walked away. The promotion had come quickly. Dylan had gone up a level, and she was moved into his vacated position. There were a number of training courses she was still to take, but she was the supervisor of this section. She had bypassed a number of team leaders who had more experience, going straight from a normal data analyst to management in one move.

She sat in Dylan's old office, and wondered how she could have been so uncomfortable in here. It was a thought that had come to her several times since she'd been given the job.

She opened one of the drawers. A crop of quivering fungi of different descriptions crowded around the edges. They all floated above the overseas account she'd been told to study, and whispered contently. The account was being used by a dictator to move large amounts of money out of his country. It was important for the bank. She smiled.

At the end of the day, she watched Paula and the others file out of the office. She kept working for another hour before deciding to finish up. The building from her floor down was quiet, except for a couple of night security lounging around.

Outside it was dark, and a chill wind blew in her face. She examined the street. No-one was near, yet she felt uneasy. The taxi she'd phoned was waiting for her, and she rushed in, unsure of what she was afraid of.

Rain swirled in the air when she got to her building. A silhouette shifted next to the entrance. She gasped.

"Bridget, I need to talk to you," Donny said.

"I thought you said I'd turned into somebody you didn't want anything to do with," she replied.

She looked him up and down. They hadn't seen each other for two and a half months. He looked clean and healthy, until her gaze went to his face. Though he was shaven and washed, there was something dishevelled about his appearance. It was his eyes, bloodshot, surrounded by bruised-looking skin.

"Can I come up? We need to have a serious talk," he said.

She shrugged. "Fine. You better make it quick. I have a load of things to do for work." She thought she saw him wince.

They walked up to the flat in silence. She had nothing to say to him. He was nervous, and watched her with some kind of horrified expectancy. She had no idea what he could be waiting for. When she opened the front door and invited him in, he hesitated, as though he expected an ambush.

She frowned at him, impatient. "Are you going to come in or not?" she demanded.

He shuffled into the flat, stopped, and started to cough. He hacked and wheezed for several minutes while she calmly closed the door and took her jacket off. Once he recovered himself he leaned against the wall, hand clamped over his mouth and nose.

"What is that fucking smell?" he said, through his fingers.

"I don't know what you're talking about. Stop being so melodramatic and come through," she said.

He bumped into something in the hall, and gasped. His eyes glittered in the green and blue light as he stared at one of the six-foot tall mushrooms that had grown in her flat over the last few weeks. Their narrow, pointed caps covered stalks that floated eight inches above the floor. A netting of mycelium connected them all, and had to be stepped over to get into the flat. She had come to accept them, had forgotten a time when they weren't there.

He lunged past her and slapped on the light. It stabbed at her eyes, and the mushrooms shivered and hissed in response. He let out a strangled cry of shock and jumped away from the fungus nearest him, only to bump into one behind him.

"Will you calm down and turn the light off?" she asked.

He stared at her, shock and terror etched in his expression. He backed away from her, mouth twitching. It was like he was trying to work out some way of describing what he saw to himself and to her at the same time. His failure made him look insane.

"What's happened to you?" he asked. "What's happened to the flat?"

"Will you stop acting like an idiot? Sit down."

He refused to go into the living room. The only things not covered by fungi were the settee and the television. She was mildly surprised at the extent of the growth. He gripped the doorframe and scanned the scene.

"Fuck this," he said, and rushed to the front door. He snapped a couple of mycelium strands, and made the mushrooms squeak.

She followed him, and found him struggling with the lock.

"I thought you wanted to talk? You're acting like a lunatic."

His look of shock and incomprehension stunned her. She didn't understand his reaction. His limp fingers fell away from the lock as he studied her.

"You don't even see a problem," he said finally. "You're up to your neck in something you don't understand and you can't even see it."

She looked around. "What are you talking about, Donny? You aren't making any sense."

"This isn't normal!"

She put her hands on her hips. "Get out if you have to. I have things I need to do for work."

Donny managed to open the door and quickly got out into the hall. He stopped there and looked at her, his expression pitying. "I'll find a way to help you, whether you think you need it or not."

*

She looked out at the empty office floor over the top of her monitor. The place had emptied three hours before, but she had no desire to leave. The reports and spreadsheets she had to go through needed her urgent attention. Going home wasn't an option at the moment. She stroked the clutch of mushrooms on the underside of her desk, and turned her attention back to the screen.

"Nice to see you taking your managerial duties so seriously," Dylan said.

"I didn't hear you there," she replied, and leaned back in her chair.

"Sorry."

"Is this a social call? Or do you have something to tell me?"

"That directness will take you far here. I appreciate you're busy, but the CEO wants to see you."

"Me?"

"Asked for you by name."

Nervous, she stood up, but this was something that needed to happen, and perhaps should have happened before now. He led the way to the lift, and for the first time, she went upwards. She'd been interviewed in Dylan's office, and had worked on the floor from her first day. There'd never been any need to go higher.

The lift opened out on to the luxuriously modern offices belonging to the CEO and couple of his other executives. Along with the glass walls, marble flooring and tasteful rugs, there were expensive paintings and strange sculptures.

She recognised the man immediately. The tramp stood in the doorway of a large corner office made mostly of glass.

"Bridget, this is our CEO, Father Polzic," Dylan said.

She held her hand out to shake the tramp's. From inside the filthy trench coat he wore, a tiny hand shot out and grabbed hers. The spindly arm pushed the coat open a little more, and she saw two small, twisted faces grinning out at her. There was a rustle of material, and both the hand and faces were hidden again.

"It's good to meet you again, Father Polzic," she said.

"You have done well, Bridget," he replied. "We were right to watch you. Father Polzic is never wrong about these things. You were a perfect source of corruption for us."

Father Polzic indicated that she and Dylan should follow him. They walked to the rear of the floor, to a blank wall. The Father pushed a panel, seamlessly hidden, that swung open to reveal a dark passage. A door at its end opened into a tunnel, rough-hewn from rock, glistening with water which ran from the rounded ceiling and down the walls. She was bewildered as to how they could be in such a tunnel. A few lanterns hung on brackets at long intervals, but although they didn't offer much in the way of illumination she could see quite well in the gloom.

Their footfalls, whether splashing in pools or clacking on bare rock, echoed in cacophony.

The tunnel wound for a long distance before coming to a large cavern. There were no lanterns here. Instead, there were huge examples of different glowing green and blue fungi. Other things stood amongst these fruiting bodies, all shapes inhuman. Some were half her height, but long, sinuous and in possession of boneless limbs. Others, like huge insects but with bat-like wings and heads like balls of tentacles, sat on some of the fungi. Hulking things with segmented exoskeletons and clusters of glowing eyes towered over even the tallest fungi. Bridget looked at the scene in awe.

Father Polzic glided through the cavern, past the strange menagerie of creatures, each of which seemed to eye Bridget with uncertainty. "Our fungal kin feed well on the spiritual corruption of humanity that oozes in enthusiastic abundance," he said. "There is so much more to take. Father Polzic guides them to the greatest feasts. You, girl, will help."

She and Dylan followed the Father to another tunnel, which eventually led to a smaller chamber. She heard weeping, and the clink of chains.

Attached to the wall by handcuffs and strong chains was Donny. He was dirty and ragged, but otherwise looked unhurt. His eyes widened when he saw her, and a spark of sympathy flared in her chest. She had married this man, loved him, and to see him so degraded and imprisoned made a forgotten part of her sick.

"Oh, Donny," she said.

"Thank god you're here, Bridget," he babbled. "They got me the second I walked out of your building. That weird old tramp was waiting for me. I don't understand anything I've seen here. All these... things. What's going on, Bridget? What's going on?"

"You've been here for three days?" she asked.

"H... have I?"

"Yes."

She turned to Father Polzic, who smiled his grizzly smile, and nodded. She knew what she had to do.

She knelt in front of Donny and held his face. "You used to have such ambition." She studied him. "You still do. I think I can help you with that. Relax, and we'll never be apart again. It will be perfect."

She touched his face and the process began.

*

"That was a wonderful dinner, Bridget. You must give us the recipe for the duck," Cybil said. She was the wife of Rob, the Chief Information Officer.

"I would do, but it was all Donny's work," Bridget replied.

Donny, slim and elegant in a silk shirt and expensive trousers, came out of the newly fitted kitchen. "It's easy. I'll send you an email," he said.

Rob looked around the flat. "You've done a fantastic job with the place. It's almost a shame you're going to move out."

"We've been here a long time," Bridget said. "We did what we could, but it's time for bigger and better things."

"That could be the motto for your career, Bridget. Overseeing a whole section in less than a year – and now there's talk of you taking an executive position ahead of Dylan. It's a remarkable climb," Rob said.

"And you were both so charming at the function last month," Cybil added.

"I've had wonderful support," Bridget said. She held onto Donny's hand and felt the mycelium beneath his skin shudder in response to her own.

Notes for a Life of Nightmares:
A Retrospective on the Work of Henry Anthony Wilcox
by Pete Rawlik

Henry Anthony Wilcox *(August 12, 1902—March 31, 1931)* was a sculptor of the Surrealist movement, notable for his work in clay and, later, marble. Born and raised in Providence, he was the son of Anthony Wilcox, a prominent businessman, and Margaret Phillips, who had some success in her youth as a songstress on the stage in Boston and New York. As a child he attended the Thomas School, were he showed aptitude in the visual arts and music.

At the age of nine he was interviewed by faculty members of Brown, and declared a precocious genius. This diagnosis only added to the attention surrounding the young man, who would often relate strange stories and odd dreams. Wilcox was doted upon by his mother, who called him "psychically hypersensitive", but the rest of the household, including the cook, butler and maid, thought of him as queer. Unsatisfied by the demeanor of his son, Anthony Wilcox often ridiculed the boy, and spent as little time as possible at the family home on Waterman Street.

In 1916, Wilcox fell victim to Sleepy Sickness, also known as Encephalitis Lethargica, which manifested initially as sleep inversion. As a consequence, Wilcox would often roam the house and streets of Providence throughout the night and into the early morning hours, and became known to the dairymen and fishermen who haunted those hours. It was during this period that he began developing an artistic style, filling sketchbooks with images of the people and things he saw on his nocturnal roaming. It was these people, his "night friends" as he called them, who found him unconscious in the street on the morning of September 3, 1917, and carried him home.

When his condition failed to improve, he was transferred to a private hospital, where he stayed until the early part of 1918. In March, he became a patient of Doctor Christopher Eckhardt, who subjected him to hydro-immersion therapy. After six weeks, the treatments proved successful, and Wilcox emerged from his catatonic state. Reports from those in attendance attest that he came to consciousness screaming two distinct but unfamiliar words. He chanted these same words over and over again for hours, until he was finally sedated. Dr. Eckhardt records them in his file as "Thulu fthan!" However, the notes of Doctor Loucks, the junior physician, record the words slightly differently, observing a strange, almost panicked lilt in Wilcox's words which suggested an interrogative form: "Thulu fthan?"

In 1920, following several years of psychological therapy, Wilcox submitted himself for examination by the local school board. These gentlemen found that despite his lack of formal education over the last few years, Wilcox was in possession of sufficient knowledge on such a variety of subjects as to be equivalent to a high school diploma. The board duly wrote him a letter to that effect. It was this letter, along with a collection of small figurines he had produced during his convalescence, that Wilcox submitted to the Rhode Island School of Design in hopes of admission. In the fall of 1920 he was granted probationary access to the college as a freshman in the Sculpture Program, with Dr. Deschanes as his academic advisor.

These early figurines, six in total—four of which reside in the RISD Museum—are collectively known as the Wilcox Submission, but each bears an individual title. These names are assumed to be sourced from Wilcox himself, although there is no documentary proof to that effect. They are a most bizarre set of clay moldings.

1. *The She-Wolf.* In the classical Roman style, an image of two infants being suckled by an anthropomorphic wolf, an allusion to the myth of Romulus and Remus. The deviation from traditional portrayals of the

she-wolf Lupa is particularly disturbing in that the anthropomorphized figure is more akin to a jackal than a wolf, and is replete with four sets of teats and reminiscent of more primitive Neolithic fertility idols.

2. *The Star-Beetle*. In the style of the Amarna Period of ancient Egypt, an image of a sphere representing the sun held by a stylized scarab. The sphere is marked with multiple concentric rings on its surface, the symbolism of which is not known. The beetle itself shows deviations from typical forms with fine protuberances in rays along the seams between the body parts.

3. *The Crucifixion of the Wyrm*. In imitation of traditional Celtic forms, a cross with two horizontal beams upon which a coiled dragon is entwined. The dragon has four limbs, all of which are severed and pinned with nails. The tail wraps around the base of the cross and then coils around it in a traditional knot pattern.

4. *The Sea Mother*. A whale or leviathan in the medieval style. Detail work on the scales, and the fount of water that curves from the front of the sculpture over to the rear, are particularly fine. Claws of all four limbs are imbedded in a stylized ocean.

5. *The Professor*. A grotesque conical form reminiscent of a barnacle with four tentacles protruding from the apex. Two tentacles end in crab-like pincers. A third tentacle bears a complex tubular organ resembling a shell or fluted flower. The final tentacle ends in the head of a man wearing glasses. In the collection of Alice Keezar.

6. *The Scion*. A man in a modern suit done in the cubist style. While the body is done in large blocks, the face and hands are done with finer pieces and create an unnerving suggestion of corruption through disease or wasting. Whereabouts unknown.

Under Deschanes' direction, Wilcox immersed himself in the routine and mundane work of formal training. This included studying under a number of staff and senior students, such as

Norman Isham, R.H. Knox, and Robert Eggleton. He was a regular at visiting lectures, particularly those given by Charlotte Perkins Gilman. During this period, Wilcox's work was perfunctory— mediocre at best—and consisted mostly of studies of human anatomy, still lifes and landscapes. There are however, some notable pieces, mostly from the spring of 1921 when he gained access to the Cooper Home for Retired Mariners. These works included clays, marbles and bronzes of various human anatomies that had suffered trauma, and were essentially twisted and broken forms. It was during this period that the Providence Art Club banned Wilcox from the premises, the trustees finding his work too disturbing for some of their more conservative members.

Banned from the club, Wilcox fell in with the like-minded painter Kenneth Hart, and the two were often seen wandering the city streets at unseemly hours. The work produced during the time Wilcox was under Hart's influence has come to be known as his Grave Period. This appellation was earned not only for the pair's melodramatic style, but also for their pervasive subject matter. Generally the most revered work from this stage of his career is *A Madonna of the Cenotaphs*, an exercise in the macabre held in the private collection of the Ward Family. However, a substantial number of critics cite *The Black Stone*, also held by the Ward Family, as a superior piece.

None of this work ingratiated Wilcox with Deschanes or the rest of the faculty, and the young man was given an academic warning. While the younger Wilcox scoffed at the censure, his father made it clear that the situation was untenable. In a conflict that reached the ears of several neighbors, young Wilcox was forcibly ejected from the family home with a single bag of belongings and a mother crying in the streets. Where he took up residence is not entirely clear, but it had long been suspected that he found a bed with Kenneth Hart in the seedier side of the city.

That arrangement soon changed through the intervention of Wilcox's mother, who found and paid for lodgings for her son at the Fleur-de-Lys Studios on Thomas Street. The residence must have been to the artist's liking, for he soon began to produce work of a more mainstream and marketable form. He seemed to have put the period of grotesquerie and the weird behind him, and turned to a more refined and accessible style. This is designated his Aesthetic Period and is dominated by nudes and semi-nudes in classic forms including *Hypnos, Janus,* and *Bellerephon on Pegasus*. Outstanding amongst these is an enthroned sea god wearing an octopus as a cowl, entitled *Oannes*, which is part of the RISD collection. This series of pieces endeared him to Professor Deschanes, and earned him good standing with the rest of the faculty.

Wilcox's Aesthetic Period lasted from 1922 to December 1924. It was brought to closure in January 1925 by a surge of bizarre dreams that, according to Wilcox's journal, prevented any serious work. He described his condition as:

> "Walking about in a muddled haze as if I was in that queer state between being asleep and awake where all sounds and other stimuli are magnified but the ability to respond is dramatically suppressed. Strange to see the world in such detail and yet not be able to react or respond in any significant manner. What a frustrating form of paralysis I find myself entrapped within! I must have relief soon or I shall simply explode out of this weird prison."

Wilcox finally gained the relief he needed on the night of February 28th, when after a nearly unprecedented New England earthquake, the artist retired to suffer from terrible dreams beyond anything to which he was accustomed. He dreamt of a strange city, ancient and forbidden, with weird, cyclopean towers, the angles of which were all wrong. Amidst this cyclopean architecture stalked a titanic creature that bore traits of a dragon, an octopus and something vaguely human. From this nightmare Wilcox awoke, and in a feverish mania produced a rectangular bas-relief, an inch thick and measuring five by six inches in area, which depicted the monster of the night before. This was surrounded with strange hieroglyphics.

The piece, which is generally known as *The Wilcox Bas Relief*—Wilcox never titled it—created quite a stir at RISD, and Deschanes and other members of the faculty praised it as a culmination of technique and talent. Many were curious concerning the symbols surrounding the central subject, and Wilcox denied any conscious knowledge of their origin. Deschanes had a vague notion that they might have been Aramaic, and suggested that the artist show them to George Gammell Angell, a retired professor of Semitic Languages at Brown University.

Wilcox met with Angell on March the first, and did so again daily for three weeks. During this brief time, his art grew evermore bizarre. It focused on the monstrosity he had created in the bas relief, but extended into figurines, busts, and even a larger piece, *The Marine Abomination*, weighing over three hundred pounds. In this three-week period, Wilcox produced an incredible eighteen masterpieces, fusing cubism, futurism and primitivism into something wholly new that is best described as his Nightmare Period. However, producing such wonderful creations at such a feverish pace no doubt contributed to what happened next.

In the early morning hours of the twenty-third of March, Wilcox suffered a severe breakdown, screaming out loudly enough to wake several other residents. Kenneth Hart, who had been staying with Wilcox for some time, found the artist ranting and feverish. When attempts to calm him failed, a call was placed, and in the wee hours, Henry Anthony Wilcox was forcibly restrained and bundled off to his family home. Placed under the care of Dr. Frederick Tobey, the young man languished, drifting in and out of consciousness. On the second of April, at around 3 p.m., every vestige of his curious illness suddenly abated. Three days later he returned to his apartment with no memory of the last ten days. His weird nocturnal visions of the titanic monster had ceased, and soon he stopped seeing Professor Angell. Sadly, with the loss of the visions went his ability to frantically create masterpieces.

This is not to say that his work ended. On the contrary, it continued apace, but now seemed focused, even obsessed, with capturing the weird and esoteric minutiae of various anatomical features of his previously more perfunctory works. Hideous wings, multi-jointed claws and queer tri-lobed eyes regularly poured out of his workshop. These pieces of the fantastic were hailed by critics as fascinating productions from a morbid genius comparable to Goya or Munch. Wilcox however took no pleasure in his notoriety, and became increasingly distant from his friends and family.

When, in 1926, police inquired concerning his relationship with Kenneth Hart, Wilcox seemed disinterested. Hart had moved to Boston and taken up with Richard Upton Pickman, but both had been unseen for weeks. Wilcox implied that the disappearances of Pickman and his friend were not at all surprising, and in fact rather predictable, but he refused to explain further. He was, however, affected by the death of Professor Angell, and following a visit from the scholar's nephew, produced a tableau of his former confidant standing amidst the ruins of an antediluvian metropolis of titanic proportions. In the collection of Brown University, the piece is entitled *Perspective*. Amongst critics it is viewed as a capstone to his Nightmare period.

In his final years, Wilcox began studying a variety of philosophies, including nihilism, anti-natalism, annihilationism, and the Buddhist concept of anatta. At one point he even investigated absurdism and the pantheon of the proto-Urartians, and corresponded at length with the outrageous Dr. Emil Thoss of Miskatonic University. These studies led to a profound shift in Wilcox's art, and he began to work in an entirely new direction that focused on a single motif, that of a tentacled wheel with a single spoke supporting a small cloudy blue ball. The first of these abstract works, *Despair*, was produced in 1928. It has a diameter of five feet, and is installed at the Morley Museum in Plunkettsburg.

In May of 1929 he joined the faculty of the Sanbourne Institute, where he taught a class in contemporary art. The course was not a success, and both students and faculty filed complaints concerning Wilcox's behavior and attendance. Wilcox was dismissed after eight months, when it was discovered that he had destroyed an acre of preserve land in creating a piece of his art. The installation was destroyed and no photographs exist, but descriptions suggest that it was a larger iteration of *Despair*.

Although no related records exist, a similar piece entitled *A Backward Glance* exists in Mexico City on the grounds of the Diaz Foundation. Signed by Wilcox and dated in July 1930, the work rises thirty-two feet into the air. It consists of steel cables entwined around each other to form vines or tentacles, some of which reach inward toward the center. The central globe is hand-blown blue and white glass supported by a single black steel wire. An in-depth investigation suggested that Wilcox designed the piece in less than eight hours, and then with the aid of a team of twenty welders completed the full-scale installation in under forty-five days.

In January 1931, the Universidad Nacional Autónoma de Nicaragua in Managua announced that they would be undertaking an unprecedented project designed and lead by Wilcox. Over the next few weeks, a ten-acre plot was cleared and a significant amount of steel, copper and lead were delivered to the site. From photographs, it is clear that Wilcox was attempting to create two circles, one vertical and one horizontal, with a central sphere supported with four spokes. The sphere was built from lead and stained glass, mostly white and blue with some green. A progression of photographs makes it clear that at this scale, the sphere is a representation of the planet Earth.

Work proceeded through February, and while notes suggest there were some engineering issues, delays were minimal. The three arcs comprising the vertical circle were completed on the second of March and hoisted into place on the fourth. The horizontal pieces were suspended on March tenth, and pinned the next day. Site work and safety inspections were completed on the twentieth of March. Entitled *Distant Vision*, the installation was opened to select guests on the twenty-fifth of March, and then to the general public two days later.

On the thirtieth of March, security was called concerning eighteen members of a local tribe who had occupied the site in order to carry out a religious rite invoking the Aztec deity Tlaloc. According to records, the intruders were allowed by authorities to complete their rite, after which they were forcibly dispersed. That afternoon, the bodies of all eighteen individuals were found dead in a church. No signs of foul play were noted and poison was suspected, but any chance of investigation was lost on the next day. On the thirty-first of March 1931, at 10:00 in the morning, a magnitude 6 earthquake struck the town. Between the quake itself and the ensuing fire, more than two thousand people were lost and forty-five thousand were made homeless. Henry Wilcox's masterwork—*Distant Vision*—was swallowed up by the earth, and lost forever. Only a few photographs remain. Henry Anthony Wilcox himself was never seen again, and is assumed to be among the dead. A marker was placed in his memory on the university grounds.

The war banished Wilcox to obscurity, but in 1948 a review of the holdings of the RISD found several pieces by the artist in their archives. This sparked a resurgence of interest in his work, and an effort to create a full catalog was made. While acknowledged to be woefully incomplete, the pieces displayed here represent the first attempt at bringing the work of the artist to the attention of the public. After four years, and significant expense, the RISD is proud to present the first retrospective of Providence native and true avant-garde genius Henry Anthony Wilcox.

The collection will open to the public on the Twelfth of August 1952, the fiftieth anniversary of the birth of the artist.

Offspring
by Evey Brett

Walks Alone was the third man found without a soul. Pale, shaken warriors brought him to my tipi. Like the first two, Walks Alone was alive. Very much so. His chest rose and fell with regular breaths, his body was warm to the touch, and he reflexively took water when a bowl was held to his lips. But his eyes...

None of the men who found him could look for long. I became queasy too, when I saw the stars reflected in his senseless gaze, pinpoints of light flickering in an otherwise endless pool of black.

A witch had done this, the warriors said. They believed I ought to confront the witch and convince it to return the stolen souls. I had no such confidence. I'd been chosen at a young age to interpret for the spirits and to wield their medicine, but this was no sort of witchcraft I knew.

As with the others, I burned sage and cedar to cleanse whatever evil remained. I sang, pleading with the spirits for whatever aid they might be able to give. The answer was the same as it had been before.

This is beyond us, they said. *The souls were taken by a being not of our time or place. We cannot help you.*

"It must be stopped," I told them. "There must be a way."

They replied with uneasy silence.

*

Two days later, one of the maidens in the village, Blackbird, went to fetch water for her family. When she did not return by sundown, her father and brothers went in search of her. The cries of grief reached me long before the men did. Blackbird's father held her crumpled figure in his arms. Her beaded doe-hide dress was torn and tattered, her legs and feet bloodied. In her eyes, she bore the same, starry blankness as the others.

Unlike the male victims however, Blackbird mumbled continuously. I had to lean close to hear the same words uttered over and over: *"Yhagni pthagi tal kai pthagiis."*

The words made no sense. Either she had gone completely mad, or a spirit possessed her to speak in a tongue I did not know.

It's an ancient language, my spirit friends said. *We will not translate. We dare not.*

Greatly troubled, I left her in the care of her mothers and sisters, but in a matter of days they sought my help once more. "Look," said her mother. She drew back the hide covering to show me Blackbird's belly, swollen with pregnancy. I held a hand just above her navel, sensing the dark energy within. I said nothing, but my fear was reflected in her mother's eyes.

*

After that brief contact, my dreams turned dark and poisonous. I wandered through caves, the walls and columns dripping with slime like some sort of hideous afterbirth. A fearsome presence loomed behind me, watching, waiting. Try as I might to track it down, I could never find so much as a single footprint, and I became certain I was the one being hunted. Blackbird's words, *Yhagni pthagi tal kai pthagiis*, echoed in my mind in a summons I dared not answer.

While Blackbird's belly grew, two more men and one woman were found stripped of their souls. Again, I was helpless, although I examined each victim with great care. The tribe had taken to blindfolding them, to keep others from getting lost in the deep pools of their gaze.

The chief ordered the tribe to move the village, and we did, but within a day of settling, a boy on the brink of manhood went missing, to be found later, breathing yet not fully alive.

"Why won't you cure them?" Blackbird's father asked me, accompanied by murmurings from other warriors. "Are you using them for your witchcraft?"

"I'm no witch," I told them but, being anxious and upset, I doubted they heard me. Gloom settled over the encampment. No one went out alone, and only the bravest hunted so that the People might eat.

I listened to the wind and earth, sun and moon for any hint as to what beast stalked my people. I circled the edge of the camp, consulting with the stone and plant nations. The answer was always the same.

There is nothing we can do. Nothing.

Despairing, I gazed into the sky late at night, searching for the meaning which continued to escape me. A light streaked across the sky, bringing with it a message: *Beware the stars.*

*

Within a moonspan, Blackbird gave birth, if the bloody, painful process could be called such. She was dead before the sun rose, leaving behind a full-sized infant with nothing between its legs to indicate its sex, and wiggling tendrils instead of fingers and toes.

The mother wailed her grief. The father caught a glimpse of the malformed baby and pulled out his knife. He turned to me. "You have brought this monster to us. It's your fault, witch. We should have let you perish on the plains, next to your mother's body."

It was true that I belonged to the tribe through adoption rather than blood. My surrogate father had found me during a hunt, a squalling newborn still covered in birthing fluids and bearing signs of being both male and female. Because of that, I felt a strange sort of kinship with this squirming child. It opened its eyes, showing the same starry blackness. All around me, the others started to pray, but I was lost in that terrible darkness, seeing at last a pattern that had also been present in the gazes of the soulless.

Terrified beyond measure, I snatched up the child and fled the only home I'd ever known.

*

I made us a shelter far from the People, at the edge of a river. The child grew impossibly fast, and fortunately seemed to have no need of milk, since I had none. It suckled on morning dew, and the broths I created from dried meat. One day it was a needy infant, the next it tottered around on wobbling legs. By the third it stared at me with its star-deep eyes.

"You're like me," the child said on the fourth day, when I returned with an antelope to skin and dress. "I can smell it."

"No," I said. I'd been born of a human mother. It was impossible to believe I bore the blood of a monster inside me.

The child reached between my legs with gentle tendrils and smiled a knowing smile.

*

On the fifth day, the child was the size of one perhaps ten summers old, and had strangled a rabbit for its dinner. On the sixth, it woke me from another nightmare by whispering in my ear, "It's time. Mother wants to meet you."

Fear settled in my stomach, heavy as river stones. I tried one last time to speak with my spirit friends, but they had grown silent, and all I could sense was their own nervousness.

Beware the stars.

It was not yet dawn. Stars lingered in the sky, moving ever closer to the pattern glittering in the child's eyes. I knew not what would happen when they reached their accord, only that it would bring grief and terror beyond all comprehension.

"This way." The child wandered off as if knowing I would follow. I did. I had no choice. Whatever evil had sprung forth, I was meant to play a part.

We traveled for half the morning until we reached a hole in the earth barely big enough for a man to squeeze through. A breeze emerged, cold and stale.

"In here," the child said, and tugged me inside. We crawled for some time, emerging at last inside a cavern more than large enough for me to stand. The walls glowed with a sickly blue light, yet it was enough to see that the slick stone pillars were covered in a viscous fluid, one I dared not touch.

With giddy horror I realized I'd been here before, in my dreams. This was the birthing canal leading back to its source.

The child tugged again. "Mother is waiting."

Tendrils curled around my fingers as the child led me deeper into the cave. Try as I might, I could sense no familiar spirits here.

They'd fled long ago, leaving the place more bereft and terrifying than anything I'd ever felt. Even the stone I wore in the pouch around my neck was a cold, dead thing, deprived of the spirit it had once held.

In the few places free of fluids, symbols had been etched into the rock. I could make no sense of them, as they represented nothing of the world as I knew it. They were strange and far beyond my comprehension, yet radiated a power that I, used to dealing with such things, couldn't help but notice. I ran my finger over one and shuddered as a deep *knowing* overcame me. Some part of me understood, although I had not the words to explain.

A pulsing echoed on the dead air like a drumbeat, drawing me nearer against my will. Words scraped against my mind. *Yhagni pthagi tal kai pthagiis,* repeating over and over the way it had in my dream. I thought of poor Blackbird, delirious and maddened by her encounter with whatever lay beyond.

Not long after, I felt it. *Her.* The creature was female. I could sense a dark, brooding nature that went against the natural order, clashing with everything I'd learned from Creator. There was no respect, no balance, only a hunger for domination that vibrated deep within my body. Creator loved all life. This creature cared for nothing except itself.

"Yhagni," the child whispered with such reverence that I knew it had to be the thing's name. The word sent a chill through me, and it was all I could do not to collapse into a ball of terrified flesh. *"Yhagni pthagi tal kai pthagiis. Yhagni dreams her own dreams."*

I'd had glimpses of those dreams—troubling, nightmarish visions of vengeance. I wanted nothing more to do with them.

Mercifully, *She* remained out of my sight, hidden somewhere in a chamber just beyond. I stood rooted to the ground, unable to force myself forward. There were dark spirits among the People, tricksters, monsters that lived in the water, but these seemed no more than ants against the incomprehensibility of the creature I faced.

The child gazed up at me, smile fixed in an obscene sort of innocence. "You are my sibling," the child said. "Created in the Mother's image. Those like you are to be her priests, meant to serve and worship her and to carry her message forth. It is time you took your place at her side."

"Those like me?"

The child giggled. "Mother needs no mate. She is all. She is father and mother, progenitor and begetter, beginning and end."

Horrified, I understood. The same duality rested within me. I was two-spirited, male and female both, a fatherless child gifted with powers I had believed came from the spirits belonging to the earth. Among the People, being two-spirited came with honor and respect. *She* had twisted and perverted that trait, making me a bane to the People, doomed to bring them to a terrible end.

I fervently shook my head. "No."

"You must. Mother insists."

"I said *no.*" I tried to pull away. I called out to my spirit friends, but they remained silent.

"Your weakling spirits cannot help you," the child said. "You belong to Mother, and she wishes to initiate you as her priest."

The tendrils lengthened and curled around my arm with such strength that I had no choice but to let the child drag me into the next and final chamber.

What I saw in that cavern cannot be told in words. *She* was so large, so incomprehensible that my sight failed the moment I gazed upon her. Cold sliminess wrapped around me, pulling me inward, and my scream was lost in the soft endlessness of *Her.*

She crawled within my mind, probing with such power that I wept from the pain of it. I was human. Mortal. No match for *Her* power or pleasure in tormenting me. I wondered if this was what the soulless had felt, this rending of mind and body, the utter rape of self as the Mother took it into herself and fed.

A thousand souls were already there, shrieking and pleading for mercy. I had no mercy to give, no means of saving myself. I knew nothing but pain and terror while *She* tore into the core of my being and uncovered the messages left there on the day *She* had conceived me, instructions I could not misunderstand or disobey.

Then *She* started peeling my very flesh, doubling my agony. For every bit of me torn away, she left something unnamable behind.

And all the while, the cavern echoed with the child's laughter.

*

She dropped me gasping and flailing onto the stone floor. I was cold, and covered in slime like some hideous afterbirth. The child eagerly devoured the flesh that had been stripped from my body. Its eyes glinted with eerie ferocity. Already, it appeared far less human than it had. Its arms had divided into tentacles, and it slithered along the ground like a snake. Only its all-seeing, starry gaze remained familiar.

I know not how long I lay in delirium. My body was little more than a vessel made to endure an intense, throbbing agony. Every now and then I tried to move, hindered by limbs that were flopping and boneless, no longer ending in hands and feet. That realization was horrible enough, but my mind spun and whirled, tormented by visions of *Her* and instructions given to me in a foul language I did not fully comprehend.

Yet I knew what *She* wanted. When the stars aligned, *She* would stir for the first time in years beyond counting. The soulless ones were nothing more than husks *She* had prepared to house *Her* children. Through them, *She* would begin her quest for dominion, and I, having survived the initiation into *Her* priesthood, would aid *Her* in this as my act of ordination.

I swiftly put my hand—or rather, the snakelike appendage that now passed for my limb—against my belly. It was then I felt *them* inside me. Hundreds, thousands of *Her* children, waiting to be reborn inside a human host.

I screamed until my throat was raw.

*

"Wake," the child said, in a rasping, sibilant voice. "It is time."

I had no idea how much time had passed, but I was chilled from lying in the water that steadily drip-dripped from the ceiling. My body ached, my belly worst of all, reminding me of that which I desperately longed to forget.

The child caressed me there, then stroked the dual sexual organs that *She*, in her peevishness, had left in place. The act brought no pleasure. The child no longer had a mouth to smile with, but I sensed its pleasure. "Go now. At midnight, the way will open. The Mother wishes her children there to greet her."

It slithered away, leaving me to my hideous task. For a long time, I could not bring myself to move. My disparate halves warred with each other. *She* had uncovered my true form, molded after *Her* essence. Mother and father. Progenitor and begetter.

Yet I was also who I'd always been. A servant of the People. Two-spirited.

A tiny, eight-legged creature crawled along my disfigured arm. My sluggish mind brought me the word. *Iktomi.* The spider. The trickster.

The spirits had not abandoned me after all.

*

Leaving the underground domain was no easy task, with my new body unbalanced and heavy with the unborn. Even so, I was a driven creature, half mad with pain and the intense urging to complete the task *She* had given me.

Slowly, I made my way upward, back to the world I'd known and loved. Tiny Iktomi rode along as a passenger, and a reminder that I was not alone.

At dusk, the warriors met me at the edge of camp, bows drawn, knives in hand. Their stout hearts could not keep them from gaping at me and trembling in horror. If each one had taken a shot, I doubt any would have been accurate enough to penetrate my skin.

"I am one you once knew." My voice came out thick and garbled. "If you wish to spare your women and children, escape with them now. Leave the soulless."

Most of them turned and fled, shouting at everyone to rise and run. Three of them stayed, staring, lips moving in prayer.

"Go," I ordered, and at last they too bolted.

I crept into the abandoned village. New life writhed inside me, eager to be transferred to an edible host. The soulless were the bodies of people I'd known, mothers and fathers, children, sisters and brothers. The compulsion urged me to follow my orders, but I remained determined that *She* would not have what remained of my people.

One by one, I used my new limbs to strangle the soulless. This was not murder so much as a cleansing, since their essence was already gone, and it was up to me to spare what remained. The hungry creatures within me cried out in anger. They clawed and nibbled at my belly, but I refused to free them.

Yhagni screamed in my mind, cursing and threatening. Each word pained me as if I'd been impaled on a knife or sharp stick. When it became agonizing to stand, I crawled from tipi to tipi.

As I reached the last, the child appeared, no longer resembling a human at all. It was a writhing mass of tentacles held together by a shapeless mass.

"STOP." It spoke with the Mother's voice, sinuous and corrosive. *"You are mine. You will obey."*

With slithering efficiency, it reached the last soulless body, that of the boy, before I could. It covered the unmoving form with undulating blackness. I caught sight of little Iktomi, the trickster on my arm, and felt sure of my plan.

"Come," the child said. *"Recall your task. Let the children feed."* One long tentacle reached toward me. The compulsion was too strong to disobey. I let the child enfold me in a horrible embrace.

With one swift, sharp punch, it tore a hole in my body and released the offspring.

They were hungry. Desperate. Crawling over one another, shoving and pushing each other aside in order to reach the undead boy, their only source of sustenance. The child released me, letting me collapse onto the dirt floor of the tipi. It now gloated over the brood, emanating feral pleasure as the offspring fed.

For a long moment, I could only lie where I was, watching the swarm of sickening creatures. Then, slowly, I realized the compulsion was gone. Now that I'd emptied my body, my task was complete. I was myself again. Mother and father. Giver of life... and destroyer.

The boy's father had been one of the People's best fletchers, which was why I'd saved this tipi for last. In the tribe's hasty departure, weapons had been left behind. Arrows, half-finished arrowheads, stone knives and more lay within easy reach.

I grabbed both a knife and an arrow. The child was first. I plunged the stone into its body again and again, thrusting with all my might. Stinking, slimy ichor spattered across my arms, face and chest. The child screamed and cursed and wailed with an eerie, unnatural tone, but I didn't care. I was of two worlds, just like my sibling, but unlike the child I intended to return balance to the world.

"STOP!" came the terrible voice in my head, echoing like thunder.

The sound vibrated through my bones, causing a new kind of agony. Even so, I dared not cease.

The offspring were next. Like Iktomi, these were small and many-legged, but unlike him, they were no tricksters. One by one, I thrust the knife into their fragile newborn bodies. The shrieks deafened me, but I kept on, striking again and again, culling tens, then hundreds. My arms ached and my skin was coated in slime and ichor, but I continued my frenzied slaughter.

As a final act, I made a torch from one of the fires still burning and set the tipi afire. The ichor burned with a nauseating stench, and the flames turned first green, then blue.

Overcome by exhaustion and illness, I collapsed. Above me, the stars made their final movements. I braced myself, terrified that the carnage had not been enough to forestall *Her*. The gateway was open... but *She* could not step through.

The ground trembled with *Her* rage, and with it came one last lash of pain that took with it the remnants of my sanity.

*

For a long time after, I lingered in the realm of madness. Every time I opened my eyes and saw the stars, I cried out with the bone-deep fear of that terrible presence emerging. What I had seen could not be unseen. That which I knew could not be unknown. The horror of it all rolled in my mind, over and over, giving me no peace. All the while, Iktomi kept watch.

At length, the drums and prayers of the People soothed me. The nightmares faded. A tipi was built around me as much for my protection as that of the People. Unable to bear the sight of me in my new form, they tended me blindfolded, bringing gifts of food and furs. In return I blessed them with the powers that still resided within me. They gave me a new name, Two-Spirit Warrior, and when their village moved, so did I.

The entrance to the Mother's womb is closed. I made sure of that. But my dreams have warned me of a time to come when the ground will be torn and the temple of pillars exposed.

Yhagni dreams her own dreams, but I will be watching. And waiting.

The People are in my care.

Out on Route 22
by E. Dane Anderson

Late Fall, 1984

Anyone who's worked graveyard shift can tell you that it completely messes with your psyche. Your entire life is turned upside down, and you only truly exist during the darkest hours. Unlike the rest of normal humanity, you do everything you can to shut out the sun during the day, so that you can rest. Because your sleep patterns have been turned so completely backwards, you can never be truly awake, never be truly asleep. You spend hour after hour in the dark fighting your instincts to slumber, go to that place where most normal people are. No human should ever have to live like this, yet so many of us do.

I dropped out of college in the winter of 1983. There wasn't any specific reason, I just didn't want to go anymore. My parents were really pissed off, and it didn't take long for my dad to cut me off. I took what savings I had, and moved from my parents' place in Suttonton to a tiny apartment in Lewisville. I'd thought Suttonton was small, but it was a vast metropolis compared to Lewisville. Out of sheer desperation and fear I took the first job that I thought I was even vaguely qualified for. That same sense of dread and complete uselessness kept me in that job.

The Jiffy Seven was a convenience store some twenty miles west of town on Route 22. The road had seen less and less traffic since being bypassed by the big interstate in the mid-1950s. The owner was an old World War II veteran by the name of Max who lived in a glorified shack behind the store, just close enough that he could always keep an eye on the place. Business had dropped off along with the traffic, and it cost him more to pay me and keep the place open all night than he ever could bring in. I never understood his logic.

The store was in a pretty desolate area, clustered together with a few other businesses. Each of them looked like they were on the edge of failure. Everything around us was bleak, a flat featureless plain without a single standing tree for ten miles. The few scrub brushes that dared to grow took on more of a gray than a green color. Since I rarely saw any of it in full daylight, it never really mattered.

Next door was a rundown bar called Dutch's. It catered mainly to the handful of truckers trying to stay off the interstate for various reasons, usually crime-related. The place was run by an ex-hippie named Barry, who looked like a child molester and still drove a barely functional '62 VW van. I learned to love the sound of the engine, because hearing it meant that my shift was close to being over. The bar was also frequented by a gaggle of drug dealers, who sold speed and coke, mostly to the truckers. The only way Barry kept the place afloat was by taking a cut of the action. An extra-creepy guy who always wore a blue tank-top occasionally sold me downers. Thank God they were still making Quaaludes at the time. Those little pills stamped with the magic numbers 714 were the only things that helped me sleep during the day.

Right across the highway was a shitty motel, laughingly called the Evergreen. It looked pretty crappy at night. I could only imagine what it looked like in the daytime. Its neon sign buzzed so loudly I could hear it from inside the store, just above the hum of the coolers and the hot dog machine. Someone told me it was a drop off point for drug shipments coming up from Florida, before they were broken up and sent west. I'm not sure I believed that. The only definable activity I saw were the hookers going there after they picked up some John at Dutch's.

The job itself was pretty easy. I did the 8pm to 4am shift, seeing very few customers after about 10:00, even less after midnight. Perhaps someone would come in after Dutch's closed at 2:00, a drunk looking for some pre pass-out munchies. On other occasions I'd get a long-haul trucker looking for a six-pack of beer from the fridge and a condom from the restroom dispenser before going across the street to the Evergreen with the hooker that he'd just picked up.

Max told me not to worry if anyone tried to rob the place. Everyone knew that he didn't have any money. On the off-chance that anyone did, I should just cooperate and hand over anything they wanted. But if the situation needed it, there was a rather large, intimidating .44 Magnum just under the till. I didn't even like touching it.

Working there became my life—existing in an artificially-lit space, surrounded by processed materials that could only vaguely be described as food, and a plethora of cheaply made plastic crap that had somehow become of value to the strange, transient population that I dealt with. I might as well have been out on the edge of the universe, peering back into the world that the normal people lived in.

*

I guess I'd been working there five months on the terrible night he came in. I didn't see the door open, didn't hear the chime of the bell, but there he was, moving towards me up the center aisle. The man must have been at least six and a half feet tall, and he was so thin I had a hard time believing his body could support such a height. He wore a very dark, tightly-fitted suit that, underneath the store's fluorescent lights, had a slight metallic green sheen about it. His skin was pale, nearly sheet white, with only the tiniest hint of red. His long, dead black hair seemed to disappear somewhere behind him. Even though it was three o'clock in the morning, he was wearing sunglasses, perfectly round sunglasses that seemed to reflect no light.

"Do you have any magic markers?" he asked, upon reaching the counter. His voice was deep, of a very low pitch, but somehow without the right tonality, as though his voice had been slowed down in a tape machine.

As his voice resonated around the room, it was the only sound I could hear. The hum of the fridges and other machines had gone totally silent.

"Aisle four, just on the right," I answered, in a voice that didn't quite sound like my own.

My memory of that night has always remained a bit distorted. I don't remember him leaving the counter, I don't remember turning away, but all of a sudden a small stack of magic markers lay on the counter in front, along with a crisp, brand-new $20 bill. I looked over to my register as I was about to ring him up, but then I looked back he was already halfway to the door.

"Keep the change," he said, his voice sounding as though he was still right in front of me. As the front doors closed behind him, all the normal ambient sounds of the room returned. A few moments passed before I could vaguely comprehend what had just happened, realizing I had absolutely no recollection of seeing his legs move. That was the moment I started seriously thinking about getting a day job, or maybe just cutting down on the 'ludes.

*

I knew before getting home I was going to have an extra hard time sleeping that morning. I just couldn't get that eerie vision of the tall man out of my head. So when I got back to my dingy studio apartment just after 8am, I quickly downed a couple of beers to try to help things along. I got up a few hours later, about the time the afternoon paper arrived. The headline got my attention, and the story quickly gave me a case of the cold sweats.

GIRL MURDERED!
"The body of an unidentified woman was discovered in a room at the Evergreen Motel out on Route 22. When police arrived at the scene, they apprehended an unidentified male who was present in the room with the body. The Iron County Sheriff's office declined to provide any further details. A press conference is scheduled for later in the day."

As I cracked open another beer, my first assumption was it had to have been the Tall Man. It just seemed obvious after seeing him. I went to work that night fully expecting the police to show up at any second to question me, but no one did. Max and I had a short conversation about the murder before he turned the store over to me. That night was otherwise routine. My shift was up when the morning papers arrived and I found out why the cops didn't need to talk to me.

'*MURDERER CHARGED*' was the headline, followed by a perp-walk photo of someone who was definitely not the Tall Man.

> "*Iron County District Attorney Mark Jensen formally charged James B. Hassell, 38, with the murder of Louise H. Avery, 20. Avery, a known local prostitute, was found dismembered in the bathtub in a room at the Evergreen Hotel on Route 22 Thursday morning. When police arrived, Hassell, a truck driver who frequented the area was discovered in the room still covered in the victim's blood and in a state of dazed shock. No motive for the brutal killing has been speculated on by either the Sheriff's office or the District Attorney. Hassell is expected to make his first court appearance on Monday morning.*"

I took another look at the man in the photo. He did seem a bit familiar, but then again most truck drivers tend to look kind of the same to me, just slight variations on the same guy. He could have been in the store at some time that night. His thick mustached face just didn't ring any bells. On any given night, he really could have been anybody.

As a lot of people expected, Hassel was declared insane and therefore not competent to stand trial. I assumed that he had been locked up in some mental institution for the rest of his life somewhere. But by that point, the press had completely lost interest in the story. Several months later it happened again.

*

It could've been April or maybe even May. When you're working exclusively at night, the time of year becomes less and less relevant to your daily life. The first thing that still clearly stands out in my mind about the evening was it was a Thursday. Two large, unmarked eighteen-wheelers were parked out in front of Dutch's. About 1:45 in the morning, a fight broke out between two drunks in the parking lot just before closing. Not the most common thing, but at least it provided a bit of entertainment.

Just after 2:30, all the lights at Dutch's shut down. A couple of minutes later Barry got into his van and drove away into the darkness as usual. I could see about half a dozen cars parked across the highway over at the Evergreen, as well as some lights on in a couple of rooms. The "Y" in the neon vacancy sign was flickering a bit more than usual. That's when the Tall Man came back.

This time, I tried to pay a bit more attention to him and anything else strange that may have been taking place, but that didn't work. Again all the ambient sounds in the store suddenly stopped. The only sound I could hear as he seemingly floated up to the counter was the rush of blood flowing past my ears, pumped by the increased pounding of my heart. I looked down at my watch to make sure I noted what time he came in. As I gazed upon the movement of the second hand for what seemed like several minutes, I knew it was moving slower than it should've been. The moment I looked away from my wrist he was standing right in front of the counter, staring down at me from behind those same reflectionless black sunglasses.

"Do you have any magic markers?" he asked again in the same exact voice and tone as before, so exact my memory insisted that it could've been a recording.

Before I even knew what I was doing, before I could even make a conscious decision about what to do, I found myself pointing to their location, answering him just as I had before. "Aisle four, just on the right." And again, within an instant, a small pile of black magic markers lay at the counter in front of me. I don't remember looking away from him, but I must have, as the next thing I remember was the single, crisp $20 bill sitting on the counter where the markers had just been.

"Keep the change," he said, just as he passed through the door.

I leapt up from behind the counter and ran to the door, desperately wanting to see where he had come from, or at least get a look at what he had been driving. I stepped outside to discover that there was not even a trace of the normal nighttime sounds. Even the buzzing of the neon sign had gone. A terrible chill ran up and down my spine. I was frozen in my tracks for at least a solid minute. As soon as I could move, I went back into the store. The moment the door opened, all the ambient sounds of the machines around me instantly returned.

I went back behind the counter and made sure that the .44 was still there. I even picked the heavy thing up to see if it was loaded. Anyone else might have just left, ran off into the night, but I wasn't going anywhere until I saw the sun come up again. I spent the next hour with my eyes going back and forth between the front door, the clock on the wall, and the .44 underneath the counter.

*

A ringing phone abruptly woke me up just after nine that morning. I jumped out of bed, loudly cursing as I stomped into the next room. Luckily, my neighbors were all at work, leading their somewhat normal lives. At first I assumed it was my mother. No matter how many times I told her what my schedule was, she never seemed to understand that I was asleep during the day and awake at night. She was a master at not paying attention to the things she didn't want to know.

It was Max on the line, though. The tremor in his voice told me he was really scared, something I didn't think was possible. There had been another murder across the street at the Evergreen. He told the cops that I had been working that night and that they were probably on their way to my place to question me. That's when I knew the Tall Man must've had something to do with it. My blood froze and I found myself unable to speak. Max continued, telling me something that I didn't really register apart from taking pity on me and giving me that night off.

Like an idiot, I tried to go back to sleep. After about an hour, I got up and made some coffee, expecting that the arriving police would want some. They finally showed up around noon. Before I was even able to ask them to sit down, in some insane, cathartic moment, I told them about the Tall Man.

I held back all of the strange details, thinking that telling them about his mere presence would've been enough. The two of them let me ramble on while they were taking notes. They didn't seem to take me seriously, or think that this had anything to do with their case. Everything changed when I told them about the magic markers. Both of them stopped their scribbling, dead cold, gave each other badly concealed looks of concern, and then turned back to me before abruptly ending the interview. They didn't even tell me who had been killed. After they left, I got into my stash and took another 'lude, which finally let me get some sleep.

*

When I got back to work a couple of days later, I made the mistake of looking at a newspaper. The recent murders over the Evergreen Motel were splashed across the front page.

"MORE MURDERS AT HIGHWAY 22 MOTEL
Early on Thursday morning, a cleaning lady at the Evergreen Motel on Route 22 discovered the bodies of three people. An unidentified man was apprehended at the scene by Sheriff's deputies. The Sheriff's office declined to reveal any more details regarding the incident at this time. Sheriff's Office spokesman Ronnie Harvey would only say that details would be released at the appropriate time. This is the second incident of murder at the Evergreen Motel within the past seven months."

I had no idea what to make of any of it. Was it the Tall Man that they caught? I still didn't even know who'd been killed. Questions rattled in my head for more than an hour before I put up a "back in 5 min" sign, locked the doors, and wandered over to Dutch's for a quick drink.

Luckily, I got in just before Barry yelled out last call. The place was almost empty. I sat down at the far end of the bar and got a beer. At the other end was a scruffy-looking guy who I thought may have been the day manager at the Evergreen. Brian, I think his name was. It was obvious that he was already pretty drunk when he ordered three more shots of whatever battery acid he'd been drinking. I overheard what I assumed was the middle of a conversation. I really wish I hadn't.

"I've never seen so much fuckin' blood in my life, man!" he was saying to Barry, leaning over the bar, thinking no one else was listening. "It was all over the place. And when the cops pulled that trucker dude out of the room, I don't know his name, Richards 'er somethin', it was like he had written crazy shit all over himself with magic markers. The cops tried to put a sheet over him so that we couldn't see nothin', but I saw that crazy, fucked-up shit! And for a second, I saw the dude's eyes, man. It was like, like they didn't blink 'er nothin'. And the dude was muttering 'Cloo-loo, cloo-loo, all has been prepared for the spawn of cloo-loo,' and other shit that made even less sense. Cops tried to shut him up, but I heard that shit, and was fuckin' scary, man."

Barry just stared at him.

"Yeah, and the really fucked part about it was that the walls in the room were like covered in all the same weird, fucked up, magic marker writing that was all over the dude. Cops told me not to tell nobody. They gave me that typical pig bullshit 'you didn't see nothin' line. And another one said somthin' like 'don't go tellin' people about no Satanism 'n' shit.' I seen some a' them Satanist fuckers over near Barstow, and lemme tell ya, this was something altogether more fucked up. But Jesus Christ Barry, I just had a fuckin' tell somebody!"

I pounded what was left of my beer and practically ran out the door. I made it to the parking lot before puking my guts out. It took about half an hour for my stomach to calm down. Then I pulled a 'lude out of my pocket, and took half a tab.

*

Little by little, the details of what actually happened came in over the next few days, some of it from the papers, more of it from people who worked at the Evergreen. The dismembered bodies of three kids, hitchhikers, had been found in the room when one of the maids went in to clean it. The trucker, Richards, was sitting at the edge of the bed, naked and babbling barely intelligible words. After the cops took him away, he was found dead in his cell before he was even formally charged. The papers didn't say much about it, but I heard later from a passing cop that he swallowed his own tongue. I don't even know how someone could do that.

There was no mention of the Tall Man, not from the cops or the press or anyone else. A couple of reporters came by to ask if I had seen anything. Max told me to keep my mouth shut. He simply wanted to stay in good with the local cops. They all probably would have thought I was some kind of junkie if I had told them my story. It was for the better not to, anyway. My stomach went into knots every time I even thought about the Tall Man.

*

Unsurprisingly, within a month the Evergreen had closed. Brian, the hotel day manager, just upped and moved out of the area, leaving all his shit behind in a crappy apartment in town. No one ever saw him again. In the months that passed, occasional groups of bored teenagers poked over the decaying motel trying to scare each other. I'd call the cops and maybe they'd send someone to scare them off, but usually not.

Eventually, winter rolled around. Traffic down Route 22 dropped to a trickle, just a few skiers coming back from the slopes across the border. I'd get a snow plow or two stopping by in the middle of the night, with tired and cold drivers looking for some hot coffee.

More often than not someone would ask me about the murders. I didn't say much more than what was already public knowledge, pointing across the street to the snow-covered ruins of the Evergreen and saying, "Yup, right over there," or something equally bland. I never said a word about what Brian had told Barry. Sure as shit I didn't say a thing about the Tall Man. No one in their right mind would have believed the least of it.

One night—it must have been around one or maybe two in the morning—I went over to the walk-in fridge to restock the beer and soda coolers, for when Max came on day shift. He got kind of cranky if he had to do it himself. I pulled the heavy door open, walked into the totally dark room, and fumbled a moment for the light switch. Not immediately finding it, I looked along the inside wall, using what little light was coming in from the next room. I was a little pissed off at myself when I found it right where my hand should have felt it. I flipped it on, turned around, and found myself somewhere else.

Instead of a small space filled with shelves stacked with bottles and cans, it was a large white room with walls that were emitting a soft glow. Above me there was no ceiling, only a black sky full of stars. But it wasn't the night sky. None of the normal constellations were there. Huge, bloated alien stars and even entire galaxies were rolling past above me, just fast enough to give me the impression that the room was spinning.

There was the sound of wind somewhere far away, an incomprehensively enormous surge of air flowing back and forth. Somewhere buried deep in the most ancient, reptilian part of my brain, I knew that it was the sound of some dread thing breathing. Just above that was the chanting, coming from thousands of voices from every direction. There were no real words to speak of, just a discordant chorus of guttural rhythms. Many of the voices were easily identifiable as being human. Many of the others were just as obviously not.

The room was totally empty, except for a tall figure at the very center. I froze, completely unable to move a single muscle. I don't even remember breathing. He was upright, but not actually standing, more like floating just a few inches off the floor. The Tall Man was almost totally motionless, except for his long, black hair, which was flowing as though it was underwater.

He may have been looking at me, or staring right though me as though I didn't even exist. Then he smiled, reaching out with both hands towards me, beckoning me to come closer. I couldn't move. I was beyond terrified. His mouth opened, as if to say something. Then sound came out, totally out of sync with the movement of his lips.

"You have been such a great help," he said. That deep, unnatural voice reverberated massively. "We have all served, in preparing for the awakening."

On the white walls surrounding us, writing began to appear, first in gray, then slowly fading in to black. The symbols were like nothing I had ever seen before. They had no resemblance to any form of human communication I'd ever heard of. Then they grew and spread across the walls, until the surfaces had become a solid sheet of black.

"When the stars are right once again, you shall be rewarded," he said. He removed his glasses. He had no eyes behind those black lenses, just two black holes filled with stars. "You will be among the chosen few who will have the great honor to be devoured first!"

*

I'm still not sure how I got out of there. I must have run off and gotten into my car, because the next thing I remember was being back at my apartment, packing what little I possessed. Without saying a word to anyone, not to Max or my landlord, I just left. In the middle of the night, I drove straight back to my parent's house in Suttonton. I didn't even go back for my last paycheck.

I was at home less than a week when the cops showed up, the same two that grilled me the previous spring after the second set of murders. They asked me a lot of questions about the night I took off. I didn't say much other than I was sick and tired of working the night shift, and wanted to go back to school. I had no way of knowing what they wanted from me. Maybe Max had reported me missing or something, or thought I had stolen something.

I discovered later that Max had gone missing that next day. So had Barry and a few others they thought had been in the area that night. Barry's VW was left in the parking lot, along with two fully loaded eighteen-wheelers, their drivers nowhere to be found. None of them were ever seen again, as I understand it. The cops had already made up their minds that the whole thing was drug-related, that the missing men had been wasted by South American drug runners. They found a stash of various narcotics in a back room of Dutch's, and it was an easy—and clichéd—conclusion to draw. I did absolutely nothing to change their minds.

I took my last Quaalude that night. For the first time in months, I slept through an entire night. Yet sometimes, I still have dreams of spinning stars and slow, wind-like breath, accompanied by droning chants somewhere at the very edge of existence. In them, the Tall Man's grin is slowly broadening.

The Red Brick Building
by Mike Davis

It was twilight, and from the sidewalk, he stared up at the red brick building. Exactly when had it been built? The real estate lady's smile had wavered when he'd asked that question. In the '40s, she'd thought, but she offered to look it up if he wanted. He had smiled and told her not to bother; he knew that when the second World War was fought, the red brick building had already been there at least two hundred years.

Perhaps longer.

Most likely longer. Photographs and documents only took you so far. From there, you had to rely on word of mouth, on stories passed down through the centuries.

On legend.

The building had most recently been used as a church, and bore a sign that read: 'I AM ALPHA AND OMEGA, THE FIRST AND THE LAST. WOE TO THE INHABITERS OF THE EARTH.'

On this side, the street side, there was a great glass door. His key did not open it. As the sun sank lower, he walked down the street and around the corner of the building. This side bordered a lonely alley, running along the backs of houses. He wondered if the residents slept well at night. If they dreamed. If they knew that this building was a blood-red monument to the past.

Here, there were two doors. One was built into the cement at an angle. Beyond it, he remembered, dark steps led down. He shuddered as he stepped past. The other door was at the top of several steps—a small porch.

He took another key from his pocket. It fell from his trembling hand, and he bent to retrieve it. He became aware of a quiet hope inside himself, a hope that this key, too, would fail. But it slid into the lock with barely a sound.

The first time he had walked into this place, he had been an unwanted orphan, without a penny. The man who entered now was so wealthy that he hadn't even needed a mortgage to buy it.

Until this moment, he had not questioned his motives at all. Did he purchase the building just to tear it down? So that he could personally take a sledgehammer to every wall and window? Or was there another reason?

The door was heavier than he remembered, and it gave way slowly. The hinges squeaked, as if in warning. A thought came to him. Words were there, if only he could make them out. This was his last chance to turn back. Outside, behind him, existed a world where his wife and daughter waited, where he had found every happiness. Inside the red brick building was nothing but a black well of terrible memories. Surely no answers. Surely no reason why.

But it felt too late to turn back, so he walked through the now-open doorway.

The place was a labyrinth. It always had been. It was a maze of several upper stories of varying levels, and at least two basements—more than two, the other children had whispered. One friend had told him that he'd found a way down through five sub-basements and had stood before stairs leading down even further before he'd chickened out and come running back upstairs.

He was in a mud room of sorts. Ahead and to the right was the worst place on this level, he remembered—the sanctuary. To the left was the room where he had spent a third of his childhood.

He walked left.

Dust everywhere. Dust and memories.

This was where they had held school five days a week. Fifty or sixty kids of varying ages, all in one large room. Each with their own desk, wooden dividers between each student so they couldn't see each other while they studied. He walked around slowly, and somehow it was easy to remember where each of his friends had sat.

And it was easy to remember where his own desk was.

He stood before it, lost in the past. He'd spent much of a childhood chained to that desk, and it had seemed that much more cruel that there was a high window above it. A window where he'd constantly seen blue sky, the brightness of the sun, birds. He'd sometimes wished that he'd had one of the other desks, far away from that window, away from the memory of Outside. It would have been easier to forget.

Enough, he thought. *Enough. You got away.*

He walked through double doors into a hallway. Before him steps led down to the left, up to the right. Down the hallway, right, led to another sanctuary door. Upstairs, he remembered, were the lunchrooms, storage rooms, and secret rooms beyond count. There was even a bell-tower, though he'd never had the nerve to sneak up there.

He walked down the steps.

They took him back down to a landing at street level, before turning 180 degrees down to the first basement. On the landing was the great glass door, but this time he was on the other side of it. He stood before it, watching cars drive past in the street beyond, watching the lights of businesses go on as the sun went down. He thought of his wife and daughter, somewhere out there. What were they doing right now? Maybe they were at a park, or already at home eating dinner. Maybe they were waiting for his nightly out-of-town call.

He could leave now, he thought. He didn't have to see the rest of the building. He could push open the great glass door, run to his rental car, drive to the airport, and never look back.

Instead, he turned and walked down the stairs. When he reached the bottom, he turned and looked through the door again just as the sun sank behind the building across the street.

It felt like a last chance.

He glanced around. Dust everywhere. Dust, and memories.

Ahead was the school principal's office. It was a room he remembered well. The door was slightly ajar, and he pushed it open all the way. Everything was just as he recalled. The desk at the back where the fat blowhard had sat, lecturing. Floor-to-ceiling shelves, filled with moldy books.

There was no need to walk into that room. There was no need to relive what had happened there.

I shouldn't be here, he thought. *I should leave.*

Instead, he walked down the hall. Another door at the end, this one leading to the dark boiler room, and beyond that, more rooms. Large rooms, small rooms, secret rooms. One room was so huge that it had served as an indoor playground for him and his friends. He had often wondered why the building was so gargantuan, what possible reason could there have been for constructing something so huge.

Past the indoor playground, he walked into a long, narrow hallway. It was so dark that once he had gone twenty or thirty feet he could barely see his hand in front of his face. He wondered why he hadn't brought a light of some kind. Perhaps he'd never really thought he would go this far.

His footsteps clacked on the stone below... and stone it was, he remembered now. He shuffled slowly forward, keeping his arms in front of him. After a while in the complete darkness, it became difficult to judge just how long he'd been there. It felt as if he'd been putting one foot in front of the other for eternity, advancing not at all.

Then he realized that the passage was gradually descending, and that he could no longer hear his footsteps. He had advanced past the stones, and there was nothing beneath him but dirt. Without warning, he tripped, and would have fallen if his outstretched arms had not found the side of the tunnel—for tunnel he now remembered it was. Instead of the cool touch of earth that he was expecting, the wall was warm... warm and rubbery. It provoked an intensity of horror within him that was almost a memory. He recoiled from it and stumbled blindly forward.

Forward, and down.

There was some kind of light up ahead, a luminescence. At first the relief at being able to see something—anything—was total. As he moved closer though, the relief slowly gave way to dread.

And then from somewhere up ahead, he heard a sound. It was faint at first, and he stood still to try to make out what it was. A voice? Voices? The blood pounded in his ears, and he knew he was still too far away to identify the sounds, so he started walking again towards the glow. In the distance, the passage swung sharply to the right. The light pulsed and the sounds grew louder. There *were* voices. Chanting? Singing?

He drew up to the corner and stopped. No. Neither of those. Crying.

He drew a shaky breath and walked around the corner.

He was in an enormous cavern. Stalactites hung from a roof so high that it was lost in the shadows. A colossal opening lay a few yards away, and on the other side, a staircase, leading down into infinity. All of that drew his attention for less than a moment. He moved toward the source of the voices, the source of the sickly light.

Children. Dozens of them. All prone on the cave floor, soft cries coming from each of them. The youngest appeared to be five or six, and the oldest were in their teens. As he staggered closer, he could see thin membranes leading from each child to something in the wall. The pulsing, luminescent wall.

No. Not a wall. Something else, something alive. It hurt his eyes to look at it. More than hurt. Offended. Offended his eyes and his mind. Each child was connected to it, their eyes closed. All of them appeared asleep, even the ones who were sobbing. Confusion gave way to resolve. Whatever was happening, no matter how terrified he was, he had to free them. He approached the nearest child and looked down at him.

He staggered back, the blood draining from his face. Eyes wide, he examined each child in turn. They were all so young. Still so young. None of them had ever grown up. The faces of his friends, everyone he'd grown up with in the orphanage. None had escaped. No one but him.

A great sadness grew within him.

He would free them. Even if that killed them, it would be better than this. Better than an eternal youth of torment and anguish. His mind made up, he walked over to the boy who had been his best friend. The membrane snaked from the back of the boy's shirt. Reaching for it, his glance fell on the face of the next child, and he screamed.

The face was his.

Tears spilled from his eyes, and as he stared, he saw tears begin to leak from his younger face. "I don't understand," he whispered.

"I don't understand," the child echoed, eyes still closed.

Yes, you do.

He whirled, facing the wall, the being, whatever the hell it was. The light pulsed with the words, whispered by every child in unison.

He thought of his family. Memories overwhelmed him. The day he met his wife. His wedding. His daughter's birth. Her first step, her first words. His wife's smile.

They were home, waiting for him.

Except they weren't. He knew that now. They had never existed. He whispered their names over and over like a prayer. "I love you," he sobbed. "You have to be real. I love you."

You never left, whispered dozens of voices. *You've been here with me all along, down in the dark.*

He wiped his eyes. "I'm leaving. I'm going home. You can't stop me." But his legs refused to work, and he fell to his knees. He closed his eyes, and the darkness took him.

The Lullaby of Erich Zann
by G. K. Lomax

My first thought was that he was having trouble with the second violins.

The conductor in rehearsal is unmistakable. The concert-going public only sees the final (hopefully polished) performance, but it's the result of hours of behind-the-scenes sessions. These are often fraught and ill-tempered, with the conductor trying to get forty or fifty disparate and opinionated individuals to do it *his* way. Frequently, this isn't easy.

Some conductors try to cajole, some are bullies, some lecture, some harangue, some plead, some throw tantrums. I could tell you some stories from my time as a rank-and-file viola player, believe me. At some point however, all conductors display the body language that says, "No, no, no, that *wasn't* what I wanted. Let's try again." That's what Erich Zann was doing, the first time I laid eyes on him. It probably says something about my state of mind that I identified with him as a conductor before wondering why exactly he was rehearsing an unseen orchestra in a deserted London square at two o'clock in the morning.

I crossed the road so that I was directly behind him, and stood in a patch of shadow caused by a defective street-light. I'm a Londoner born and bred. I'm not afraid to walk its streets, day or night. I'm not naïve, however – a woman on her own is wise if she displays just a little caution. The difference between a harmless eccentric and a dangerous nutter is not always obvious before it's too late.

"Once more from the top, please. One, two, two, two..."

It's often the second violins, by the way. The clue's in the name, really. There's usually a couple of them who consider the label to be an insult, or think that the best way to progress to being a first violin is to stand out in a crowd. They're rarely right, and can end up passed over and embittered. Which is part of the reason why, early in my career, I switched from second violin to viola, before deciding that my true vocation lay in another direction.

I watched the performance. *Allegro*, common time. An intricate bit of counterpoint, it seemed, with a lot of input from the brass section. I found myself beating the measure.

He was a small, spare man somewhere past sixty, somewhat stooped and almost completely bald. He was wearing a dark overcoat which was rather too large for him. He had no baton, though his right hand seemed to clasp an imaginary one.

Crescendo. Fortissimo, with the timpani giving it plenty of welly. A long build to a climax, followed by rather abrupt finish, almost mid-bar. The mad conductor shook his head sadly, then turned round. I thought at first that he was going to take a bow as he received the adulation of an audience as invisible as his orchestra, but you don't take a bow after a rehearsal. Instead, he looked directly at me. I got the feeling that he'd been aware of my presence throughout. He started to walk towards me.

The difference between a harmless eccentric and a dangerous nutter is not always obvious before it's too late. It occurred to me for a fleeting moment to make myself scarce. It might have been better if I had, though not for the reasons my mother warned me about. I stood my ground, however. Partly this was because the man walked with the slow and painful gait of the elderly whose joints are troubling them, and I could see that he posed no physical threat at all – but mainly because I was overwhelmed with curiosity. I wanted to know more about him.

*

It's peaceful in here. Tranquil. Everyone walks quietly and talks in hushed tones. They tell me that I need to rest, and I smile in reply. They tell me lots of things – that the visions are nothing to be afraid of, for example. That there's a perfectly rational explanation. They're right, of course, but they don't know what the explanation is, and wouldn't understand if I told them. They haven't been where I've been. They haven't seen what I've seen, heard what I've heard. They weren't chosen by Erich Zann.

*

I suppose I'd better introduce myself properly. My name is Michelle Hinton, and I'm a jobbing composer. "Jobbing" in this instance means that you won't have heard of me. I'm unknown to concert-goers, don't feature in the classical charts, have never had a *Radio Three* programme dedicated to my works. I write advertising jingles, theme-tunes for minor TV shows, incidental music for this, that and the other. I tell myself that this is because I'm still working my way up the ladder, though in truth I'd hoped to be a few rungs higher by now. Still, I can take comfort in the fact that when your average couch-potato spends an evening surfing through a hundred TV channels, there's at least a fair chance that he or she will hear something by me, without realising it.

Which is all very well, but I've not abandoned my loftier ambitions, even if they've begun to seem distressingly like pipe-dreams. My unperformed First Symphony has been gathering dust for almost a decade now, my unfinished Viola Concerto ditto. And though I accept that life rarely goes according to plan, I can't help thinking that there's something else that's holding me back. Something rather fundamental, and desperately unfair.

Stop anyone in the street and ask them to name half a dozen composers. The chances are that they'll start with Beethoven and Mozart and Tchaikovsky and Brahms. What do these composers have in common? They're all men. Ask the same people to name a female composer and you'll get a lot of blank looks. No-one will mention Ethel Smyth, for example. She went as deaf as Beethoven, by the way, though in *his* case it was a tragedy. In some fields, emancipation still has a long way to go.

Does this make me angry? Well, yes. Do I think that if I'd been born male I would've been taken more seriously? Yes again. Please don't get the impression that I'm some sort of virago, or a dyke in dungarees or anything like that (Ethel Smyth *was* a lesbian, incidentally – had a crush on Virginia Woolf at one point). I admit that I've got a chip on my shoulder, but that just makes me more determined. Rather than expecting things to be handed to me on a plate, I accept that I've got to work for them. If the fact that I'm female means that I have to work ten times as hard, then so be it.

Which is another reason why I know so much about difficult rehearsals. Advertising jingles and TV theme tunes need to be played by someone. Whilst I admit that the ensembles I get to lead are pared-down shadows of full orchestras, it still takes a certain amount of brass neck to stand in front of a bunch of professional musicians and tell them that, "This is the music I've written and *this* is how you're going to play it." When you can see in their eyes that they don't take you seriously because of your gender – that takes things to a whole new level. I try to be diplomatic, but it's not always easy.

About a month ago, it seemed that my hard work was finally beginning to pay off. I was commissioned to write a film score. I was overjoyed. Film scores have cachet. They get you noticed, and played on Classic FM. There's a belief that composers who, a century ago, would have written symphonies and sonatas are now working for the film industry. This may well be true, but the severe lack of gender equality hasn't changed much. Not that I'm denying the genius of John Williams or Hans Zimmer or Danny Elfman, but surely there's room for *one* woman at the top table?

I set to with a will. I knew that I'd been given an opportunity which I had to grasp with both hands. If I made a mess of it, it was long odds against me being offered another. Which may have been where the trouble started as, in my determination to come up with something remarkable and memorable, I became hyper-critical of my own work.

I sat for days on end at my piano, trying this combination of notes and that, scribbling down vague sketches and germs of ideas, then playing them back and being dissatisfied with all of them. I began to get angry with myself, and with the anger came stress, and a growing realisation that my deadlines were looming ever closer. I've heard some people in the business say that deadlines concentrate the mind wonderfully, but all they induced in me was a rising sense of panic. I was going to blow it, because the ideas wouldn't come.

Now, I don't want you to get the idea that all a composer does is sit back and wait for inspiration to strike. Composing is a job of work like any other. There are established ways by which an initial fragment can be shaped, moulded and built up into a finished score. It's hard work, and can involve long and pretty stressful hours. But you cannot make bricks without straw. The initial spark has to come from somewhere.

Which explains why I was walking the streets at 2am. I'd fielded a difficult phone-call from the producer's hatchet-man – the one whose job it was to shout and rage and fire people as required – and I don't think he was totally convinced by my assurance that I'd have a piano sketch at least within the next few days. Actually, I know he wasn't convinced. He didn't shout and rage or anything, but he has a way of menacing people down a phone line whilst hardly saying a word. I could see my career slipping away before it had really started, which only made me worry more. On top of that, the advance was returnable, and I'd already spent half of it.

So I went back to my piano and banged away at the keys, and screamed, and cursed, and pulled at my hair and did all the things that temperamental artistic types are supposed to do. Nothing. Nothing that seemed good enough, anyway. Various ideas arose, but even as I wrote them down to save them for possible future use, I saw that they were trite and banal. Not what I was looking for.

Around ten o'clock, I ran myself a bath. Sometimes a long, perfumed soak does the trick. I use the word "trick" advisedly. On occasion, it's possible to fool your subconscious into believing that you've given up, and an idea will just pop into your head. It's happened before. It didn't work this time, probably because I simply couldn't switch myself off. After the bath I tried the usual distraction techniques – television, toe-nail painting, ice-cream – but nothing seemed to work. I couldn't even go to bed in the hope that things would look better in the morning, as I was as wide awake and restless as I've ever been.

Finally, in desperation, I decided to go for a walk, hoping that London's streets in the small hours would provide the longed-for inspiration. Either that, or I'd make myself tired enough to sleep.

*

They tell me that I've been here for a week. I don't reply. They don't know that time is unimportant. A second, a week, a year, an aeon, it's all the same in the end. I've been to the Centre, where time bends in on itself to create the eternal Now.

*

The mad conductor approached me slowly. It seemed to be up to me to initiate the conversation, though.

"Bravo," I said. I'm not sure why. Possibly I was being ironic.

He stopped in front of me, seemed to pause for thought, then said, "The music must be played."

His voice was croaky and hesitant. I wondered if he was one of those lonely old people who can go from one week's end to the other without talking to a human soul – one whose speech muscles begin to degrade from a combination of age and lack of use.

"The music must be played," he said again, waving a bony finger at me. "You will play it, perhaps?"

"Me?" I answered, taken by surprise.

"You," he said. "Yes, you. You are a composer, no?" His accent was hard to place, given the rasp in his throat. He certainly wasn't English, but then, so few of London's inhabitants are, these days. I thought he sounded a bit German.

"Yes," I told him. "I'm a composer. How did you know?"

He didn't answer me directly. Instead he repeated, "The music must be played." Then, possibly sensing my confusion, he added, "I left it unfinished. I have been waiting."

I suppose I could have simply walked away, but something stopped me. Maybe it was the pricking of my conscience, which wouldn't let me turn my back on someone so old and seemingly helpless – particularly on a night that was none too warm for all that summer was supposed to be around the corner.

"What's your name?" I asked him.

"I am Erich Zann," he said. "You *will* have heard of me." The name meant nothing to me, though the tone of Zann's voice suggested that he was making a statement, rather than asking a question.

"I'm Michelle Hinton," I told him. He seemed uninterested in this piece of information. "Where do you live?"

"It was in Paris," he said. For a second I thought that he'd said that he lived in Paris, but then he continued. "It was in Paris that I started to write it, but I never finished. Someone else must finish it for me. You must finish it, for the music must be played."

OK. Old, helpless and several marbles short of – whatever a set of marbles is called. I had a vision of dialling 999 and trying to persuade the police to call round the local care homes to ask if any of them was missing a resident. It didn't appeal, so I settled for plan B, which was to ask the old man if he fancied a coffee.

"Coffee," he said, as if essaying an unfamiliar word. "Yes, coffee perhaps."

I led him down a side-street to an all-night café I knew of. It's run by a couple of brothers, Turkish, I think, or possibly Bulgarian. They serve decent coffee, anyway. The old man walked extremely slowly, and I revised my estimate of his age upwards. He had to be eighty, perhaps more.

Inside the café, I sat him at a table and approached the counter, where I got the slight nod due to a customer who wasn't quite a regular. I ordered the coffees. I asked the old man if he wanted a latte or a cappuccino, but he didn't seem to know what either of those words meant. After a few words of explanation, he settled on an espresso.

I took him his coffee and sat down opposite him. "How did you know I was a composer?" I asked him again.

He seemed surprised by the question. "One composer should know another, no?" He stared at me. His face was veined and blotchy, but his eyes were bright. They were a most peculiar pale blue, the like of which I'd never seen before. For an instant, I got the impression that he was anything but senile, and that he was studying me intently. "Yes," he said, waving his finger at me again, "the music must be played. You will finish my music, and you will play it." He reached forward slowly, and touched the tip of his finger against my forehead.

I was about to protest when the brother behind the counter called out to me. I'd been so distracted that I'd forgotten to pick up my change. Honest of him, I thought, as I got up to fetch it. When I turned back to the table, Erich Zann was nowhere to be seen.

I stood there for a second, blinking stupidly. I'd only had my back turned for a moment. Not even Usain Bolt could have made it out of the café in that time, certainly not without me hearing the scrape of a chair or the sound of the door. And yet Erich Zann had simply vanished. His untasted coffee was still on the table, but it sat in front of an empty chair. I turned back to the guy behind the counter, seeking some form of confirmation, but he'd already turned away and was busying himself at a sink. The only other customers were a pair of shabby middle-aged women, each staring fixedly into their cup of tea.

I opened my mouth to say something, but realised that I could hardly ask, "Excuse me, but did anyone see an old man vanish into thin air?" without sounding stupid. That left me no other option but to leave the café with as much dignity as possible, and to head home in search of a stiff drink, and possibly the realisation that I'd been dreaming.

*

They tell me that I've been working too hard, and that I need to rest. I don't mind. I probably need to save my strength anyway, for what is to come. They give me something from time to time. They say it will help me to sleep. I think I sleep, but I'm not sure. I know I don't dream. What would be the point of a dream within a dream?

*

Feeling confused, embarrassed and more than a little annoyed, I made my way back home. For me, home is a detached house on a leafy street in a district which is predicted to be the next boom area. Not that I care. Though I never tell a direct lie, I sometimes let people believe my house was purchased with my earnings as a composer. The truth is that it was bought by my grandparents back in the fifties, and was left to me, their only grandchild, when my mother declared that she'd moved out of it once, and that it would seem too strange to move back in. It's far too big for me – there are rooms I have to remind myself to dust once a month or so – but I feel it that leaving would be disloyal. My mother keeps telling me it will be ideal when I start a family, and lets her disappointment hang in the air. It's not that I don't want to start a family. I do, but all I've managed so far in that direction is a succession of ex-boyfriends.

One major plus my house does have, courtesy of a loft conversion, is a music-room, and it was there that I headed, large vodka in hand. I stopped on the threshold. The music-room has a skylight, through which a shaft of moonlight was shining directly onto the piano. I suppose that due to the workings of celestial mechanics this happens on a regular and predictable basis, but I'd presumably been asleep on all the former occasions. Come to that, I didn't remember seeing the moon at all during my nocturnal comings and goings. But then, who looks up at the night sky when they're preoccupied with other thoughts?

The effect was striking. It was as if the piano was on a West End stage, attracting the attention of a mega-watt spotlight. The rest of the room, by contrast, was veiled in gloom. Its clutter of drums, guitars, music stands, and synthesisers was formless, indistinct and unimportant. The piano was the only thing that mattered.

Not wanting to spoil the effect, I decided against turning on the light, and approached the piano. It's an ordinary upright, which surprises some people. Certainly I'd like to have a Bösendorfer, but such a beast needs a concert hall with big acoustics. Even if I could afford one, it would be cruel of me to confine it in my loft. I have long believed that a piano is, metaphorically at least, a living thing, and that the reason that truly great pianists – the Ashkenazys of this world – can give such magnificent performances is that they are able to tap into the instrument's soul. That night, my piano passed way beyond metaphor. The white keys shone painfully bright in the moonlight, and the black ones seemed to suck light into themselves, until they became the embodiment of nothingness. As I sat on the stool and set my glass aside, I swear my piano was expectant, and hungered to be played.

I ran my hands lovingly over the keys, then raised them high in the dramatic gesture that has become a habit. I paused, then brought them down, and was dumbfounded. I had played, or had intended to play, four random chords. And yet those chords in that sequence formed a phrase that instantly set my heart pounding. I played it again. Yes, there was something there, something I could work with. I seized a sheet of manuscript paper and scrabbled around for a pencil. One should always write new ideas down straight away. As well as being elusive and unpredictable, inspiration is transitory, and disinclined to repeat itself – a lesson I learned the hard way. To me, *The Lost Chord* is not a comic song. Then it was back to the keyboard, and suddenly ideas were tumbling out. One phrase led to another. A graceful treble melody suggested itself, with a portentous bass counterpoint. Themes begat themes, interwove with each other, shifted from major to minor and back again, developed themselves with labyrinthine complexity.

I was frenzied. I played, I scribbled; I played and scribbled again. I remember feeling that I'd finally come up with something truly significant. This was no advertising jingle or ephemeral TV theme tune. This was... This was something that would finally make my name.

*

They tell me that my mother's been to visit me each day. She's been staying in my house. She's probably spring-cleaned it. I should feel sorry for her. I've been the only family she's had since my father died two years ago. Cancer. Soon I'll be gone, too. I'll have gone with Erich Zann to stand at the Centre, and my mother will remain trapped in time. I would explain it to her, but she'd never be able to comprehend.

*

I've no idea how long I sat there, covering sheet after sheet with bars and phrases and measures. Two or three hours, maybe, though it could have been much longer. As far as I remember, I transcribed everything by moonlight. I seem to remember thinking that I ought to turn on the light, but the ideas were coming thick and fast, and I didn't dare get up for fear of losing the flow, or of spoiling the weird atmosphere. It must have been a strain on my eyes, as I was seeing spots before them by the time I finished.

Eventually, I reached a point where I knew that I had everything. I'm not sure how I could have been so certain of that, but I was. That's not to say that there wasn't still a lot of work to be done. I was far from finished, but I had all the *pieces*. They would need to be ordered properly, then refined and polished, then orchestrated. This, however, was a matter of technique, not of inspiration. Exhausted yet exhilarated, I went to bed.

If I'd been less tired, however, I might've noticed something strange. If I had truly sat at my piano for several hours, surely the moon would have set, or at least moved to a different part of the sky? It certainly shouldn't have continued to shine at that precise angle through my skylight the whole time. Yet my memory insists that it did.

*

I woke with a start, sat bolt upright, and looked over at the clock beside my bed. Half past twelve. It's sometimes said that you can tell a musician by their habit of getting up early in the afternoon, but I try to keep more respectable hours most of the time. I made myself some coffee, and took the mug up to the music room.

The floor was littered with manuscript paper, and the place smelled of vodka. Without realising it, I'd knocked my glass over the previous night, and it had shattered on the floor. I ought to have swept up the broken glass, especially since I was barefoot. Instead, I stepped around it.

I gathered up the sheets and started to go through them. The writing was appalling, a feverish scrawl at best. Nevertheless I took the pages over to the computer and started to transcribe them. I don't know how composers managed before computer software. They say that Mozart could hear an entire orchestra in his head – every part from piccolo to timpani – just by looking at a score. But, well, he was Mozart. Nowadays, it's possible to enter a piece of music and hear it back, played by any instrument, pretty much straight away. Then you can develop it on screen. You can transpose it to another key at the click of a mouse, move a line from the horns to the bassoons, program in harmonies... Well, you get the idea. Some composers, I'm told, actually do their primary entry at the keyboard. I mean the computer keyboard, not the piano one – technology may have advanced, but the vocabulary hasn't caught up yet. Either way though, I have to start with paper and pencil.

Even with my computer's help, it took a long while before I had anything near a finished article. It was basically a fugue, the exposition of which – starting softly on the cellos and building steadily as more and more layers were added – would serve as the theme of the film itself. The development introduced two competing themes, which would be the motifs of two of the subsidiary characters of the film. One was plangent and woodwind-led, the other was brasher, and featured some slightly dissonant brass. I was particularly pleased with the latter. It would be developed into the creature's theme, rhythmic and repetitive, and just jarring enough to set the audience on edge without making them complain about the racket.

It occurs to me that I've not said much about the film whose score I'm supposed to be composing. Frankly, I'm a little in the dark myself. I've been given a copy of the script – after signing an agreement stating that if I let anyone else see it I would attract the attention of men with sober suits, no sense of humour, and a reputation of winning extortionate damages for their client – but it didn't knock me out. As far as I can see, it's a horror. Unsuspecting heroine unearths bizarre artefact, which is then stolen from her. It turns out that the said artefact can be used to summon or banish demons (hence my "Creature's theme") from another dimension. They've given me some pictures of these demons, as dreamed up by a conceptual artist. They're really rather gruesome, and made me feel uncomfortable when I looked at them. Goodness knows what the effect will be when they've had the full CGI treatment.

Anyway, the heroine enlists the aid of a nerdish professor, who turns out to be an Indiana Jones clone. Together they battle to prevent the deranged bad guy from unleashing the apocalypse. Not my sort of thing at all, but I was hardly going to say that when they offered me the gig.

Actually, I think that part of the reason I *was* offered the gig was that CGI is taking up so much of the budget that corners needed to be cut elsewhere. I'm not saying I'm cheap – but I'm cheaper than hiring anyone the audience will have heard of. Even then, they tried to beat me down. I was eventually obliged to accept a reduced fee in return for an increased share of the royalties on the soundtrack album. If any. But this no longer matters. Even if the royalties run into millions, I'll never see a penny, nor wish to. Money will not be of the slightest importance in that place.

I completed a first draft, with partial orchestration. That is to say that for the most part I scored a top line for the first violins, with the violas, cellos and double basses echoing it (thanks to the software) at intervals. Oh, and the second violins, of course. Mustn't forget them, much as I'd like to. Similarly, the brass was playing *tutti*, and the clarinets, oboes and flutes were playing follow-my-leader in fourths and fifths. It's a useful way of getting an idea of the finished product in a relatively short time.

Even so, it took many hours. When I reckoned I was just about done, it was deep into the small hours. I saved the score to a file which, after a pause, I labelled Erich Zann. Then I belatedly fixed myself something to eat.

Fortified, I lay down on the floor and closed my eyes. This may sound an odd thing to do, but I find that to give music my fullest attention, it's best to shut out the other senses as much as possible. I pressed *play* on the remote.

The music played, and I listened. I tried to do so objectively – as the audience, not the composer – but I have to say that I was transported. I've attended a lot of classes on composition and musical theory, and the upshot of them all was that music doesn't really have any rules. It has norms, it has guidelines, but these are constantly being rewritten. Beethoven was considered dangerously avant-garde in his day, for example. Some of his harmonies would have shocked Haydn to the core, but he would have been appalled in his turn by, say, the atonal stuff of the Second Viennese School.

I'm not saying that the piece I'd just written was a wholly radical departure, but there was something in the chromatics that I didn't believe I'd heard before. Something ethereal, even unearthly, particularly in the brass-led passages. Since I was supposed to be writing something to accompany supernatural beasties from the beyond, I was quite pleased with myself. I smiled gently as I lay on the floor.

"The music must be played."

I swear that I actually heard the voice of Erich Zann, repeating the phrase he'd uttered so emphatically in the café. The surprise made me open my eyes – at which point hearing voices became the least of my problems. Colours were pouring from the speakers which my computer was hooked up to. Colours formed and moderated by the music. Greens for the strings – a dark Lincoln for the double-basses, lightening up to a bright Chartreuse for the first violins – various blues for the woodwinds and, pulsing throughout, a lurid orange that chimed with the brass.

I didn't stay to watch the performance. Seized with a sudden panic, I bolted from the house and ran.

*

They tell me that my mother found me, and raised the alarm. She'd become concerned by my failure to answer her calls or to respond to her messages, so she'd "popped by." She has a key. She says she found me on the floor of the music-room, mumbling something incoherent about colours in space. She told the people here that I hadn't eaten or slept properly for weeks. I didn't argue, or ask how she could know this. Mothers always know. It may well be true. She also found the gruesome pictures the film people had given me. They shocked her, but then they were designed to. So here I am.

I don't blame my mother. Indeed, I feel sorry for her, because she doesn't understand. She cannot understand what I will become.

*

I didn't run far. There's a small park about half a mile from my house, where I sometimes go jogging. When I got there, I slumped down on a bench, panting heavily, and forced myself to think.

Had I gone mad? I began to reason things through. Erich Zann's voice had clearly been my imagination. I'd been thinking about him – had even named a file after him – and it was entirely understandable that my brain would make the association between him and the music. This was especially true given the frenzied strain of composition, not to mention my lack of sleep. As for the colours, well, there was a rational explanation for them as well. Synaesthesia. The way that, for some people, certain words or sounds really do appear to have colours associated to them.

There have been many documented cases. They say that Franz Liszt was one. During rehearsals, he was prone to saying things like, "Not blue enough, gentlemen," or "A little too much yellow in that passage." People thought he was mad, or joking, or both, but it turned out he really did see colours whenever music was played. Synaesthesia is a known phenomenon, and nothing to be frightened of. I didn't recall hearing of any case where the condition had occurred spontaneously in a new subject, but it was hardly something I'd studied in depth. Several composers have had it, and found it useful. Sibelius, I think, and Rimsky-Korsakov.

I calmed down, and my breathing slowed to normal. There was light in the eastern sky, and I watched the play of colours as dawn broke. I wondered idly if I'd now be able to transcribe a sunrise for full orchestra.

"You have done very well. The music will be played."

I turned my head. Erich Zann was sitting next to me. I have no idea how he'd managed to approach the bench and sit down without me noticing him, but his appearance neither alarmed nor truly surprised me. I realised that I'd been expecting him without being aware of the fact.

Still, there were questions I wanted answers to. "Who are you?" I asked.

"I am Erich Zann." He didn't look at me, but stared fixedly to his front.

"I need more of an answer than that."

"The music is the answer. The music is always the answer. It must be played. It will be played."

"When?"

"There is no When. There is no Where, either. For the music, it is always Now, and always Here. Music always was."

"Music always was what?"

He finally looked at me, and I found myself transfixed by his shimmering blue eyes. They seemed to hint at unfathomable wisdom and unguessable secrets. "I mean that music always was. Before everything, there was music. Before all this." He waved his arm vaguely, though his meaning wasn't clear. "Music will still be after all this," he went on, gnomically, "and will remain until the Dreams start anew."

"The dreams?"

"Not yet. Not new ones, if it can be prevented. That is why the music must be played. You have done well."

"Done well? What do you mean? And how do you know what I've done?"

"I started it. In Paris, many years ago. I did not finish it, though. I was prevented. The young man. He did not know what he was doing. The music touched him in a way that overcame his reason. He tried to silence me. It was a very high window."

I looked at him blankly. What young man?

"Since then, I have been looking for someone to complete it for me," Erich Zann went on. I am fortunate that I found you before..." he tailed off.

My mind went back to the moment in the café when he'd touched my forehead. Was he trying to suggest – but no, that was absurd. I gave an exasperated sigh, and in so doing I took my eyes off Erich Zann for a moment. Just a moment, I'm sure, but in that moment he vanished.

*

I walked slowly back to my house. Out of curiosity I called up the on-line version of Grove's Dictionary of Music and Musicians. Every composer and significant musician who's ever lived has a biography in Grove – about seventeen thousand all told, all the way back to 1450. I found an entry for Erich Zann, but was disappointed to read of a player of the bass viol, born in Nuremberg circa 1830, who had composed for the Paris theatre, and who had died in a fall in 1897. Clearly not my man – though the German origin and the mention of Paris made me think that the Zann in Grove was an ancestor of my mysterious acquaintance.

I played Fugue of Erich Zann (as I had come to think of it) again, this time sitting in front of the speakers and watching carefully. The colours came again. Each instrument had its hue, each note its shape. They performed their dance as I watched them, writhing, intertwining, inter-blending and supporting each other.

That is, until the arrival of the creature theme, with its pulsing brass and lurid shades of orange. These came out of the speakers and seemed to attack the blues and the greens, gradually strangling them and subsuming them – until the recapitulation, when the main theme was re-stated. Haltingly at first, but eventually triumphantly. Though the orange seemed to resist, it was soothed, lost its angry hue, and became calmer and more warming, more in harmony with the rest.

The piece ended. I wondered whether I'd see the exact same performance if I played it again, but instead tried a different experiment. I picked a piece of music at random from my library – Tchaikovsky's Swan Lake Suite – and played it expectantly, waiting to see what colours the swans would be, and whether I'd see them dance, and transform themselves into ballerinas.

I was to be disappointed. I saw no colours. I let the piece play through to its end, and really *tried* to see colours, but I didn't. Not a vestige. It seemed that I was selectively synaesthetic, if that's the right term. I googled synaesthesia and read a couple of learned articles, plus a few less-learned ones. They told me nothing. No-one knows how or why the condition arises, and no two synaesthetes describe it in the same way. As to whether the condition could arise spontaneously, I found no answer, because no-one had thought to ask the question.

*

They tell me that seeing colours is not a reason to panic. They tell me it has a medical name, synaesthesia. They seem surprised to learn that I already know this. They seem puzzled when I tell them that the colours I see only come when I play my own music, but they shrug. Possibly they're humouring me. They tell me not to worry. Although synaesthesia is little-understood, no-one has ever died of it. I think they mean this last bit as a joke. I don't laugh. They give me something, and tell me to relax.

*

Experiment over, I once again felt the fierce pull of the Fugue, and I was soon deep in the detailed orchestration of the work. I was pleased with it, in a way that no other piece I've written has pleased me. It occurred to me that it was too good to be a mere film score, certainly not for a second-rate schlock-horror. I had a vision of conducting its debut performance during the Proms, and humbly acknowledging a rapturous ovation. I thrust the thought aside. Day-dreams are all very well, but they don't pay the bills.

I ploughed on, deep in the minutiae of major thirds and minor fifths that is the stuff of orchestration. This is where composing becomes close to drudgery, but on this occasion I worked faster and more easily than I ever had before. Often, when searching for exactly the right note for the second beat of the third bar of a certain phrase, I have been reduced to trial and error, finding myself wavering indecisively between two options. Now, however, I knew what was right because I could see it. If a note was wrong, it remained just a note. If it was right, then it became a flash of colour. Composition by colour chart – a sort of reverse paint by numbers.

Swiftly though I worked, I once again lost track of time. It was dark by the time I was done. I didn't lay on the floor, as I wanted to see as well as hear. I positioned a chair in front of the speakers, sat down, and pressed play.

The Fugue began as before – though richer, now that it was finished. The colours were richer also, sharper, more animated, with subtler differences of hue to reflect the more detailed orchestration. I smiled a self-congratulatory smile. Then the orange theme began.

I was too strongly fixated on the kaleidoscopic dance before me to notice it at first, but belatedly became aware that my room was becoming faded and blurred. I initially thought it was just an illusion, similar to the way that the moonlight on the piano had made everything else seem indistinct.

After a while, however, the effect became unmistakable. The music-room was fading, and something else was taking its place. I tried to stand up, but couldn't.

The music played, and the colours danced. I wondered if it was the music itself that was somehow making everything else fade. I tried to switch it off, but my fingers passed through the remote as if it was made of smoke.

The room vanished completely, and I got the impression of a vast emptiness – too vast to be properly perceived. It was dark, and icy winds blew, first in one direction and then another. I shivered, and the music played on.

*

They tell me that a rather rude man has tried to see me. They're apologetic, but I smile to show that I don't blame them. I know who the man is. He's the hatchet-man who works for the producer of the film. The film for which my music was supposed to be the theme, but now won't be, for it has a mightier purpose. I smile to say let the man come, for he doesn't frighten me. They don't let the man come, which is a shame as, after what I've seen, I can frighten *him*.

*

Slowly, so slowly that I cannot describe it, I became aware that I was not alone. I was one of a multitude – one of a million millions – yet so vast was the emptiness that it was not filled beyond an infinitesimal fraction. Every one of the multitude was staring at the same spot in the unguessable distance.

I stared, too. I don't know what it was that I saw, but it filled me with awe. It was vast, as vast as the night sky. It was many-faceted. So many and so varied were these that it was impossible to focus on one part without the mind being distracted by a myriad of others. There was an impression of cubes and spheres and other, more complex, forms. Forms that only a mathematician could name. Forms so intricate and fantastical that that they defied naming at all. There were loops and whorls and clusters, spirals and planes and curves. There were parallels that were not parallel, and angles that couldn't be. It moved, or parts of it moved within itself, twisting and coiling, and passing through each other as they challenged the dimensions. It shone darkly with a thousand colours, all of them black. I gazed at it, and it filled me with horror, the sort of horror I'd felt when gazing at the picture of the film-creature, but magnified untold times. It was the sum of all nightmares – portentous, malevolent, all-powerful, nausea-inducing. Above all, it was a *presence*.

A presence that was becoming restless. A presence that was awakening.

Through it all, my music played. The colours went out into the void and performed the dance. The orange melded with the greens and the blues, and submitted to them, and was quieted. The restlessness of the presence seemed to diminish very slightly.

"The music has been played."

I couldn't take my eyes off the vastness, but I knew that Erich Zann was by my side.

"Where are we?" I asked.

"At the Centre."

"At the centre of what?"

"At the Centre. The Centre is everywhere, and it is at the centre of everything. The Centre is the beginning of all things, and also the end. It is the eternal Now."

"And what is that – that *thing*?"

"That is Azathoth, though he has many other names. Azathoth is the Centre and the Centre is Azathoth. Azathoth is the Beginning and Azathoth is the End. Azathoth is the Dreamer of Dreams. Azathoth dreams all things. Everything that is, is but a dream of his. You and I and all that we have known are dreams of Azathoth. But Azathoth stirs. Azathoth starts to wake, and when Azathoth wakes he will dream no more. And what will become of the stuff of Azathoth's dreams then? Azathoth must not wake."

"Who are you? I mean really."

"I am Erich Zann. I was born in Nuremburg long ago, though the time of my birth is also Now. I was called upon. I was not the first. There have been many. Multitudes. They are all around you. They are the Choir. I was called upon to make music with the Choir, to contribute a small part to the whole. I failed of my task. I was prevented, and did not complete it. Because of this, an imbalance was caused. I have been searching for one to finish what I began and restore the balance. You have done so. By your work, Azathoth shall not wake. Not yet."

"You are the Erich Zann of Nuremberg? That would make you more than a hundred and eighty years old."

"I am neither old nor young. I am but a dream of Azathoth. But hearken: the Choir will take up your music."

And they did. Cued by I know not what, the entire multitude lifted their voices in song, though neither "Voice" nor "Song" adequately describes their music-making. There was every kind of sound – woodwind, brass, strings, percussion, yes, but every other conceivable and inconceivable sound also. There was the music of the oceans, the music of the winds, the music of electrons in their orbits, and the music of stars imploding. There was every kind of pitch, from notes so low that they might have been the thrumming vibrations of an abyss vast enough to swallow galaxies, to bitter, piercing trills fit to shatter a quark.

The Choir sang. It sang my music, and it sang many other musics, a hundred, a thousand, too many to count. Musics from every corner of the cosmos, from every race that has ever walked or crawled or slithered or swum. From every race that has ever aspired. Musics of multitudinous forms, some ethereally beautiful, some cacodaemoniacally alien – and yet all somehow blending into a monumental whole. The Choir sang, and the presence slowly became less agitated and more still.

*

They tell me that I need to relax, that I will feel better in time. They play me music. They've been told that I like music, and they are glad, because they think music will calm me. They don't play *my* music. No-one plays *my* music. Not here.

*

I came to, lying on the floor of my music-room, with no idea what time it was, or what day. I sat on the floor and hugged my knees, thinking of Erich Zann and the Choir – and the presence that was called Azathoth. The presence that stirred in its sleep, and was charmed back to deeper slumbers by music. Music that was constantly played, constantly renewed.

I had written the music, or at least a part of the music. A fragment which, combined with a myriad of others, formed the vast mosaic of song that sooths Azathoth as he dreams the cosmos. I smiled at that. What I had actually written was a lullaby.

*

They think I'm mad. That's the one thing they don't say, but I know they do. It doesn't matter what they think. I've been here a week, or I think I have. It doesn't matter. Time doesn't matter, not at the Centre. When time doesn't matter, waiting is not waiting.

I'm waiting and not waiting for Erich Zann. I know he'll come for me. He'll come for me, and together we'll go to the Centre, and we'll join the Choir. We'll stand before the Dreamer of Dreams, and we'll sing the music, and the Dreams will go on.

Cymothoa Cthulhii
by Gethin A. Lynes

Leaning on the railing of the upper deck, Patrick listens to the sound of the river against the hull. The lights of other boats bob gently out on the dark river. Tiny motes of phosphorescence drift by. He watches as they're carried upstream by the slow, incoming tide, minute cogs in the great machine of existence. Below him he can hear the lazy murmuring of Prue and Charlie, drifting out the window of their cabin in the blessedly quiet aftermath of their fucking. Downstairs, on the lower deck, Blake and Daisy have stopped talking. Blake is probably trying to convince her to go to bed.

Daisy giggles.

A moment later Blake's drunken whisper hisses out over the lower deck. "Why is he here?"

Patrick smiles. He knows where this is going.

Daisy's a little less smashed than Blake. He almost can't hear her. "Because he's my friend."

Patrick doesn't mind Daisy using him as a buffer against the affections of her boyfriends. He's a patient man. Blake seems okay, like most of them. Uncomplicated. Simple. He understands games—sports, or cards even. He likes to drink, to have fun. His taste for good scotch is surprisingly sophisticated. It's a struggle to dislike the guy, even if he's a little sceptical of Patrick. Not really threatened, just doesn't get him.

He's not the first.

"He doesn't even seem like the boating type," Blake's saying, all pretence at whispering abandoned.

"It's a fucking houseboat," Daisy says. "It hardly qualifies as *boating*."

"That's not the point," Blake says. "I just don't understand why—"

The door to Charlie and Prue's room bangs open, and Charlie declares that it's time for a swim.

"Shots first," insists Prue. The peace of the night is broken by the jangling chords of *Jumping Jack Flash*.

Patrick rolls his eyes. Boozing and the bloody Stones. Original. He pushes himself off the railing, and climbs back down to the main deck. Passing on tequila and skinny dipping is only going to make things worse.

*

Patrick's concern for the tranquillity of the other boaters nearby is gone by the time the tequila is. Everyone spills noisily out onto the rear deck and into the river. He's first in, his nakedness covered by the black water. Prue stays onboard, sitting on the gunwale in her swimmers, smoking and watching. Charlie tries to coax her into the water while Blake and Daisy splash and carry on, a drunken dance of groping, shoving and laughter.

He strokes gently away from the boat on his back. He realises the water is full of little glowing specks, making their way upstream with the tide.

Blake and Charlie start doing back flips off the deck, trying to outdo each other. Before long, Blake is holding on to the wire railing of the upper deck, back to the river, on the verge of asserting his dominance once and for all.

Patrick is well away from the boat now, the ripples from their games barely disturbing the water around him. No one seems to have noticed, and he lies back, floating, gazing up at the slow wheel of the stars above. They're like a reflection of the myriad little bioluminescent lights floating past him in the river.

With his ears below the waterline, the music and the carrying-on is muted. He floats in near-silence, weightless in the water. The world disappears. He is timeless, lost in the depths of the stars above and below.

*

Something brushes the back of Patrick's head and he jolts upright, forgetting where he is, inhaling warm, brackish water. Coughing and spluttering, he splashes around in a panic, trying to see what touched him in the darkness. He is close to shore. A fallen branch, fresh and leafy, lies partly submerged in the now-dark river.

He puts his feet down in relief, and stands up in the shallows, heart thumping. He is suddenly aware of the others calling his name. He has drifted a long way from the boat.

"I'm fine," he calls back. "I'm coming."

The river is still and high, like a held breath, paused before the tide turns. Drunkenness swept aside by the adrenaline, he glides back into the water and swims for the boat.

*

"Sorry," Patrick says again, one hand raised to ward off another slap. "I must have fallen asleep."

Daisy looks furious, her slap-hand twitching.

"Uh-uh." He shakes his head. "Save the beating for Blake. I'm sure he'll enjoy it."

They're standing at the stern, wrapped in towels. Prue and Charlie are in their room getting dressed, or something.

"I think I bit my tongue during that last dive," Blake says, holding his face. "Damn it."

Patrick smirks. "Drink some whisky," he says. "It'll sterilise it. Good for the personality too."

"You're a dick," Daisy says, after Blake has gone inside.

"I thought that was Blake's job." He grins.

She elbows him in the ribs. "You scared me."

She leans her head on his shoulder, and he drapes an arm around her. "I was fine. Besides, I really didn't need to hang out while you lot played grab-arse."

"Um, yeah, sorry."

"I don't care," Patrick says. "I just don't want to watch. Now," he gives her a squeeze. "Piss off while I get dressed."

*

"What do you think those little phosphorescent things were?" Charlie asks. They're sitting around the dining table, playing rummy.

"Probably some sort of parasite," Patrick says, reaching for the whisky.

"Careful." Blake nods at the bottle. "Wouldn't want to fall asleep."

"Ha ha." Patrick turns to Charlie with a straight face. "You didn't pee in the water, did you? One of them might have swum up your willy and lodged there. They'll have to amputate."

Charlie blanches.

"He's not serious," Prue says.

"I know that," Charlie replies.

Blake snorts and flashes Patrick a grin.

"The whole swimming up your pee stream thing is a total myth," Prue says. "And anyway, Candiru are only found in the Amazon."

"Could be tapeworms," Patrick says.

Prue shakes her head. "Tapeworms are not bioluminescent. There are hardly any fresh water bioluminescent animals, and most of them are insect larvae."

"Could be those tongue-eating lice."

"Those what?" Charlie asks.

"Cymo-something or other," Patrick says. "They eat your tongue, and then take it's place, feeding off the food you put in your mouth."

"They *don't* eat your tongue," she says. "They only affect fish. And they're a marine species, not freshwater."

"Well technically, Missus Marine Biologist, this is an estuarine system right here," Patrick says. "Maybe they're—"

"Stop it," Daisy says.

Patrick cocks his head to one side and wriggles his little finger in his ear. "Water in my ear," he says, ignoring Daisy. He looks at Charlie. "Could be Dracunculus medinens—"

"Whose deal is it?" Daisy interrupts.

*

Patrick carries his bedding up to the top deck, and drops it in a drunken heap. He sits and watches the reflection of the stars on the glassy river, trying not to listen to the grunting and moaning from downstairs.

The phosphorescent dots—whatever they were—have long since disappeared, and the water is black and silent with the outgoing tide. He wonders if he should have stayed at home, if he is making things harder on himself.

Eventually the fucking stops, and in the quiet he lies down and stares up at the stars. The seemingly chaotic swirl of countless suns moves in patterns beyond the ken of humans, infinitely complex but perfectly balanced, structured. Beneath that vast display he should feel like a speck of dust, but he feels instead a part of everything, small but essential. He was right to come.

As his eyelids droop, and the heavy sleep of drunkeness claims him, the momentary spark of a shooting star flares across the sky above him. A violent end to an insignificant lump of rock.

*

He is in darkness. It is absolute, no sound, no air, the cold blackness pressing in around him like the crushing weight of the oceans. There is ground beneath him, soft and deep, sucking at his feet while he is tugged this way and that, as if by shifting currents or the pull of waves rolling above. Disoriented and off-balance, he feels like everything is tumbling, his stomach lurching, like up and down keep changing places in the dark. The pressure is squeezing the air from him, tighter, heavier. His heart thunders, strength fails. The blackness pushes into his mind, lungs burning with the strain, burning...

*

Patrick wakes up in blazing heat and for a moment, eyes closed, he doesn't know where he is, who he is, which way is up.

He half-opens one eye. The sunlight, a bright spear, slants through the crack, piercing his head. He drapes a forearm across his face with a groan, and tries to go back to sleep.

It's useless. He has rolled out from the shade of the canopy. His brain feels like a raisin, a shrivelled little grape with every last drop of moisture sucked out of it. He's not ready to be alive, but the heat is merciless.

He tries to convince himself he's still asleep, that this is a dream...

He *was* dreaming. He can't quite remember what it was, but it's still there in the back of his mind, a great pressure in his skull.

Or perhaps that's just the hangover.

He sits up, unsure of whether he's capable of standing. His ear is still full of water, and he can hear his pulse in that side of his head. He feels off balance. It takes a while, but eventually he turns over onto his knees, and pushes himself to his feet.

*

"Ugh, whose idea was it to hire a boat?" Daisy is emerging from her room, making her way unsteadily to the table.

Patrick is nursing a tepid cup of coffee. He's barely able to manage that, let alone getting up to cook breakfast. He musters just enough equilibrium to pour Daisy a cup.

"Pretty sure it was yours," he says, pushing the coffee across the table at her.

She stares at the coffee briefly, and then lays her head on the table in defeat. "What's for breakfast?"

"Just making the coffee nearly killed me," he says. "I was hoping you were going to make eggs."

She grunts, possibly in amusement, possibly in horror at the thought of actually eating.

After a while, he's not sure how long, he looks up from his coffee. Daisy appears to have gone back to sleep. She's drooling onto the table. Prue and Charlie's door springs open and slams against the wall.

Daisy wakes up with a start as Charlie saunters out whistling. She wipes the drool from her cheek.

"Do you ever open a door like a normal person, Charlie?" Patrick asks.

"What do you mean?"

"You know, not trying to kick it down."

Charlie looks at him blankly for a few seconds. "I'm famished," he says finally, opening the fridge. "Everyone for bacon and eggs?" He doesn't wait for an answer.

Daisy looks at Patrick. "God," she says. "How is he so chirpy?"

He shrugs, and the two of them sit in dazed silence.

After a minute, Charlie looks up from digging in the fridge. "Where's the bacon?"

*

Patrick is lying on the upper deck, pretending to be asleep and trying to ignore the thump of his heartbeat in his blocked ear.

Daisy and Charlie sip carefully at gin and tonics, and lounge in the heat.

Patrick stares off at the river. They are moored in a wide bend, windless and bright with the sun. In the distance the river bends into the trees in a humid haze, and disappears behind the rising hills. It's alluring, like a pathway to some exotic adventure or hidden treasure. He is struck by a desire to follow it, to take the boat as far upriver as he can and find what is there.

His fantasy is interrupted by Blake climbing into view up the step ladder from the bottom deck. He looks haggard, and still half asleep. He reaches into the esky, pulls out the gin, and takes a mouthful straight from the bottle. Daisy and Charlie stare at him, mouths agape.

Blake swishes the gin around his mouth and spits it over the side. "Jesus, don't know how you guys drink this shit."

The others simply look at him.

"It's my tongue," he says. "Nearly fucking bit it clean off." He sticks it out in emphasis. There's a bloody, swollen mess down one side.

"Christ," says Charlie. "There's nothing clean about that."

"Exactly. I'm trying to make sure it doesn't get infected." Blake takes another swig from the bottle. He swallows it this time. "I'm starving," he says.

"You should have got up earlier." Daisy looks over her sunglasses at him. "You missed a great breakfast."

"Would have been better if there was any bacon," Charlie says.

Daisy slumps back in her deck chair. "I fucking brought the bacon."

Blake turns around and heads back down the ladder.

Charlie arches an eyebrow at Daisy. "Uh huh."

*

It's late afternoon by the time Prue gets up. Patrick is still lying on the deck, fantasising about what he might find upriver. He's been in a post-drunken haze all day. It's not helped by the dub that's droning out of the stereo.

The other three, well on their way to finishing the bottle of gin, are sitting on the deck playing cards. Prue comes up the ladder and sits down on top of the esky. She looks slightly ill.

Blake looks her up and down. "You guys had fun last night, huh?"

"Oh, sorry," she says. "Were we too loud?"

"Yes. But that's not what I meant." He points at her shoulder, where her loose shirt has slipped off to reveal a bite mark that has broken the skin.

Prue looks. "Shit," she says, pulling her shirt back up. She glares at Charlie.

Charlie looks at his cards.

The silence is starting to get awkward when Prue, eyes still fixed on her boyfriend, says, "Is someone going to make dinner?"

"Right," he says, and makes his escape down the ladder.

Patrick rouses himself as the others pack up the cards, and sits up. Another boat has raised its anchor, its motor muttering softly as it heads upriver. He watches it go. He hasn't noticed the other boats fleeing them, but they are the only ones left now.

*

Patrick doesn't last long after dinner. His attempts to clear the water from his ear have been unsuccessful, and his head feels clogged and uncomfortable.

"Don't be such a pussy," Blake says, as Patrick heads for the door.

Patrick looks back with a smile, but Blake has already turned away, leaning in to kiss Daisy on the neck.

She gives Patrick a questioning look, whilst Blake tongues his way up to her ear. Patrick just rolls his eyes at her, and heads upstairs.

He watches the bioluminescence float upriver with the tide again. It's mesmerising, and he is drawn along with it in his mind, riding currents and eddies of light. For a while he forgets the dull thud of his pulse in the side of his skull.

"I don't know why you're so nice to him."

He looks over his shoulder. Prue is sitting on the esky, rolling a cigarette.

"Who, Blake? He's not such a bad guy."

"He's a dick."

Patrick shrugs, and Prue cups her hands to light her rollie.

"It's always the same, Pat. I don't get it."

"What do you mean?"

"Don't be obtuse. Daisy's boys. You're always so fucking nice to them."

"Why wouldn't I be? What's being an arsehole going to achieve."

She looks at him, legs crossed, cigarette dangling between her fingers. "Are you ever going to do anything?"

"About what?"

"About Daisy."

"I don't know what you're—"

"How long have we been friends, Pat?"

"Are we?"

"Fuck, you can be such hard work. You know, I'm surprised Daisy still bothers. It's painful, watching you every time Daisy parades some new fuck-bull around in front of you. Just do something about it."

"If we're meant to be together, she'll—"

"Are you kidding me? *Meant to be together?* What, are you waiting for the stars to align or something? Or just for the fairy godmother to show up? She didn't ask you to come on the boat so you could sit up here and listen to her fuck Captain Biceps down there."

"Yeah? Then why did she ask me to come?"

"Jesus." She stands up and flicks the dog-end of her cigarette out into the river. "Sometimes I can't tell if you're daft or just stupid." She disappears back down the ladder.

Patrick turns back to the river. They are in starlit blackness tonight. There is no moon, and since their party chased off all the other boats, no lights to break the darkness either. The volume is starting to creep up again downstairs, with Blake leading the charge. He's been hard at the booze since he got up, but the others are at tipping point now too. Soon they'll be beyond help, with unconsciousness or sex the only ends to the party.

Patrick stares out into the dark, mulling over Prue's words. He knows it's ridiculous, the whole fate thing, but he can't help it.

He lies down on the deck, his blocked ear muting the noise downstairs. There are only the stars in the sky and the water, and the boat, floating in between. The noise of drunken conversation disappears, and he loses himself in the mirrored patterns of light above and below.

*

The breath has gone from his lungs, and with it the fire and the panic and the crushing pressure. The blackness has filled him. His density matches that of the void outside.

He begins to walk—without thinking, without intent, pulled forward by a will not his own. He moves slowly, like the newly blind, hands stretched out before him. Each step is an effort to pull free of the muddiness beneath his feet.

He is certain now that he's in water, deep and boundless. He is buffeted by currents that change direction wildly, and the strange feeling of movement persists, the loss of up and down.

There is no sense of time. He might have been walking forever. Ahead, he thinks he can make out a few spots of light, wavering in the dark. They give him an anchor, something to focus on, and the disorientation recedes. But after what seems an age, they have come no closer. He rubs at his eyes to make sure he is not seeing things.

When he opens them, the lights have gone, and the shifting of the world resumes. He is pulled onwards.

*

Patrick wakes up in total darkness, curled up on his side. His head pulsates, each throb of his heartbeat a burst of speckled dream-light in his skull. There is no sky, only pitch blackness. He can see nothing. He can hear nothing.

No sound of the river. No noise of the boat shifting on the water. He is alone, and the world is spinning. He sits up, his heart racing, hammering in his ears. He puts his hands out, feeling around himself in a panic.

His bedding is there, and the deck of the boat. And then he sees the green, luminescent dial of his watch. He forces a deep breath, and another, and gradually calms himself.

When his pulse has slowed, quieted, he can make out the gentle movement of the deck beneath him and, in his good ear, the faint lap of the river against the hull.

He sits, lightheaded, a little confused, like a heavy blanket of flu is draped over his mind. After a while, a ragged hole opens in thick clouds. He can see stars through the gap, and the faint light shows small details of the boat around him.

He rolls onto his back, and closes his eyes in relief.

*

He has no idea what time it is when he wakes up again. The clouds have mostly gone. Mist hangs low on the river, shrouding the boat, chill on his skin. Patrick gets to his feet. His ear is still completely blocked, deaf, but his head feels clearer. The sound through his other ear is clean and sharp.

He looks over the side of the boat. He can barely see the water, and there is no sign of the phosphorescence.

When he climbs down to the main deck, a single, dim light is on over the stove. He drinks several glasses of water. The sound of swallowing is loud in his blocked ear.

He puts the kettle on, and while it is boiling, looks at the map of the river on the wall. It winds upstream into the jungly hills, narrow and serpentine. There is a wide circle on the map, marking the limit of their territory. Everything outside it is shaded red, off limits. All house boats are tracked by GPS.

He pours water, lets the tea brew, checks the GPS unit at the helm to find where they are moored, and looks at the map again. They are not *that* far from the exclusion zone. Most of a day's motoring, judging by the time it took them to get here from the marina.

This branch of the river stretches well beyond the red line, disappearing off the edge of the map. His idea of motoring upriver, following the luminescent trail, is largely out of bounds.

A little disappointed, he grabs his tea, and turns to head back upstairs. Daisy is standing right behind him, as though she's just appeared from nowhere. He jumps in surprise, spilling the tea.

"Jesus, Daisy," he says, trying to keep his voice down. "You scared the shit out of me."

She's standing so close he can feel her breath hot against his neck. Her eyes are closed. She is unmoving, apart from the steady rise and fall of her breasts as she breathes.

"Daisy?" He says, uncomfortable, stepping back against the sink. Her nipples are hard through her oversized t-shirt, and she is not wearing any pants. He looks over her shoulder. The door to the cabin she shares with Blake is closed. She inches closer, her nipples grazing his chest, her lips almost against his throat.

He feels himself getting hard, and opens his mouth to say... something, when she looks up at him.

"I'm so cold," she says. She stares at him blankly, as if she doesn't quite register that he's there.

And then, perfectly normally, she says, "Well, are you going to make me a cup of tea or what?"

Patrick just looks at her, stunned.

"Hello," she says, stepping back and snapping her fingers. "What's wrong with you?"

"Sorry," he mutters, and puts his tea down to boil the kettle again.

"You should go and put some clothes on," he says, glancing over his shoulder as he drops a teabag into a cup and spoons sugar into it.

Daisy looks down at herself. "Um, yeah," she says, and creeps back into her room.

She does not come back. After a while, he leaves her tea on the sink and goes back up to the deck.

*

In the thin light of false dawn, he watches the glassy water. His blocked ear is worse, if it's possible to get more deaf. The pressure is slowly building, and his head is getting stuffy again. It makes everything feel lopsided, as though the boat is listing to one side. He's having trouble thinking straight.

The mist has receded slightly, though the banks of the river are still obscured. He feels untethered, like he is floating, like the boat and its little stretch of river are slowly spinning in a foggy nothing.

He is thinking about the lights in the water again, their passage on the tide. He doesn't know much about bioluminescence, but he's pretty sure that whatever the things are, they should still be glowing when the tide is going back out. There's never any sign of them, though. It's strange that nobody has mentioned them. The marina was filled with information about things to see on the river. The old coot who gave them the run down on the boat hardly shut up about the place the whole time. He sounded like he's lived here forever. Looked like it, too.

At any rate, this can't be the first time these things have appeared. They're so beautiful, he can't understand why they're not a big attraction, or why Daisy and the others barely seem to notice them.

He stares upriver until the sun is over the horizon, the mist receding back into the trees. He wonders if the lights are simply being carried on the tide, or if they're swimming, migrating upriver like salmon. A moment later, he discovers he's intent on finding out. While the others are still sleeping, he goes down to the main deck and starts the engines. He pulls up the anchor, letting the boat drift while he stows the chain. Then he takes the wheel, and turns upriver.

*

"What's going on?" Daisy asks, coming up behind him and looking over his shoulder.

"Just a change of scenery," he says, eyes on the river. He can feel her breasts pressed against his back as she leans against him, following his line of sight. He tries not to like it, to will her away from him.

"Cool." She leans further over him and looks down at the GPS. "Where are we headed?"

Patrick glances sideways at her. He is struck by sudden feeling of mistrust, of wanting to keep his thoughts to himself.

He says nothing, considering the absurdity of his formless suspicion. She stays settled against his back.

Eventually, he shrugs. "I'll know when I get there," he says.

*

A door bangs and a moment later Charlie is standing at Patrick's elbow. He looks out at the front deck where Daisy is sunbathing naked, directly in front of Patrick, then glances sideways at Patrick and shakes his head. He leans out to the deck. "Jesus, D, put some fucking panties on would you?"

He gives Patrick another disapproving look, but Patrick just watches the water ahead. Charlie goes back to the open kitchen in the middle of the cabin.

A minute later Prue wanders silently past, and out onto the deck. Patrick looks at her absently as she sits down next to Daisy, his mind still filled with swirls of light.

As Prue sits, her loose dress shifts on her shoulders. The movement catches his attention, and he sees another livid bite mark before it is quickly covered up again.

Daisy looks up and says something, but he can't hear it. A moment later she sits up, a look of concern on her face. She pulls her dress on over her head, and moves next to Prue. They talk quietly, heads together.

"Hey," calls Charlie, striding up to the door and sticking his head out. "Where's the fucking sausages?"

Daisy turns to him with a scowl. "Don't look at me. They were in there yesterday."

"Well, where are they then?"

"How the bloody hell should I know?" She turns back to Prue.

Charlie glares at her for a moment, and then looks at Patrick, who looks at the river.

*

Patrick sits down at the table, having finally been pestered into mooring the boat so that everyone can eat and have a swim. He really wants to keep going, but he's trying to be casual about it. He still doesn't know why he doesn't want the others to know what he's doing, but he wants to make the red line today.

Then he can be ready to row the boat's dinghy further upstream tomorrow.

Charlie seems to have adopted the role of chef, and cheerfully serves up a late, lavish breakfast of huevos rancheros and Bloody Marys.

Daisy knocks on the door to her room. "Get up, babe," she calls. "Breakfast is ready." There is no response, and she sits at the table with a shrug.

Breakfast is nearly over by the time Blake emerges, pale and puffy-eyed. Charlie has been eyeing up Blake's breakfast, and, obviously disappointed by Blake's arrival, turns to Patrick. "Are you going to eat that, Pat?" He nods at Patrick's barely touched food.

Patrick pushes the plate across the table with a shake of his head. His stomach is seething again.

Blake sits down, and after staring sullenly at the food for a minute, pushes the plate away and reaches for the Bloody Mary.

Charlie raises an eyebrow. "You are a machine, fella, but maybe you want to slow down a bit?"

Blake mutters something, his voice thick and hard to understand.

"Why don't you eat some breakfast?" says Charlie.

Blake drinks the Bloody Mary in one long swallow, and gets up without a word. He walks out to the rear deck, puts the empty glass down on the gunwale, and dives off the back of the boat.

The others look at Daisy, who shrugs.

Charlie reaches for Blake's breakfast.

"I think I'm going to lie in the sun," Prue says, getting up.

Charlie glances after her and then starts on his third enormous helping. He's too busy eating to notice the dark look he gets from Daisy.

Daisy gets up and follows Blake.

Patrick watches in disgust as Charlie ploughs his way through the eggs. When he can't look any more, he too gets up and heads up to the deck. Charlie is oblivious.

*

Patrick is losing his patience. His blocked ear has become an ache, and he is agitated, pacing the main deck while the others lounge upstairs in the sun and take it in turns to swim. Most of the afternoon has disappeared, with someone always in the water, as if deliberately sabotaging his desire to keep the boat moving. Three boats have passed them while they've been stopped, headed upriver, and he is frustrated that the good moorings will be gone by the time they get there.

Charlie has just climbed out of the river, and gone up top. Patrick is waiting, trying to judge his timing. He doesn't want to give someone else the chance to go for another swim, but he doesn't want it to look like he's desperate. He's knows he's being a little ridiculous, but can't help himself. He holds off as long as he can stand it, and then sticks his head over the top of the ladder.

"Hey, can someone give me a hand with the anchor?"

Daisy and Blake, cuddling at the far end of the deck, pay no attention. She's giggling as Blake nibbles the back of her neck, and Patrick's pretty sure she's got her hand down his pants. Prue looks over the top of her book, but says nothing.

Charlie, sprawled on a deckchair, beer in one hand, opens his eyes. "What for?" he asks.

"So I can move the boat."

"Why?"

"Because we're moored in the middle of the river. Not really the smartest place to stay."

"Mate, just sit down and relax. You look like you could use it."

"Never mind," Patrick says, and climbs back down the ladder.

He starts the engines, and winches up the anchor. When the last of the chain rattles up over the bow, he goes out to the front deck. While he is untangling the chain, the engine dies.

Charlie is standing at the helm.

Patrick storms back inside. "What the fuck?"

Charlie's holding an ice bucket, a bottle of champagne in it. He has the keys to the boat in his other hand.

"Chill out, Pat," he says. "Nobody cares where the boat is. Come and hang out, have a drink."

"I don't feel like a drink. And being in the middle of the river is stupid if the weather changes."

"Don't be such a worry-wort. And you should have a drink. You look like shit. Whisky will kill whatever you're coming down with." Patrick snatches at the keys, but Charlie jerks his hand away, and takes a step back. "Seriously, Patrick. Calm down, mate."

"Give me the fucking keys."

Charlie stares at Patrick for a moment, then without warning, pitches the keys out the door. Patrick spins around, and catches a glint of sunshine as they sail over the gunwale and hit the water with a splash. He rounds on Charlie. With a yell, he runs at him, bashes the ice bucket out of his hand, and knocks him over, coming down on top of him. The surprise only stuns Charlie for a second, and before he knows it, Patrick finds himself flung aside, and then Charlie is on him, holding him down while he snarls and thrashes.

"What the hell is going on?"

His frenzy broken, Patrick looks over to see Daisy, hands on hips, with Blake and Prue behind her. Charlie is still straddling him, pinning his arms to the floor.

"He fucking attacked me is what's going on," Charlie says.

"He threw the keys into the river," says Patrick.

Charlie sits back, letting go of Patrick's arms, and pulls the keys out of the back pocket of his board shorts. He dangles them in front of Patrick's face.

"It was a joke," he says. "I threw a chunk of ice."

"You're a dick. Get off me." Charlie doesn't move. Patrick looks beseechingly at Daisy.

"Don't look at me," she says. "I'm not your bloody mum. You two children sort your own shit out." She turns away, shaking her head, and heads back up to the deck with Prue. Blake stands there smirking for a moment, and then follows the others, leaving Patrick and Charlie to it.

"Are you going to calm down?" Charlie asks, a warning finger in Patrick's face.

"Just get the fuck off me."

Charlie lets Patrick up, and hands him the keys. Patrick takes them without a word, and goes back to the helm. They have drifted close to the river bank. He starts the boat and turns it toward the middle of the river, heading upstream.

By the time he turns around, Charlie has cleaned up the spilled ice and disappeared.

*

The light is beginning to fade. Patrick is squinting through a headache. His glasses are upstairs, and half his head is almost bursting with sinus pressure. But they are within swimming distance of the red line, and he is heading toward a sheltered inlet, with a little beach. Another boat is moored there, but there is enough room for them to drop anchor.

Daisy appears at his side. She says something he can't make out.

"I can't hear you," he says. "Ear's completely blocked."

"Are you ok?" She asks, stepping round him, resting an arm on his shoulder.

"Yeah, I'm good."

She grabs his chin and turns him to face her. "Are you sure?"

He looks her in the eye. "I'm fine," he says.

"Well, are you going to come and hang out with us, with me?"

"Go and get one of the guys to help me with the anchor, and then I'll come up."

Hand still on his chin, she looks at him for a moment. "Ok." She kisses him on the mouth, slowly, hungrily, and then turns around and saunters off.

He stares after her. He can't even think, just sits, feeling the lingering heat of her lips on his. He is still staring, mind blank, a minute later, when Charlie comes in.

"You trying to beach us there, mate?"

Patrick spins back to the bow. They are heading directly in for the shore. He turns the wheel hard to starboard, backing off the throttle. The boat slowly comes about, and Charlie hops up on the prow to watch the anchor.

It's completely dark by the time they get it to take, and Patrick cuts the engines.

There is a dim light inside the other boat as Patrick climbs up to the deck, but no sound, and no one visible onboard.

*

Nobody seems to notice Patrick make his escape. The atmosphere has turned positively weird. They are ostensibly playing cards, but the game seems only to provide each an excuse to be in the same room.

Charlie is eating. His appetite seems to know no bounds, and he is sitting amid a growing pile of empty containers, snack packets and boxes.

Prue is quiet, drinking red wine straight from the bottle, and ignoring the no smoking inside policy. She appears mostly amused by the proceedings, but there's a bitter edge to her smirk. Patrick suspects it's got something to do with Charlie, and probably the bite marks. Charlie seems oblivious.

Blake, as usual, is drinking heavily, reduced to a state of inarticulate childishness, grabbing at people's cards and looking at them, spilling their drinks and laughing. His words are thick and incomprehensible, and Patrick isn't sure if it's due to inebriation or the state of his clearly infected tongue. If he gave a shit, he might insist they head back and get him medical attention. He does not. He dislikes the man.

He's not sure he feels much different about Daisy right now, either. She is clearly turned on. He can see the telltale flush across her neck and chest, and she lets Blake paw at her and suck at her neck and ear between his bouts of guffawing foolery. Patrick doesn't know what she finds attractive about it, but he has no interest in it.

His headache is excruciating, and he wants to lie down, somewhere he won't be disturbed. He climbs down the ladder, quietly unhitches the dinghy from the back of the boat, and shoves off. He waits until he has drifted a distance before setting the oars in the locks and rowing out into the stream of lights.

*

The houseboat is lost around several bends in the river, and at last Patrick can take no more and ships the oars, letting the dinghy drift with the current. He slumps in the bottom of the little boat and closes his eyes, squeezing them against the building migraine.

Eventually, when sleep refuses to come, he opens them again. He seems to have drifted close to the bank. Branches reach out above him, their undersides lit by an eerie light.

He lies there for a minute or two, his mind slow to register what he is seeing. Then, headache forgotten, he sits up.

The water is bright with the bioluminescence. The surface of the river is alive, covered in a shifting blue-white glow.

Leaning on the gunwale, he gazes into the water. It is thick with the creatures, clouds of them, tiny and almost indistinguishable from one another. They are too small to identify. They look more like they are swimming than being carried on the tide, and he sticks his hand in the water. They veer away from it, parting like a school of fish.

As if in response, there is a sharp pain in his ear. Patrick falls back into the dinghy, clutching his head. The pressure builds, sudden, severe, spreading from his blocked ear until he thinks his eardrums will burst. Eyes clamped shut, mouth open in a silent scream, he passes out.

*

He opens his eyes. The headache is gone. His ear hurts, a slight, diffuse pain, but it's external, and the pressure in his head has dissipated. Sound is still muted.

He touches his ear gingerly, and feels wetness. His finger comes away dark with a smear of blood.

Wiping it on his shirt, he sits up. The river is dark, the dinghy tucked in against the bank. Not far away, he can make out the pale, ghostly shape of a small yacht low in the water against the bank. It lists heavily to one side, as though scuppered, and is dark and silent. It is too dark to make out any detail, but there is something disquieting about it, so he sets the oars and shoves the dinghy out of the darkness beneath the trees and into open water.

There is only the barest sliver of moon, but the stars are bright enough for him to make out the surface of the water against the dark mass of the banks. He looks upriver briefly, considering, but the lights are gone. Instead he makes his slow, careful way back to the houseboat.

As he rounds the last bend, the houseboat floats into view, lit only by a dim light on the rear deck. He can hear voices, low and angry, hissing across the water. It is indistinct without his glasses, but he sees two people—Daisy and Charlie by the sound—having a whispered argument on the deck.

Patrick stops rowing, letting one oar trail so the dinghy spins and he is facing the houseboat front on. He drifts close enough to see, and sits out in the dark watching. He can't quite make out what they are saying, but Daisy is clearly giving Charlie an earful about something. Eventually she stops talking and Charlie stands there in silence for a minute. He says something, and lets out a short bark of laughter. Daisy slaps him, so quick and hard it snaps his head to the side, and turns on her heel. He grabs at her, catching her wrist and pulling her back toward him. She tries to hit him again, but he pulls her back against him, wrapping his arms around her and pinning her arms.

Patrick is caught in inaction for a moment. And then Charlie leans forward and sinks his teeth into Daisy's shoulder.

Patrick digs the oars into the water, turning the dinghy around, and pulling hard for the boat. He looks over his shoulder as he nears, and stops. Daisy has Charlie hard up against the gunwale, hands on either side of his face and her lips locked to his. As though struck in the head, a flash of jealous rage strikes Patrick, and then he goes limp and drops the oars. Their blades catch the water and whack him hard in the chest, nearly knocking him over backwards.

Disengaging himself, he looks back at the boat again. Daisy is gone. Charlie is still bent back slightly over the gunwale, mouth open, arms limp by his sides. He straightens up and goes inside just as the dinghy drifts into the light and thuds into the boat.

Patrick sits in a daze for a few minutes. He feels drained. He is not patient, he realises.

He's a fucking idiot.

Suddenly, he can't be bothered being on this boat, or following the bloody bugs upriver. His ear probably needs to be looked at by a doctor, and he wants to go home, back to his work, away from these people. From Daisy. He pulls himself out of the dinghy, throws the towline over the cleat, and climbs the ladder to his bed on the top deck.

*

Around him, above him, they swirl in a great spiral—stars and planets in their billions, the brilliance of their light staggering. The momentum is building. At the centre of the maelstrom, he is spinning, each turn faster, steeper. The darkness is pulling at them, dragging them down into the blackness.

*

When Patrick wakes up, he's at the helm. The pull of the void is a cold fear in his chest. It takes him a moment to work out where he is. He looks around in confusion, his hands limp on the wheel. How the fuck did he get here? He was dreaming... darkness.

The cabin is filled with the rumble of the outboard motors, and the rasp of Charlie snoring on the sofa to one side.

The motors.

The fucking boat is moving.

It is still black outside, the river little more than a hint of movement in the night. He can barely see a thing out there. He eases off the throttle, and looks down at the GPS.

It has been pulled partway out of the dash. A cable runs from it to the floor, connected to his laptop. Their position claims to be just below the red line, unmoving. What the hell is happening? He cuts the engine altogether. The boat coasts, slows, eventually stops. When he's sure they won't immediately drift into the bank, he lets go the wheel and picks up his laptop.

He hardly needs to look at the code.

The script stopped when the boat did. The GPS's signal is steady, in approved waters. He unplugs his laptop. They could be anywhere now. How long was he at the wheel? He looks at his watch. It is a couple of hours before dawn, but that doesn't tell him anything. When did he start?

Putting his laptop to one side, he releases the anchor, and goes out to the bow to make sure it catches. He sits up on the gunwale to watch their position.

He has no idea what the fuck is going on. Most people walk into a wall in their sleep, if they make it that far, but piloting a boat? Writing code? It doesn't make sense. He feels like he's blocking something out.

The last thing he really remembers is Daisy and Charlie. Daisy... He feels a hot flush of shame. How many of her dickhead boyfriends have looked at him, and then laughed while they fucked her?

Did he ever really think—"Fuck." He spits the word over the side of the boat.

He's angry now. At himself, at Daisy. He has a sudden vision of his hands around her throat, and she screams.

Daisy really screams.

He is on his feet, running. Past Charlie, slowly sitting up, dazed, on the sofa. He yanks at the door to Daisy's room. It's locked. The noise of struggle is coming through the thin wall.

"Daisy," he yells, rattling the door violently.

"Patrick," her voice is laboured, choking. He can hear a strange moaning noise. He is bracing himself to pull at the door again when the cabin light goes on and Charlie shoves him aside.

Back against the opposite wall, Charlie kicks the door. The flimsy wood splinters inward, tearing away from its lock and hinges.

They rush through the narrow opening.

Daisy is backed up against the wall beside the door, trying to fend off Blake. He has his hands around her throat, pulling himself closer. His mouth is open, reaching, moaning. Sticking out of it is what used to be his tongue. The mangled appendage is a knot of twisting tentacles. It is clearly straining to get to Daisy's face.

Charlie smashes into the man, knocking him back against the bed. Patrick shoves Daisy into the corridor, standing in the doorway. The Blake-thing throws Charlie aside like a child, and is on its feet instantly. It reaches for Patrick, pulling him into the room and tossing him effortlessly against the wall. From the floor, Patrick sees Prue standing in the door of her room opposite. So does the Blake-thing, and it latches onto her, pulling her close.

Her scream is cut off with a gurgling choke.

Patrick scrambles to his feet at the same moment as Charlie, the two getting in each other's way as they try to get through the door. Then Daisy reappears in the corridor, and plunges a wide-bladed kitchen knife into the thing's neck.

Everything stops, the moment frozen, everyone in shock. Blood gushes over Daisy's hand.

She lets go of the knife, and the thing falls sideways, pulling a long tangle of tentacles out of Prue's mouth. The other three stand motionless as Prue's eyes roll back in her head, and she slumps to the floor.

*

Patrick sits on the top deck, Daisy curled up in his bedding beside him with an arm draped across his lap. Upriver, the first hint of dawn separates the line of hills from the sky. He is weighing up outcomes. The tightness of fear clutches his gut. The inevitable police involvement and the consequences of the killing seem mundane, insignificant, compared to the loss of memory, the blackness in his mind.

He can't stop thinking about the Blake-thing's face, reaching for Daisy, pulling her closer, the cold blank eyes, the hunger.

And then he sees Charlie in his mind, sitting on the deck, surrounded by a growing pile of snack packets, and then the bite marks on Prue, and Charlie biting Daisy. He sees Daisy and Charlie kissing, and remembers the hungry pull of Daisy's lips on his own. He feels an almost overwhelming urge to lie down with her, to give in to sleep. To the darkness. Fighting the pull, he gently lifts Daisy's arm and slides out from under it, heading for the ladder.

He does not like their chances of making it back to the Marina, but the Houseboat rental company has speedboats ready to respond to emergency calls. If he radios, they should be here in a matter of hours. He ignores the broken door, propped against the doorway to hide the dead thing where they dragged it back into the room.

He is about to pass the door to the other room, but something stops him. There is a dim light ahead in the kitchen, but he turns away from it, and eases open the door a crack to peer inside. The room is dark, and it takes a moment for his eyes to adjust. He can dimly make out Prue, splayed naked across the bed on her back, her head hanging over the far side. One breast and shoulder are a bloody mess, and there are dark stains splashed across the sheets. She does not appear to be moving.

There is a rustling noise in the kitchen, so he treads quietly along the corridor. Peeking around the corner, he sees Charlie squatting on the floor in front of the open fridge. He has a bag of raw mince between his legs and is shovelling handfuls of it into his mouth. His eyes are empty, staring.

Patrick reaches out, picks up a heavy cast-iron pan that sits on the end of the counter, and steps carefully past the kitchen, keeping his back to the wall. Charlie's head follows him as he moves. He is just about to step out of the light from the fridge, into the main cabin, when Charlie leaps at him. Patrick swings the pan as hard as he can, smashing Charlie in the head with a clang. The man drops to the floor, unmoving.

Patrick drops the pan, rushes to the helm, and turns on the two-way radio. He lifts the transceiver from its cradle only to see the coiled cable dangling free, its end a bundle of torn wires.

There is no choice but to try for the marina. He hopes that they come across another boat.

He hopes that he can stay awake.

With a glance over his shoulder, he starts the motors and eases the boat forward. Looking over the bow into the grey dawn, he winches up the anchor, turning the boat toward the middle of the river. Hearing movement, he spins around just in time to get his hands up before Charlie is on him, knocking him back into the helm's high stool. They go down in a heap. Patrick flails, punching and clawing, but Charlie has both hands around his neck. The weight pins Patrick to the floor. He can't breathe. His struggles get weaker as Charlie's face looms closer, mouth wide.

There's a thin tentacle reaching up from the back of Charlie's throat. He shoves a hand in Charlie's mouth, but he can already feel himself growing faint. He's falling into blackness, the roar of nothing in his ears. The last thing he sees is Charlie slump to one side, Daisy standing over him with the frying pan. The pressure around his neck releases, but he is too far gone.

*

The arms of the spiral spread wide, an eternity from one side to the other, countless worlds between. But they are not here to bring life. Their fire is meaningless. The great vortex of light, everything there is, it is but a spark in the blackness. It is being sucked down to feed the endless hunger of the sleeper. The idea that there was ever anything else to existence would be laughable, if he could remember what laughter was. He falls inwards.

*

And then he is no longer falling. He feels fire, warmth in the cold dark. He rises, as if floating to the surface from the depths.

Patrick wakes up on his back. Daisy's lips are hard against his own, her tongue in his mouth. She is straddling him, one hand around his cock, tugging at him. He catches himself for a moment, confused, and pulls his mouth away, turning his head to the side. It is dark. They are naked on the top deck, and the water is filled with the blue-white glow of the lights.

Daisy keeps going, sucking his neck, biting his ear. She grabs his face and pulls it back to her, kissing him again. He can't help himself. Her breasts are heavy against his chest, her skin hot beneath his fingers. He lets himself go.

She lifts herself up slightly, and then something grips tight around his cock and balls, squeezing, pulling. Painful. He pushes her face away, and looks down between them. A mass of tentacles writhes between her legs, wrapped around him, pulling him in toward her.

He screams, shoves her to one side, rolls and pushes her away from him. The thing grips him harder, and he goes into a frenzy, rolling over and over, screaming and punching her. The woman he loves is limp, but the thing inside her is squeezing him tighter and tighter. They bang against one of the uprights of the railing. Then Daisy flings her arms around him and rolls under the bottom wire, and together they hit the water.

*

Around them in the dark water, the lights swirl in a great spiral, brilliant, mesmerising, slowly pulling them down into the black depths.

An eldritch tribute to

H.P. LOVECRAFT

TIM DEDOPULOS · JOHN REPPION
GREG STOLZE · LYNNE HARDY · GABOR CSIGAS
GETHIN A. LYNES · E. DANE ANDERSON
PIERS BECKLEY · JOFF BROWN · JEREMY CLYMER
HELMER GORMAN · MICHAEL GREY
G.K. LOMAX · IAIN LOWSON · MARC REICHARDT
PETER TUPPER · ADAM VIDLER

with a foreword by
LEEMAN KESSLER *of* 'ASK LOVECRAFT'
afterword by

S.T. JOSHI

Cthulhu lives!

edited by

SALOMĖ JONES

GHOSTWOODS

A Quick Word

If you enjoyed *Cthulhu Lies Dreaming*, please consider leaving a brief review where you obtained it, or spreading the word a little. You'd be surprised what an immense help it is for the book!

For advance notice of upcoming Ghostwoods releases, and special member-only offers, please sign up to our (very) occasional mailing list at:

http://www.gwdbooks.com/mailing-list-sign-up.html

We have a very strict policy of not being annoying email jerks. We'll never spam you, sell your details to anyone else, or broadcast any third-party offers.

a *darkly magical* story cycle

RED PHONE BOX

Warren **Ellis**

Tim **Dedopulos**
Dan **Wickline** *and more*

edited by Salomé **Jones**

Contributor Bios

Listed alphabetically by last name

Seattle-based writer **E. Dane Anderson** grew up in Spokane, Washington. He attended Eastern Washington University and University College London, and holds masters degrees in both History and Archaeology. He is currently employed as an archaeologist for an Environmental consulting firm. He is also a photographer and musician.

Lucy Brady is a London-based writer and researcher of speculative fiction and occult history. She discovered Lovecraft as a teenager, which inspired an enduring love of the literary Weird in all its many forms. After a brief foray into fiction as a teenager, she spent several years studying literature and classical languages, before returning to writing in 2013. She has contributed to anthologies including *Dreams from the Witch House: Female Voices in Lovecraftian Horror* from Dark Regions Press, and is the editor for *Project Praeterlimina*, a hyperstitious journal of demonology and the occult.

Evey Brett lives in southern Arizona with two cats and a Lipizzan mare. She's been published with Lethe Press, Cleis Press, Pathfinder Web Fiction and elsewhere and has attended workshops such as Clarion, Taos Toolbox and the Lambda Literary Retreat for Emerging LGBT Writers. Visit her online at www.eveybrett.wordpress.com

Matthew Chabin is a writer from Portland, Oregon. He was a journalist in the US Navy and studied literature and philosophy at Southern Oregon University. His writing is a mixture of memoir, journalism and fiction. He is the winner of the 2015 Miglior Press Essay Contest, and is currently pursuing larger publishing goals. He lives in Nagano Prefecture of Japan with his wife and two cats.

Daniel Marc Chant is an author of strange fiction. His passion for H. P. Lovecraft and the films of John Carpenter inspired him to produce intense, cinematic stories with a sinister edge. Daniel launched his début, *Burning House*, swiftly following with the Lovecraft-inspired *Maldición*. His most recent book *Mr. Robespierre* has garnered universal praise. He also created *The Black Room Manuscripts,* a charity horror anthology, and is a founder of UK independent genre publisher The Sinister Horror Company. You can find him amongst the nameless ones on twitter @danielmarcchant, at facebook/danielmarcchant or his official website www.danielmarcchant.com.

In the deep wilds of Scotland, hunkered down in a sylvan bunker, **William Couper** churns out works when he's not hunting and foraging. Well, he claims 'deep wilds' — all evidence points to him being somewhere in the Greater Glasgow area, although there are reports of a lot of cats, so there could be some veracity to the 'wild' thing. There's a possibility his 'hunting and foraging' are over-long visits to the supermarket. He does churn out works. Much of his output is fiction, with strange stories in science fiction, fantasy and horror floating around in print and online.

Mike Davis is a writer and editor, as well as the publisher of *The Lovecraft eZine.* He lives with his wife and son in Texas, and is at work on his first novel.

Lynnea Glasser is an award-winning independent game designer who draws on her science background to create strange and beautiful worlds that speak to our humanity. She loves mischievous cats, deep oceans, creative cooking, and trying to make order from chaos. More of Glasser's works can be found at MadeRealStories.com.

Originally trained as a biomedical research scientist, **Lynne Hardy** was first introduced to Lovecraft's work through Chaosium's *Call of Cthulhu* roleplaying game whilst at university. Having failed to escape the mind-rending insanity of the Mythos, she now works on Modiphius Entertainment's *Achtung! Cthulhu* game as a writer, editor and line manager, and can be found on Twitter @ CogsandCakes

Thord D. Hedengren is addicted to words, and the stories they make. He writes fiction, short and long, as well as freelance articles and columns for various media outlets. He's a renowned web developer and designer, and the author of *Smashing Wordpress: Beyond the Blog* and *The Writer's iPad*, among other techy things. You'll find him wasting away on Twitter as @tdh, or spewing words at tdh.me. Thord lives in Sweden, the Land of Kings.

Kenneth Hite is the author of the *Trail of Cthulhu* roleplaying game, *Cthulhu 101*, *Tour de Lovecraft*, the "Lost in Lovecraft" column for *Weird Tales*, four Lovecraftian children's books, several Mythos short stories, and *The Cthulhu War: U.S. Battles Against the Mythos* for Osprey Publishing. He lives in Chicago with two Lovecraftian cats and one non-Lovecraftian wife.

Matthew J. Hockey left a nice, stable, boring job in the North of England to teach elementary English in Seoul, South Korea with his fiancée. Though his days now contain more screaming and snotty noses, he finds it a lot easier to concentrate on writing. He has been previously published by Thuglit, *All Due Respect* Magazine, Spooky Words press, Shotgun Honey and the Akashic Books *Mondays are Murder* series.

Yma Johnson is a first generation Sierra Leonean immigrant who began her writing career in 1996 as a journalist in Puerto Rico. She has written articles on topics ranging from the criminalization of the mentally ill to Japanese swordsmanship. She is a master's candidate in creative writing at Eastern Michigan University where she recently taught rhetoric and composition. She also taught poetry at a women's prison. She won first place in the 2012 Current Magazine Fiction and Poetry Contest as well as an honorable mention from 2014 Glimmer Train's Very Short Fiction Contest. Her work has appeared in the St. Petersburg Review. She also has a story forthcoming in the *Encyclopedia Project*, an anthology of experimental literature. Yma currently serves as grants director for a nonprofit agency dedicated to protecting the environment.

Salomé Jones is a writer turned editor who enjoys stories where reality meets the strange and wondrous. Though she can now be found wondering around Europe, her native habitat includes the American Midwest, Northwest, and East Coast. Her favorite place is London, where she often sets her stories. Find her on Twitter at @call_me_salome.

Morris Kenyon is a freedom fighter, jungle explorer, international mercenary, Riviera jewel thief, jet pilot and gigolo. He's done them all. In his dreams. Mostly specialising in fast-paced crime, horror and science fiction, he has been writing for several years with his main literary influences ranging from HP Lovecraft to Elmore Leonard. You can connect with him by emailing morris. kenyon@ymail.com.

Ayobami Leeman Kessler is a Nigerian-born American actor who spends his time impersonating HP Lovecraft for his show *Ask Lovecraft*. His writing can be found in Ghostwood Books' *Cthulhu Lives!* as well as in Martian Migraine Press's *Resonator*. He can also be heard discussing elements of horror and pop culture on his podcasts, *Miskatonic Musings* and *Geekually Yoked*. His story, *Babatunde*, is dedicated to Baba Ayobami Adupeo Pupo-pupo.

G. K. Lomax is a pseudonym. Behind it lies a strangely reserved and camera-shy individual from the fair English county of Essex. Contrary to rumour, he is mostly harmless. He writes short stories which are sometimes favourably received, and longer works whose time has not yet come, mostly because they're unfinished. Oh, and verse, which is best glossed over. He has appeared under his real name on four broadcast quiz shows, performed on stage at the Albert Hall, and been cursed by Sean Connery for the errant nature of his golf. His signs himself "GKL" which, he contends, is pronounced "Jeckyll." Go figure.

Gethin A. Lynes is a novelist, comics writer and a general peddler of parables. For some reason (having lived in such exotic locales as Worton, Maryland) he now resides in Perth, Australia with his remarkably tolerant darling wife and two cats. His shameless cynicism, love of whisky and expletives, and uncanny talent for speaking before thinking regularly get him in trouble.

Former rock singer/guitarist **Samuel Morningstar** is the author of several books, including the *Dirk Garrick Occult Detective* series. He has been studying meditation, martial arts, the occult, magick, tantra and kundalini for over twenty years. He has Master's degrees in Psychology and Business Management. He lives in Kansas City with his wife and three cats.

Saul Quint is the pen name of a middle aged British academic living in the north of England. He grew up by the sea playing *Dungeons and Dragons*, *Traveller* and *Call of Cthulhu*, from which his admiration for Lovecraftian literature derives. He enjoys history, novels, warships, wine, cats and marriage.

Pete Rawlik, a long time collector of Lovecraftian fiction, is the author of more than fifty short stories, a smattering of poetry, and the Cthulhu Mythos novels *Reanimators* and *The Weird Company*. He is a frequent contributor to *The Lovecraft eZine* and the *New York Review of Science Fiction*. In 2014 his short story *Revenge of the Reanimator* was nominated for a New Pulp Award. His new novel, *Reanimatrix*, a weird noir romance set in H. P. Lovecraft's Arkham, will be released in 2016. He lives in southern Florida where he works on Everglades issues.

Marc Reichardt continues to reside in the Other World of Ypsilanti, Michigan, with two demons that purport to be cats. He's a repeat offender with Ghostwoods (*Cthulhu Lives!*) and still plots to replace the US government with something even marginally sane. He can be found on Twitter @jackwraith and on his occasional blog: dichotomouspurity.blogspot.com

Brian Fatah Steele has been writing various types of dark fiction for over ten years, from horror to urban fantasy and science fiction. Growing up hooked on comic books and monster movies, he originally went to school for fine arts but finds himself far more fulfilled now by storytelling. Steele lives in Ohio with a few cats and survives on a diet of coffee and cigarettes. He spends his time still dabbling in visual art, vowing to fix up his house, acting as a part-time chaos entity, spending too many hours watching television, and probably working on his next writing project. His work has appeared in various anthologies as well alongside his collections and novels.

Greg Stolze was born in 1970 and in the intervening decades has written games (*REIGN*, *A Dirty World*, *Better Angels*), novels (*Switchflipped*, *Sinner*, *Mask of the Other*), and ever so many short stories, which are archived at www.gregstolze.com/fiction_library, where you can read them for free. There's a fair bit of Mythos stuff in there too. He has also written one comic book, *A Softer Apocalypse*. He's tired. Oh so tired.

M. S. Swift lives by the banks of the Mersey in the North West of England. He is paying off his accumulated karmic debt by working in the English education system but he is happiest amongst ancient stones in the dripping rain. His work has been previously published in the *Schlock* webzine and the *Schlock* Bi-Monthly.

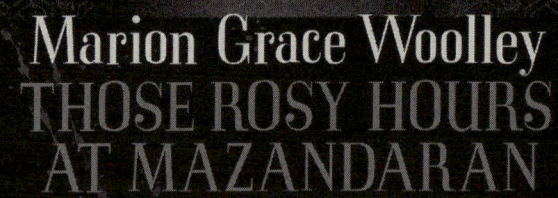

Marion Grace Woolley
THOSE ROSY HOURS
AT MAZANDARAN

15476839R00227

Printed in Great Britain
by Amazon